A BLAST F

"No!" President Norfie ... ...
"That is my simple and fi ...
have solved our problems s ...
and shall continue to do s ...   ...uld you
kindly go to hell!"

"Oh dear." On the screen transmitting from twenty-seven years in the past, the then-President of the United States shook his head sadly in the manner of one forced, reluctantly, to broach something that he would rather have left unsaid.

"Mr. President," he said, "I suspect that you have not yet had time to appreciate fully the realities of this situation. My proposal to you was not so much in the nature of a request, as an ultimatum. If you reflect for a moment, you will see that your position gives you no leeway for bargaining. In short, you have no choice but to comply."

"How so?" Norfield demanded. "What is there to bargain over? There's no reason why we should send you anything back in time. You haven't got anything to trade."

"Possibly true," Garfax conceded. "But on the other hand, you will agree that our relationship here, to you there in our future, does put us in a unique position. Whatever we choose to do now must affect your world of twenty-seven years later. However, the converse does not apply. The effect is completely one-way, as it were."

Norfield rubbed his temples and looked confused. "I'm . . . not sure I understand you," he said. "What are you trying to say?"

Garfax made an exaggerated show of being patient. "Let me put it to you this way. We are sitting on the planet that you will be occupying twenty-seven years from now. If you were to reject our proposals, we would be in a position to embark upon various activities—I'm sure I don't need to be distastefully specific—that could make life very . . . difficult for you." Norfield emitted an outraged gasp. Garfax leered openly and nodded. "I trust, Mr. President, that I have made my point," he said.

By James P. Hogan

CATASTROPHES, CHAOS & CONVOLUTIONS

JAMES P. HOGAN

CATASTROPHES, CHAOS & CONVOLUTIONS

Copyright © 2005 by James P. Hogan

"Convolution" first appeared in the anthology *Past Imperfect*, edited by Martin H. Greenberg and Larry Segriff, DAW Books, New York, October 2001. "The Tree of Dreams" first appeared in the anthology *Cosmic Tales: Adventures in Far Futures*, edited by Toni Weisskopf, Baen Books, New York, February 2005. "Decontamination Squad" first appeared in Guy H. Lillian's magazine *Challenger*, Issue 22, July 2005. "The Sword of Damocles" is based on an original story of the same title that was included in *Stellar 5 Science Fiction Stories*, edited by Judy-Lynn Del Rey, Ballantine, May 1980. "Take Two" first appeared in the anthology *Silicon Dreams*, edited by Martin H. Greenberg and Larry Segriff, DAW Books, New York, December 2001. "The Falcon" first appeared in *Apex Science Fiction and Horror*, Summer 2005. Cryptic Crossword copyright © 2005 by James P. Hogan.

A Baen Books Original

Baen Publishing Enterprises
P.O. Box 1403
Riverdale, NY 10471
www.baen.com

ISBN-13: 978-1-4165-0921-9
ISBN-10: 1-4165-0921-6

Cover art by David Mattingly
Interior drawings by Randy Asplund

First printing, December 2005

Distributed by Simon & Schuster
1230 Avenue of the Americas
New York, NY 10020

Production & design by Windhaven Press (www.windhaven.com)
Printed in the United States of America

Dedicated to the Irish midge—a tiny, pesky fly that comes out in swarms in warm, humid evenings. Hence, even with the summer sky still showing light close to midnight, we retreat indoors at a reasonably early hour from hours of pottering in the garden or just idling in the sun. Without the midge, this book would possibly not have been written.

CONTENTS

The Guardians

"God in His wisdom made the fly;
And then forgot to tell us why."
—Ogden Nash

"It's been declared an emergency, official from Earth," Nordsen said over the desktop in the cubbyhole that served as his office in the Lab Section of the Eurussian compound. "Which means that under the rules that everyone out here has contracted to abide by, the Chinese are empowered to take charge. They're the biggest contingent, and they've got the most at stake in the operation. If they say they need a metallurgical physicist at Tremil, we're obligated to comply." He paused, eyeing Kerry dubiously. "If it's any consolation, they will recompense us for your time. So look

1

on the plus side. You can think of it as a spell of paid leave. Being paid to get away from this place for a while . . ."

Yeah, right, Kerry thought to himself. To get sent to a place where everyone just got wiped out and nobody knows why. One of the reasons why he'd signed up to come out to this god-awful swamp of a world that some administrator with either a terminally warped sense of humor or none at all had christened Priscilla had been to get away from home-style bureaucracy's strangulation of rules and procedures.

That Kerry's enthusiasm lay distinctly to the nether side of total must have showed. Nordsen located a pink memorandum denoting Directorate business beneath the litter of paperwork and equipment parts and pushed it across to change the subject. "They want you over there right away to fill you in. The person you need to ask for is a Xiang-Chu Juanita, Office of Security."

"Juanita?"

Nordsen shrugged. "That's what it says."

Kerry picked up the slip and read it. A small detail that Nordsen had omitted to mention was that the only military presence on Priscilla—reinforced several times now with the general heightening of preparedness as relationships with the Eks deteriorated—was also predominantly Asian and under Chinese command. So not only was their word law for all under an officially declared emergency, they had the means to back it up.

It seemed that Kerry was going to Tremil.

* * *

Okay, so their culture went back thousands of years to when Europe was home to barbarian tribes, and they had emerged as a superpower after America balkanized into self-run racial and ethnic enclaves. That made it all the more amusing that, out of the assortment of state, corporate, private, and other interests whose conglomeration of structures made up Langtry "city," the Chinese should be the ones whose internal environmental management had goofed. Everyone else had set up strict controls at the locks in the communications tunnels connecting to the Chinese compound, and so Kerry went across via the surface route, taking one of the GP robobuggies that provided the main means of getting around outside Langtry and in its immediate vicinity.

It was still called a compound, although the original dome put up after the Eurussian founding of the base had by now grown to a complex of towers and launch facilities, with enclosed plazas and residential zones standing above more than a dozen subterranean levels. Somehow, a consignment of insect samples en route to an experiment being conducted at some distant research station had gotten loose and found the surroundings conducive to multiplying their various kinds. As a result the entire Chinese sector was overrun and under effective quarantine to prevent the invasion spreading to the rest of Langtry. Not that there was anything hazardous to be concerned over. But conditions on Priscilla were oppressive enough as things were, without having to deal with other people's bugs on top of all else. And besides, there was that feeling of satisfaction that comes with being in a position to dictate to the high and haughty that the administrative chiefs in the other sectors weren't going to miss the opportunity of relishing.

Enclosed working and living spaces were not essential for survival on Priscilla. The atmosphere was breathable but drippingly humid, and it stank just about everywhere with fetid emanations from the swamps and mudlands that were the closest the planet came to mustering an ocean. The location had been deemed suitable for a long-range logistics consolidation and forwarding base to support the string of farther-flung outposts proliferating into the nearby regions of the Galaxy since macro-coherent entanglement toppled and superseded Relativity. Soon, ships from every outreaching organization with a cause or a product or a creed to promote were bringing down pilot groups to begin a new construction on the periphery of what the Earth media had dubbed a "spacerush" town, and stake out their claim in the operation.

Kerry had a good view of the area as the buggy came over the hump of bulldozed excavation debris between the south side of the Eurussian sector and the twin domes housing the shared power-generation and materials-extraction plant. In a way that said a lot even if it hadn't been by design, the layout and groupings on the ground reflected pretty closely the pattern of ideological affinities and aversions back on Earth. The Eurussian sector was connected to the New American. (On Earth this referred to the white Caucasian remnant, comprising the bulk of the Midwest and much of Canada, with coastal feet in Texas and New England straddling Ebonia, which ran from Louisiana to the Carolinas above the Cuban south of what had been Florida.) Zion—its namesake had been rebuilt in southern Argentina in the aftermath of the last global conflict—sat as a smaller appendage also connected to the New American complex but on the opposite side from the Eurussian. Yenan, which was the Chinese sector's proper name, dominated the central part of Langtry, having absorbed the original landing area for its military facility as impudently as its empire was expanding across Siberia. And equispaced from both, but the only other structure to rival them in size, the Muslim sector stood apart in a symbolic balancing role, incongruously complete with minarets and finials. Among these major edifices, the outposts of lesser representations had sprung up nearer or far according to their allegiances, like Gothic hamlets huddled under the walls of their lords' castles.

After three serious attempts at destroying what progress they had made in the direction of being able to live together in a civilized way, Kerry had thought people would have had enough. And, for a while, it had seemed that they might indeed have learned something of value finally. The tribal divisions that found expression in places like Langtry city reflected tradition more than effective reality, and by and large the assortments of humanity that found themselves clustered together on strange worlds orbiting alien suns light-years from home got along remarkably well.

For Kerry, "Priscilla" had never fitted the image of easygoing acceptance and everyone getting along. The name had too much of a prim and proper ring about it. There was nothing prim and proper about the bars and clubs that did a round-the-clock trade in Langtry's "downtown" strip that everybody went to but nobody owned. But they made a better mixing ground and forum for the conduct of social affairs than any parliament or congress back on Earth had ever done. The people you ran into there could be rough and blunt at times, but they were not judgmental, accepted others as they were, and if you stayed out of their business they stayed out of yours. Some wondered if it could be a preview of how the new worlds that were coming into being in the Outzones might be run. Hadn't it been the meddling moralizers who always caused all the problems? Live and let live would be the new guiding philosophy. The reason people don't trust each other and end up fighting is that they think others are different. But out here, everyone is so small compared to the vastness around them that they realize they're really the same now. So the old way of handling life is over, right? We've changed. Inside, where it matters, we know that everyone is just like us, moved by the same feelings, harboring the same fears. So when I take a deep, honest look inside myself, I see you. Isn't that right? Right!

And then the Eks showed up.

As missions from Earth probed farther into the surrounding reaches of interstellar space, they encountered various other forms of life—some looking surprisingly familiar; others, completely alien. Biologists of opposed persuasions all claimed support for theories that contradicted each other, and Kerry had never really followed the arguments why. Most of the life was primitive, and for a long time the rare instances of what could rightfully be classed as "intelligent" were rudimentary. However, as was probably inevitable, the collision with another advanced, technological culture happened eventually.

The "Eks," as far as could be ascertained, appeared to be at a comparable stage of development to Earth's, pushing out their own horizon of expansion and discovery, but coming the other way. So, they should have been just like us: motivated by the same reverence for knowledge, awed by the same wonder at the mysteries of the universe, and kindred spirits in all the ways that the new philosophy of enlightenment said mattered. And maybe they were. But they were also built to a body plan of arthropods, with exterior plates of black armor; double-jointed, stick-like limbs covered in bristles and hair; and snoutish heads sporting mandibles and large, multifaceted eyes suggestive of giant, mutant insects or riot police in full gas-masked battle garb. The name was a derivation from "Exoskeleton," but alternatives that quickly caught on included "Roachies," "Stickleheads," "Beetle-Peeple," and "Mantis-Men." Predictably, things had gone downhill from there. The taunts, boasts, and thinly disguised threats that seemed to be the nearest approach to diplomacy that the Ek mind could manage didn't help matters much either.

Kerry hadn't followed the details of who had allegedly said or done what as relationships deteriorated, despite the media's hysterical blow-by-blow coverage. That it followed the usual pattern of screwups by the best and the brightest that everyone else trusted to run the ship, he had no doubt. He had long ago grown too cynical to have much faith or interest in politics. He'd had enough dealing with his own domestic politics back home. That had been another reason why he signed up to come out for a tour at Langtry.

*   *   *

Tremil was a peculiar body on the fringe of the Xerxes system, of which Priscilla was an inner planet. It was peculiar in possessing a habitable surface with life-bearing oceans, despite being too small, as planetary standards normally went, to retain any atmosphere at all, and at a distance from its parent star where whatever did exist should have been frozen solid. Analysis of data from probes sent out to check the neighborhood following the first human arrivals at Xerxes suggested that Tremil contained a hot, superdense core, which at once sent imaginations racing. Theories spanned the gamut of exotic objects from miniature black holes and coherent neutronium plasmas to artificial bioforming devices constructed by aliens, and proposals for further research programs had poured in from all quarters.

While the scientists and funding authorities were still arguing, a rogue prospecting consortium called Midas Holdings had sent in a private expedition to assess the territory and take first dabs on any pickings. The laws as to who owned what or had the right to authorize such actions were still vague, and with a sharp legal department it was generally possible to get away with things like that. On this occasion, however, the move to get in ahead of the game had backfired tragically. A garbled distress call had come in from the Midas base camp on Tremil, indicating that they were in some kind of trouble, and then cut out. Almost at the same time, signals from the navigation beacons and communications relays placed in orbit as a matter of routine had ceased. Finally, the Midas expedition ship had come through briefly again, sounding as if it was attempting a hasty departure. Since then, there had been nothing. Fifty-three individuals had been involved in the expedition. It could only be feared that the worst had befallen all of them.

That much was common knowledge from the news coverage. Juanita Xiang-Chu—if they wanted to write their names backward that was their prerogative, but Kerry thought of them the way he was used to—filled in the few remaining details in an outer office of the Chinese Security Section. They were waiting for Kerry to be called in to a selection panel headed by a Colonel Hinjao, who would be commanding the mission being sent to Tremil to investigate. A bank of screens along one wall showed images of Tremil from orbit, along with the view of the Midas base camp that had been filed with its certificate in the Titles Registry before the disaster overtook it. The visible background was sandy and rocky, with a stretch of water opening out on one side and yellow cliffs beyond—about as different from Priscilla as it was possible to get.

"You'll be able to see the actual message transcripts later, when your temporary transfer is confirmed. . . ." Juanita began.

Kerry's eyebrows lifted. "Why the secrecy? Is there something more about this business that's security-sensitive?"

"No. It's just that the extra time would be better justified when we know for sure that you'll be coming. It will be decided later today."

"Coming?" Kerry repeated. "Does that mean you're on this too?"

"Yes, Dr. Kaplinsky. I shall be going with the mission also."

"Okay." Something buzzed past Kerry's ear on the

edge of his field of vision, causing him to swat at it reflexively. He had noticed the flies on the walls; another walked across the screen showing Tremil as they watched.

"I must apologize for this inconvenience," Juanita said awkwardly. She was clearly embarrassed. "We are doing what we can until things arrive from Earth to deal with the situation. It wasn't an eventuality that Langtry was equipped for."

"Oh, I'm sure we'll all pull through," Kerry said with a grin that he tried to make look sympathetic. Truth was, he was enjoying it.

He had to admit to being guilty of carrying something of a stereotype of Chinese women around in his head—particularly intellectual, academic, or otherwise officious ones—as being genderlessly baggy and toothy, with ring-rimmed glasses and their hair tied up like schoolmarms. "Priscilla" would have fitted it well. But Juanita shattered the caricature totally. She was perhaps in her early thirties, he judged—for what that was worth; he had a habit of being hopelessly wrong with Orientals—with a slim figure that managed to look shapely even in the high-necked, trousered suit that was standard casual working dress for the Chinese uniformed services. In the case of the Security Branch the colors were off-rust with black tabs and trim, which seemed tailored for her skin, more umber than yellow, and the hair sweeping to her shoulders with just enough bend not to look lank. Her eyes were the ever-alert, watchful kind, set in pert, finely formed features, which just at this moment were held in cool, unyielding lines that gave away nothing. Kerry had the feeling that was due more to a sense of professional correctness than to anything innate within. Off-duty, she could have turned a few heads in the bars downtown, if she ever had a mind for it.

Juanita continued, "From what we were able to make out before communications ceased, they seemed to be having equipment failures."

"What kind of equipment?" Kerry asked.

"All of it. Multiple failures, as if everything was going down at once. We had messages that would start coming through on one band stop suddenly, and resume on a different kind of channel. One talked about surface vehicles being immobilized, and another cut off in mid-sentence after saying that the power was going out." Juanita gestured in Kerry's direction, as if signaling something of particular relevance. "The crew of a reconnaissance platform left in orbit reported that they had structural failure in the hull. They said it was disintegrating before their eyes as they watched. Did you ever hear of anything like that in orbit before, Dr. Kaplinsky?"

"This is flattering, I'm sure," Kerry interjected. "But it's just mister. I'm called other things too."

"I apologize. My assumption. I should have read the records more closely."

Kerry frowned as he went back to her question. "In free fall, outside the atmosphere? . . . Meteorite stream, maybe?"

"No, it was nothing like that."

"How many people were up there?"

"Three."

"What happened to them?"

"The platform was equipped with an escape capsule. But whether they ever got down, we don't know."

Not that it would have made a lot of difference by all accounts.

"I see," Kerry said. Although at that stage there really wasn't much yet to be seen. It was just something to say.

However, one thing he could see now was why they had wanted a metallurgical physicist included in whatever kind of team was being organized to go there. Although, it seemed strange that *he* should have been singled out. There were numerous others of the same kind of specialty around Langtry, including more than a few who could boast a more exalted handle to their name than just "mister."

He ran his eye over the orbital shots of Tremil again. It looked like a tropical panorama of desert coasts and islands set amid cobalt oceans. Yet by rights it should have been solid ice and frozen methane. An interesting place under any other circumstances.

And then the obvious finally hit him. They didn't want to risk the Prof's and the Dr's, and the others with expensive, fancy titles. Nobody knew what to expect out there. They wanted someone more expendable!

The interview with the panel went smoothly, and Kerry's selection was confirmed early that same afternoon. The mission to Tremil departed from the Chinese launch area less than forty-eight hours later.

Kerry was prepared to swear that they could walk through metal walls. They had gotten into here too. Less than a day out from Priscilla, and the ship was turning into an insectarium.

"*I hate them!*" Juanita slapped at her arm as she sat behind Kerry on a folding seat in a recess at the side of the instrumentation fitting bay, where scientists were working to get their equipment ready. Kerry was running a calibration test on the grating assembly of an X-ray spectrometer lying partly dismantled on a bench. "My skin feels as if its crawling, even when there's nothing there," she said. "What use are they to anybody?"

"Over three quarters of all known Terran species are supposed to be insects," Kerry murmured without looking up. "Maybe they could ask the same question about us, but with a better reason." He read off some numbers to a red-bearded optronics engineer called Elliott, who repeated them while adjusting the shape of a curve being displayed on a screen. Juanita sniffed behind Kerry's shoulder. There was a pause.

"Okay, we're done on this," Elliott said. "Time for coffee, guys. I'll get 'em." He cocked an inquiring eye at Juanita. She shook her head.

"They don't seem to trouble you," she commented to Kerry as Elliott rose and moved away. "These bugs everywhere."

Kerry sat back on the lab stool. "Well, they're just being what they are, same as the rest of us. . . ." He tried biting his lip but couldn't resist adding, "Anyhow, I'm not the one who thinks his country's image is disgraced. You do it to yourselves, Juanita. Nobody else thinks so. It could have happened to anyone."

"Perhaps not everyone feels the same obligation to maintain exemplary standards, Mr. Kaplinsky."

"You know, to us that has a kind of stiff and formal sound about it. 'Kerry' would really do just fine—especially out here in a situation like this."

"Kerry." She repeated the word distantly, then fell silent again—as if she were thinking about it.

The first, most obvious suspicion was that whatever had happened at Tremil had something to do with its strange internal composition, possibly involving a hitherto unknown type of radiation associated with a matter-annihilation process. But nobody had any ideas of trying to learn more by landing on the surface and seeing what happened. Walking into a den is not the smart way of finding out if the bear is at home. The first step would be to put robot instrument packages in close orbit and down on the surface, while the ship stayed well back and its complement of chemists, physicists, electronics, communications, structures, materials, and other specialists monitored developments remotely. And that was about as far as anyone had been able to plan ahead in the time available. Where they went after that would depend on what transpired.

"Kerry's an Irish name, isn't it?" Juanita said at last. "But it doesn't seem to fit with the other part."

Kerry got asked this all the time. "I'm from the part of Eurussia called Poland," he replied. "My parents bought a lucky ticket in the Irish state lottery shortly before I was born, and that was how they celebrated." He wrinkled his nose and rubbed it with a knuckle. "Anyway, who are you to ask? How does 'Juanita' come to be connected with Xiang-Chu?"

Juanita's face softened into the concession of a smile. It was the first time Kerry had felt a moment of real person-to-person contact. He wasn't sure what she and the several others from her department were doing here at all. It wasn't as if there was likely to be much call for security precautions on Tremil. The Chinese just seemed incapable of doing anything without its having to have a political dimension.

"Oh, my mother had a Mexican grandfather that she was very fond of," she replied. "You know how it is with us and our illustrious ancestors. I'm pretty sure that had something to do with it."

"Do you miss it much?"

"Earth, you mean?"

"Uh-huh."

Juanita sighed. "I suppose there are always some things. I try not to think about it much. This is where I am. This is where the things are that it is my duty to do. . . ." She inclined her head. "How about you?"

Kerry shook his head. "It's a madhouse back there. Everyone has some reason for getting militant about why everyone else shouldn't be allowed to do what they want to do. Getting through to most of them is like trying to talk to a fire siren. I prefer life in the Outzones, even if the attractions might not make for the best tour brochures. People value each other for the things that matter, because they depend on them. Phonies don't get very far. You learn to be honest with yourself."

"I saw in your records that you are divorced," Juanita said.

"Hey, that's not fair. I didn't get to see your records."

"I was never married. I got involved in politics when I was at university, and decided on a career in that direction."

"Hm. So weren't there any like-minded politically attractive males there too?"

"If there were, I never met one." Juanita paused for a moment, acknowledging the need to be delicate. It struck Kerry as very gracious. "What happened with you? Things just didn't work out?"

"Oh . . . her only measure of a meaningful life was impressing worthless friends. She'd never have lasted a week out here. You see, we weren't meant for the same world. Literally."

Elliott returned with two plastic mugs and passed one across to Kerry. Before Kerry had taken a sip, Colonel Hinjao came in from the corridor, wearing ship fatigues and accompanied by an adjutant. He looked around, raising a hand to indicate that he had an announcement. A hush fell over the scientists.

"We have more news from Langtry, just in from Earth," Hinjao informed them. "It appears that our task is more complicated. Two more occurrences have been reported, each in a different star system. So we can forget any idea that this is something peculiar to Tremil. I will, of course, keep you updated as soon as we learn anything further. Thank you."

Earth had been strengthening the deep-space defenses protecting the outposts around the periphery of its domain in response to the perceived threat from the Eks. One of the new incidents was at a gamma-laser battle station in orbit over a gas giant in the Cyrus-2 system. The platform also housed an advanced military research and testing laboratory that possessed all the right equipment and expertise to investigate the phenomenon from its earliest beginning. It was from here, therefore, that the first insights came back as to what was going on.

The station was being "digested"—which was the best word that the scientists there could come up with. Its outside was corroding under the combined assault of countless microscopic objects that attacked metals, utilizing oxidation energy and incorporating the products. Nobody knew where they had come from. They seemed to have drifted in from space, and found the artifacts of advanced technical civilization to be just what they needed to thrive on. Built in the way and to the scale generally thought of in connection with nano devices, yet exhibiting more of the function of a bizarre form of digestion enzyme, they had been dubbed "nanozymes." Arguments broke out immediately over whether they were of natural or artificial origin but the issue was soon settled. Before the scientists in the ship were even through studying the preliminary data, reports of new attacks were already coming in. As the locations were plotted on charts of the surrounding regions, an ominous pattern became discernible. The nanozymes were appearing roughly in a hemisphere centered upon Sol. And the latest ones were getting closer.

Things didn't move that quickly between star systems. Not naturally, anyway. It was being orchestrated deliberately, for a reason, by something with the means to exert an influence across light-years. And at a time like this, that could only mean the Eks.

"A nano-scale weapons system," Katsumi Yoshida, the head of the scientific group, summarized. He had called the others together on the ship's mess deck for a review session. "And frankly, I think we may have a major problem on our hands. How do you defend against something like this? You can't even see it. Our latest orbital bombardment systems and interplanetary beam defenses are just sitting out there, literally being eaten, with nothing to target. They're effectively junk." He looked around as if seeking suggestions. A heavy silence hung in the air.

"Are we making any overtures to the Eks diplomatically?" somebody asked finally. The tone sounded as if it already presumed capitulation.

Hinjao answered from where he was standing by the wall to one side, carrying a fly swatter wedged under his arm like an officer's baton. "As far as I am aware, the Eks are being derisive and admitting nothing. If I had to bet, I'd say that they are letting us sweat for a while and enjoying it." Angry and frustrated murmurs came from around the room.

Dominic Behas, an organic chemist from Pasadena, in northern New Aztlan, raised his head. "I can't help wondering . . ." He hesitated, rubbing his chin, as if checking for something he might have missed. "What I'm trying to say is, don't you think we might be overreacting? I mean, sure, it's a crazy, different kind of weapon and all that. But I've been going through the numbers. Nothing's really happening that fast. It's more like a corrosion of the outer skin. Those new places that it's affected are all still functioning."

"Huh! Try telling that to the guys who were in the Midas place on Tremil that got hit," Elliott challenged, turning from a seat at the front. "And all their sats. Everything came apart like igloos in Hades. You saw the clips."

"But we don't know how long it had been going on there," Behas persisted. "From what's being measured, the erosion rates right now are not that high."

"So what are you suggesting, Dominic?" Yoshida asked.

"I'm not really sure. . . . But we might have more time to work on this than some people are assuming. There could be a simple chemical answer—maybe something you can spray on the outside that neutralizes them. Something like that."

"I believe that experiments of that kind are already being tried," Colonel Hinjao put in.

Kerry nodded in silent agreement where he was sitting near the back. He had nothing to add at that point, but the same thought had occurred to him too. It was true, as Behas said, that nobody knew how long the nanozymes had been active before the structures on Tremil finally disintegrated. But Midas had only been there for so long, which put an upper limit on it. And from the estimates Kerry had made using the same data that Behas was referring to, the numbers still didn't add up. Even if the erosion had been going on from the first day that the Midas expedition arrived, there still hadn't been enough time for the damage to become catastrophic. Kerry had the uneasy feeling that what they were seeing in these new attacks was just the first phase of something that was going to get worse. Perhaps the Eks were holding back because they knew the biggest laugh was still to come.

The ship arrived at Tremil thirty hours later. Although the planet itself no longer seemed implicated, it was decided to keep to the original plan of conducting a preliminary reconnaissance using robots remote-directed from orbit. Kerry was on duty, manning one of the monitoring consoles in the Control section when the main pod landed a thousand feet from what was left of the Midas base camp. The pod's outer doors opened to disgorge an assortment of drones, minirovers, and camera mobiles, which dispersed to assess the surroundings and obtain some general views of the area before moving in closer to the site itself.

The structures that had been the camp's main quarters and attendant installations were not even shells or stripped-down remains, just a few frayed slivers of metal left standing, and a scattering of debris in the sand. Of the Midas ship itself, last heard from making a getaway attempt, there was no sign. The most likely conclusion seemed to be that it had been overwhelmed in the same manner as the base installation and the orbiting satellites, in which case anything left of it would by now be a mass coffin far from Tremil, receding on a trajectory that was anyone's guess.

Juanita had joined Kerry to follow the event. Despite—or perhaps because of the mutual challenges stimulated by—their different backgrounds they were getting to like each other's company, and spent most of their off-duty time bantering about the relative merits of politics and science. For Kerry, simply listening to someone whose priorities in life were ideals and principles instead of material preoccupations made a refreshing change. What his attraction to her might be, he wasn't sure. Maybe as a different kind of subject for honing her not inconsiderable dialectic skill, he sometimes suspected. The cynic in him said it couldn't be anything else.

Displays alongside the main screens showed readings being taken from orbit. In addition to breaking down metals, the nanozymes also emitted "quanco" radiation collectively—a macro-coherent quantum wave function of the kind that provided the basis of interstellar communications and travel. This had been one of the first clear pointers to their being of artificial as opposed to natural origin. They seemed to be broadcasting, though to what purpose nobody had even a guess.

An alert indicator began flashing on one of the spectrum analyzers. Kerry killed it, studied the data, and then voiced a command to connect an auxiliary screen through to Yoshida, who was looking over the shoulder of the operator at another console across the room. "Quanco emission being detected from Lander One," Kerry reported. "C and H modes."

"Yes, we've got it," Yoshida responded. "It seems to be building. There's a reading from Orbiter Three as well."

"What does it mean?" Juanita muttered in Kerry's ear.

"The lander down there has started q-radiating. It's got nanozymes aboard. It sounds as if one of the orbiting pods that we put out does too."

"So they know we're here? They've found us already?"

"Looks like it."

Juanita took in the scenes as the rovers moved to new angles, and Kerry switched between different zoom magnifications. Some patches of debris to one side of the site turned out to be the remnants of general-terrain survey vehicles. Even the heavy-duty balloon tires had been reduced to a few hanging tatters of rubberized threads. "Those tiny things that you can't even see did this?" She shook her head. "I thought you said soap and water would wash them off."

"If you got there early enough, maybe." It puzzled Kerry that everything could have the appearance of being picked so clean. Even if the structures had been eaten away, the materials from them should still be lying around. For the most part, they seemed to have evaporated. It seemed odd.

He ran a routine check from the camera covering inside the equipment bay of the lander pod. The access doors were open, and just a couple of specialized instrument carriers were left, awaiting calls to the outside. . . . And then something black and leggy settled on the camera lens, took several quick steps across in blurred silhouette, and was gone. "I don't believe it!" Kerry breathed.

"What?"

"I just saw a bug. Surely they can't have gotten down there as well!"

Then Elliott's voice called out to the room in general. "Hey, people, what do you make of this? Rover Two, visual."

Kerry brought the channel up on another of his screens. The view was from an open area on the far side of the site from the lander. It showed what appeared to be the beginnings of a shining structure, sprouting from the ground. But what kind of structure was a good question. It was metallic, yes, and looked like a skeleton of struts and peculiar geometric shapes that more was to be built around, but beyond that there was no clue as to its likely function. The only two things that could be said for certain were that it was unlike anything that any human designer would have conceived, and that it hadn't been there when the last shots from the ill-fated Midas venture were sent.

"Man, if that isn't a piece of Ek inspiration, then my name isn't Elliott Sweeney."

Every console in the room switched to the view. Somebody brought one of the drones over to get a shot from above. No comment was really needed. It was evidently an early stage in the construction of something. The materials must have come from the disassembled Midas base structures, which at least answered the question of where they had gone. "Guesses?" Yoshida invited. Nobody had any.

The other obvious question was: What was doing the constructing? Surely it was beyond the capabilities of nanozymes. They seemed to be specialized for breaking materials down; in any case, without a liquid or other apparent substrate to operate in, where would they get the mobility?

The answer came with a series of zoom shots showing details from around the surfaces of the strange alien construction. It was alive with tiny mobile creatures—not nanozymes, for they were orders of magnitude above a molecular scale in size, but still small enough to have been missed at first sight. Then, as the astounded scientists continued watching and following them, doubts began growing as to whether "alive" was the right term at all. They seemed to be more of the nature of weird, elaborate micromachines. There seemed to be a number of different kinds cooperating to transport grains of materials that were being carried in from somewhere—the direction indicated the Midas site—and attach them into the growing structure. Some had jointed grabs and rotating manipulator appendages, which had been the first things about them to suggest machines rather than living objects; others seemed specialized for joining and fixing, while yet more took care of cutting, trimming, and cleaning up. What had given the first impression of their being alive was their odd method of locomotion, which involved a deformable, moving underpart that flowed to lay down a tread for the body to move over, and then picked itself up again behind, somewhat like a plastic form of caterpillar tread but able to realign in any direction. Their speed and efficiency and the precision they were able to achieve were amazing. The scientists sat, fascinated, watching as they contrived integrated channels and ducts, chambers and connecting holes, all with a finesse comparable to the finest etching. Elliott Sweeney came up with "microbot" as a generic to describe them.

Closer examination of the Midas camp remains confirmed yet more kinds busily engaged in dismantling what was left there. But more significantly, it finally provided a credible answer of the kind Kerry had been looking for as to what could have provoked the Midas people into a panic evacuation and caused the crew of their orbiting platform to describe the hull as disintegrating before their eyes. He outlined his theory of what he thought it meant to Yoshida and Colonel Hinjao in the ship's officers' dayroom. Juanita, who had gone to fetch them, was sitting in.

"It's a two-stage process. The nanozymes are the scouts. They're transferred to a target star system and dispersed to search for signs of an advanced culture." He made a gesture to excuse stating the obvious. "Refined metals and alloys are a good indicator. When they find a concentration that's too extended and consistent to be natural, they call in the backup wave—the microbots. That's what the broadcasting is all about. How the microbots navigate and steer, I'm not sure. Maybe they use some kind of radiation absorption and re-emission with a reaction. The kinds we've observed so far are not necessarily the space-mobile forms. They could be transported by other types, or conceivably transmogrify on arrival."

"Intriguing," Yoshida pronounced, steepling his fingers under his chin. "Do go on, Kerry."

Hinjao put in, "But the initial ones, the nanozymes. They do more than just find suitable structures and send signals. They are destructive in their own right too. They're described as corrosive."

Kerry nodded. "Yes. But I think that's just incidental to their main function."

"Which is? . . ."

"Setting up advance supply dumps. They create stocks of fuel molecules for the microbots, and produce a reserve of startup materials. But the action doesn't really start until the microbots arrive. They're the heavy-duty demolition and construction crew."

"Do you have any idea what this construction might be that they have commenced down there on Tremil?" Yoshida asked.

Kerry could only spread his hands. "Who can say? Ek minds work in a different conceptual realm from ours. This is apparently their way of making war. Microbot spearheads move in and take out bases, weapons, vehicles, machines—anything that could form part of an infrastructure capable of organizing a resistance. At the same time, they transform it into different structures that serve their purpose instead." He shrugged. "It could be some kind of forward installation or base. We'll no doubt find out when the Eks decide to move in."

Juanita was looking strained as the enormity of the situation they were facing unfolded fully. "Is there any way we can defend ourselves against something like this?" Yoshida asked.

Again, Kerry could only shake his head. "I can't think of any. You put it perfectly yourself on the way out here. None of our weapons have anything to target. They're effectively junk."

Two further developments followed in rapid succession that were even more alarming. The Orbiter Three package that the ship had deployed, from which nanozyme quanco emissions had already been detected, ceased functioning completely. Telescopic inspection from the ship showed that it was visibly changing shape, shrinking at one end while growing at the other. Hinjao ordered a reconnaissance drone launched to investigate from closer quarters. It revealed Orbiter Three to be already swarming with microbots. Even given that they hadn't needed to be summoned from afar but were already at Tremil, the rapidity with which they had concerted their attack was stupefying. And so was the form that the attack was taking. Without space available to transport their materials to a new location as was being done down on the surface, the microbots were managing the two operations simultaneously, digesting the orbiter down into its constituent substances in one part, while rebuilding them into something completely different at another.

And then the same thing was reported from the

gamma-laser battle station at Cyrus-2. Systems there were failing one after the other, just as Juanita had described in the garbled messages from the Midas base. Structures were already compromised in several places and deteriorating rapidly everywhere. When the latest findings from Tremil were relayed via Priscilla, Command HQ on Earth ordered immediate evacuation at Cyrus-2. The first battle had been lost in a rout with the enemy not even sighted.

The Eks opened a channel to Earth less than an hour later. Although their ultimatum was not put out on the public grid, a recording was forwarded to Tremil, which Colonel Hinjao replayed for the benefit of the scientists and the mission's officers. It showed three of the beetlelike heads tilting from side to side and making curious circular motions in what could only have been the alien equivalent of chortling. The nearest rendition the translator computers were able to make from their halting, clickety-clack speech came through as:

"So, ho-ho, human jelly-worm people see now Ek superweapon is invincible. Eks rule Sol worlds now. One Earth-day to agree surrender. Then we come to Earth and accept. Otherwise we send in transmute-everything plague. You have no answers. Much jolly fun then to see, ho-ho, hee-hee. One day is all. Good morning."

Kerry sat, staring despondently at the screens. The others in the Control section were equally subdued. All of the low-level orbiters were dead. Orbiter Three was almost completely consumed and turning into something resembling a Ferris wheel mounted on an eggbeater. Orbiter Seven, the farthest out from Tremil, had commenced quanco emissions. The ship was at readiness to pull out at an instant's notice. Nobody had come up with any suggestions, let alone answers.

"What do they *want*?" Juanita asked beside him. "I mean, what can we have that they possibly need? Everything about them is so different. It can't be technology or resources. They've already got the technology to create any kind of resource."

"Who knows? Maybe a green, warm world to retire to. Or to get us working plantations for them. For all we know, silicates and carbonates might taste nice. Somehow I doubt if it's our women, Juanita, so don't lose sleep worrying about that."

"Then why can't they just say whatever it is? There might be some way of coming to an accommodation without any of all this."

"They seem to like it this way. It must be how they do things. Maybe they find power trips addictive."

Juanita sighed and fell silent for a while. Then she looked up. "Did we just collide with them by accident, do you think, the way we assumed? Or did they have a surveillance net set up that detected our technology and steered them to us?"

Kerry had been wondering the same thing. If they looked for advanced technologies, that could maybe provide a clue as to what they wanted. "That's a good question. But since nobody's going to be able to answer it in the time we've . . ." His voice trailed away as he realized that Juanita wasn't listening. She was staring past his shoulder, her eyes wide.

"Kerry," she whispered.

He turned back to face the console. Framed in the

screen showing the video channel from one of the minirovers down on Tremil was a bedraggled human figure, a man. He approached warily, looking down at the rover, at the same time swatting at something near his head. Then he said, "Can anybody hear me?"

His name was Arvasse. There were two of them, from the Midas orbiting platform. The third hadn't made it into the escape capsule when the structure started to break up. The capsule had long disappeared, along with everything else that had been at the base. Arvasse couldn't add anything further regarding what had happened to the rest of the expedition. By the time they got back down, the ship had gone, and that was all he knew. They had watched the base and its equipment decomposing and kept their distance, living on survival rations from the capsule, eked out by fungi and cactilike offerings from the surroundings that tested okay.

"So these micromachines don't attack people?" Yoshida said. He had been called in and was standing beside Kerry. Hinjao was on Yoshida's other side. Everyone who could get away was cramming into the Control section to see this.

"What micromachines?" Arvasse asked. He looked weary, haggard, and not all that interested.

"They're what have been eating your base away."

"I don't know anything about that. Like I already told you, we weren't about to come anywhere close to whatever was going on here."

The other survivor had joined Arvasse by this time. She was dark-skinned, equally ragged and exhausted, and her name was Vonne. "Look," she said, clearly at the end of her patience. "Can we forget all these questions for now? I'm not sure who you people are, but you're somewhere up there, right? Will you just come down and get us out of here? Do you know how many days we've been sitting around in these rocks, sleeping in hot sand?" She brushed irritably at her arms and face. "And now we're being eaten alive by goddam bugs."

At that moment, the operator at the panel showing the ship's condition called out, *"Alert condition registering! Q-mode emissions from the outside hull. They're here!"* It meant that nanozymes had found the ship. The microbots wouldn't be far behind. This was the point where it had been decided the ship would pull out. But all of a sudden the decision was fraught with an unexpected complication. Kerry looked at Hinjao's face as the colonel agonized over giving the order.

"We have to, Colonel," Yoshida muttered in a low, somber voice. "I know it will be slow for those two people. But you have no choice. We'd lose the whole ship down there."

And then Kerry became conscious of a very strange fact: *The lander pod, its rovers, and the other devices down on the surface were all still functioning.* Unlike the satellites dying on orbit, nothing was interfering with them!

He brought up the image from the inside of the lander's equipment bay, still open to the outside, and magnified it. Sure enough, there were microbots there. But they were lying still and inactive. They seemed mangled and dismembered. He noticed then on the other screens that the agitation and bustle that had been going on all over the strange Ek construction and the ruin of the Midas base had ceased. Pieces of microbots lay littered in piles everywhere. Even as he watched one of the views, something crawled in from the side, seized a microbot that was still moving, practically bit it in half, and disappeared again. And then it came to him what it meant.

"*No!*" he said, jerking his head around at Hinjao. Hinjao blinked at the sharpness of Kerry's voice. "Trying to get away won't do any good. We'll be a quanco beacon everywhere we go. If you want to save the ship, get us inside the atmosphere. Put down on Tremil as fast as you can, and open all the hatches!"

Earth agreed to the Eks' demands and prepared a site to receive the Ek delegation with their surrender terms. The site they chose was carefully selected amid swamplands of the lower Amazon. The Ek ships landed and disgorged a great showing of representatives and entourage, which proceeded in a swaggering parade toward where the Terran deputation was assembled. At which point the Terrans uncovered hidden weapons emplacements to the accompaniment of flyovers of warplanes—almost as if they didn't know that their machines were already marked by nanozymes. The Eks responded by unleashing their plague of micro-disassemblers, as they had said they would.

The result was a massacre. Hornets, flies, mosquitoes, and bugs came out of the swamps in clouds. Nanozymes triggered the same responses as sexual pheromones, but with the difference of priming the recipients to seek out microbots. When the arousal-crazed insects failed to elicit the requisite responses from the objects of their passions, they tore them to pieces. Upon which, being of a disposition to iterate the same loops of program over and over rather than reflect on the meaning of it all, they would then go on to find another. Repeatedly. Such were the frenzies instilled, that they could tear through a population of microbots like foxes set loose in a chicken farm. As a bonus that the Terrans hadn't expected, several varieties turned out be quite partial to whatever the outsides of Eks were made of too, and the whole debacle ended with the Eks fleeing in panic and disarray back to their ships to beat a hasty and decidedly inglorious departure.

They were deferential and mannerly after that, agreeing to mind their own affairs and keep to their designated part of the Galaxy until Earth saw fit to concede otherwise. In the course of the negotiations that followed, they also revealed that Tremil was a construction of theirs, which answered that mystery. It was the transfer port through which the initial scouting screen of nanozymes, and then, subsequently, the follow-up waves of microbots, were injected into the Xerxes system. The Eks staked out many star systems with such devices to monitor for signs of advanced technologies. Making the outside look like a planet was the "bait" to lure any civilization sufficiently advanced to realize that something was wrong into coming to investigate.

It also appeared that there were no insects on the Eks' world. They assumed them to be products of a fiendishly advanced Terran technology, and interpreted the event at the Amazon as a masterful ploy to demonstrate its potency, devised by minds they couldn't hope to equal. Nobody on the Earth side, naturally, chose to dispel their illusions.

The tunnel locks were open again, and Kerry rode a car through to the Chinese sector. Emergency pest-control supplies had arrived from Earth as ordered, but nobody was using them. People kind of liked having the little guys around. After all, it was as much their home too, right? Right. And simply opening the doors to the outside more often kept it from becoming too much of a home. They just seemed to love those swamps and marshes out there, all over the surface of Priscilla.

Juanita was waiting outside the Security offices, looking trim and fresh out of uniform in a lilac blouse with a design of flowers and dragons, and a calf-length skirt slit tantalizingly to four inches above the knee. "Wow!" Kerry greeted. "Politics just took on a new dimension. They should use you for a recruiting ad."

"I thought you'd want an acceptable partner. You are still going to show me how to dance?"

"You bet. We'll knock 'em dead—the whole downtown."

"Which place did you decide on?"

"I couldn't make my mind up. So I figured, what the heck? We'll take in all of them. It's not exactly as if it's the Boulevard Saint Michel down there."

"Oh, who needs Paris?"

"But we'll start at one that I think you'd like. It's got a quiet bar and an early-evening seafood snack bar. We can always eat properly later."

"Sounds great. What's it called?"

"They just changed the name. It used to be the

Cuddly Kitty. But since they did it up and reopened, it's the Friendly Firefly."

"I love it!"

"Everybody does. Come on, let's go have some fun."

Juanita slipped her arm through Kerry's. They began walking toward the access elevator that would take them to the tunnel connecting to downtown.

Getting Better Connected

It was my agent, Eleanor Wood, who started it all. By the mid 1990s I had sold the Irish answer to the Taj Mahal that we had been renovating in Bray, County Wicklow (see "Sorry About That," in *Rockets, Redheads & Revolution*), to Phil Coulter, the well-known songwriter. Phil and Geraldine have six children too, and it was gratifying to see Killarney House continuing to be used as a family home that would be appreciated, instead of being turned into a pile of greasy flats for students as happens to so many fine old houses these days. Jackie and the boys had used part of the proceeds to acquire a place in northwest Florida, where the climate and general laid-back way of life were congenial to exercising the torpidity that comes naturally to cats and teenagers, while I had put the rest into a town house near the seafront in the center of Bray and converted it into a couple of apartments. One, I rented out to generate some useful extra income, while the other I kept for my own use when in Europe.

I was fortunate in finding an ideal tenant—an elderly widow with a son who was a construction worker in the town, and could take take care of repairs and maintenance when I was away in the U.S. The old lady would always be ringing the bell five minutes after I came back from abroad, saying she had heard me come in and put a pot of tea on the stove. We sometimes got embroiled in arguments of a distinctly unusual kind for landlord and tenant.

"I see you've put up an outside light over the alley to the entrance at the back. How much was it? I'll give you a check."

"Ye will not, so!"

"Why wouldn't I? Isn't it my house that you've added to the value of?"

"'Twas our own decision. Ye weren't asked. So shut up and have a cup of tea."

The quality of life improves so much when maximizing the bottom line doesn't become the sole measure of everything.

Anyway, life was drifting into one of its tranquil periods again, which experience has shown invariably to be the prelude to some kind of upheaval. I was across in Florida—it would have been around the time I was working on *Bug Park*, or maybe *Outward Bound*, when Eleanor called from New York to say, "Jim, you need to get yourself a Web site."

"What for?"

"It's the way things are these days. The whole

world is going online. All the writers are setting up Web sites."

"But you know I think everything invented after I turned fifty was unnecessary—and the world would probably have been better off without."

"It's the way to be visible and stay in touch. Really, it's something you should think about."

There was no way I was going to be dragged out of book-writing mode to start getting involved in HTML programming and whatever else this would need—I had only recently, grudgingly, converted to a PC, having been probably one of the last people left on the planet to be still using the TRS-80. (I'd also had a great time with the Commodore 64, writing rudimentary graphics games for the boys before most people had heard of them. That had to have been one of the neatest machines for its time.) But, hey, wasn't this the kind of thing that teenage sons are there for? So I took the matter to Alex, then aged around fourteen, whose bedroom had already become a computer assembly shop and meeting place for the local juvenile hackers, and said, "Why don't we put together a Web site?"

And so the first version of www.jamesphogan.com came about. It began as simply a reference resource for my novels, short stories, and other works. A decision that we made early on and have stuck to since was to keep a strongly text-oriented flavor. Much of the mail we've received indicates that visitors appreciate it. The purpose was to inform people, after all, and it's the text that tells you things. Even back then, the amount of fancy graphics, banners, wallpapers, and other ornamentation was irritating and made dial-up downloads infuriatingly slow—even before the appearance of ads, pop-ups, animations, and other rubbish proliferating today. (Excessive graphics and overelaboration are still the most effective things for making me tune out of sites that I visit—usually running out of patience before any content has appeared at all. Newspaper sites seem to be the worst offenders. The ones I like best are those that post in plain-text format—fast, and compact to store. The *Thoth* catastrophism newsletter is a good instance, at http://www.kronia.com/thoth.html. Where nothing of interest is lost, I prefer to store downloaded pages as text files.)

Of course, the inevitable happened. Once you've got a shop window to the world that people are coming to look at, you find all kinds of thoughts, opinions, and "takes" on various issues that you just have to air. But at least it's better to vent them in a place that anyone interested can choose to visit, than to insist on bogging your books down and turning them into pulpits, with the consequences that we've all seen and groaned at. So we added the Bulletin Board, featuring comments on areas of science that I tend to hold forth about if given the chance, politics, puns, and anything else that I happened to be of a mood to share on any particular day. The Board turned out to be quite popular, stimulating a lot of mail calling for responses that I hadn't exactly bargained for. But such is the price of leading with one's chin, I suppose.

It's customary for a book-publishing contract to specify a quantity of copies for the author when a new title or edition is released. With hardback and paperback editions, various reissues, UK and foreign-language subsidiary-right sales, an entire room of

Jackie's house was by this time taken up with storage. I think it was Alex who suggested adding an ordering section to the site to see if we could sell some of them. I thought it was a good idea and told him to go ahead, adding in a fit of magnanimity that he could keep any proceeds as his "fee" for all the project work. He did quite well out of it, as things happened, getting orders from all over the world, not infrequently topping $100—not bad for a high schooler in the late '90s, before the dollar started turning into used bus tickets. Some people reading this might have been following the site long enough to remember "Mr. Toad's Book Ordering Page." That had been Alex's nickname since babyhood, owing to a slight tendency to pudginess not uncommon in early years, which he had clung to proudly ever since.

We began by keeping the ordering process simple, accepting just checks and money orders. But it wasn't long before requests started coming in from readers for us to add online electronic capability too. The site had been steadily growing in size and complexity, and since I had not really made the time to keep up with developments and trends in the computer world since leaving DEC in 1979—writing, family issues, and a recurring compulsion to mess around with old houses adds up to a pretty much full-time commitment—it was becoming apparent that just maintaining the site, never mind adding more to it, involved more than we had bargained for.

Fortunately, the situation was ameliorated by the appearance on the scene at around this time of one Tim Gleason, in Connecticut. Tim's name began appearing in the reader e-mails, and our ensuing exchanges grew to a regular correspondence. An ex-Vietnam-era Marine, he had gone on to become a computer engineer, working also for DEC in Maynard, Massachusetts, it turned out, in the same years that I had been based there and at Framingham. Afterward he had spent time with Data General, and eventually set up his own systems consultancy. From starting out by helping Alex with some of the technicalities, Tim was drawn progressively deeper into our Web-site dealings and today functions as the regular site administrator—as well as keeping up pressure on me, as a matter of professional pride, to do things like upgrade from Windows 95 to 98 long after the rest of the world had already gone to XP or whatever.

Taking all considerations into account, we decided that, to consolidate and clean up the various layers of Alex's experimenting that the site now embodied, add the online ordering that readers were asking for, and streamline the business of maintenance and some further enhancements that we had in mind, the time had come to transfer everything over to being database-driven. Although Alex had created several small, special-purpose databases, converting a system of the mix and size that the site had become would have been asking a bit much. So we started shopping around to see what utilities for this kind of thing might be available commercially. Software had long been a peeve of mine. So much of what I'd come across seemed to have been inspired conceptually by the designer's knowledge of the inner workings, rather than approached from the viewpoint of a user seeing the outside. (When I wrote technical sales manuals for DEC, I used to collect comments on the draft from the secretaries who would be using the product, not from the engineers who knew how it worked.) Just about everything we looked at had something about it that made it no good for what we wanted. The standard choices for adding the shipping cost to an order, for example, were based either on the number of line items or the total order value, neither of which was much use for a mixed consignment of hardback and paperback books. It was astounding how often the program would accept only addresses conforming to the standard U.S. format. (Try force-fitting a few addresses from, say, Germany or Japan.) I grumbled that Amazon.com seemed to be able to deal with everything in a comprehensive and flexible manner. True, I was told—but they probably paid five or six million dollars for it. So we resigned ourselves to probably having to draw up our own specification and putting it out to be specially written. A somewhat less ambitious undertaking than Amazon's, no doubt; but we were only talking about listing my titles, after all.

This was where life produced one of those learning experiences that come about from sallying forth blissfully into a realm of which one has no prior experience and naivety is all but total, where the most that can be hoped for is to come out of it a bit the wiser with the gain of something that might stick. That expression comes to mind of confidence being what you feel when you don't really understand the situation. Word of our needs had propagated around, and brought a stream of offers to help from various quarters, with the general gist that playing a part in producing Jim Hogan's new Web site would be payment enough in return for the books that people said they had enjoyed over the years. Well, this sounded like the kind of thing it would be foolish to refuse. Buoyed by the assurances that I was dealing with professionals who would polish something like this off in their lunch hours and breaks, I told Alex to retire Mr. Toad's page and posted an announcement that the new site with its expanded ordering capability would be up in a matter of a few weeks. That must have been around 1999 or 2000. Three or four years were to go by before we saw my books being offered for sale via the Web site again.

I'm not saying that the volunteers didn't mean well. But I should have kept in mind something that I had learned in my experiences of renovating old houses, and that was to be suspicious of self-promotion and people who tell you what great work they do. The ones who really do good work just do it and let it speak for itself. Some that we tried to deal with were unable even to grasp what we wanted. Others rushed in with commendable enthusiasm, only to founder when it became plain that they didn't know as much as they thought they did, and a number of dialogues that were going in circles had to be diplomatically ended. A recurring pattern that I noticed here, for the benefit of anyone interested in human psychological traits, was a seeming inability to simply accept being in over one's head, admit it, and retire gracefully—which would have been respected, and the effort nevertheless appreciated. Instead, what happened was that some reason would be given for putting back the date that had been estimated, and this would turn into a steady succession of excuses in which we were always another month away. As they say, you get what you pay for. Tim had always been skeptical of this being a way to get worthwhile results, but having expressed his view, didn't see it as his place to be telling me what to do on my own site. Maybe he'd been in the business long enough to know that letting people find out the hard way is probably the only way they'll learn. Anyway, it gradually became clear to all that this wasn't going to get us anywhere, and so we went back to our original position of accepting that the way to go was to put the job out commercially to professionals.

Our thought was to tackle the proposed changes in two phases. First, we would keep the existing site as it was and link it to a separate shopping-cart facility that might be on the same server or elsewhere. Once that was working, we would upgrade the original site to be database-driven as planned. An attraction of this approach was that by focusing initially on the shopping cart, we would restore a book-ordering capability in minimum time. I checked out ads and blurbs, sought recommendations, and ended up talking to an outfit on the West Coast that had supplied the shopping-cart software for a number of online order operations. We got a written quote outlining the work, setting out a payment schedule, and giving time estimates for the milestones. All very impressive. I okayed the deal and sent a check for the down payment. Nothing could go wrong this time, right? Oh, boy.

I still suffer from flashbacks to the horror story that followed, which makes it difficult to recount coherently. A warning bell should perhaps have sounded when the head of the company—let's call him J—said that things would go more smoothly if we transferred the site from its present server to theirs, so that everything could be hosted in the same place. There was no real need for this, but I could see nothing wrong with the suggestion at the time and authorized the transfer of my domain name accordingly. A firm stipulation of the arrangement was that the existing site was not to be changed in any way. It would be reproduced in its existing form and the new order page and shopping cart simply added to it. The JPH site had been written to be transportable without modification, and there should have been no problem in getting it up and running on the new host virtually immediately upon loading.

Several days later, however, attempts to access www.jamesphogan.com at the new site were still not working. Then I learned that J had asked the original hosting company to keep their version running for a further two weeks, which they agreed to do. Still oblivious to the undertones that this should have signaled, I put the delay down to a touch of the preliminary overoptimism that often characterizes these situations, and reimmersed myself in the book that I was writing.

A month later, the site still wasn't functioning. E-mails from readers were piling up, asking what was going on. J's people were concentrating on setting up the shopping cart, seemingly indifferent to the fact that the site that the cart was supposed to attach to wasn't working. A second warning should have rung when they kept asking for the weight of each catalog item rounded up to the nearest pound, for their software to calculate shipping costs. This didn't make any sense. A typical paperback might weigh seven or eight ounces. For a package of, say, five books, rounding each one up separately would produce an absurdly inaccurate overall weight. Rounding should be done afterward, on the total. In any case, post-office rates are figured to the nearest ounce, not pound. Besides which, we had stated from the beginning that we had our own formula for calculating shipping, tailored to the way we worked, and so their software that calculated post-office rates wasn't needed. But nothing made any difference. The same questions kept coming back, as if none of the previous correspondence or conversations had taken place.

When I finally brought the matter up with J, it turned out that he was under the impression that the site was working, and hadn't even realized there was a problem! Only then did the full ghastly scale of the incompetence that we were up against begin to reveal itself. Yes, these people had implemented online ordering sites before. But they possessed no concept as to any other purpose that a Web site might serve. Web sites were for selling stuff. Period. When J said he thought the site was working, what he meant was that the home page came up okay when he entered the URL. But none of the links from the home page went anywhere. J was unsure where else links needed to go, other than to the shopping cart that his people were working on. We described the other pages of the site—information on my books, new events and releases, Bulletin Board topics . . . He remained nonplused. Why would anyone need that kind of stuff on a Web site? Look, don't worry yourself thinking about it, we told him. Just get it done, okay? There would be no further discussion concerning other aspects until the basic original site was reproduced, up, and working.

It seemed straightforward enough. All they had to do was follow what was there, in front of them.

A week later, nothing had changed. Tim couldn't understand it, since the original site should simply have been loaded and running in minutes. If J's people couldn't fix it on their own host, he would do it himself; but he would need the appropriate access codes to their server. His requests for the codes were not answered. E-mails to J were bouncing with the message that his mailbox was full. I sent a letter to him and his head programmer, copies by mail, giving a seven-day deadline for the situation to be cleared up, otherwise I would consider the order canceled and expect a refund of the amount paid. Jackie also tracked J down on the phone, just to be sure that he understood. He assured us that the problem would be fixed by the deadline I had given.

It wasn't, but it would be by the following day—in any case, not later than noon of the day following that. The time passed. No change. I called J to demand an explanation. He sounded surprised. Everything was fine, wasn't it? No, it wasn't. He brought the URL up on his machine while we were talking and insisted defiantly that it was working. Astoundingly, all he had looked at and checked was the home page. He *still* didn't grasp that this was not the complete Web site. It was as if none of the e-mails, letters, and phone conversations of the previous few weeks had ever happened. So even at this stage, his company was not yet in a position even to commence the work that it had contracted to do. I wrote a letter formally canceling the whole thing and sent it by certified mail, again with e-mailed copies. It was subsequently returned by the post office, marked "Refused."

The day after I sent the letter, J called me to insist again that the site was working, and if I was having problems it had to be something on my machine or out in the Internet. Attempts to explain yet again were futile. He wouldn't listen, but talked incessantly about the virtues of his shopping cart. I reaffirmed that the deal was canceled and ended the conversation. For the rest of the day, J went into a round of calling everybody remotely connected with the project—Alex; Jackie; Mark Luljak, another consultant friend of mine who was by now involved; Tim—and delivering the same rambling monologue, even to Tim's wife, who had simply picked up the phone and knew nothing about the affair.

The fact that the order was canceled didn't deter J and his company, who carried on working to fix what they had been saying for weeks didn't need fixing. By "fix," it turned out that they meant tearing the Web site apart and rewriting it to try and make it work on their server—never mind that this wouldn't have been necessary for anyone who knew what they were doing, and that it flatly violated the stipulation made from the beginning that the site wasn't to be altered. This would have been bad enough if what they were "fixing" was an imaged copy of the site running as a development system, which would have been standard system-engineering practice—you run the new system in parallel until it's clean, before you phase out the old one. But that wasn't what they were doing. They were tearing apart *the live site, to which my domain name had been transferred—online, publicly, before the eyes of the world*! Mark sent me an agonized e-mail describing how he had been watching them online for several hours, taking www.jamesphogan.com apart before his eyes, not fixing it, but wrecking it.

Since nothing we said was being heeded, the only course left was to transfer the domain name back to the original hosting company and restore the original site as it had been from backup files that Tim had kept. Normal policy for the registry where domain names are filed required the domain-name owner—that was me—to instruct the present hosting company—J & Co.—to initiate the transfer back, and so I called J accordingly. He at once launched into his spiel of claiming that all was as good as fixed. I stopped him to say that was no longer an issue and told him I wanted my domain name transferred back to its original host. Would he please initiate it? He began arguing. I cut him off to state my request again. This happened several times before I said there was nothing else to talk about and hung up the phone. It should be stressed here that he had no legal right to hang onto what was my property after I had instructed him to relinquish it. It gets even more unreal. That evening, J called Jackie—I had nothing further to say to him—and asserted that the problem was fixed. She walked him through some of the links on the home page that didn't go anywhere. But he *still* couldn't get it, and spent an hour and a half—she assured me she wasn't exaggerating—talking nonstop about irrelevancies after she gave up trying to communicate.

By the next day, it was plain that J was not complying. I called him and asked for the name of his company's attorney. He began again the same line that we had all heard over and over—like a tape being replayed. The exchange went something like:

"I haven't called to discuss anything. I'm asking for the name of your attorney. Are you refusing to give it to me?"

"There's nothing wrong with the system. Our shopping cart is the—".

"Please, shut up. Will you, or will you not give me the name of your attorney?"

"I want to talk to you first."

"You are impossible to talk to. Everyone who's tried has given up. You won't listen. Are you refusing to tell me who your company's attorney is?"

"I'm not refusing. But I'm going to tell you first that—"

"*Will you shut up!* I have clearly requested that my domain name be returned to its previous host. Will you comply, yes or no?"

"Huh, well, I can write books too. There's nothing wrong with the site. I just need to prove to you that we can—"

I hung up. Tim and Mark both called J to emphasize the seriousness of his attitude from a legal standpoint. Mark told me wearily that after two hours on the phone with J and two of his programmers, J still seemed unconnected with reality and unaware of the difference between the home page to my Web site and the rest of it. The upshot was that we called the people at the registry direct and described how my Web site was effectively being hijacked. Although it went against their normal protocol, they agreed to transfer the domain name back to the original host. Before the end of the day all was up and running once more, just as it had been two months before.

Alex finally did the job himself, developing an order page built on a database that offered our old mail-order choices as per Mr. Toad's Page, with the addition of a PayPal option. We called it the "ManyWorlds" order catalog, added to the still undatabased original site. My youngest daughter, Tina, in California, took on the job of handling the order processing. It has proved quite popular. More recently, Tim added a separate "Heretics' Bookstore" section, listing titles mentioned in some of the Bulletin Board postings, along with others of general interest or that aren't always well-known or easy to find, usually concerning controversial scientific topics that I sometimes get into.

I never did get the money back from J. I talked to several lawyers in Florida, but none of them were interested in handling it. When I tried the small-claims court, I was told that a claim needed to be filed in California. So I took it up with an attorney in Los Angeles, recommended by a mutual friend who described him as specializing in computer-related issues, but after a lengthy exchange of e-mails and phone calls, it became obvious that he was all talk and would never get around to actually doing anything. Fortunately, I had pinned him down to agreeing to a contingency basis with no retainer up front, which at least meant I wasn't sending more good money after bad—and perhaps explains the lack of luster. On the last occasion that I talked to him he brought us back full circle by suggesting that I should take it up through the courts in Florida. I'm told that Los Angeles has more lawyers than the whole of Japan.

(Q. How many lawyers does it take to roof a house? A. It depends how thin you slice them.)

Alex moved on to college in Orlando, from there went to work in Boston for a year, and then moved back to Orlando again as a 3-D graphics programmer. With a demanding work schedule, a girlfriend, and things like apartment matters to contend with as part of those commitments that impose themselves in the course of getting a life of one's own, it became evident that expecting him to take on in addition the further plans that we had talked about over the years wouldn't be realistic. Nevertheless, by the time this gets to print, it might be that the full databased Web site along with its ordering system might have become a reality. As further enhancements, we'll be introducing a discussion-thread capability, which a number of readers have asked for, and a comprehensive search-and-index facility, which should make everything on the site more accessible. When we met yesterday for a review meeting in McGarrigle's Pub in Sligo center, things were looking promising. Dare I say it? We might see the final product up and running in a matter of weeks now.

Meanwhile, a few selected items that have appeared on www.jamesphogan.com over the years are included through this book to give an idea of the kinds of thing that get posted there. Maybe a sampling will induce some who haven't tried it yet to visit the site itself. And who knows? If they stop by the ManyWorlds bookstore while they're at it, we might even recover a little of what's gone into finally making it all happen.

From the Web Site

A couple of pieces from the early days.

IMPOSSIBLE RHYMES

Posted in the "Humor & Diversions" section of the Bulletin Board, August 16, 1998 (http://www.james-phogan.com/bb/content/081698.shtml)

WITH A LITTLE INGENUITY

I got a note from somebody claiming that no word in the English language rhymes with "month," "orange," "silver," or "purple." Well, a challenge is not something to be passed over lightly by an Irishman, and for somebody of my profession, certainly not one with a literary connotation. So, after retreating pen-in-teeth into a period of some solitary meditation on the matter, I emerge to present the following modest offerings:

> *The animalth rathed three timeth*
> > *latht month,*
> *The hare won twithe and the*
> > *tortoithe oneth.*

> *An Irishman Green,*
> *Can take the potheen.*
> *But an Irishman Orange*
> *Ends up on the flooranj'*
> *Ust doesn't seem able,*
> *To stay at the table.*

> *When you're choking,*
> *Turning purple,*
> *A hearty slap and one good burp'll*
> *Usually fix it.*

> *Gold and silver*
> *presents willvir*
> *Ginity tend to*
> *Put an end to.*

FROG FANTASIES

Posted in the "Environmentalism" section of the Bulletin Board, March 12, 1998 (http://www.jamesphogan.com/bb/content/031298-2.shtml)

MORE EFFECTS OF THE UV INCREASE
THAT NEVER WAS

The early part of this century witnessed the "N-ray" fiasco, in which scientific true believers solemnly observed and recorded the behavior of a supposed new form of radiation shown subsequently to exist only within their own imaginations. These days, it's revealing to see how far politically funded and approved science will go to find politically pleasing results of causes that have never been shown to exist.

In the March 1998 issue of *The Energy Advocate* (http://www.jamesphogan.com/bb/content/032697.shtml), Howard Hayden reports on a big flap that has been going on for some years over a certain species of frog that lives high in the Sierra Nevada mountains, whose population appears to have been declining. Investigators have jumped to attribute this to increased UV radiation due to ozone depletion—although without presenting any actual data of a UV increase, which is assumed unquestioningly to have occurred because the prevailing dogma says so.

Yet after all the arguing over CFC breakdown, chemical reaction pathways, Antarctic "holes," skin cancer, and so on, the one single fact that would follow if any of the scare stories had any merit, and before any effects could be experienced—a real, measured increase of ultraviolet at the Earth's surface—has never been observed. In 1988, Joseph Scotto of the National Cancer Institute published data from eight

U.S. ground stations showing that UV-B (the wavelength band affected by ozone) *decreased* by amounts ranging from 2 to 7 percent during the period 1974–1985. A similar politically wrong trend was recorded over fifteen years by the Fraunhofer Institute of Atmospheric Sciences in Bavaria, Germany. The response? Scotto's study was ignored by the international news media. He was denied funding to attend international conferences to present his findings, and the ground stations were closed down. The costs of accepting the depletion theory as true will run into billions of dollars, but apparently we can't afford a few thousand to collect the data most fundamental to testing it. In Washington, scientists who objected were attacked by environmentalist pressure groups, and former Princeton physics professor William Happer, who wanted to set up an extended instrumentation network, was dismissed from his post as research director at the Department of Energy. The retiring head of the German program was replaced by a depletionist who refused to publish the institute's accumulated data and terminated further measurements, apparently on the grounds that future policy would be to rely on computer models instead. (So much for a reality check, which used to be known as observational science.)

The whole doomsday case boils down to claiming that if something isn't done to curb CFCs, ultraviolet radiation will increase by 10 percent over the next twenty years. But from the poles to the equator it increases naturally by a whopping factor of fifty, or 5000 percent, anyway!—equivalent to 1 percent for every six miles. Or to put it another way, a family moving house from New York to Philadelphia would experience the same increase as is predicted by the worst-case depletion scenarios.

Which leads one to wonder why so much fuss should be directed to high-altitude frogs, when the layer that absorbs the UV supposedly affecting them exists high in the stratosphere, far above the world's highest mountains. Any change capable of affecting them would affect frogs at sea level equally. And if that were so, how could any survive at all, say, two hundred miles farther south, where the UV is and always has been way above anything experienced in the Sierras?

Howard does mention that lakes in sporting areas such as the Sierras have been stocked with fish in recent times. And guess what these fish love to eat. Frogs' eggs. But saying so apparently doesn't get the glamor and the applause. Howard's source for the above gem was Candace Crandall at the Science Environmental Policy Project, founded by S. Fred Singer, who developed the backscatter photometer used for satellite measurements of atmospheric ozone. Those interested to learn more can check it out at http://www.his.com/~sepp.

Convolution

Professor Aylmer Arbuthnot Abercrombie looked up irascibly from the chore of tidying up his notes as the call tone sounded from his desk terminal. He moused the screen's cursor to the Call Accept icon and clicked on it. "Yes?"

A window opened showing the head of a youth aged twenty or so, with collar-length, studentish hair, a wispy attempt at a beard, and shoulders enveloped in a baggy sweater. "Oh, er, Jeremy Qualio here, Professor." He was a postgraduate that Abercrombie had assigned a design project to, in one of the labs below in the building. "We were expecting you here at ten-thirty, sir."

"You were?"

"To review the test of the transcorrelator mixing circuit. You were going to help us set the power parameters for the output stage."

"I was?"

"We've completed the runs with simulated input data and normalized the results. They're here ready for you to check through now."

"They are?" Abercrombie's brow knitted into a frown. He cast around the littered desk for his appointments diary on the off chance that it might give him a way out, but couldn't see it. He was cornered. "Very well, I'll be there shortly," he replied, and cut off the screen.

Abercrombie left his "public" office at the front of the lab area, which he used for receiving visitors and dealing with routine day-to-day affairs. On the way out, he stopped by the open cubicle and reception desk from where the stern, meticulous, and fearsomely efficient figure of Mrs. Crawford, the departmental secretary and custodian of all that pertained to proper procedures, commanded the approach from the elevators.

"Do you have my appointments diary, by any chance?" Abercrombie inquired. "I appear to have mislaid it."

"You took it back this morning."

"Did I?"

"*After* I found it again, the last time." The pointed pause, followed by a sniff, invited him to reflect on the enormity of his transgression. "You know, Professor, it really would be more convenient if you'd keep your schedule electronically, as do other members of the staff. Then I could maintain a copy in my system, which wouldn't get mislaid. And I'd be in a position to give timely reminders of your commitments—which it seems you are in some need of."

Abercrombie shook his head stubbornly. "I won't go into that again, Mrs. Crawford. You know my views on computerized records. Nothing's private. Nothing's safe. They can get into your system from China. The next thing you know, some fool who doesn't know a Bessel function from a Bessemer furnace is publishing your life's work. No, thank you very much. I prefer not to become public property, but to keep my soul and my inner self to myself."

"But that's such an outmoded way to think," Mrs. Crawford persisted. "It's absurd for somebody with your technical expertise. If I may say so, it smacks of pure obstinacy. With the encryption procedures available today . . ." But Abercrombie had already stopped listening and stalked away to jab the call button by the elevator doors.

"Oh, and by the way," he threw back over his shoulder while he waited, "has that FedEx package arrived from Chicago yet?"

"Yes. I've already told you so, Professor."

"When?"

"Less than half an hour ago."

Abercrombie checked himself long enough to send back a perplexed, disbelieving look before stepping into the elevator. Mrs. Crawford shook her head in exasperation and returned her attention to the task at hand.

Jeremy Qualio and Maxine Turnel, his bubbly, bespectacled, blond-haired partner on the project, were waiting in the prototype lab with the bird's nest of wires, chips, and other components connected to an array of test equipment. The results from their trial runs of the device were displayed on a set of monitors. Abercrombie jutted his chin and scanned over the bench with a series of short, jerky motions of his head. The layout was neat for a lab prototype, with careful wiring and solid, clean-looking joints; the data had been graphed onto screens showing time and frequency series analysis, along with histograms of statistical variables, all properly annotated and captioned. A file of hard copy was lying to one side for Abercrombie's inspection. He looked at the circuit work again and grunted. "You've used nonstandard colors for the board interconnections. I expect the approved coding practices to be observed."

"Yes, Professor," Qualio agreed, looking a bit crest-fallen.

But Abercrombie couldn't fault their experimental design and procedure as they went through it and discussed details for over an hour. The analysis was comprehensive, with computation of error probabilities and the correct algorithms for interpolation and best-curve fits. Maxine took the absence of further criticism as indicating a rare opportunity to probe the obses-sive screen of secrecy that Abercrombie maintained around his work. She and Qualio had been given just this subassembly to develop to a specification in isolation. Abercrombie hadn't told them its purpose, or the nature of the greater scheme of which it was presumably a part.

"We're still trying to figure out what it's for," she told him, doing her best to sound casual and natu-ral. "What, exactly is a 'transcorrelator'? The inducer stage seems to create an electroweak interaction with the nuclear substructure that stimulates a range of strong-domain transitions that we've never heard of before."

Qualio came in. "They're not mentioned in any of the standard references or on the Net. It's as if we're dealing with a new area of physics."

"That's not for you to speculate about," Abercrombie said. "All you've done is graduate from basic training in the army of science. It doesn't give you a voice in deciding strategy. Leave the big picture to the generals." He gave a curt nod in the direction of the bench. "Satisfactory. Have the report written up by the end of the week."

"Yes, Professor," Qualio said. Maxine flashed him a look with a shrug that said, *Well, we tried.* Abercrombie picked up the folder of hard copy and turned to leave.

"I told you. It has to be something military," he overheard Maxine whisper as he went out the door.

After stopping for lunch in the cafeteria, Abercrombie took the stairs back up through the warren of partitioned offices and labs that now filled the space amid the massive brick walls and aged wooden floors of the original building. The City Annexe of Gates University's Physics Department occupied a converted warehouse on the downtown waterfront of what was no longer a major trading port. Hence, it had been acquired at a knock-down price and qualified for the city's urban-renewal grant scheme, making it a fine investment property for the university trustees. It was also where the department secluded its oddball projects and other undertakings that the governors preferred to keep out of sight, away from its main, prestigious campus. They were retained, as often as not, to humor some high-paying source of research grants or other primary influence on funding.

No premature publicity, Abercrombie reiterated to himself as he emerged on his own floor and weathered Mrs. Crawford's Gorgonesque stare to return to his lab. When this project came to fruition, it would be the news event of the century. And not just with the public media. Everyone who was anyone worth talking about in the entire physics-related sector of the scientific Establishment would learn of it in a mass-announcement that Abercrombie had been preparing as methodically as the design studies and calculations that had occupied him for eight years. He had all the names listed, covering academic, private, and government science elites throughout the world. This would be his ticket to a Nobel Prize and permanent fame as surely as geometry had immortalized Euclid and the laws of motion were virtually synonymous with Newton. Maybe even more. The things that Nobels had been awarded for seemed mundane in comparison. Perhaps, even, a new grade of award would have to be instituted especially for him.

He came to the inner, windowless workshop area that he had designated as the place where the device would be assembled, and stopped for a moment to picture it completed. It wouldn't be especially heavy or bulky—little more than a metal lattice boundary surface to define and contain the varichron field, with a control panel supported on a columnar plinth, and the generating system and power unit beneath. If anything, it would resemble an oversize parrot cage with a domed cap, standing on a squat cylindrical base.

Howard Jaffey, the dean, and the few others from the faculty who were in the know as to the aim of Abercrombie's project, were polite in avoiding mention of it; but with a billionaire like Eli Zaltzer writing the backing, and the amounts that he lavished on the university as a whole, nobody had been inclined to turn the proposal down, even if they secretly thought Zaltzer was an eccentric. Well, let them think what they liked, Abercrombie told himself. The parts were coming together now, and the initial tests were under way. It wouldn't be much longer before the full system was assembled—three months, maybe, in his estimation. They'd be singing a different tune then, when the whole world came flocking to his door. Never mind for a better mousetrap. Abercrombie was going to give them a working *time machine*!

He stood, savoring the moment in his imagination for a few seconds longer, and then proceeded through a door and along a corridor to his inner, private office at the rear of the lab area. This was where he conducted his more secretive business. Inside, he locked the door, cast a wary eye around instinctively, even though it was obvious there could be no one else there—and at once spotted the missing appointments diary on a corner of the desk. Tut-tutting to himself, he went over to the wall cabinet and released the catch that allowed it to slide aside, revealing his hidden safe. Armor plate, sunk into the brickwork of the original walls. No electronic security for him, whatever the administrators tried to say about how solid it was these days. How could anyone believe it, when half the people in the world seemed to spend their lives trying to make computers do what they were supposed to do instead of contributing to anything useful?

He dialed in the combination sequence and swung the door open to disclose his trove of files, papers, and notes from the time when he first met Eli Zaltzer and the dream began the course that would one day make it reality. He took out the file box reserved for test results, added the hard copy that he had brought from downstairs, and was just replacing the box, when he heard footsteps in the corridor outside. They sounded furtive, as if someone were creeping past warily. Normally, Abercrombie always locked the door when he opened his safe, but on this occasion, after the momentary distraction of seeing the appointments diary on the desk when he walked in, he was unable to recall whether or not he had. "Who's there?" he called out, fearful of being found with the cabinet open. There was no reply. The footsteps hastened away.

Hurrying to the door, Abercrombie found that he had locked it after all and had to fumble for his keys before he could get out, by which time the corridor was empty. He followed it to the back stairs and the freight elevator but found no sign of anyone there. As he began retracing his steps toward his rear office, a peculiar, low-pitched whine emanated from the other side of the door to the workshop area ahead of him. He increased his pace, heading past his office door. "Who is that in there?" he yelled ahead, but the noise ceased just before he burst in, and he found the place empty. With rising agitation he carried on through to Mrs. Crawford's post, but she had seen no one go that way. Then Abercrombie realized that he had committed the cardinal sin of leaving his private office door unlocked with the safe open.

Abandoning Mrs. Crawford in mid sentence, he raced back through the workshop area, slammed the office door behind him, and rushed across the room to check the contents of the safe. Moments later, he emitted a horrified groan. The master notebook, in which he had brought together and summarized the essential design information for the time machine—the distilled essence of his past eight years of intensive labor—was gone.

He had to inform Eli Zaltzer and the university governors that the project had run into unexpected difficulties, forcing him to put the schedule on hold. Zaltzer remained as trusting and optimistic as ever, but the faculty members who were privy to Abercrombie's crazy scheme chortled behind raised hands and told each other it had only been a matter of time—deriving added glee from the intended pun. Abercrombie became convinced he was the victim of a conspiracy to either sabotage or steal his project. Several times, he thought he heard prowlers about in the labs, but he never managed to catch anyone. On one occasion, late in the evening when the lights were turned down, he did actually accost and pursue an intruder; but on rounding a corner was met full-force by the discharge from a fire extinguisher, and by the time he had cleaned the froth from his eyes and recovered, the trespasser had vanished.

And then, a week or so after the loss of the notebook, he heard the strange noise again. He was on the phone in his public office at the front near the main elevators, wearing a dress suit in anticipation of an honorary dinner he was due to attend that night, when the same low-pitched whine as before reached him through the wall from the direction of the lab and workshop area. He excused himself, saying he would call back later, and hung up. Then, giving no advance warning this time, he rose and went over to the door, checked the corridor beyond, and crept stealthily to the double doors leading through to the workshop. The noise had by now ceased. Turning one of the handles gently, he eased the door open far enough to peer around it and inside . . . and almost fell over from shock and disbelief. The time machine was there, standing in the middle of the floor, exactly as he had envisioned it! But there was nobody with it.

He stepped inside the room, closing the door behind him, and walked past it warily—almost as if fearing that a sudden movement might cause it to vanish—and secured the doors leading to the rear before coming back to study the machine more carefully. It stood over seven feet high from the bottom of the cylindrical base frame, crammed with circuit boxes, generator manifolds, and coil housings, to the top of the field delimiter capping the cage. The ticking and clicking of hot parts cooling came from beneath, as from the hood of a car after a long run. Abercrombie reached out and touched part of the structure gingerly, as if unsure if it might be an illusion. It was solid and real.

And as he thought through what it meant, his indignation rose in a hot flush climbing slowly from his collar. Evidently, at some eventual future time, somebody would build the machine. So was he now supposed to go through the protracted effort of redoing all the work he had lost, in order for someone to steal it and go careening around through time and having who-knew-what kinds of adventures? Dammit, he had been though all that once. And here he was, seeing the fruits of his own labors for the first time. It was his!

Furious now, he opened the access gate, stepped up into the cage, and stared at the control panel atop its plinth. He wasn't really sure what he intended to do. And as he looked over the keys, lights, and the command lines displayed on the screen, it slowly came to him that he wouldn't have had a clue how to go about doing it. The machine was based on his original design, yes; but a lot of detail that he was not familiar with had been worked out in the final stages. But it was rightfully his, wasn't it? Maybe he could turn things around and be the one to benefit from his interloping future self's labors instead. That would require studying the construction and wiring and trying some tests, which could take a while. It couldn't be done here; his other self who had arrived in it for whatever reason could return at any moment. He needed a safe place to hide the machine, where he could investigate it at leisure.

But could such a plan work? He frowned, bemused by the bizarre logic. Surely, whatever he decided to do, his future self would remember having decided, and be able to pursue him accordingly. Unless the time line somehow reset itself to accommodate changes. Or maybe some multiple-universe explanation applied, in which the possibly similar past that a person returned to was still different from the past that was remembered. He had long speculated about such alternatives, but a working machine was the prerequisite to being able to test them. And now he had one! Forget all the questions for now, he told himself. Worry about getting the machine to a place where he could devote himself to the only prospect in sight—without having to repeat eight years of work—for finding some answers.

It would need to be reasonably close but unfrequented by people. Anywhere in the City Annexe itself would be out of the question because of the comings and goings of staff, students, visitors, and a host of others. But a short distance away along the waterfront there was a disused dock building, a former customs warehouse still owned by the Port Authority, earmarked for development into an indoor market and restaurant mall one day, but derelict for years. The cellars beneath would provide a suitable place—not perfect, maybe, but they would do until he found something better. And with the limited time at his disposal, that was good enough. He stepped back down out of the machine and went through to the rear part of the building to find a means of moving it.

By the freight elevator he found a hand dolly that was used for moving equipment cabinets, machinery, and other heavy items around the labs. A utility room nearby, where maintenance and decorating materials were stored, yielded a painter's floor tarp that would serve as a cover. He hurried the dolly back to the workshop, eased the lifting platform under the time machine's base, elevated it, draped the machine with the tarp, and trundled it back through to the rear. The freight elevator took him down to the goods-receiving bay at the back of the Annexe building, where he signed for use of the departmental pickup truck. He brought the truck around to the loading bay, and minutes later was driving his purloined creation out through the rear gates of the premises, onto the waterfront boulevard.

He had gone no more than a few hundred yards, when he heard the wail of a police siren behind and saw red and blue lights flashing in his mirror. For a sickening moment his heart felt as if it were about to fall into a void that opened up in his stomach. Then he realized it had nothing to do with him; a car a short distance back was being pulled over. Exhaling loudly with relief, Abercrombie entered the weed-choked lot surrounding the derelict dockside building, drove around to the side, where he would be less conspicuous, and parked in front of a once-boarded-up entrance, its planks long ago stripped and broken up for firewood by vagrants. He climbed out of the truck and went in to reconnoiter the interior for a suitable hiding place for the machine.

The figure who had observed Abercrombie's arrival retreated to a hideaway in the cellars below the front part of the building, screened by fallen debris but commanding a view of the ramp down from the ground-floor level. His name was Brady. He was long-haired and bearded, dressed in a military-style camouflage parka with paratrooper combat boots. As Abercrombie came out of the room into which he had wheeled the strange contraption, and disappeared back up the ramp to the side entrance, the watcher murmured into a cell phone to a person that he referred to as "Yellow One."

"I dunno. It looked like a machine."

"What kind of machine?"

"I never saw anything like it before. A man-size birdcage. Maybe some kinda surveillance thing. I don't like the look of it."

"What does the guy look like?"

"Tall, about sixty, maybe. Thin. Could be kinda mean. Hair white and gray. Wearing a black suit."

"A suit? There's only one kind of people that wears suits. They're onto us, man. Get—"

"Wait!" Brady interrupted as the sound came of tires squealing to a halt outside the front of the building, close to where he was concealed. Moments later, footsteps pounded in on the floor above, followed by crashing sounds and metallic clanging. "There's more of 'em breaking in upstairs!" Brady said, sounding alarmed.

"It's a bust," Yellow One told him. "Get yourself out!"

Professor Abercrombie came back out onto the waterside boulevard and drove the truck back to the university Annexe. Just as he was turning in through the rear gate, a dull boom and a whoosh sounded from a short distance away as the building he had just left exploded and collapsed in flames.

Police and fire-department vehicles arrived by the dozen, and the ensuing spectacle meant that little work was done anywhere in the nearby university buildings for the rest of the day. Curious officials from the Annexe went to find out what they could from the officers in charge, and the gossip in the staff coffee room by the end of the afternoon was that an extremist group of survivalists, who trained in the hills with guns and believed in preparing for catastrophe or nuclear holocaust, had been using the place to store weapons and explosives. The police had been waiting for a special shipment, due within the next few days, before moving in, but evidently there had been some kind of accident in there first. Rumor had it that the charred remains of one of them had been found in there. Nobody else had been caught.

All of which was of peripheral interest to Abercrombie, who was now left without either design data or machine, after having had the completed, working model literally in his hands. And just to make his day, when he left the office to go home, he found that his car had been stolen.

That night, in a fit of dejection, he took out the folder with the lists of media contacts, scientific notables, and others that he had prepared for the day of his great announcement, which he kept in the desk at home in his apartment, carried it downstairs to the basement, and threw it into the building's incinerator.

The next day, Abercrombie stood at the window of his private office, staring despondently out in the direction of the old customs warehouse. What was left of the shell had been pronounced unsafe and reduced to rubble by a demolition crew, who were now fencing off the site pending a decision on eventual disposal. But the professor's thoughts were not on how the Port Authority should best manage its piece of still-prime downtown waterfront real estate.

Why, he asked himself, was the obvious always the last thing that occurred to people? Probably for the same reason that a lost object always turns up in the last place one looks: Nobody is going to carry on looking after they've found it. The mysterious intruder of the day before, and no doubt those that he had suspected previously, hadn't been from any conspiracy at all. It had been *himself*, coming back from a future where the machine had been built! It had taken the discovery of the machine for him to realize it. He no longer possessed the notebook containing the design information necessary to build it. Could it be that the notebook had been used, nevertheless, stolen from the past by means of a machine that will exist in the future? It sounded preposterous, but the evidence was there. However, if so, that raised another logical conundrum. For if, somewhere in the future, he had built a working machine—possibly after having to work it all out again—then what motivation would he have for going back and stealing the design? He wouldn't need it!

No. He shook his head decisively. He wasn't going to get embroiled in any more of those impossible tangles. He had problems enough as things were. Just take the facts one at a time and let philosophers or mystics worry about the contradictions and deeper meaning of it all, he told himself.

Yet the implication remained that at some point in the future he would find himself the owner of such a device. He stared distantly out along the waterfront and allowed himself to relish the thought. If he ever did go back to regain the notebook, he would take out some insurance to prevent anything like this from happening again, he resolved. Computer people were always impressing the importance of keeping backups.

Well, maybe they did have a valid point there, he conceded grudgingly. Very well, he would follow their advice. If—or when?—such a day came, he would leave a backup copy of the notebook in some secure place, back there in the past. Then, if he ever lost the original, had it stolen, or found himself without it for any other reason, from then onward, anytime in the future, the backup would always be there, waiting to be retrieved. It was so breathtakingly simple—once again, eminently obvious now that he had thought of it. Had he done so before, he would have taken the simple precaution of maintaining an additional copy to the one that had been in the safe.

He turned his head unconsciously from the window toward the wall cabinet concealing the safe while he thought this. And his jaw dropped as the bizarre realization hit him of what the very act of his thinking it signified. The fact of having made this decision meant he would carry it with him into the future. And the decision would still be in his head when he traveled back via the machine to what was now the past. Provided, then, that he abided by that decision, it had already been done! Somewhere, right now—unless his penchant for forgetfulness were to reach impossible proportions in the future—a hidden copy of the notebook existed! That must have been how he had built the machine! He looked around the office, licking his lips in the excitement that had seized him, as if now that he had worked the implication out, the hiding place would somehow leap out and advertise itself. He cast his mind over all the places there were to choose from. Somewhere in the Annexe? His downtown apartment? Somewhere else in the city? . . . Where, out of all the possibilities, would he have picked?

And that was when the full craziness of it all finally hit him; he realized that *it didn't matter*! There was no need for him to try and second-guess himself at all. For all he had to do was pick a place—any place—right now, and be sure to put the backup copy in that place when he came to travel back. And that would be where he would find it today!

Surely it couldn't be that easy. He went back in his mind through the insane logic, looking for the flaw, but couldn't find one. Okay, then, where would he hide the copy? He looked around again. And his eyes came back to the window and the site where the demolition crew were finishing the fence around the ruin of the old warehouse. Down there in the cellars beneath, where he had taken the machine yesterday, there were bound to be corners and cubby holes left beneath the rubble. Nobody would be going in there for a long time now, probably years. With the design information available, building the machine would only take about three months. It was close by, being posted with Keep Out and hazard warnings. . . .

Then his eyes blinked rapidly as the inevitable complication reared its head. There was another version of himself at large out there somewhere—the version who had arrived in the machine. And his disposition would not be very friendly, since by now he would have discovered that the machine had been stolen and he had no way of going back. But if this Abercrombie—the one looking out of the window, trying to make sense of it all—now chose a place to hide the backup in, then the other one of him would not only have remembered it too, but have known it all along while he (this Abercrombie) was still having to figure it out. On the other hand, knowing it wouldn't have helped his other self to do much about acting on it, since the place had been swarming with firemen and demolition people since yesterday. So did that mean it would be a race to see which of them would get there first, probably tonight?

And then a malicious twinkle came into his eyes as the last skein of the tangle unraveled itself. He couldn't lose! For the machine *had* come to be built. He was here, installed in the Annexe, with all the resources at his disposal to build it, while the other Abercrombie was somewhere outside in the cold. Therefore, somewhere in the strange convolution of causes and effects that he didn't pretend to grasp yet, events must have shuffled themselves out in such a way that *he* had obtained the information he needed—and hence the other Abercrombie, presumably, had not.

But the other Abercrombie would just as certainly know all this, and yet was out there somewhere, unable to change it. Knowing himself, he pictured the rage of frustration that the other version of him must be experiencing at that very moment. Not a pleasant character to cross, he told himself. Better be careful not to bump into him. A frown darkened his face then. But wasn't he destined to become that version eventually, and have to undergo the same frustration? Surely not. If knowledge had any value at all, there had to be a way to avoid it. But there was no way to be sure of any answer at present. He turned away from the window and sat down at the desk to consider his plans. One step at a time, he told himself again. Just follow where it leads.

The police found his car abandoned less than a mile away. Late that night, wearing dark coveralls and a woolen hat, Abercrombie parked by the remains of the warehouse building, forced a gap through the fence, and followed around the outside until he found an opening under a tilted slab of concrete that gave access to what was left of the cellars. Using a flashlight, he worked his way down to a part of the center gallery that had survived, and from there found a collapsed room almost buried in rubble and mud still wet from yesterday's hoses. On poking around, he discovered a run of pipes low on one wall, and beneath them a row of recesses between the support mountings, almost like pigeon holes. A perfect place!

The first slot that he examined was empty, but the one next to it was blocked by a brick outlined in the congealed muck—just as would have been placed by somebody wanting to conceal something. He pried the brick loose with a jackknife he had brought, and pulled it clear to uncover a rectangular shape. It proved to be the end of a flat, plastic-wrapped metal box. His hands shaking, for surely this couldn't mean what a rising premonition was already telling him it did, he slid the catch from the hasp and opened the lid of the box to reveal . . . a notebook and documents!

But they weren't his. Flipping rapidly though them, he found names and pseudonyms, addresses, contact numbers, and a section on what looked like codes and encryption procedures, but none of it was familiar. This wasn't possible, he told himself. He couldn't have reasoned things through and have gotten this close, only to have it all go wrong now.

All but whimpering aloud in dismay, he turned the flashlight beam back and prodded frantically among the other recesses. And sure enough, the next one along was also closed by a mud-encased brick, which also divulged a package. And this one, indeed, turned out to contain a full set of copies of the information from his master notebook! Exultation swept over him. No other version of himself had materialized to interfere. His only thought now was to leave, before anything could go amiss. Stuffing his finds into a bag that he had brought for the purpose, he clambered back to the gallery and picked his way up through to the opening that led back outside. His car was there, untouched, and he left without incident.

Even after his success, Abercrombie was mindful of the presence of his other self still at large somewhere, probably bordering on homicidal by now and capable of causing mischief. He approached Eli Zaltzer to say that the problems were resolved and the project could move ahead as scheduled. However, he had reason to believe there was some kind of opposition movement afoot who had gotten wind of the project and were opposed to it. In view of the precedents seen in recent times of protest groups sabotaging scientific research that they disagreed with, perhaps security around the lab should be tightened up. Zaltzer talked to the authorities, who were ever ready to appease his whims, and a private security firm was contracted to provide twenty-four-hour guards for Abercrombie's lab and office area, and to control access. His life became a fever of activity day and night, and as weeks passed by, the machine began taking shape in the center of the workshop.

And during that time, there were indeed several attempts by unknown persons to get into the labs. On one occasion, an alleged repairman who had come to check the air-conditioning produced credentials that didn't pass scrutiny, and on checking turned out not to be from the company he claimed. Abercrombie himself was elsewhere that day and so wasn't able to confront the imposter, and a slick lawyer intervened who prevented the security people from detaining him, so his identity was never established. But the description didn't sound anything like Abercrombie, and Mrs. Crawford confirmed it. So his other self was using fronts to test the waters, Abercrombie concluded.

Another time, somebody actually did get in under cover of what was almost certainly a contrived power failure, but one of the guards accosted him, and he got away without accomplishing anything. Inwardly, Abercrombie was impressed by what was, after all, effectively his own resourcefulness in an area where he had no prior knowledge or experience. He had never suspected that he had such talents in him.

And eventually the day came when the machine was ready for the first live tests.

Eli Zaltzer had to be there to see it, naturally. So was Howard Jaffey, the dean, along with Susan Peters and Mario Venasky, two other members of the faculty. Abercrombie briefed them, cautioning them to stand back, and announced that he was initiating a control program in the machine that would activate automatically ten minutes from now and send the machine back that far in time. Everyone watched the open area of floor expectantly. Moments later, an eerie whine filled the room, and a copy of the machine appeared beside the first. Even Abercrombie, though he had seen tangible evidence before that it would work, was astonished.

"My God!" Venasky breathed, staring pop-eyed. "It's real. I mean, really real."

Susan Peters was staring at Abercrombie with a mixture of awe and mortification. "Aylmer . . . you were right all along. The things some of us said behind your back for all that time . . . I'll never know how to make it right now."

"Quite understandable," Abercrombie condescended in a paternal tone.

"There, you see!" Zaltzer pronounced triumphantly. "I am not the nutball that you think I don't know you think. Next we talk about changing the name to Zaltzer University. Okay?"

Howard Jaffey just stood gaping, without, just for the moment, being able to say anything.

In the stupefied words and semicoherent comments that followed, nothing really meaningful was said through the next few minutes, at which point Abercrombie, enjoying his role as master of the show, called one of the security guards in from outside and said they needed help to move the machines. Looking puzzled but asking no questions (up till then there had been only one machine), the guard draped his jacket over a nearby chair. Then, following Abercrombie's directions, Jaffey and Venasky shifted the duplicate machine a few feet farther from the original, while

Abercrombie and the guard moved the original into the space where the duplicate had stood. The guard turned to leave at that point, but Abercrombie's intoxication made him crave a greater audience. "No, stay," he commanded. "It doesn't matter anymore. Twenty-four hours from now, the whole world will be talking about this."

The guard waited obediently. Moments later, the original machine suddenly emitted a series of warning beeps followed by its characteristic whine, and then popped out of existence. At the same instant, a new voice from somewhere shouted "*Get down!*" in such an imperative tone that everyone automatically obeyed—just as the gun holstered in the guard's jacket still hanging over the chair exploded, sending bullets ricocheting around the room.

"Calm down, all of you. It was just an oversight," the voice continued, while they were picking themselves up and looking about dazedly. Another machine had materialized, this time with a copy of Abercrombie inside. He made no effort to contain a look of smug amusement at the expressions on the others' faces. Even Abercrombie-One was stunned. "The varichron radiation induced by the process evidently triggers unstable materials like cartridge caps," Abercrombie-Two went on. "Now that we are aware of the fact, we will know to avoid such instances in future."

Abercrombie-One was about to ask how far in the future his other self had come from, when A-Two looked at him loftily and supplied, "Thirty minutes."

A-One collected his wits raggedly. But it made sense. "Which you knew I was about to ask, because you were me," he said.

"Exactly," A-Two confirmed.

"So in the next thirty minutes I'll figure out it was the radiation that did it, and decide it's something we can work around?"

"No, you won't have to. I've already told you."

"In the same way you were told?"

"Yes."

A-One still couldn't make sense of it. His other self had the advantage of having had more time to think it through, which irked him—and which, from the expression on the other self's face, the other self was also well aware of. "So I presume too that you also know how irritatingly supercilious you appear just at this moment?" A-One said.

"Of course," A-Two agreed. "But then I don't care, because I can assure you that you'll enjoy it every bit as much as I am right now, when you come to be me."

Harold Jaffey was finally managing to find his voice. "This is crazy," he croaked. "How can he tell you what you'll do, like some kind of robot executing a program? You're a human being with free will, for heaven's sake. What happens if you plumb decide you're not going to do it?"

Susan Peters was frowning, trying to reason it through. "No machine or copy of you came back from, let's say, an hour ahead of now. But what's to stop us setting the machine to do that, just like you did before? Let's go ahead and do it. So why isn't it here?" She directed her words at Abercrombie-One. He didn't know either, and looked appealingly at Abercrombie Two, as if the extra thirty minutes might have conferred some superior insight.

"Those are the kinds of things we'll be testing in the weeks ahead," A-Two told them. "But for now, enough of the mundane and methodical. I've been shut up in this lab, working virtually nonstop for three months." He went over to Zaltzer and draped an arm around his shoulder. "This is the man who believed in me, and he'll share in the glory. Tonight, Eli, we'll go out and celebrate, and talk about how this will be the sensation of the century. Tomorrow we'll be the talk of the world."

This was becoming infuriating. "You seem to be taking over," Abercrombie-One told his other self peevishly. "Might I remind you that I had some little part in bringing this about too?"

"Yes, but that doesn't really come into things, because in a little under thirty minutes from now, you won't be here, will you?" A-Two replied.

That did it. "And suppose I refuse to go back?" A-One challenged. He folded his arms and sent Jaffey a look that said, *Good point. Let's try it right now.* "What are you going to do—hit me over the head and throw me into the machine?" he asked A-Two. "Even that wouldn't work. You came out of it in good shape."

A-Two grinned back as if he had been expecting it—which of course he had. "Later, is when we test the paradoxes," he said. "You know as well as I know how full of uncertainties this whole business is. We pursue it methodically and systematically, isn't that what we've always said? And now you want to jeopardize years of work by giving in to a fit of pique. Is that what you want?"

A-One felt himself losing ground at hearing his own

often-reiterated principles recited back at him. But it would need more yet to dissuade him. "A cheap debater's ploy," he pronounced. "You'll have to try better than that, Aylmer."

"No I don't. All that's needed is for you to think about it. You've got about twenty minutes to figure out that if somebody doesn't go back and warn them, some of these friends of yours back there might very well get killed. I don't know the ins and outs of the logic either, yet. That's what we have to look into. But for now, are you going to risk it—just for the sake of that stubbornness of yours?"

A-One felt himself wilting. He knew already, with a sinking feeling, what the outcome would be, as he could read his other self knew perfectly well also. He didn't need twenty minutes. He was trapped.

"All right," he said in a voice that could have cut seasoned teak. "I'll do it."

But Abercrombie's elation had subsided into gloom and wistfulness by the time he and Zaltzer sat down to what was to have been their celebration dinner at the five-star Atherton Hotel in the heart of the city. "The most staggering discovery in the history of physics, Eli," he lamented. "When it happened, we said that the world would know. I had a list of all the names, the contacts . . ."

Zaltzer nodded enthusiastically "Yes, I know. You showed it to me. It—" He checked himself as he saw the look on Abercrombie's face. "Why, Aylmer? What happened?"

"I never told you this before. But there was a period . . . you remember when I almost put everything on hold? Oh, it's a long story. But it seemed everything was over." Abercrombie looked up. "The short answer is, I destroyed it."

"What?"

"The file with all the lists. I burned it."

For a few moments Zaltzer seemed taken aback. Then his irrepressible ebullience resurfaced as always. He waved a hand. "So . . . the announcement won't be as widespread as you planned. I still have contacts. We'll get the word around. It's hardly the Dark Ages."

"But it won't be the same," Abercrombie said. "The lists I had prepared were the work of years. Not just the regular media hacks—with respect, Eli, but you know what I mean. They covered the whole scientific establishment too: Nobel laureates, directors of the national labs, national advisors . . ." This time it was Abercrombie's turn to break off as he saw that Zaltzer wasn't listening but staring across the table suddenly with a strange, inscrutable smile. "What is it?" Abercrombie asked. "What do you find so funny?"

"You've already forgotten this afternoon," Zaltzer told him. "Your own machine. You don't have to be without your file now, Aylmer. You can go back and get it!"

The problem was, Abercrombie had no way of knowing just what days in the past, or times in the day—it was over three months ago now—he should aim for to avoid running into people and being apprehended. To compound the difficulty, the short-range tests that were all he had experimented with so far did little to help him calibrate for longer hops back, and he was unable to set an arrival time with accuracy, even if he had known which one to select. His first few attempts were cut short when he realized he had been detected—on one occasion culminating in a narrow escape when an earlier version of himself actually chased him, and he escaped only by remembering that he had used the fire extinguisher. (He never was able to work out who had thought of that.)

But he persevered, and eventually succeeded in rematerializing in the workshop at a time when the surroundings seemed empty and quiet. He still didn't know exactly when it was; and even if he had, he had no way of knowing what his earlier self had been doing on that particular day, and hence how much time he was likely to have. He needed to get out of the Annexe and to his apartment, which was where the folder was, make copies of the contents, conceal them in the cellars of the pre-demolition customs building nearby, and then get back to the machine with the original folder, and away. Planting the backup seemed a bit odd now, he had to admit, if by that time he was going to have the original in his possession; but he had resolved to adhere rigidly to his plan. He was taking no chances. The thing that would tell him what he had been doing that day would be his appointments diary, which was usually in his public office.

He came out of the workshop and padded toward the main-elevator end of the lab area. When he was about halfway there, the door at the far end of the corridor opened, and Mrs. Crawford came through. Abercrombie froze; but she gave him only a cursory look and disappeared into one of the offices. As he began moving again, she thrust her head back out.

"The FedEx package that you were waiting for from Chicago has arrived," she informed him.

"It has?" He had no idea what she was talking about. "Thank you. I'll pick it up later." Mrs. Crawford's head disappeared back through the doorway. Abercrombie scuttled quickly to his office, found the diary, and retreated with it to his private office at the far end of the facility.

That had been the day when he'd gone downstairs to review Qualio and Turnel's project assignment, the diary told him. He thought back. He had spent over an hour with them in the prototype lab, he recalled, and then lunched in the cafeteria. He had enough time. But he couldn't afford to leave the machine standing in the workshop that long, inviting discovery. He went back and sent it away under automatic control to a quiet period in the middle of the night, programmed to return after ninety minutes. The alarm on his watch would warn him fifteen minutes before it was due to reappear.

He left the building via the back stairs and drove home using the keys already in his pocket. The same keys let him into his apartment, where he retrieved the contacts folder and took it to a commercial copying store to make the backup.

And that was when he discovered the master notebook containing his design calculations for the machine. It hadn't been stolen from his safe in the office at all! At some time he had taken it home to work on and inadvertently dropped it among the papers in the contacts folder. Oh well, too bad. There wasn't time to do anything about rectifying that now. He did copy the notebook's contents as well, however, and sealed them in a separate, plastic-wrapped package before leaving for the old customs building.

Down in the cellars, he located the room where he remembered finding the documents—intact now, of course, but still conveniently obscured and out-of-the-way—and went to the recesses between the piping supports. There were even some bricks lying handily close among some rubble. He placed the packages in two of the slots and covered the openings. Just as he was about to leave, he remembered something odd. When he found them, the notebook had been there, sure enough, but the other package had contained things he'd never seen before. He turned back uncertainly and stared down at the pipes. Had someone else changed the other package? Had he himself revisited this place on some future errand that he was as yet unaware of? But then his wristwatch beeped, warning him that it was time to be heading back to the machine. Shaking his head and telling himself that it would all be resolved somehow, he hurried back toward the ramp leading up from the gallery.

He almost didn't make it. By the time he emerged from the freight elevator in the Annexe building, his earlier self was already back from lunch and in the private office—putting Qualio and Turnel's test results in the safe, he remembered now. He heard his own testy "Who's there?" as he crept past the door. He ran to get out of the corridor, hearing keys being fumbled into the lock on the inside of the door behind him. He let himself into the workshop, remembering that his other self had mercifully chosen to investigate in the other direction along the corridor first. The workshop was empty. He gazed frantically at his watch, as if sheer willing could make the seconds count off faster. The door at the far end of the corridor was opening, footsteps approaching. Then came the blessed sound of the machine arriving right on time.

"Who is that in there?" his voice demanded loudly from just yards away.

Clutching the documents that he had brought from the apartment, he threw himself into the machine, stabbed at the control as he latched the gate behind him, and was gone. . . .

And so it was done—apparently without mishap. Abercrombie stood in the machine, looking out over the familiar scene of the workshop. He had the contacts file with him, which was what he had gone to get, along with the original master notebook as a bonus. He'd had thoughts of maybe returning that to its proper place in the private-office safe before returning, but time had run out on him and that had proved impossible. Now, for what it was worth, back-ups of both were secure in their hiding place from the past. There were still loose ends of unanswered questions dangling in his mind, but all in all everything seemed to be working itself out. He didn't pretend yet to understand precisely how.

Zaltzer had hoped to be waiting for him when he got back, but in view of the imprecision still bedeviling the process, his absence was understandable. Abercrombie climbed down from the machine and drew in several deep breaths of relief. He hadn't realized how tense the undertaking had made him. He let himself out the rear door of the workshop, went back to his private office, locked the door, and stowed the two sets of documents in the safe. That essential task accomplished, he sank down into the chair at the desk to unwind. A vague feeling of something not being quite right had been nagging from somewhere below consciousness since he came out of the machine, but just at this moment he was too exhausted to give it much attention. His mind drifted; he might even have dozed. . . .

Until the muffled sound of something being moved along the corridor outside brought him back to wakefulness. By the time he had sat up and let his head clear, the noise had gone. He rose from the chair and was about go to the door and check, when his gaze traveled across to the window and he caught the view outside. He stared in confusion for a moment, then crossed to the window to be sure. The old customs building along the waterfront was intact. . . . Yet it was supposed to have burned down three months ago. And then he realized what was wrong that he had noticed but not registered: There weren't any security people around the lab. This was no minor error. He hadn't returned to anywhere near the time he was supposed to be in. So when, exactly, was this?

Infuriatingly, nothing in his office would tell him. He came out into the corridor and headed for the front of the building, either to seek some sign in his other office or find out from Mrs. Crawford, but stopped dead the moment he entered the workshop area. The time machine, in which he had arrived only a short while ago, was gone. His mind reeled, unable to deal with what seemed an insurmountable hurdle. But as he forced himself to think, the pieces of what it had to mean came together. If the customs building was still there, this had to be before it was demolished—pretty obviously. Then this could only be the day that he had been in the public office, heard the strange noise, come back to investigate, found the machine unattended, and stolen it. The noise that aroused him had been himself moving it to the freight elevator. He thought back rapidly, trying to recreate the sequence of events. Knowing what he did, if he moved quickly enough, there would be time yet to intercede.

He ran back through to the rear stairs, started down, and then halted as a cautionary note sounded in his head. After all he had been through to get them, would it be wise to leave the notebook and contacts file here? No. Until he was a lot clearer about this whole business, he wasn't going to let them out of his sight. He ran back to the office and removed them from the safe. Then, deciding it was too late to intercept himself in the loading bay—and in any case, he didn't want a scene involving two of him in front of the service people there—and knowing that he still had his keys, he raced instead to the front lot, where he parked his car.

He screeched out onto the waterfront boulevard without stopping and saw the truck carrying the tarp-covered time machine exiting from the rear gate a few car lengths in front of him . . . a split second before a horn blared, brakes squealed, and something hit him in the rear. And that was when the police cruiser that just had to be there turned on its siren and pulled him over. He remembered it too late, while he sat through the ritual of insurance information being exchanged, radio check of his license number and record, and the ponderous writing out of the ticket. By the time he got moving again, the truck had long since disappeared.

Nervous about the time now, instead of going around the long route to the side entrance that the truck had taken, he drove straight up to the front of the building, leaped out, and ran inside, in the process knocking over a pile of steel drums just inside the door and causing enough noise to make any thought now at concealing his presence a joke. But by this time he didn't care. All that mattered was getting to the machine.

"Wait!" Brady, interrupted, sounding alarmed. "There's more of 'em breaking in upstairs."

"It's a bust," Yellow One told him. "Get yourself out!"

Brady looked around at the boxes of gelignite, HMX, PETN, rocket-propelled grenades, and other explosives, along with the cases of detonator caps and fuses. "But the stuff . . . It's taken months," he protested.

"It's all lost anyway. What we don't need is them getting you to talk too. Get yourself out!"

Brady nodded, snapped off the phone, and pulled himself together. The fastest exit was up a service ladder to the front entrance. He emerged without encountering anyone and found a car right there with the keys left in. There was no arguing with a gift from Providence like that. He jumped in and accelerated out onto the boulevard, failing, in his haste, to wonder why, if the place had been busted, there were no other vehicles in the vicinity.

*   *   *

While down in the cellars, surrounded by explosives, incendiaries, and sensitive detonating devices, Professor Aylmer Arbuthnot Abercrombie started up the time machine that emitted varichron radiation. . . .

One thing that Yellow One did want from the ruins, however, if it could be retrieved, was the group cell leader's book of codes, contacts, command structure, and other information that could prove disastrous if the law-enforcement agencies got their hands on it. The next night, after the fire crews and demolition teams had left, Brady went back down to the place where the documents had been concealed. He found a package in one of the recesses beneath some old pipes as described, but then he was forced to hide when he heard someone else coming. From behind cover he watched as the same figure whom he had observed wheeling the strange machine down from the truck the previous day entered and extracted another package from one of the other recesses. The contents didn't seem to be what he wanted when he examined them with a flashlight, and he became agitated until he located yet another package, checked it, and then left taking both of them. Brady followed him back up and looked out in time to see him depart in the same car that Brady had "borrowed" the day before, just before the building went up. Brady reported all the details when he handed over the package that he had recovered.

But it turned out to be the wrong one, containing lists of names and details of media people, scientists, political figures, and others who were of no interest to the group. The stranger, therefore, must have taken the group's code and organization book. With the help of a friend in the police department, they traced the car's number from the records of stolen vehicles. It turned out to belong to a professor who worked in the university Annexe nearby.

The organization sent a couple of its bagmen into the premises to see if they might be able to uncover something further, one posing as a repairman, the other under cover of an arranged power outage, but the security arrangements they came up against were astonishingly strict for a university environment. Eventually, the leaders gave it up as a lost cause.

All of it very odd. It turned out that there hadn't been a police bust at the old warehouse that day, after all. Brady often puzzled about the professor, because he had assumed him to be the body that was found in the ruins. In his own mind he was sure there had been nobody else there. Yet there the professor was, still coming and going for months afterward. Brady decided he probably never would figure it out.

The Modern Medievalism

In his monumental work *The Decline of the West*, the German philosopher Oswald Spengler held that the academic practice of dividing subjects of study "vertically" is misleading in a number of ways. In creating categories of Art, Mathematics, Literature, and so on, and structuring them historically to reflect such "periods" as Classical, Medieval, Renaissance, Modern, we construct an illusion of continuities that never existed. More seriously, in taking an epoch of human culture apart and distributing its constituent parts across artificial groupings that we impose upon the world, we lose sight of the essence defining the great human civilizations that time has seen. Hence, we fail to understand them as expressions of a unique cultural soul that is born, grows, flourishes for a while, and then, like any other living organism—which they are—dies. It would be as if, having consigned the business of circulatory systems, nervous systems, digestive systems, and so forth, each with its own history of discovery and development, to separate departments, we were unable to put together a horizontal slice through all of them as an entity having attributes of "personhood" at all.

Every culture embodies a central guiding idea, or worldview, that determines its account of the universe and dictates how it will interpret its perceptions to shape what it sees as reality. Everything that speaks in its arts and its sciences, its social and political institutions, and its conceptualizations from architecture to economics express its inner nature as inevitably as biological form and behavior express a genetic imperative. The classical world of Greece and Rome was finite and bounded, shrinking back from confronting infinities of space and time. Its pictures show only foregrounds, avoiding the challenges of distance and unlimited extent, while its sailors followed the coastlines, rarely venturing out of sight of land. Mathematics confined itself to the study of static geometric figures, and the number system contained nothing that went beyond what was needed to enumerate finite, tangible objects. Is it mere coincidence that the leading art form was sculpture—finite volumes bounded by surfaces?

That age ended when Rome fell, and in Europe there followed the era of Christendom in which spiritual concerns took precedence over the material values that we take as synonymous with progress, and which we consequently term the Dark Ages. And then came Western Man, who not only took on the notions of change and infinity, but delighted in them, and whose every innovation exulted in the newfound freedoms that they symbolized. The calculus of Newton and Leibnitz was the language that described a universe no longer static and bounded but dynamic and unlimited, to be explored through scientific discovery, the testing of limits, and the voyages of the global navigators. Mastery of perspective, soaring arches and buttresses, and the new astronomy rejoiced in the experience of boundless, endless space. And what else was the music of Mozart and Beethoven but flights of woodwind and strings exploring vast, orchestra-created voids?

From origins in the Renaissance, through the seventeenth–eighteenth century "Age of Enlightenment," the philosophical ideology underpinning the Euro-American Western culture in whose legacy we live today was a commitment to scientific rationalism: the belief that the universe would prove explainable in purely material, mechanistic terms. The hand of God, which an earlier age had discerned as guiding every facet of existence from the individual's station and fortune in life to the courses traced by the planets, was unnecessary. And if that were so, it followed that the God-given right of hereditary elites to rule, upheld and defended by the authority of traditional religion, could be challenged. In the idealistic vision of science, beliefs are arrived at impartially from objective evaluation of the evidence. But when a deeply rooted predisposition pervades an entire cultural movement, it is easy for objectivity to give way to ideology, even in those rarer instances where the conflict registers consciously. I have come to the conclusion that in some important areas, modern science, far from replacing old, outmoded ideas with new insights in the way that is presented, has let principle rule over evidence in ways that actually represent a retreat from truths that were closer to being understood more than a hundred years ago.

I've written at some length elsewhere[1] about the Immanuel Velikovsky affair that was precipitated by the publication of his book *Worlds in Collision* in 1950, and continued through to the inquisitorial exorcizing of his theories under the guise of the AAAS meeting in San Francisco in 1974—which has been described as "one of the blackest episodes in the history of science."[2] Essentially, Velikovsky proposed that the Solar System has not always displayed the repeating orderliness that we observe today. We live in one of a series of quiescent periods occurring between times of convulsive change, in which the motions of the planets and other bodies are disturbed before settling down into a new pattern of stable orbits. Such events have involved the Earth in encounters that have had profound effects on its geological, climatic, and biological history. The most recent of these events took place in historic times and are recorded in mythologies and legends handed down through cultures the world over.

All of this was completely at odds with the reigning scientific views of the time, which admitted none of the catastrophic influences that are finally being recognized today (so long as they are kept comfortably remote in the distant past). But the dominant thinking of the mid twentieth century held doggedly to notions of a lawful, nonthreatening universe, cycling endlessly and predictably from the indefinite past to the indefinite future. Despite diverse evidence that Velikovsky marshaled to support his contentions, and some daz-zlingly successful predictions that would have been applauded as triumphs had they been noncontroversial and made by an acceptable insider, he was greeted with a campaign of vilification and misrepresentation of an intensity seldom seen in professional circles, which remains largely successful to this day.

Yet his picture of a relatively tranquil Earth being periodically beset by immense cataclysms that bring on entirely new ages was not something innovative and revolutionary. Two centuries ago, evidence for the occurrence of major catastrophes in shaping the Earth as we know it had been considered self-evident and ubiquitous. The trouble, however, was that to the minds of many, such notions were inseparable from the doctrines held by the wrong side of the broad-based religious and political ideological clash that was coming to a head at the time.

Conflicting views on whether the universe has always existed pretty much as we find it, or arrived there either convulsively or through steady change go back to the time of ancient Greece and no doubt further. Such early accounts were inevitably inspired by religion and mythology, reflecting more than anything their proponents' predisposition to see the powers that ruled the cosmos as wrathful and capricious or protective and dependable. Homer's cosmos was a turbulent affair filled with selfish, insensitive gods. Plato saw it as an imperfect and sometimes troubled attempt at imitating unattainable ideals of form and harmony, while Aristotle, whose version eventually prevailed as the model for the medieval Scholastics, presented eternal stability in a system of celestial spheres centered upon the Earth, moving in perfect circles under the guidance of a Prime Mover who epitomizes everything good.

By Newton's time the subject was taking on more of the appearance of what we would consider a science, i.e. conclusions arrived at through study of the actual world rather than deduced from axiomatic preconceptions of how things must be. And what the early studies showed unequivocally was a record of the Earth's being subjected to episodic destruction on a vast scale. The evidence came in the form of large-scale faulting and dislocations of its surface geography, tremendous folding and uplifts of mountain chains—in many places of rock that had once lain beneath the ocean—and vast fossil graveyards testifying to sudden and violent mass extinctions, after which the essentially re-formed world was repopulated with new breeds of life. Initially, the Church opposed such notions as being sacrilegious to the doctrine of changeless order that Thomas Aquinas, primarily, had forged by reconciling Aristotle with the Bible. But as the evidence for change mounted, and such riddles as the existence of fossils showed an allegedly omniscient creator apparently capable of imperfection, or at least of having second thoughts, the new facts were coopted as demonstrable proof of divine retribution and the Great Flood, support for Mosaic chronology, and hence as a reaffirmation of Scriptural authority.

Christianity began as an ennobling of the worth and dignity of the ordinary individual, and an opposition movement challenging the right of Rome to rule through force and military conquest. By the time the emperor Constantine became a convert and proclaimed it the official Roman religion in AD 313, what he unveiled was a counterfeit. While preserving the symbols and slogans that had given the original movement its appeal, in essence it had become an arm of the state. Far from being a nonviolent opponent of imperialism, the refashioned institution championed it, fielding its own armies and conniving in the schemes of kings and princes to secure its share of power, wealth, and landholding across the map that emerged out of medieval Europe, the founding ideals effectively forgotten except, for a while, in a few places along the western fringes. What did the genocidal wars of the Middle Ages, the manic persecutions of witches and heretics, ferocious crusades against neighboring peoples, and the horrors of the Inquisition have to do with the original teachings of love, compassion, tolerance, and forgiveness?

The Renaissance is celebrated as a revival of Classical learning and the freeing of intellect from subjugation by repressive dogma to open inquiry and the objective pursuit of knowledge. But in a way that becomes apparent from the perspective of hundreds of years later, it also rekindled the earlier spiritual vision as the pioneers of the newly idealized Science came to see the mathematical laws they were uncovering as proof of perfection and harmony in a manner ideologically closer to medieval Scholasticism.

In the minds of most people, Isaac Newton towers as a virtual embodiment of the philosophic revolution that ushered in the age of science and reason. And, of course, his scientific achievements were indeed stupendous, creating precedents in thought and method that would serve as models for the next three centuries. It should be stressed, however, that the prime aim of Newton's science was not to show a universe functioning without God, but to reveal the creator's perfection through the workings of the cosmos and their conformity to mathematical precision. His scientific work was ancillary to theological preoccupations, which formed the major part of his unpublished writings and absorbed more of his time.[3]

In 1696, nine years after publication of the first edition of Newton's *Principia*, William Whiston, a fellow of Cambridge University and devoted pupil of Newton, presented the manuscript of a book entitled *New Theory of the Earth*. With uncanny similarities to what Velikovsky would claim over two centuries later—and which Velikovsky acknowledged fully—Whiston argued from historical evidence and astronomical considerations that the cataclysm implied by the Old Testament account of a universal deluge was caused by the impact of a comet at the end of the third millennium BC, prior to which the solar year had been 360 days long. At first, Newton was impressed and sympathetic to Whiston's views, but later he became hostile to their radicalism. If traditional views of the cosmic order were abandoned, the foundations of morality would be undermined and the chief arguments for the existence of God—the wise adaptation of the natural world to the preservation of living creatures—eliminated. In 1710, Whiston was dismissed from his teaching position because of heresy and then formally tried before a body of bishops of the Church of England. Nevertheless, the astronomer Edmond Halley, who had himself, a year and a half before Whiston's book, read a paper before the Royal

Society explaining the deluge as a comet impact but not printed it lest he might "incur the censure of the sacred order," proposed Whiston for membership of the society, upon which Newton threatened to resign. By the time the second edition of the *Principia* appeared in 1713, refutation of Whiston and proving the universe to be stable and unchanged since the creation had become Newton's major preoccupation.

But in a way that can only be described as ironic, the lawfulness and precision first demonstrated in Newton's mechanics provided the inspiration for those who were seeking to break from traditional religion. Following his mathematics but not his theology, the thinkers of the Enlightenment period moved from theism to deism—in which God was removed from intervention in day-to-day human affairs and relegated to setting up and starting the clockwork universe to operate under its own laws thereafter—and thence to the mechanistic atheism of the later eighteenth century. Hence, while they believed they were freeing themselves from religiously determined predispositions, the Newtonian ideals that they projected upon the world represented a philosophic return to medieval tenets of changeless, eternal heavens. Thus, in what was really a reversal of the roles that are popularly perceived today, a worldview that owed more to the theology of the Middle Ages than to impartial evaluation of the evidence mounting from Renaissance researches became the underlying ideology guiding what was seen as science, while genuinely new factual accounts and unbiased reviews of ancient records were dismissed as too uncomfortably evocative of biblical wrath and retribution to be acceptable.

Studies comparable to "geology" as we understand it had not really figured in the medieval world. The Earth was deemed corrupt and fallen, and hence not a subject worthy of academic study. The wisdom of God was reflected in subjects like geometry, numerology, harmony, and astronomy. But what the findings being made in the new spirit of discovery were showing was not a picture of serene changelessness, but of abrupt discontinuities in the formations of rocks and the stories told by fossils, of immense deposits of sediments, mountains rising where there had been oceans, and graveyards filled with the bones of countless animal forms that no longer existed.

After the notoriety it had earned previously in opposing new ideas, the traditional Church largely accommodated to the new findings. But the Protestant Reformation, with its fervor to demonstrate the literal truth of a Bible that taught not only its creation story but also of the deluge as divinely decreed punishment for sin, sought an interpretation that would reconcile these findings with the book of Genesis. A stream of books and publications appeared in England from the close of the seventeenth century onward, explaining such features as the stratification of rocks in terms of Noah's flood, and provided the Tories with one of their major weapons in defense of the monarchy against the liberal Whigs. In both England and France, upholders of the traditional order argued that monarchy was not only the most ancient and the most common form of government, but also the most *natural*. Hence, the king was emulating the divine monarch in ruling with absolute authority. In the course of the eighteenth century, ideas of liberalism and democracy challenging this doctrine took hold throughout Europe and in America. But to show that monarchy was not "natural" in a way that would be acceptable at the time required alternative explanations for the origin of the world and its living things, and a refutation of catastrophes as the punishment for sin.

It is difficult for most people today, when geology is thought of in connection with university laboratories and rock-filled museum cases far removed from politics and religion, to imagine it as a subject that was regarded as inseparable from passionately held beliefs. Two principal, strongly antagonistic schools emerged, impelled to conflicting interpretations of the same facts for reasons that were to a large degree ideological. The "neptunists" attributed the Earth's strata and sediments to precipitations from immense flooding and saw the faulting of its surface as the result of catastrophic episodes, while the "vulcanists" or "plutonists" accounted for it all in terms of volcanic activity and the slow erosion of massive uplifts. The language had become scientific, but beneath it lay the old association of catastrophe and violence with biblical authenticity and revelation. The Scottish geologist James Hutton, author of the influential *Theory of the Earth*, which made the case for strictly natural processes—also a friend of Adam Smith, the promoter of laissez-faire economics ruled by natural market processes—believed that when we became "free of the mental shackles of rigid adherence to biblical doctrines" we would see that "the operations of nature are equable and steady."[4]

Repudiating violent upheaval as the natural mechanism of change also had more immediate implications.

Hutton's book was published in 1789, six years after recognition of America's independence and on the eve of the French Revolution. Following the French bloodletting and the subsequent Napoleonic wars, England fell into a severe depression with the cessation of demand for military supplies, demobilization of nearly 400,000 soldiers, and laws passed to protect farmers from imports of cheap grain, which had devastating effects on industrial towns and the laboring class. In 1819 a political meeting of the unemployed in Manchester turned into a riot and was fired on by the militia, which resulted in the passing of a series of repressive acts by the monarchist Tory government, bringing the country to the verge of revolution itself. But after witnessing the French experience, the people wanted reform in Parliament, not violence. Reforming Parliament, however, would first entail defeating a highly effective system of natural theology—required reading before a student could graduate from Oxford or Cambridge—which taught that sovereignty descends from God to the king, and "it is the will of God that the established government be obeyed."[5] And the only way to achieve that would be by destroying the scientific foundations upon which that system rested.

The London Geological Society had been formed in 1807. Remarkable about it was that none of its thirteen original members was a geologist. Four were doctors, one of them a former Unitarian minister and another a refugee from the French Revolution, along with four Quakers, two booksellers, two independently wealthy amateur chemists, and a member of Parliament. Its growth thereafter was brisk, attracting 26 Fellows of the Royal Society in the following year, 400 members by 1817, and reaching 637 at the time of its incorporation in 1825, almost all of them still drawn from such ranks as doctors, clergymen, lawyers, and politicians. England was heavily engaged in canal digging and mining at this time, so there was no shortage of people actively engaged in geologically related work. William Smith, for example, a drainage engineer who pioneered the technique of dating strata by fossils, is cited in modern texts as a noted geologist of the era. But he was not invited to join the society. The business that drew such exalted attendance had to do with theological and political implications and their impact on the system that would shape the country, not with canals, mines, and hammering rocks.

In the same year that the London Geological Society was incorporated, 1825, George Scrope, who later bought himself a seat as a liberal in Parliament, published *Considerations on Volcanos*, which flagrantly applied Hutton's ideas to transforming all of the Torys' arguments, ascribing to volcanic activity every event that they ascribed to God. So effective was this mechanism at achieving the results observed, Scrope maintained, that there was no more need of God to interfere in the business of the universe than there was for a king to interfere with the natural laws of economics and society. Scrope's head-on approach proved somewhat too radical and impetuous for the times, and achieved little immediate effect. It did, however, set the tone of co-opting facts that the opponents presented as arguments and accounting for them by natural means. This tactic was taken up in a more subtle fashion by Scrope's Whig lawyer associate Charles Lyell with devastating success. In his three-volume *Principles of Geology*, published between 1830 and 1833, Lyell established "uniformitarianism," or gradualism, as the exclusive guiding force in shaping the world we see.

The essence of the uniformitarian claim is that all features the Earth's surface as it exists today can be accounted for by the same processes that are observed working today, operating at the same rates, over immense spans of time. Lyell's book was not, primarily, a scientific report as is generally depicted, but "a treatise devoted to the presentation and defense of a new system."[6] Steady, cumulative transformation, working insensibly and patiently, could bring about extreme change. World cataclysms and violent upheavals were not necessary.

By the middle of the nineteenth century the catastrophist school had been vanquished in the eyes of intellectual trendsetters. Its leading proponent was the French comparative anatomist Baron Georges Cuvier, also known as the "father of paleontology." Solid English rationalism and gentlemanly restraint, tempered by a proper sense of allowing things time to mature, had saved the day against those excitable continentals with their rioting mobs and guillotines. It was more a religious and political battle than a scientific one, characterized by demonization of the opponents and fanatical attacks. In a well-funded and coordinated campaign, catastrophists were popularly depicted as crazed supernaturalists forcing facts to fit their delusions and bent on imposing a Mosaic account of history on the world, while uniformitarians were presented as sober, sensible, and intellectually sound. All and any data pointing to the possibility of catastrophes were rejected, suppressed, or ignored.

There were no grounds for compromise, and by the end of the century an enormous body of inconvenient findings had disappeared from textbooks and university teaching. To a disturbing extent that remains true to the present time.

Not only did uniformitarianism gain acceptance as the explanation of geological phenomena to the exclusion of all rival theories. It was adopted into biology by Darwin, and became the unifying paradigm that enabled astronomy too to be fitted comfortably into the emerging Victorian worldview of progress, predictability, and security. As Stephen Jay Gould described it: " . . . scientists began to see change as a normal part of universal order, not as aberrant or exceptional. Scholars then transferred to nature the liberal program of slow and orderly change that they had advocated for social transformation."[7] Science took on the role of presenting a universe that was in accordance with its cultural worldview: safe, stable, nonthreatening, not quite timeless but changing imperceptibly, and then in the direction of constant improvement, carrying mankind onward toward ultimate perfection at the top of the Great Scale of Being.

The vision might have been one of progress and enlightenment. But what the embodiment of this Victorian fantasy really represented was an ideological retreat to a medieval faith in cosmic benevolence and the inherent constancy and protectiveness of Nature. In the spirit of empirical discovery that came with the Renaissance, Cuvier and others had begun putting together the picture of how the evidence said things were in the real world, but the prospect was too alarming to face and the new ecclesia buried it.

The world of the Victorians and Edwardians exploded in 1914, and the time might have been ripe then for a deep-searching reappraisal of the precepts that it had been founded on. On the other hand, perhaps, in the chaos of world wars, revolutions, and economic catastrophes that followed, science needed more than ever the reassurance of a more fundamental stability and orderliness beyond the world of human affairs with all its follies and transience. And so things pretty much remained until 1950, when Velikovsky resurrected all the specters of catastrophism that had been safely laid to rest, amid a blaze of publicity that couldn't be ignored.

In some respects, the timing couldn't have been worse. The world was still recovering from World War II, ended by twin man-made catastrophes of nuclear explosions, with communist paranoia in the U.S. at its height and drawing the lines for the Cold War. His proposals were greeted with a level of hysteria and vehemence perhaps unique in the professional circles of modern times. Every device of ridicule, vilification, ad hominem attack, misrepresentation, and denial of means to respond was employed, and continued even as evidence mounted from space probes, archeological findings, revised historical accounts, and elsewhere that was in accordance with his claims and refuted the authorities that he had challenged. One can only note the striking parallel to the tone of the early-nineteenth-century ideological battle in England and wonder what deeper, possibly unconscious psychological terrors might have been triggered.

In more recent years, catastrophist notions have

begun to regain some respectability with the much-publicized theory of the dinosaurs' extinction being due to an impact event—although that is now (late 2004) being challenged. Also, we're suddenly hearing a lot about the hazards in the form of wandering asteroids, near-approach comets, and the like threatening the end of the world as we know it—which may have a lot to do with an ailing space program and the kind of funding opportunities that tend to follow any campaign of scaring the public. Impacts by relatively minor objects have become permissible, but any thought of major Solar System instabilities or encounters between the planets themselves remains off-limits. Newly discovered swathes of ancient cratering are reported seemingly every week, along with another major historical event or turning point being linked to some postulated climatic change or geological upheaval. The science press and popular media treat these revelations as breaking through into new realms of inquiry and conceptual insight. Yet what they really represent are the first steps toward recovery from a backward-looking mind-set that has held sway in some of the major departments of science for the best part of two hundred years.

The shabby side of all this is that it's hard to find one of the ideas that Velikovsky proposed, which was once derided and rejected with ill grace, that isn't today being quietly coopted and sneaked in through the back door of Establishment science with no due acknowledgment. Electromagnetic influences beyond Earth and across the Solar System have been confirmed by space probes, and cosmological models have been developed giving them a major role in shaping the universe. Such topics as ancient cometary encounters, revisions to ancient history, mass extinctions, sudden climate changes and pole shifts, and the fission of the minor planets from gas giants are standard fare today for scientific conferences and journals. But such is the political tone within mainstream science that to associate one's name with the originator of concepts that are still beyond the pale of conventional acceptability would be tantamount to committing career suicide.

Fortunately, not all minds are so easily intimidated or deterred. A lively school of catastrophe theorists outside the citadel walls, publishing its own journals and convening its own meetings, continues developing and debating the lines of inquiry that Velikovsky's questions first opened up. In some ways their work may be closer to the spirit of original science, being motivated first and foremost by curiosity and the urge to know, not by any need to attract political approval and funding, and pressures to conform. It took about a hundred years for Copernicus's fairly straightforward suggestion—if you put the Sun in the center, everything becomes simpler and makes more sense—to get past the professors of his day.

Velikovsky believed that the disturbances to the Solar System brought about by Venus's encounters with Earth, and later Mars, represented the final phase of even greater cataclysmic events that went back much earlier. In his studies of the world's ancient mythologies, he was struck by the repeated descriptions of a past age in which the skies has been ruled not by the Sun but by other deities that turn out over and over again to be references to the planet we know today as Saturn. Pursuing this line of investigation led him to speculate that Earth might once have been a satellite of Saturn, which was then a protostar somewhat larger than the object we know today. He suggested this might explain, for example, the apparent adaptation of most plant life to red light (they absorb and utilize mainly redder wavelengths, which is why what's reflected is predominantly green), and the mystery of how early life could have survived unshielded ultraviolet radiation from the Sun, which disrupts the formation of biological macromolecules. The configuration broke up when Saturn flared in a novalike instability that involved the loss of much of its mass. Velikovsky connects these events with the seven days of light that cultural traditions worldwide attest to as ending a time of darkness before the skies changed, an immense deluge that predated the Venus events, the receding of Saturn to a position of minor importance, periods of cold and ice, and massive extinctions of life, followed by the appearance of new forms.

Although reliance must be primarily on mythological interpretations because the physical evidence no longer exists, the Saturn theory has taken on a life of its own, giving rise to a variety of alternative forms that continue to be the subject of energetic debates, carried notably by the journal *Aeon, Chronology & Catastrophism Review*, and the Kronia Group.[8] One of the most controversial features that these models share is a linear configuration of Earth, Mars, Venus, and Saturn as a kind of celestial shish kebab, in which Saturn remains stationary over the northern hemisphere. The daily rotation of its sunlit crescent as seen from Earth is said to explain the countless stories in mythology and legend of wheels, mills, horned heads, and the like turning in the sky, while the strange electrical and gravitational conditions produced at the common axis along which all the planets were aligned provides the basis for once-again widespread accounts of awe-inspiring ladders, stairways, pillars, columns of light, mountains, and other edifices extending away into the northern heavens. Some researchers have identified Adam and Eve with the celestial spectacles presented by Mars and Venus, the four rivers that flowed out of their abode being radiant filaments of light emanating from Venus to cross the surrounding halo of Saturn's disk.

In a further dissension, some proponents of the Saturn theory, while agreeing with Velikovsky on Venus's being a young, recently hot object and not something that has existed for billions of years as the conventional picture maintains, contend that it originated by fission from Saturn in the course of these events, not from Jupiter. A bolder version still of the theory holds that Saturn and its companions, including Earth, constituted a separate interloping system that met up with an originally smaller Sun-Jupiter configuration of some form, and the Solar System that we know is what came out of it. In this interpretation, the lineup results from the smaller planets being strung out behind the primary in the final stages of acceleration toward the larger Sun, somewhat in the manner of the pieces of Shoemaker-Levy comet before its spectacular plunge into Jupiter in 1994.

And then we come to further developments of the theme that propose events even more fantastic than anything imagined by Velikovsky himself. The

Velikovsky-Angiras scenario[9] results from years of research on the part of the latter, a physicist, into deriving new translations of the Hindu *Vedas*, the oldest written records available to humanity, interpreted from the point of view of their being accounts of cosmic and cataclysmic events. Angiras's conclusion is that Velikovsky was right in identifying Venus as a young body, but wrong in his dating of its encounters with Earth. By Angiras's account, Venus as a white-hot proto-planet is identified with the Hindu fire deities Aditi and Agni, which seared the Earth on two occasions fairly close together but two thousand years before the time of the Exodus, causing immense devastation that is still recorded in the band of desert stretching from West Africa to Mongolia, and almost ending the human race in the process. Venus then dislodged Mars from what was originally an internal orbit (closer to the Sun), and the three bodies entered into a resonant cycle in which Mars periodically approached close to Earth, locking synchronously with it like a binary star for stretches of fifteen years or so at a time, ending only when Venus returned to break up the configuration.

If Angiras is right, this pattern continued for something like 2,000 years! During each encounter, Mars hung stationary in the sky above northern India, appearing ten to twenty times the size of the Moon. Its surface was clearly visible, possessing oceans and, quite possibly, a biosphere. The mutual tidal effect caused the oceans of both planets to pile up around the crustal bulges forming the points of closest proximity—the Tibetan plateau in the case of Earth, and the Tharsis region of Mars, the latter being submerged. This, according to Angiras, is where the Atlantis was that Plato was trying to describe—which could be, perhaps, why nobody is having much luck finding it here.

The only real reason for the incredulity with which most people greet this proposition on hearing it for the first time is its contradiction of so much that we think we know. But it's consistent with the well-publicized mystery of where all the water went that Mars evidently did possess at one time. According to Angiras's reconstruction, as a result of a matter-transfer process similar to that which can be observed taking place between some binary objects, it's right here! And it's true that Earth's sea levels apparently rose several hundred feet at around this time for reasons that conventional theories have never really explained. All this, of course, would make nonsense of the official position that the surface of Mars we see today dates back millions or billions of years. I've never understood how this could seriously be believed. The comment heard over and over again from researchers studying pictures of the floodplains, water channels, canyons, and other surface features is how sharp and uncannily fresh they appear. Even by their own figures for wind speeds, dust transportation, and meteorite infall, all such traces should long ago have been obliterated.

The scenario is consistent also with such factors as the repeated inundating of regions from China to the Middle East that surround northern India, the layers of archeological finds that testify to cycles of flood devastation and rebuilding, and the reinterpretation as flood defenses of many puzzling massive structures assumed to be fortifications when no other explanation seemed to fit. And, finally but not least, of course, it would mean that the object responsible for the upheavals recorded at the time of the Exodus would have been Mars, in one of its recurring visits, and not Venus as Velikovsky believed.

Many of the foregoing contentions are contradictory or mutually incompatible. I take this as a sign of vigorous and healthy inquiry in action—science the way it should be, in which standing by what seems to be true, even at the risk of isolation and ridicule, takes precedence over being acceptable to the ranks of the exalted. Whether one takes the view that Velikovsky had the right picture even if he was wrong on some details, or the converse, as is the case with some schools among his followers, his genius lay in being one of the first to recognize the myths handed down by ancient cultures as accounts by people who lived under different skies of terrifying events that they actually witnessed but were unable to comprehend. He was the first to ask why objects that we see as insignificant pinpoints, which few people today could even find, should be depicted as harbingers of the end of the world and titanic celestial battles between gods, inspiring awe and terror across the Earth. Here, surely, are the cosmic origins of the rituals and attempts at placation that were to become the foundation of all religions, and beyond that, conceivably, the roots of many of the phobias, insecurities, and obsessions that continue to haunt humankind today.

Officially promulgated science clings to its doctrine that—apart from the relatively minor impacts that it has conceded to admit in the last couple of decades or so—the major bodies of the Solar System have remained essentially unaltered for billions of years, and the heavens look much the same as they always did. Yet the observational basis for these confident assertions extends back only for a matter of a few centuries. Is there some unconscious fear at work that accepting the interpretations of ancient myths as cosmic events that took place in recorded human history would be to acknowledge they could happen again? On the one hand we have faith in a principle that enables us to infer how things must have been; on the other, if the catastrophists are correct, we have the records of what the people who lived then say they saw.

The spirit of unprejudiced inquiry that began to emerge with the Renaissance, of following where the evidence seems to lead, was quashed by forces that viewed themselves as progressive, but which in fact had more in common with the Aristotelean-medieval yearning for a safe and predictable universe shaped by benign forces for the continuing betterment of man. As a consequence, we still labor under the legacy of a largely forgotten nineteenth-century religious and political struggle that has no bearing upon the modern world.

Notes:

[1] James P. Hogan, "Catastrophe of Ethics," Kicking the Sacred Cow (New York: Baen Books, 2004), pp. 151–224

2 Irving Wolfe, "The Original Velikovsky Affair: An Idea that Just Would Not Go Away," *Stephen J. Gould and Immanuel Velikovsky*, (New York: Ivy Press Books, 1996), p.1.

3 Livio C. Stecchini, "The Inconstant Heavens," included in *The Velikovsy Affair* (New York: University Books, 1966), pp.101–105

4 Andrew Hallam, *Great Geological Controversies*, second ed., (Oxford: Oxford University Press, 1986), p. 31

5 William Paley, *The Principles of Moral and Political Philosophy*, fifth edition (1793)

6 Hallam, p. 49

7 Stephen Jay Gould, *Time's Arrow, Time's Cycle*, (Cambridge: Harvard University Press, 1988), p. 21

8 See www.aeonjournal.com, www.knowledge.co.uk, http://www.kronia.com/kronia.html

9 See www.firmament-chaos.com

From the Web Site

Bulletin Board, "Catastrophism" section, November 4, 2000 (http://www.jamesphogan.com/bb/content/110400. shtml)

GLOBAL FLOODING

As I've said in early postings, I'm pretty convinced that the doctrine of slow, gradual geological and biological change is wrong, and that things happen far more rapidly and more recently than is conventionally taught. This apparently causes some people to leap to the conclusion that I must be a Creationist. I'm not, in that I don't buy their answer either (showing that the butler didn't do it doesn't prove that the chauffeur did) although I think that some of their work pointing to what's wrong with the orthodox line is more solidly based than it's fashionable to admit. One person wrote a rather derisive note asking if I believed in a global flood too. Apparently, the answer to the question is taken as an indicator of one's political stripe and has nothing to do with what actual evidence from the surface of our planet might say. Well, below are a few facts consistent with the idea of immense, planet-scale oceanic surges from the equator toward the poles, resulting from an axial shift or crustal slip caused by a recent close encounter with a large astronomic object of the kind Velikovsky proposed.

- Immense deposits of sediment where such surges would have slowed or encountered barriers. Seismic reflections of the Arctic Ocean, where huge inflows would result from the northward narrowings of the Atlantic and Pacific oceans, show stratified sedimentary layers from a minimum of two miles in thickness to five miles—much more than can be accounted for by the rivers emptying into that basin. The foothills of northern India—where a north-rushing tidal flow would plow into the wall of the Himalaya—extend for hundred of miles and consist of sediments 2,000 to 3,000 feet deep. Sediments forming the seabed of the northerly enclosed Bay of Bengal, extending east into the Gulf of Siam, average 20,000 feet and reach over 50,000 feet.

- If seabeds were formed only by slow spreading outward from the ocean ridges, the sediments would be thinnest at the ridges and become progressively thicker with distance as the ocean bed grows older. Some textbook writers were so confident that this would be the case that they wrote it as fact before the evidence was in. Actual drillings showed, paradoxically, deep sediments at the flanks of the ridges, then little progressive change until sudden thickening at the continental margins—precisely where huge oceanic flows would be slowed and shed their burdens.

- Enormous fossil beds containing the remains of millions of animals, torn-up trees, deposits of "muck" made up of gravel, soil, clays, and mineral and organic matter, forming a circumpolar ring across Alaska, upper Canada, Siberia—where the reverse flow from the polar surge would inundate the northern continents. Some islands off northern Siberia, several hundred feet high, consist of practically nothing but animal bones and broken tree trunks. The Siwalik Hills north of Delhi have been described as containing fossils of such variety and profusion that the animal world of today seems impoverished by comparison.

- Loess. A second circumpolar ring of lighter slurries (which would be carried farther) found deep inside North America (Texas, Colorado, Louisiana) and Eurasia (China, Mongolia, Turkestan, Russia), along the northern sides of mountain chains where floods from a south-flowing polar source would deposit them. Often grading into huge areas of sand beds (e.g. Nebraska, 21,000 square miles averaging 25 feet deep) difficult to reconcile with wind-borne origins but nevertheless usually explained that way. Smaller belt in the southern hemisphere, found in the Argentine Pampas, southern Australia, New Zealand.

- Erratics. Large rocks transported far from places of origin. The usual explanation of their being carried by glaciers runs into trouble with the physics of how glaciers actually move themselves and other objects. Essentially, glaciers move by melting at the base and flowing over, which gives them no way of moving large boulders uphill. Many large erratics are found at high elevations. The force exerted by water flows, however, varies with the sixth power of velocity, meaning that while current moving at 2–3 mph might not be able to move more than a small pebble, 10 mph can move upward of 5 tons, and 50 mph, many thousands of tons. Further, erratics occur in great numbers in places that were never glaciated, such as Uruguay, Jamaica, Maryland, Georgia, Spain.

- Whales, whalebones, and other deep-sea remains found hundreds of miles from the ocean in North Africa, southeastern and western USA, Central Europe, sometimes atop mountains.

So yes, maybe there's something to the 120-odd world-flood legends apart from that of the Old

Testament, which range from the Hindus and Iranians, Lithuanians and Norsemen, Lapps, Voguls of the Ural Mountains, Kalmuks, Chinese, Eskimos, North American Indian tribes, Caribs, Mexicans, Peruvians, Polynesians, Fiji Islanders, Australians, Philippine Islanders, Andamans . . .

The above extracts are from Vol. II, No. 4 (1994) and Vol. IV, No. 1 (1998) of *The Velikovskian* (http://www.knowledge.co.uk/velikovskian/)—click for subscription information.

WORD GAMES

Bulletin Board, "Humor & Diversions," April 1, 2000 (http://www.jamesphogan.com/bb/content/040100.shtml)

HOW MANY HADS?

Many computer programs have delusions of being smarter than they are. One of my spell-checker's irritating examples is its flagging of any word that it finds repeated, which is often intentional and correct. An instance is with many uses of the word "had," where "had had" is required by the intended tense. Commenting on this led a friend and me into one of those contests to see who could compose a valid sentence containing the greatest number of successive "hads." I finally came up with one containing eleven, which when properly punctuated makes perfect sense:

*In the English language test, Smith, where Jones
had had "had," had had "had had"; "had had"
had had the approval of the examiners.*

Anybody got a better one?
(And yes, my spell-checker just threw a fit when
I typed it.)

Note added May 15, 2000

Okay, somebody outdid me. Aristotle Jones sent
me the following (with twelve "hads," to save you
counting), which he got from Max and her dad, Ron
Read, in B.C., Canada.

"John, where James had had 'HAD HAD,' had
had *had had*. 'HAD HAD' had had the editor's
approval."

Note added August 10, 2002

And then I got this from Scott Ryan, which weighs
in at forty-one.

"Aristotle Jones, where you had had <had had
"had," had had "had had"; "had had" had had>, had
had <had had 'HAD HAD', had had *had had*. 'HAD
HAD' had had>; <had had 'HAD HAD', had had *had
had*. 'HAD HAD' had had>; had had a temporary
victory until I wrote to you."

This could obviously be extended indefinitely until

every particle in the universe was pressed into service to encode them ("hadrons"?). The whole nonsense is therefore hereby formally closed.

The Tree of Dreams

The far-space exploration vessel *Hayward Kermes*, operated by the Kermes-Oates Restructuring consortium on license from the Sol Federation to promote cultural advancement among the outer regions, blipped back into 3-space two months ship's time after leaving the fitting-out station above Ganymede. It entered the Horus system, and four days later took up a parking orbit over the star's second planet, Lydia.

As stated in the preliminary report beamed back by the reconnaissance ship *Oryx* three years previously, Lydia was a warm, Earthlike world with two moons, slightly smaller than Earth but with a surface closer to three-quarters water rather than five-sixths. It had five major continents, spread across greater extremes of tropical, desert, temperate, mountain, and polar climates. Pictures obtained from orbit and lower-altitude probes confirmed Lydian habitats ranging from village communities to moderate-sized towns that exhibited colorful and picturesque architecture rendered in wood, brick, adobe, or stone, according to the locality, with spectacular central buildings in some areas, suggestive of religious or imperialistic societies. Technology did not appear to have progressed beyond primitive or early agricultural in any area. Of the *Oryx* itself, there was no sign. Its preliminary assessment was the last to be heard from it.

Lydian skies could be spectacular, mixing a palette that ventured from the palest of streaky greens unveiling the sun at daybreak, to full-bodied violets, lilacs, and lavenders that turned the western clouds into towering castles of light in the evening. One of the biologists with the *Kermes* had put forward a theory attributing the displays to photodissociation in the upper atmosphere of exotic molecules produced by the planet's lush and varied flora, which made even the tropics of Earth seem unassuming in comparison. The biologist had been challenged by the mission's head physicist and head climatologist, both of whom claimed the subject as belonging rightfully to their domain, and a motion was already being filed back on Earth for the issue to be brought before a scientific arbitration court.

Chelm was seldom drawn into such things. As an archeologist, his field was more self-contained and defined, and territorial disputes with other disciplines tended to be rare. Colleagues warned him that invisibility equated to obscurity, and having a low political profile was tantamount to committing career suicide.

Wilbur Teel, his section head, would come poking around, looking for possible areas of overlap that could be used to pick a fight with the linguists or paleosociologists, maybe, and hinting that Chelm could help his future promotion prospects by taking a more aggressive stance himself. Chelm sometimes wondered if perhaps he *was* too accepting and passive. But the thought of a future supposedly broadened by getting involved in the perennial rivalries and infighting that went on among the upper administrative echelons back on Earth simply didn't excite him. He wasn't, he supposed, if he was honest with himself, really that competitively disposed by nature—not that he would have admitted it to the ship's psychocounselor. The fact of the matter was that he *liked* his work and its challenges, especially when it took him out in the field and among the natives. Times like right now, for instance. . . .

He sat on the end of one of the log pilings supporting the boat dock that formed the lower level of Ag-Vonsar's house, watching the old man scrape an upturned wherrylike craft that had been hauled up for cleaning and repair. The house was built on stilts like the rest of the settlement at the bottom end of the lake, with storage space immediately overhead, the general living area above, and sleeping rooms above that again. The houses were all interconnected by stairways and bridges to form what was essentially a village over the water. The workmanship was rich, ornate, and precise, bringing to mind a combination of ancient Mesoamerican pattern work and colorful Chinese intricacy. Besides making boats, Ag-Vonsar also constructed sluice gates for the system of water channels and locks that irrigated the surrounding area and allowed the level to be controlled during the season when the river feeding the lake was in flood. The dry dock and shop that he maintained for this heavier work were part of a boatyard built along the shore.

What had first attracted Chelm's interest to this place was a long, low, square-formed block protruding from a hillside and into the water to provide a breakwater and jetty bounding the upper end of the yard. He had assumed it was cut natural rock, until closer examination showed it to consist of an artificial material similar to concrete. Some Lydian structures, such as temples, aqueducts, and bridges in cities and other locations that Terran exploration teams had visited did, it was true, use forms of concrete. But the type was invariably reminiscent of the kind the Romans had developed: tough, virtually immune to demolition in some instances, deriving strength from the filiform binding of carefully blended minerals. The block at the upper end of the lakeside yard, however, was of coarser composition, reinforced internally by metal ties in the style of Terran patterns that had come into use millennia later—as if the arrival of heavier industry had rendered the earlier reliance on finer-grain chemistry superfluous. Could it be that an advanced culture had existed at one time on Lydia, and then vanished practically without trace? If so, what kind of calamity could have overtaken it?

This was the kind of once-in-a-lifetime occurrence that sent an archaeologist's blood racing with excitement, and—unless Chelm was truly missing something—relegated such alternatives as chairing a peer-review committee in some academy or university, or becoming a familiar face on the academic social and cocktail-party circuit, to the depths of irrelevancy and tedium.

And then had followed the seismic images showing broken outlines of even more massive and extended structures deeper down. The mission's steering group had higher priorities than archeological searches, however, and the possibility of even a pilot excavation was on hold indefinitely at that stage. Chelm had made overtures to see what the chances of recruiting native labor might be. The Lydians seemed amiable and willing enough in principle—but he had to be careful of the ship's sociologists and psychologists, who considered any activity of that nature to be part of their turf.

"They suggest structures like levees," Chelm said. "As if this might have been part of the river before the lake formed. They look like bits of levees."

"Levees?" Ag-Vonsar repeated, without looking up. The exchange took place via the transvox channel in Chelm's wristpad, but the process had become so familiar that he barely registered it. He was making an effort to learn the local Lydian tongue, but the number of languages identified already, each with endless dialects, made it a daunting business. The transvox was trained primarily in the speech of a region about the size of Europe's Iberian province, centered on a city called Issen, fifty miles or so from the lake settlement. Landers from the *Hayward Kermes* had established a Terran surface base just outside Issen.

"Artificial embankments built along the sides of rivers," Chelm said. "To stop them flooding over low-lying land."

Ag-Vonsar peered at the strip of the boat's underside that he had cleaned, running a finger along a seam that was showing signs of opening up. He had a surprisingly muscular and well-contoured body for what Chelm judged from his grizzled, crinkly hair, craggy features, and veined hands to be by Terran standards sixty or even seventy-plus years of age. As with most Lydians, his skin had the hue and tone of polished walnut. He wore a loose, red, knee-length tunic with a pouched leather tool belt, and laced boots of a soft material that looked like suede or felt. The doctrine that had once been taught of species developing uniquely, as never-to-be-repeated accumulations of accidents, had long been discredited and forgotten. Genetic codes seemed to be universal—the reasons why were still not understood, and hotly debated—expressing themselves similarly in similar environments, and the missions probing ever farther from Earth were no longer astounded to find Earth-like life on Earth-like planets.

"Why would you stop the water that brings life to the crops?" Ag-Vonsar asked finally. "Tame the waters, yes—like the wild horse. But you would kill the horse. Then it can no longer work for you."

"The floods caused a lot of damage to the towns," Chelm pointed out.

"Then they built their towns in the wrong places. The floods deliver the silt that revives the fields. And the *darvy* fish that hatch in the early spring when the floods come eat the eggs of the shiver-fever fly. So it seems that your levees would bring sickness as well."

There really wasn't any arguing with that. Chelm

smiled and looked away at the hills tumbling down
to the upper reaches of the lake in forested folds and
rocky outcrops decked with necklaces of waterfalls. A
group of *egani*—ponderous, buffalolike creatures with
shaggy hair the color of an Irish setter—had come
down to drink on the far side. The Lydians seemed
to have it all figured out. The water here seemed
corrosive to metals, eating away the reinforcement
bars in the concrete slab to leave little more than
stains and residues in the surrounding matrix. Ag-
Vonsar used no metal fastenings in his boats, Chelm
had noticed, the parts being joined by precise-fitting
wooden dowels and pins. The same seemed to be
true of the houses and other constructions forming
the settlement. Ag-Vonsar said that the woods used
for the houses were of a mix selected to repel the
local varieties of bug pests.

The opening bars of *Eine Kleine Nachtmusik* sounded
tinnily from the unit on Chelm's wrist. He turned
it toward himself and pressed the ANSWER stud on
the band. The inch-square screen showed the face
of Praget, calling from the folda-cabin set up as the
local field camp on a rise below the end of the lake,
where the flyer was parked.

"We're about ready to head back," Praget said.

Chelm looked at the old man. "The flyer is leaving.
I need to get back."

"Moishina will take you," Ag-Vonsar said, and
then louder, directing his voice upward at the house,
"Moishina. Our guest is leaving. Will you take him
back to the shore?"

"Yes, of course."

"Okay, I'll be right over," Chelm said to the face

on his wristpad. Moishina was Ag-Vonsar's grand-daughter. Chelm had left her unpacking and sorting the items he had brought back from some digging farther up along the lake. The family let him use a bench in the lower part of the house. He preferred working there on his own, away from the stifling filtered and conditioned air of the cabin. It was supposed to be "safer" than prolonged exposure to the raw unknowns of the Lydian environment—but the ones who seemed to be sick all the time were those who stayed cooped up in the base. In any case, some kind of soil microorganism had developed a partiality for the plastic that the folda-cabin was made from and eaten through the floor, with the result that the place was overrun by insects.

"Do you know when you will be back?" Ag-Vonsar asked Chelm.

"Well, there are some routine chores I have to take care of back at the base. Not tomorrow, but probably the day after."

"I may not be here. I am due to journey into Issen on business shortly, but the day has not been fixed yet. If I have gone, your work space will still be available, naturally."

"You're sure it's not an imposition?"

"You are always welcome among our family, Stan-islow Chelm from Earth."

Chelm thought for a moment. "You know, we could take you there right now if it would help. There's plenty of room in the flyer."

Ag-Vonsar smiled thinly. "I thank you, but I will not be alone. And we prefer our own ways of traveling."

"If you want to contact me while you're in Issen, just have someone enter my name into the Terran comnet. It will find me."

"What is this 'comnet'?"

"Just ask any Terran."

"I will remember. . . . *Moishina!* Are you taking a bath up there? Stanislow's people are waiting."

"Coming. I was just cutting some flowers for Quyzo." Moishina appeared at the top of the stairs as she spoke. Chelm guessed her to be in her twenties. She had the brown, sharply angular features that were typical of Lydians in these parts, and straight, black hair that fell halfway down to the waistband of the short saronglike garment that she was wearing. The stairs were steep and narrow but she descended them nimbly, facing toward them like a ladder, one hand sliding on the guide rail, the other holding a bunch of brightly colored blooms with the stems wrapped in leaves.

As she reached the bottom, the voice of Moishina's nephew Boro called from above, saying something that Chelm's transvox channel didn't catch. "Then tell him to hurry up!" Moishina called back. Boro called out again, shouting this time. A figure that had been approaching across the connecting bridge from one of the other houses—another boy, maybe about ten—broke into a run. A woman's voice came from somewhere, telling them in tones that would have been unmistakable anywhere, in any language, on any planet, to be quiet. Boro came scampering down as Moishina moved toward a boat moored at some steps leading down from the dock. "A couple of extra passengers," she explained to Chelm, intoning it in a way that seemed to ask if that was okay with him.

"Sure." Chelm shrugged. It was their boat, after all.

He followed her, stepping down inside and sitting himself on the center cross board facing aft. Moishina gave him the flowers to hold while she took up the oar and remained standing in the stern. Boro's friend arrived, climbing aboard behind Boro after expertly untying the mooring line behind him, and the two boys squeezed past Chelm to crouch in the bow. Ag-Vonsar raised a hand in farewell as Moishina pushed the boat away from the dock. She propelled the craft deftly with a rhythmic sculling motion, evoking lithe, supple movements of her body. Chelm had to make a conscious effort to stop himself staring. The boys chattered behind him, trailing their hands in the water. One of them almost caught a fish, and then lost it.

"Quyzo. Is that one of the spirits?" Chelm asked, as Moishina turned the prow shoreward. The Lydians had a spirit for just about everything. Mountain passes, waterfalls, dells in the forest, each one had a shrine to the dedicated being who safeguarded travelers entering its domain, dispensed good fortune or bad, or danced capriciously over the world in the form of the elements. Ag-Vonsar had told Chelm about the *Fessym*—mountain sprites who teased the land into crying tears of laughter, producing the springs that made the river that fed the lake. Chelm had asked him out of curiosity if he really believed magical spirits existed.

"It doesn't matter," Ag-Vonsar had replied. "People should live their lives as if they do, anyway."

"Quyzo lives in the lake," Moishina confirmed. "But he watches over the whole valley. So the village is his family."

"Is he a happy spirit, do you think?" Chelm asked.

"Oh yes, very much. He catches stars to make the water sing and sparkle. You can see them in the lake at night."

They tied up at a wooden jetty below the jumble of slipways and painted roofs that constituted the yard. Boro and his friend disappeared along the shore. Moishina walked with Chelm in the opposite direction, up the rock steps that led toward the rise where the Terran field camp was situated. They came to Quyzo's shrine on the way. It did indeed convey the impression of him as a cheerful little fellow, perhaps somewhat inclined toward the mischievous: a finely worked, abstract sculpture of variously tinted stones, set in a rocky niche above a running pool and gazing out at its lake abode over a low stone parapet smothered in flowers. Lydian artists never tried to depict the actual likenesses of their spirits.

Some figures were sitting on the rocks beside the terrace in front of the shrine. It was only when Chelm and Moishina had approached to within a few yards that Chelm realized from the empty expressions on several of the faces, and the simple, guileless smiles on others, that the group was partly made up of *jujerees*, probably being taken on an outing. The nearest English translation was "child-people." They were harmless and incapable of malice, having reverted to a condition of infantile trust and dependency, greeting each new experience with the awe and delight of eyes beholding the world for the first time. The Lydians didn't seem to know what caused the affliction, but the *Kermes'* Principal Medical Officer guessed it to be a genetic condition. There were moments, such as when the petty jealousies and rivalries of life at the base got to him, or some particularly inane and exasperating edict came through from Earth, when Chelm came close to envying them.

Moishina unwrapped the flowers she had brought and placed them in one of the vases along the parapet, picking out the previous withered occupants and dropping them in a receptacle to one side, provided for the purpose. She fell silent for what Chelm assumed was a quick prayer or moment of reflection, and then turned toward one of the women minding the *jujerees*, who had come over. "Forgive me if I intrude," the woman said.

Moishina smiled. "Not at all."

"I just wanted to say welcome to the Terran. I have seen them at their work up above, but never spoken with one."

"Stanislow Chelm," Moishina said, extending a hand to introduce him.

"My name is Norelena. We have come from Veshtor, over the hills to the east, to bring our charges here to see the valley and the lake." Norelena's voice dropped to a more confidential note, as if confessing the true reason for wanting to talk with them. "And you *have* to take a break from them sometimes—otherwise I'm sure you'd end up the same way."

Moishina chuckled. "I can imagine it."

Chelm sensed a movement nearby him and turned. One of the *jujerees*, who had previously been gazing rapturously at the lake and the mountains, had stood up and moved over. He was lighter-skinned than most of the Lydians that Chelm had met, with rounder eyes and less angular features. On Earth, appropriately dressed, he wouldn't have looked out of place on a typical street. Chelm did his best to act naturally and mustered a grin. "Hi."

The child-person grinned back. His eyes were depthless as they looked into Chelm's, interrogating him as if he were a new sight to be analyzed and registered, but conveying no hint of any shared thought or percept that could enable communication. And yet, just for an instant, Chelm had the feeling of something searching, reaching out toward what some instinct said should be there, but not knowing how to recognize it if it were.

And then the *jujeree*'s gaze fell to the Sol Federation Exploration Division emblem on Chelm's lapel—a gold-on-blue spiral motif with flashes, representing the galactic structure and unleashed energy. His face widened into a smile.

"You like the badge, eh?" Chelm said. The *jujeree* didn't speak, but reached out to touch the embossed metal surface. It seemed to fascinate him. "Here, you can have it." Chelm unpinned the badge and pressed it into the *jujeree*'s hand. The eyes looked at it, then up at Chelm once again. Chelm nodded encouragingly.

"It's yours," Norelena told her charge. "You can keep it." She glanced at Chelm. "Thank you so much . . . Stanislow Chelm. You have no idea what such things mean to them." Moishina was staring too, as if seeing him in a new light.

On the top of the rise higher up behind the shrine, Chelm could see the team standing around the flyer, obviously waiting for him. He picked out Praget, making impatient gestures and waving down toward the terrace. Praget's arm came up to let the other hand stab at his wristpad, and a moment later the call tune sounded from Chelm's unit. "Okay, okay, I'm coming up now," Chelm said before Praget could start.

"Well, hurry it up. What have you got going down there, a union meeting? The rest of us would kinda like to get back sometime between now and the next ice age."

"On my way," Chelm said again, and snapped the call off. He was about to bid his farewells, when he noticed the *jujeree* staring at the wristpad. Chelm shook his head. "Uh-uh. Sorry, but that's different. I can't let this go."

"Mozart," the *jujeree* said.

Chelm blinked in astonishment and looked from Moishina to Norelena. "Where in hell did he learn that?"

"What does it mean?" Moishina asked.

"That bit of music that it played. Mozart was the person who wrote it. But that was hundreds of years ago, back on Earth."

Moishina looked perplexed. "I don't know. . . ." She faltered. "There have been Terrans all over Lydia for a while now. I suppose it's amazing how such things can be picked up."

Although the Lydians showed no hostility toward the Terran presence—indeed, they seemed to have little concept of such things—Issen Base, with its lander pads, situated five miles outside the city, had been "secured" inside a double-layer chain-link fence protected by sensors, surveillance, and guards. Regulations and routine procedure required it. When the Principal Medical Officer, after conferring with the Scientific Advisory Committee, declared the base to be also microbially "safe," the facility began expanding and taking on additional comforts as more administrators and officers, along with their staffs, tired of more than two months of being in the ship, began moving down to the surface.

Chelm sat in front of Wilbur Teel's desk, staring out through the window of the cubicle appropriated by Teel as his office in the blandly rectilinear assemblage of prefabricated modules that officialdom in a dazzling flash of creativity had designated "Block 3." Teel was turned toward one of the screens, taking a distress call from Chuck Ranneson in the Cultural Exchange Center, set up in the city to give the Lydians a preview of the benefits they stood to enjoy from being subsumed into the Sol Federation economic system.

"What do you mean, not interested?" Teel challenged. "Are you telling me you can't even *give* the things away? You're supposed to be a sales negotiator. How do you think this is going to look on your review?" A routine ploy in the opening up of new worlds was to distribute portable screenpads to the natives with a chart of easy-to-use icons to whet their appetites. The assortment of included games and advertisements was designed for appeal to the younger set.

"They're not interested in talking to people on the other side of the planet, or watching things happen on Earth or anyplace else," Ranneson answered. "They don't see the point of it. They say their ... I'm not sure what you'd call it; the best the transvox could come up with was 'awareness circle' . . . isn't shaped by what happens on the other side of the planet."

"There have to be kids there. Have you shown them the games and the movies?"

"They laugh at them. A bunch that I talked to couldn't see why people would want picture-lives when they can live real ones. But they thought things like that might be something to amuse . . . what do you call those smiley-face retards? *Jujerees.*"

"What about the merchandising catalog? Look at what we're offering: fingertip-control environments and appliances, modern transportation systems, planned health care and psychiatry, entertainment in the home. . . . I thought you knew how to *sell* things, Rannelson. Maybe we should think about relocating you to a clerking slot up in the ship. . . ."

Outside, just inside the gate, a work crew was setting up an isolation-and-decontamination tent that the ship's legal counselor had insisted on, even though the doctors deemed it unnecessary. Although he thought the chances would be slim, Chelm had put in for approval to move his quarters out of the base. He had mentioned the thought to Ag-Vonsar, who had arrived in Issen on his planned visit, and Ag-Vonsar had said he would introduce Chelm to a friend who could arrange accommodation. Out of curiosity, Chelm had arranged to go into Issen and meet them anyway later that day. Even if nothing came of it, it would be an excuse for spending an afternoon away from the base.

"Okay, where were we?" Teel had finished his conversation with Ranneson and was ready to continue. Chelm switched his attention back from the window.

Teel had a long, pallid face made up of furrows that arched from the forehead to hang vertically at the jowls, putting Chelm in mind of the lines of a Gothic cathedral. He seemed born to endure all the woes and afflictions that could beset a man, venting the resulting biliousness on his subordinates with a relish that, in unguarded moments, came close to revealing a capacity for enjoying at least that aspect of life.

"Scraping the barrel of the budget," Chelm answered.

"Right . . . Look, you know as well as I do that archeology isn't exactly what you'd call high on our list of priorities. A mission like this only has so much in the way of resources. The things that advance our primary objectives get first bite: economic reform, geology and resource prospecting, introduction of an energy and transportation infrastructure, political restructuring . . ."

"But there's symmetry down there. It's clearly geometric. Those patterns didn't form by themselves through any accident." Chelm was referring to the latest series of ground-penetration radar scans taken from orbit, which had revealed what could have been the remains of vast structures or engineering works extending sometimes for miles beneath tracts of what were now jungles and deserts.

Teel shook his head. "You still don't grasp it, do you, Chelm? We're in the business of creating new worlds, not digging up old ones. The potential returns are huge for opening up a backward place like this. Twenty years from now it will be as profitable and progressive as the Los Angeles–San Diego Strip. And they have no concept of effective political organization here. No military. When we've appointed regional governors and set up local systems of provincial administration and control, the markets for defense and security alone will be worth tens of billions. Investors are already lining up back on Earth to get in on a share of Lydia."

Chelm hadn't seen anything on Lydia—apart from the armed Terran guards watching the perimeter fence—that anyone might need to be defended against. Before he could put the thought into words, however, Teel rose from his chair and came around the desk to stand looking out of the window, as if in his mind he could already see a complex of office towers, malls, and freeway bridges replacing the arches, alleys, temples, and domes of Issen's center, and the hills behind cleared and cut into leveled industrial terraces.

He went on, "Now, *those* are the people who have to come first: the ones in charge of the activities that the consortium is interested in. And we have to back them, because the consortium generates not only our direct funding but also our political support. Now, if you were to help us keep them sweet, then who knows? Anything might happen. Maybe, even, brighter prospects for archeological research. But you have to learn to play the game."

"I'm not sure I know what you mean," Chelm said, although he did, perfectly well.

Teel sighed and turned from the window. "We've been through this over and over. I'm talking about your general attitude and refusal to fit in with the system. If you want to run your own life and professional career into a dead end, it's your business, and frankly

I don't care. But when it affects the performance of *my* section, that's something else."

"But you've just told me that nobody's interested in what I do," Chelm protested. "What else is it you want?"

"That's for you to figure out."

Chelm turned up his palms helplessly. He had never been able to play these kinds of games. "You're losing me. I put in the requisitions for what I need. They were thrown out. You obviously endorse that decision. What more am I supposed to do?"

"What you're supposed to do is understand the politics of scratching other backs if you want them to scratch yours. Nobody's going to be interested in supporting your agenda unless it helps advance theirs too. Is that simple enough? What you have to do is get more involved in what's going on around here and develop a nose for *opportunity*." Teel stamped across to the desk and picked up a piece of paper that had been lying in the center. It was Chelm's application to be billeted in the city. He wheeled about, brandishing it aggressively. "But what do we get? Instead, you want to run away and hide from what's going on. Do you really think that's the way to build the right kind of relationships with the people here who can get you what you want?" He tore the offending document in two, then again, and dropped the pieces into the disposal unit. "No way, Chelm. You need to learn how to become a functioning member of the team here first, before you even think about something like this. Request categorically denied."

✳   ✳   ✳

Chelm had booked a ride into Issen with a utility shuttle bus running personnel and sample wares to the Cultural Exchange Center. But he always found confrontations like this one with Teel unnerving. On leaving Teel's office, he popped a tranquilizer from his medical pouch and went over to the rest lounge in the Lab Block to calm down. Thankfully, it was empty. While he sat savoring the moment of solitude and feeling the pill kick in, he checked his mail via his wristpad. Among the items listed, he saw that a communication had come in from Ursula, his fiancée for more than three years now, back on Earth. He selected it and tapped in the code to download it from the ship.

Ursula was tense and edgy as always, like an over-wound spring about to fly off its mounting. Chelm put it down to interactions between the medications she took for executive stress syndrome, high blood pressure, neuronal hypersensitivity complex, and emotional oscillatory metabolic reaction, but Ursula insisted that it simply reflected the heightened activity that came with the lifestyle of a high-achieving professional. The latest scandal back home was that the drug mandated for trans-System travelers following the cosmic-radiation sickness panic had been shown to be worthless despite the miraculous success rates claimed for it, and the whole episode was unraveling as a gigantic fraud. The legal and medical associations and involved government departments were all claiming innocence and blaming each other, while the Sol Fed health secretary, having promised full investigation and exposure of the culprits, had resigned following revelations of massive family stock holdings in the prime corporation raking in the take. A Titan Liberation Alliance nuke was believed to have taken out the Federal Security Agency's orbiting bombardment station there, and construction contractors on Mars had put a moratorium on further work and were organizing protest boycotts of supply ships in response to a forty percent hike in insurance rates.

Closer to home, Ursula's rival for a big promotion opportunity was out of the running, having suffered a breakdown following the failure of a hostile takeover bid that he had masterminded—which was good news; Ursula needed the extra money that the position would bring to cover the deferred loan she had taken to pay off the called-in option on the Sirius-B transmutator scheme that hadn't worked out. Two militant atheist sects were waging legal battles and disrupting each other's meetings in a dispute over whose were the *correct* reasons for not believing in a God. California was going ahead with banning home cooking on the grounds that nutrition needed to be regulated and should be dispensed by licensed professionals. Chelm's nephew Toby had gotten his medical certificate and permit to ride a pedal cycle. Sister Celia had suffered traumatic shock after falling off a barstool from disorientation caused by the lighting, but she was expected to recover. Oh, and yes, did he have any idea yet when he would be coming home? She had found a bigger house with *gorgeous* landscaping, domestic robotics throughout, Olympic-equipped exercise room, and a full VR simulation deck, but the loan would be more than she wanted to take on by herself—especially with this Sirius-B business. . . .

At that moment, the door slid open and Jen from

the exopsychology section came in. "Hi, Stan," she greeted, going across to the autochef to punch in the code for a straight black coffee, and reconfirming it without waiting for the health warning to appear in the window. Since just about everything came with health warnings; their effective information content was close to zero.

Jen was one of the few people that Chelm felt at ease with. She was open and honest by nature, good at what she did because she liked it, and uninterested in cultivating faked imagery and "style," all of which added up to a fair guarantee that she would never rise far on the generally accepted scale of recognition and success. But the most delightful thing was that she cared about as little as Chelm did—if that were possible; and she harbored fewer inhibitions about saying so.

"Oh-oh." She took in Chelm's strained look and dropped the everything-going-well-with-the-world smile that she had been wearing. She had wavy red hair cut short, and a freckly, snub-nosed face to which smiles came easily. Her ancestry, she had told Chelm once, was from a Celtic people who had inhabited central Turkey in Roman times. "You look like your face was hung on you to dry. Dare I ask? Would the problem be something that begins with tee and ends with el?"

"You're uncanny. How do you do it?"

"Oh, it's a gift that I have. They didn't put me in the shrink shop for nothing. So . . . what's he done now?"

"Given me all the reasons why I can't have what I need to do my job; then more or less told me it's my fault for not knowing how to get them. What's so infuriating is that I'm sure I'm onto something big, and he knows it. He's reveling in the power trip."

Jen nodded knowingly. "It's the same old story. He wants you to fight for it."

"If that was my way of doing things, I'd have joined the security forces. Tell me, Jen, is there really no other way of relating to human beings other than antagonism and confrontation? Everyone trying to screw everyone else first all the time. No trust, no integrity. Or is there simply something wrong with me? I'd really like to know."

Jen took a moment to sip her coffee before answering. "There are other ways. At least, there used to be, so I believe. But we seem to have created a culture that excludes them."

"Not everyone feels that way—you and I don't, for instance," Chelm pointed out.

"Yeah, right. And how much of the world takes any notice of what people like us think? Let's be honest, Stan. We're the sheep, and the wolves have taken over. Maybe it's some kind of inevitable, natural law, like the one about bad money and apples."

"God, I wish I could say you were wrong. But . . ." Chelm shook his head. "At least it doesn't seem to have affected the Lydians yet."

Jen made a face. "Don't speak too soon. I heard this morning that if Yassik doesn't come around and start playing ball soon, some of the Directorate are pushing for just going in and imposing a hard-line, military style. Investors are getting impatient. The argument is that there's nothing to stop us, so why mess around? Lydia doesn't have a single militarized state, let alone any capability to defend the planet.

Yassik was the ruler of the surrounding area, which he governed from Issen city. The usual pattern in Terran programs of planetary "cultural advancement" was to recruit native rulers who could be relied on to manage the local populations in ways that kept order and served Terran interests. In return for cooperation, the Terrans guaranteed wealth and prestige, military assistance in the elimination of foreign rivals, and help with security and civil control at home. Not a bad deal for the typical shakily ensconced nabob or ambitious upstart. The problem with Yassik was that he seemed anything but insecure or ambitious, and had been unresponsive to attempted bribes, flattery, grandiose promises, and the other routine approaches.

It took Chelm a few seconds to absorb the ghastliness of what Jen was saying. Was it really about to come down to this: unprovoked aggression and military occupation to exploit an inoffensive and defenseless planet? Jen had said on a previous occasion that greed and power-lust could become addictions, stimulating the same neural chemistry as hard psychotropic drugs. "We don't have that kind of firepower, surely," he said, more to convince himself. "Just this mission. . . . A whole planet? Even if it's wide open."

Jen shrugged. "So we call in backup from Earth. They could be here in under three months. You know as well as I do how easily a pretext can be concocted for the folks back home."

Chelm looked at her glumly. "Well, thanks for really making my day complete, Jen. As if it wasn't bad enough already with—" A peal of squeaky Mozart from his wristpad interrupted. "Excuse me." He took the call.

"Dr. Chelm. Shuttle bus driver here. We need you out here, sir. Departing in ten minutes."

"I'm on my way." Chelm clicked the call off. "I have to go. I'm taking a break this afternoon. Going into town. Strictly unofficial."

"Playing hookey, eh?"

"I think I need it." Chelm winked. "Promise you won't tell Teach?"

"How could I? I never heard a thing."

The road into Issen followed a river with steep, rocky banks, winding its way between hills planted in rows of small trees reminiscent of Mediterranean olive fields and vineyards, with open pastureland above. Houses huddled along the valley bottom among orchards and gardens watered by systems of interconnected ponds that reminded Chelm of the irrigation scheme he'd seen around the lake settlement. As at the lake, the designs were intricate and lavish with ornamentation, and yet carefully balanced—as if pleasing the eye and harmony with the surroundings were as important as function, warranting every bit as much thought and effort. For Chelm, this was a revolutionary concept. It flew in the face of all the accepted principles of cost-effectiveness. And yet, thinking about it, he was unable to come up with a good reason why the practices he was familiar with should be considered a better way of utilizing the vastly superior wealth that he was assured his own culture possessed, if the result was the stark, styleless, but eminently practical configuration of blockhouses that made up the base he had just left.

The contrast became even more marked at the

outskirts of the city itself, where the bus left the river at a lock gate that also served as a swing bridge. The buildings clustered closer and higher, eventually linking together across the streets in a bewilderment of connections and bridges, among which narrow alleys and stairways twisted their way out of sight on mysterious errands to hidden reaches of the city. Although alive with the bustle of shops, stalls, and crowds going about their daily business, the surroundings were well kept and clean. This was even more so in the central precinct, where the architecture took on more grand and imposing proportions, boasting minarets and columned frontages facing terraced plazas, and animal traffic was excluded. It could have been pieces of ancient Athens, Rome, and the Arabian Nights all blended together incongruously. To one side, across a square bounded by a canal and walled gardens, a new construction of high arches and onion-shaped domes was nearing completion amid a labyrinth of ramps, scaffolding, and ladders. Rendered in orange and green, it in some ways suggested the former Taj Mahal—before its destruction in a federal air strike during the Indian and South Asian Uprising against the Terran central authority. The stepped bridge connecting the square to the far side of the canal, where several tiers of buildings rose below a line of figures cut into a cliff face, added a dash of Venice to the mix.

The bus halted by several other vehicles that were parked outside of the building that one of Yassik's ministers had made available for the Terrans to use as their Cultural Exchange Center—a three-story affair of protrusions, gables, and balconies, rising to a riot of

blue-tiled roofs and turrets. The Terrans had draped
the outside with plastic sheeting to confine the air
from the conditioning-and-filtering plant that they had
installed, and hooked up a mobile fission generator for
power. Chuck Ranneson was on the steps in front with
one of his assistants, plugging to passersby through a
megaphone, while a screen set up behind him showed
a commercial clip for an Australian amusement park,
but the only attention being paid was from a small
audience of curious young children. Chelm avoided
them and crossed over the street to where he had
already spotted Ag-Vonsar waiting as promised. With
him was a man with a short, tousled beard, clad in a
gray, knee-length tunic and a dark brown cloak with
the hood thrown back. Ag-Vonsar introduced him
as Osti, who had space available that Chelm might
find suitable. They crossed the river in the center of
the city, which seemed to be devoted to public and
administrative buildings, and from there came back
into the peripheral area.

Chelm was impressed by the brisk, powerful pace
that Ag-Vonsar was able to maintain—without benefit of
aging retardants, energy boosters, or exercise machines.
Or perhaps he had not yet learned to judge a Lydian's
years. Very soon, he had lost all sense of direction in
the maze of alleys, squares, bazaars, and arcades. He
felt himself becoming strangely euphoric. The scents of
the blooms in vendors' displays and window planters
along the streets blended with the odors of fruits and
strange foods being cooked on curbside stalls and in
open shops to produce a constantly changing background of exotic aromas that made him heady. His two
companions kept up a commentary on curiosities and

points of interest that they passed, but Chelm was too absorbed by the hubbub of voices and sounds punctuated by peculiar music, the patterns and the colors, the unintelligible signs and banners, and the curious faces turning to watch him wherever they went, to more than half listen. It was as if the vibrancy and vigor around him on every side had energized a part of his being that had been dormant throughout what, up until now, he had called life.

Osti was a potter, and the place they eventually brought Chelm to consisted of two rooms above his workshop, approached from the rear via stairs from an alley descending erratically through a tangle of interconnected architecture. Two sons had lived there previously, but the older one had moved out to start a family of his own, whereupon the other had left for the coast to seek adventure at sea. The interior was open and airy, with windows at the front and a small balcony overlooking a cobbled court that led down to a quay by the river. All the essential furnishings were there—even a countertop built along one of the walls, which would make a good desk and worktable. It was ideal. Chelm found himself wishing that he hadn't let his curiosity bring him here. The thought of having to go back to the base was almost painful.

The rooms had been recently cleaned, and there was a scent in the air from a vase of flowers beaming color in one of several niches built into the walls. Somehow, Chelm couldn't see this as the work of Osti or Ag-Vonsar. But the question was answered almost immediately, when Ag-Vonsar's granddaughter Moishina came in carrying a flask in a wicker container, and a dish of hot, spicy-smelling food that she had brought from somewhere. "Our lives come together again—yours from Earth, mine in Lydia," she said, in one of the peculiar Lydian forms of greeting. "The cupboard was left empty, so I went to get something. This is called *kinzil*. And some wine."

"You needn't have . . . but it's appreciated," Chelm said.

"But it would be unforgivable to invite someone under one's roof without offering food." Moishina sounded surprised, as if stating something that was well known.

"And the flowers? Are they for another spirit too?"

"No, for you. To brighten your new home. Companions for you, you see."

"It's not my home yet," Chelm cautioned. "And might not be at all. There could be a problem getting approval at the base." He couldn't bring himself to say that it had already been refused outright. There might still be an angle.

"You have to have permission for where you live?"

"The place needed opening up and airing anyway," Osti said. "We are grateful to you, Moishina." He looked at Chelm. "How long will it take before you know? . . . Not that there's any hurry."

"A couple of days, maybe." Chelm gazed around again, for a moment savoring the feeling of acting like a serious buyer. Then he looked back at where Osti and Ag-Vonsar were standing. "Out of interest, if I did get clearance, how much would we be talking about?"

Ag-Vonsar made a brushing-away motion in the air.

"Ah, don't worry, Stanislow Chelm. We can talk about that at the appropriate time."

"Really. I'm curious."

Osti looked a little awkward and pursed his mouth. "Oh, I had been thinking of around, say, ninety *zel* for a week. Or we could make it by the greater-moon month."

Chelm was thrown off-balance. He had done some checking around, and from what he could make out, the figure was substantially below the going rate. His first impulse was to actually offer more, to bring it up to what seemed fair. . . . But then, on the other hand, he couldn't be sure that all his impressions were accurate. And in any case, he didn't want to come across as a pushover—especially since he was still feeling sore after his run-in with Teel. So in the end, he merely nodded vaguely.

"You are too generous," Osti said.

The meal was like a pita bread with a filling of meat and vegetables; the wine somewhat on the dry and tangy side, but Chelm decided he could get used to it. They talked about Osti's sons and some of the antics they had gotten up to here, the news from Ag-Vonsar's part of the world, and things for Chelm to do and see if he did end up moving into Issen. Ag-Vonsar and Osti were curious about Chelm's interest in the past history of their planet's cultures. Chelm got the impression that such a concept was new to them. A civilization in its early stages wouldn't have developed much concern about unearthing the past, he supposed—which was galling, since precisely for the reason that it was young, it would be in a position to preserve priceless information about its roots that could only be recovered with so much effort later—and incompletely at that.

"You should talk with some of the *nejivan*," Ag-Vonsar said. "They preserve knowledge of the ways of past ages. They would be able to help you. I will inquire for you." The *nejivan* were a caste of priest-judges, as far as Chelm had been able to make out, who served in the temples and courts, officiated at such ceremonies as marriages and funerals, and provided the society's foundation of law and teaching generally. They probably wouldn't have much that bore directly on Chelm's area of interest, but Ag-Vonsar had made the offer in good faith. Chelm accepted it, and thanked him.

Then Chelm checked with the Cultural Center for the schedule of transportation back to the base, and declared reluctantly that he would have to be leaving. Ag-Vonsar and Osti had business to attend to elsewhere. Moishina said she would take Chelm back across the city to the Center.

They took a different route this time, through a garden of pools and cataracts, where the rocks had been exquisitely carved into animal forms, then along the river past docks and wharves surrounded by boats. People who wanted to be invisible could lose themselves permanently in a place like this, Chelm thought to himself. No scans, ID profiles, or registration with any authorities required; Lydian doctors were surprisingly skillful, and would easily be able to remove the implanted microchips that most Terrans possessed—in some cases mandated—that could be tracked to within a few feet by satellites.

Which brought to mind the still-unsolved mystery of the vanished *Oryx*.

"Tell me," he said to Moishina, "do you know of other Terrans ever having been here? Another ship like ours, that came . . . it would have been around five of your years ago?"

"I have heard of such questions being asked. But no. I'm afraid I have no answers that I can give you."

But the ship *had* been in orbit over Lydia. That didn't prove it had sent down landers, of course. But having come this far, what reason could there be for it not to have done so? Then again, there was nothing that said they had to have chosen the same area to land in. All the same, from what Chelm had seen of the way things worked here, it would be strange if any news hadn't reached Issen during all that time.

They came to an open market exhibiting wares of every description, with musicians and street entertainers playing to small crowds among the stalls. Seeing the vendors and buyers haggling reminded Chelm of the uncertainty he had felt about dealing with Osti. "I wondered if I was being too easy," he said to Moishina. They had stopped for a moment to look at a stall hung with pictures and tapestries.

"You were gracious to agree," she replied. "We were impressed."

Chelm felt relieved. "I thought the expected thing might be to offer him less. But the figure seemed low anyway. And in any case, somehow it wouldn't have felt right . . . as a guest, not knowing this world well yet."

Moishina frowned, evidently puzzling over what he

had said. "Why would you want to offer him less?" she asked.

"Force of habit, I guess," Chelm replied, with a shrug. "Business is business. I know it was a good rate to begin with, but . . ." He let the rest hang, seeing that she wasn't following. "Well, isn't that what you do here?"

She shook her head. "No . . . You always give a little more, ask a little less. That is the way we are taught. You must return more to the world than you take. Otherwise, how could it feed us all?"

It was then that Chelm registered the exchange that was going on between the stallholder and a prospective customer who had taken a liking to a carved wooden relief showing boats passing under a bridge.

"I'll tell you what. I'll give you eight *zel*," the buyer said.

"Do I look as if I'm hungry or incapable of managing my affairs? Five would be quite sufficient. . . . Very well, make it five and a half."

"And do I look so tattered and ragged that I need to rob a trader who brings us such fine works? It is surely worth seven. Any less, and you can keep it."

The buyer was insisting on the higher price, and the seller was trying to bid it down. Chelm looked at Moishina perplexedly. "I don't understand. They're both trying to give money away."

"Yes," she agreed. And then, as if to explain, "As much as they can afford to, at least."

Which didn't explain anything. "You mean people don't try to get more of it?" Chelm asked, becoming increasingly bewildered.

"Why would they want more than provides for their needs?" Moishina replied. "Getting it would just take time out of their lives, which they would rather spend doing the things they want."

"But wouldn't more money mean they could buy more of what they want?"

Moishina shook her head. She seemed to be having as much trouble understanding Chelm. "Money is necessary for fulfilling obligations that you would prefer not to have. Needing more means being less free." She thought about it some more, as if trying to make sense of how it could be any other way. "On Earth it is not the same?"

"Not at all. It would be considered inefficient. Impossibly inefficient."

"So, what is efficient?"

"Being profitable. Making as much from a deal as you can."

"As much what?"

"Money." Chelm waited, saw that he still hadn't gotten through, and elaborated. "Buy low and sell high. It's really very simple. The bigger the difference, the more you get to keep. So everyone makes a living."

Moishina rubbed her brow with a knuckle. She was obviously having a hard time with this. "So that is the way you are taught? On your world, everyone takes as much as they can, and gives as little in return as they can get away with? But if everyone is trying to take from you, you would have to protect yourself. Is that why the Terrans have built the fence around their base?" Chelm recalled that he had seen nothing resembling a lock or bar on the door into the rooms that Osti had shown him. All of a sudden, a lot of things that he had always taken as self-evident didn't seem so obvious anymore.

"It's the way to create wealth for investing in better things," was the best answer he could come up with.

Moishina seemed to take a long time thinking through what that meant, and then shook her head again. "I don't think that Quyzo would be very happy in that world at all," she replied.

Two days later, Chelm received a summons to Teel's office. He arrived to find that Carl Liggerman, the mission's Chief Security Officer, was there too. Liggerman was a heavy, thickset man, with close-cropped black hair, a permanently blue chin, and pugnacious, beetle-browed features. He suspected everyone and everything, was devoid of humor, and Chelm had always found him intimidating to the point of devastating. Chelm had no idea what transgression might have prompted a confrontation with the two of them in concert. Surely it couldn't be his unauthorized jaunt into Issen, which would have warranted a rebuke from the section head at most. He steeled himself for the worst. Their manner, however, came close to being conciliatory.

Teel began. "When we talked before, I said that by showing more awareness of the mission's priorities, you might do yourself a favor when it comes to getting support for your own objectives. Specifically, it's possible that the questions you've been raising with regard to archeological research could be reviewed in a more favorable light."

"Oh?" Chelm was immediately suspicious and responded neutrally.

Liggerman leaned forward to take it, as if Teel were mincing around the subject. "The big problem we've got out there right now is that Yassik doesn't understand progress and can't recognize an opportunity when it's being waved under his nose."

"Utterly uncooperative," Teel said.

Liggerman continued, "When we've run into this kind of situation before, there have always been rivals or disaffecteds of some kind that we could install, from at home or abroad, who would see things more realistically." He made a resigned gesture in the general direction of the city. "But in Lydia, we haven't been able to identify anyone who would fit that role. The ones we've approached either act like they don't understand, or they pretend they're not interested. What it has to mean is that they're holding off until they get a better handle on why we're here and what's in it for them—and that's not altogether a dumb move. But we've got a ball to get rolling. We don't have time to sit around admiring the scenery until they decide to show their hands."

Chelm nodded that he understood, at the same time asking with his expression what any of this had to do with him. Teel chimed back in. "You seem to have developed a closer rapport with some of the Lydians than most of us, Chelm. Even—and I don't mind saying it—the professional ethnic psychologists. That could make you the ideal person to sound the Lydian situation out for us." He paused for a moment to let Chelm digest that. "You see my point? Maybe *you* could get them to open up and be more forthcoming; find out who and where the potential movers are. Then it's just a case of dealing with the more ambitious ones and seeing what motivates them. Everyone wants something. There's always an angle, eh?"

Chelm could see the picture now. The mission's program was stalled because the people who were supposed to do the political groundwork had failed to recruit the native leadership and were getting nowhere trying to find a more "responsive" element that could be used to foment trouble as a pretext for Terran intervention. Teel had seen a possible opportunity for his department to reap big credits with the ship's Directorate, which in due course would be communicated to Kermes-Oates Restructuring and the authorities back home. The deal for Chelm, as Teel had said, would be a more receptive attitude toward his work. There was more too, he realized as he leaned back to consider the proposition. Liggerman voiced it.

"Naturally, this would make a big difference to the application you filed to move into the city. With your leads and contacts, it would be the perfect place to be based for collecting the kind of information we want. So there it is. How long do you need?"

There really wasn't anything to think about. In his mind, Chelm was picturing the two rooms above the pottery workshop already. In any case, what did the alternative have to offer? "I can give you an answer right now," he replied. "Okay, I'll take it."

Chelm's clearance came through later that same day. Within hours he was packed and ready to go. His quarters in the base had already been claimed by a Kermes-Oates development planner from the ship, who cited her work as requiring her to be in proximity to the city. She was drafting an outline proposal for the first phase of restructuring and listing the sites to be scheduled for demolition. But it was equally an instance of anyone who had the right authority or pull getting themselves a posting down on the ground. For those who didn't, it worked the other way. Chuck Ranneson, as Teel had threatened, was consigned back up to a ship-bound job to make room for one of Liggerman's aides to move down.

Chelm moved out to his new abode the first thing next morning. He was even able to arrange for his pay to be issued in Lydian *zel*. The Lydians had supplied a list of Terran products and equipment that they required, presumably out of curiosity or for evaluation, and which they insisted on paying for. Hence, the Terran administrators found themselves flush with Lydian currency that they were happy to dispose of. Presumably some system of regularized currency exchange would follow. Chelm wasn't really an expert on such things, but in the meantime it meant that he had the wherewithal to do some shopping.

Jen was at the Cultural Center in Issen that morning and took a couple of hours off to come and see Chelm's new abode, immediately falling in love with it. They went out together for some household items and comforts to make the rooms homey, in the process making some headway in getting to know the neighborhood better. Chelm explained to Jen about the custom of always trying to give a little more and take a little less, which she laughed at delightedly and thought was wonderful. Nevertheless, they emerged as patsies when it came to Lydian bargaining, somehow ending up with a lamp, some towels, and a serving dish that they had allowed to be foisted on them for nothing as "welcoming gifts" to the alien.

"How did you get approval to move out?" Jen asked when they got back, obviously taken by the thought of trying something similar. "Do you think it might work for me too if I applied?"

"It couldn't hurt to try, I guess," Chelm told her. He tried not to sound too hopeful. Going into the deal he had struck with Teel and Liggerman would have spoiled the day. "Maybe I just got lucky."

The next day, Chelm was visited by a young man in a yellow robe and hooded green cloak who introduced himself as Troim, an acolyte of a high *nejivan* called Xerosh. Xerosh had heard word of Chelm's interest in Lydia's past ages—presumably from Ag-Vonsar—and humbly offered to share what knowledge he possessed. And in any case, he wished the honor of meeting the traveler from afar who had come to live in their city.

Troim took Chelm into the center of Issen, arriving at a large building of stone with inlays of what looked like polished marble, set atop steps that converged toward high doors framed by a triangular architrave bearing reliefs of human forms and supported by pillars. The building was a peculiar mixture of designs, with lower walls sloping back like the base of a pyramid, a stepped, ziggurat-style center portion, and the top part culminating in a large, silvery dome. Inside, they passed through a succession of arched and columned halls, carrying a continuous flow of people coming and going, that seemed to combine the functions of temple, public forums, and city offices. A broad central stairway took them up to an overlooking gallery behind balustrades, from which corridors diverged in several directions. They found Xerosh in a chamber along one of these, poring over charts laid out on a table set among shelves crammed with manuscripts and bound volumes.

Chelm had pictured a patriarchal, Moses-like figure, with flowing white hair and a beard. Xerosh was wearing a robed tunic similar to Troim's, with a dark red cloak and the addition of a thick, braided belt and a silver medallion hanging from a cord about his neck. Otherwise, he was fiftyish, maybe, clean-shaven with dark, cropped hair, and square and stocky in build. He had smooth, rounded features that carried fewer lines than his years should have produced, and large, deeply intense, dark brown eyes.

"Xerosh, *Kal-nejivan* of Issen," Troim said, addressing him. "Stanislow Chelm, archeologist-scientist from Earth."

Xerosh extended his hands. "Our world is yours. May life return to you what you give to life. Welcome to Issen."

"You are too generous." Chelm gave the standard Lydian response.

"Thank you, Troim. You may leave us," Xerosh said. The acolyte bowed his head toward Xerosh and Chelm in turn, and departed. The two men exchanged formalities and politenesses for a while, Xerosh asking Chelm about the differences between Lydia and Earth, and the impressions he had formed since arriving. Finally, he came to the subject of Lydia's past, and how could he be of assistance?

Chelm tried to convey the idea of archeology and

its purpose. Was there anything along the lines of a
museum in Issen, which might start him in the right
direction? His transvox channel had trouble finding a
Lydian equivalent to the word. "A place where things
are preserved that have survived from long ago," Chelm
said. "So the story of the people who lived then can
be reconstructed."

"Ah, yes. We have stories of long ago," Xerosh
replied.

He conducted Chelm back to the gallery with the
balustrade, and from there to a rear stairway leading
down—smaller than the one Chelm had ascended
with Troim. A passage brought them to a space that
seemed to form a rear vestibule into the building.
The way from the interior—through which they had
just emerged—was flanked on either side by massive
square pillars, tapering upward, carved with intri-
cately interwoven linear designs. Xerosh turned and
motioned for Chelm to look up at the tablet set into
the wall across the space above, between the pillars.
It must have been fifteen to twenty feet long, of a
smooth, dark rock, almost black, and was inscribed
all over with depictions of stylized human forms
involved in undecipherable events; animals, artifacts,
and enclosed spaces with apertures, that could have
been fixed constructions or vehicles; and patterns of
signs and symbols written in rows above and beneath,
and interwoven among the scenes to divide them into
what looked like a narrative series.

"This tells the story from the earliest times, when
the world and the sky were born from the thoughts
of the spirits, and only the animals walked the land,"
Xerosh said. Staring up at the tablet as if reading, he

recited, "And then there came giants, who rode upon stars and possessed powers beyond those known to men. They could turn night into day. They commanded fire from rocks, that shaped matter into whatsoever form they desired. They imprinted their will into the very designs that cause living things to grow. Neither distance nor time, nor vastness nor minuteness, nor limits of memory or thought, were impediments to their knowledge. Yet their hearts burned with covetousness and rage, and they fought ferocious battles that laid waste the earth to possess that which cannot be possessed, and as the Dark Gods they perished. And the spirits created mankind to spread and multiply, to restore and heal and tend the world; and so have we been entrusted."

Chelm waited a moment and then nodded solemnly. It sounded like the typical creation myth of a primitive culture—interesting for the cultural anthropologists, maybe, but not exactly his line. Of course, he wouldn't have been ill-mannered enough to say so, and thought up a few questions to ask for form's sake. This only seemed to encourage Xerosh, however, who answered them, and then confided, "There's more."

Chelm followed him out through the rear portico and along a tree-lined terrace to more stairs, which descended to a side entrance to another building. The surroundings here were plainer and less spacious than the imposing public halls and galleries of the building they had just left, suggesting more of a workaday environment. They passed through a library; a room like a large office, where somewhere between a half dozen and a dozen people were writing and copying, and two operating what looked like a hand-driven rotary press—a surprise to Chelm; and then two rooms each containing a central worktable, side benches bearing charcoal burners and retorts, and lined with shelves of bottles and glassware, which could have been some kind of laboratory, a pharmacy, or an alchemy shop. Beyond this, they emerged into a cloister bordering a garden enclosed by high walls and filled with rows of closely spaced shrubs and small trees, herbs, flowers, and plants of every kind. The emphasis seemed to be on variety, with just a few specimens of each kind. A local stream had been captured to create a pond in the center, and from the twittering and movement, it appeared that the place was popular with the city's community of birds. Several figures were at work here and there, tending, watering, and weeding.

"This is just a small establishment that we keep in the city to try new ideas and consolidate our repository of learning, you understand," Xerosh said. "The original knowledge comes from the experience and wisdom of people everywhere, passed down over time." Chelm didn't really follow, and looked back questioningly.

Xerosh explained, "Another story that goes back to the ancient times of our race is of how the magic that exists within plants was studied and put to use. In the beginning, they provided just simple foods. As knowledge was gained over the ages, they came to be recognized as gifts from the spirits, which would ease cares and pain, bring sleep and new life to souls weary from toil, heal the sicknesses of body and of mind, and open the inner eyes of the soul to the purpose of life. The Dark Gods, too, sought these things, but they looked for them in the forces that are outside, not the soul that dwells inside, and the fruits of the seeds they sowed were violence and fear, the lust to compel others and possess all. They believed they would be as the spirits that had created the world. But the spirits let them destroy themselves, and the world was begun once more."

They were now walking along a path between some beds containing seedlings. Chelm couldn't but think how strange it was that a world as far-flung as this should have evolved its own version of the Fall legend, practically universal among the cultures of Earth. But what Xerosh was saying about the ways of life since was too idyllic. From what Chelm knew of human nature—and the natures of all the humanlike species that Terran expansion had encountered—the impulse toward power and personal aggrandizement, and readiness to resort to force in order to achieve them, were too powerful not to have asserted themselves.

"But the people of Issen and the lands around obey the laws of Yassik," he pointed out. "How does Yassik come to exercise that authority? Wasn't the office that he holds as ruler established by predecessors who fought and disputed at some time? It had to be, surely."

Xerosh didn't quite seem to understand. "The people obey Yassik because he accepts the burden of taking responsibility." He went on to describe a system whereby the villages and other communities sent representatives to an assembly that met every two years to proclaim the ruler. The ruler then offered ministries and other official positions to selected individuals to form the governing body. It sounded like a rudimentary form of a republic—but a surprisingly enlightened one, nevertheless, for the planet's level of technical development.

"What about his rivals for the position, or others who might want to impose a different system?" Chelm persisted. "How would they achieve their objectives? Isn't some kind of confrontation inevitable? When all else fails, that leads to conflict. Then only superior strength will prevail."

Xerosh frowned while he turned this over in his mind. "You make it sound as if others would *want* his position," he observed finally.

"Well, yes, after all, isn't that the universal . . ." Chelm stopped as he saw that Xerosh wasn't following at all. "Are you telling me they wouldn't?"

"No. Not if given the choice . . ." Xerosh eyed Chelm uncertainly, as if hesitating to state the obvious. "Ruling the land is a wearying and unnerving task, filled with responsibility and worries. It takes great fortitude, character, and dedication to serve the people. Not all of those asked are willing to accept."

Chelm felt his whole foundation of reality shift again. It was like the time in the marketplace, with Moishina. "You mean it isn't something that's forced on the people?" he said.

Xerosh shook his head, evidently mystified. "The people are grateful. They know that for two years Yassik will have to pass judgments, make decisions, and that he will give of his best. And so they are sympathetic and supportive, and they do what they can to make his term easier. Abuse of a public office would be the worst of crimes. . . . Why do you look at me so strangely, Stanislow Chelm? Are our ways somehow in error, do you think?"

Just at that moment, Chelm could only shake his head mutely. In error? Just the converse! In one simple statement, Xerosh had undermined the rationale that had been taken as the axiomatic, unavoidable root of just about all of Earth's troubles for thousands of years. Somewhere, once, Chelm had heard it said half-jokingly that anyone who *wanted* the job of President of the Sol Federation shouldn't be allowed to have it. Ambition for power should be its own automatic disqualification. Now something else that had always seemed unquestionable was being turned on its head. Suddenly, it felt as if what Xerosh was saying was the only thing that made sense. Small wonder that the mission was having no luck finding opponents and power rivals to install in Yassik's place.

Yet nothing in life was ever that simple or easy. "Your way is not in error," Chelm replied at last. "But there will still be people who feel differently, whose compulsion is to command and control the lives of others, to take and not to give. And they will find ones who will help them. Wolves will emerge in the flock. What do you do then?"

Xerosh stopped walking and thought for several seconds. Then he nodded, beckoned, and led the way along a side path running through a grove of mixed trees bright with blossoms and fruits. "Yes, it is so," he agreed. "When a wolf appears, the other animals must become wolves too; unless the wolf can be tamed." They came to a shrub about five feet high, with a maze of twisty branches something like a monkey puzzle tree, leaves of bright green and orange, and small, purple berries hanging in clusters. Xerosh stopped and gestured toward it. "In our world, such people find the answer to their desires here. It is called the Tree of Dreams."

Hallucinations of grandeur, Chelm interpreted. It was Xerosh's way of saying that Lydian culture had become immune to such perturbations, and the only recourse left for those harboring such cravings was escape into drug-induced fantasizing. Ordinarily, he wouldn't have thought that the problem could be solved that conveniently; but who was he to argue with someone who lived here that it couldn't be so? He left it at that.

That evening, Xerosh attended a meeting of the Inner Chamber of Issen's Governing Council. Yassik was present, along with his senior ministers and advisors. They gathered in the debating room at the rear of Yassik's official residence, across the square from the building in which Xerosh had first met Chelm earlier.

"My observations agree with what the boatbuilder, his granddaughter, and others say," Xerosh informed them. "Rapacity and the hunger to subdue might be what drives the Terran federation, but it is not a universal trait in all Terrans. The voices of those who would dissent are not heard. To adjudge guilt equally would be to commit a grave injustice."

"Are we not, then, guilty of injustice before?" Yassik asked.

"That was not your decision, Yassik," one of the ministers said. "It happened before your appointment."

"*All* responsibilities of the office I hold are my responsibilities," Yassik reminded them.

"The flower cannot return to the seed, nor the hatchling into the egg. It is done."

"But the flower produces a new seed, and the bird, a new egg. If we have learned more, we can be wiser this time. What was done cannot be repeated. Justice requires that we be more selective. But how?"

There was a long silence. Eventually, Xerosh spoke. "I talked with Stanislow Chelm about his decision to move into our city. It seems there is a broader pattern. The envy that Terrans are conditioned to feel produces rivalry among them for accommodation down on the ground. They also measure status by their ability to command the services of others. I think there might be a way. . . ."

Jen called Chelm the next morning with glum news. Not only had her application to move out of the base been rejected, but she was being reassigned to a position back up in the ship. Apparently, exopsychology didn't figure strongly enough in the mission's current planning to warrant her continuing to use base accommodation that was needed for others whose work was more pertinent. In reality, of course, it was just another part of the jostling by higher officers and administrators for a place—literally—in the sun.

Granting her request would have freed up the space just as effectively, but that was ruled out on account of a further development. Even the professional paranoids had gotten it into their heads by this time that the Lydians represented no threat and the environment was wholesome, and partly as a consequence the competition for surface assignments had taken on a new dimension. Prefab modules within the base area were regarded as mundane, and the new status symbol among the upper echelons was to be able to boast a real native-built house outside. And the Lydians, as always, were cheerfully obliging. In fact, they seemed to encourage the fad by taking Terrans to see places that they thought would appeal to them. Some said the Lydians had instigated the idea in the first place. Practically the entire Directorate and their wives moved into a group of villas on a hillside about a half mile from the base. Anyone of department-head level or above needed at least a three-room chalet or one complete level of a multistory town abode. It followed that to confer a comparable privilege on someone of Jen's lowly standing was unthinkable. The mission was effectively dividing into two castes, the privileged and the empowered down on the surface, and second-class citizens removed to orbit. Chelm's, of course, was a special case that it was convenient to forget about.

However, living without things like computer-managed kitchens and household inventories, self-regulating environments, and shipboard services that had been taken for granted did not come as easily as the newcomers would have thought, had they thought about it at all. Creating an edible meal from an assortment of strange liquids and powders, raw vegetables, and pieces of dead animals was something that few Terrans from the professional classes had ever contemplated, let alone practiced or mastered. What did one do with dirty clothes without a laundry machine, when laundry, by that definition, is something a machine does? And then there were all those endless things that needed fixing or cleaning, adjusting or restocking, that made existence impossible without a maintenance crew to call on.

Again, the Lydians came to the rescue. They had been thinking about things the Terrans had been saying, and they agreed it was only right that they should pay for all the things from Earth that they stood to gain. In the absence, as yet, of a currency-exchange system, they offered their services as domestic help for their new neighbors. This rapidly caught on as the indispensable mark of having any status at all among the Terrans, and the bragging at cocktail soirees thrown to show off a newly possessed mansion, or across the dinner table of an apartment overlooking the river in Issen, centered around the number of native cooks, maids, stewards, and gardeners that the household commanded. Even the security people were persuaded that the Lydians possessed no weapons apart from those used for hunting, which were easily spotted, and began allowing them into the base to perform their duties—albeit after the standard ritual of scanning and screening. It was not long before even the most jaundiced, lower-echelon occupier of a prefab single module had a part-time Lydian domestic to rustle up a change from the routine autochef fare, or send ostentatiously on errands as visible affirmation of respectable standing—superior, at least, to those banished to the dreary confines of the ship.

The security procedures looked for knives and axes—guns, had there been any—and other potential implements of violent assault of the kind that security-trained minds envisaged. What they didn't take into account were the various exotic delicacies that the Lydian cooks brought to titillate the appetites of their new employers, or the ingredients that went into their preparation. In particular, nobody paid attention to an essence distilled from the juice of a pale red berry, picked before it turned purple, and combined with an extract from a certain seed, that could be blended into a sauce or garnish, cooked with the stuffing of a fowl, added to a compote of fruits, or introduced into a dish in a dozen other ways. The berry came from a twisty-branched shrub that Lydians called the "Tree of Dreams."

There were exceptions, of course. Not *every* Terran who dwelt down on the surface was of a disposition that would be found threatening. Some were decent enough people in themselves, caught up in a way of life that was not of their choice or making, and which they couldn't change. But after a week or so, a telling measure of which kind was which could be had from the way they spoke to and treated their Lydian housekeepers. In effect, the servants became the judges of their masters.

An evening meal was the best time, allowing the potion all night to work, after which the victim would awake a changed person. The effect was irreversible.

The first Chelm knew of it was when Jen called him from the ship early one morning. "Stan, thank God you're okay. What's going on down there?"

"What do you mean?"

"You don't know?"

"What are you talking about?"

"Something's happened to . . . it seems, just about everybody down on the surface. Some kind of sickness.

I managed to raise two people at the base, but they were just shift operators in the com room and not making much sense. People up here are getting a lander ready to come down."

"Did you try anyone here in the city—at the Cultural Center?"

"I was more concerned about you first."

"I'll try and raise someone there. Will you be coming down too?"

"I'm not sure yet. Yes, if I can. I'll call you back when I know."

"Later."

Chelm called several numbers at the Center, finally getting through to a secretary. She, a couple of technicians, and a security guard had come out on an early shuttle bus, and other than the driver were the only ones to have shown up. They hadn't been able to make any more sense of what had happened back at the base than Jen had. "We need to get back there," Chelm said. "Can you guys pick me up here in the bus?" The secretary took a moment to check with the others.

"Sure," she replied. "Where are you, exactly? Give me some directions."

The first strange thing to strike Chelm as the bus approached the base was the number of Lydians both inside and outside the perimeter fence, along with a collection of mounts and carriages of various kinds that many of them had presumably arrived in. The gate was wide open, and the only guards he saw were standing in a huddle to one side, looking bewildered and very much out of things. As the bus maneuvered its way

through the throng, he saw numerous *nejivan* robes
and other symbols of office among the Lydians present.
This was not some street crowd that had wandered
in out of idle curiosity. And then he spotted Xerosh
and his acolyte Troim with a group standing near the
entrance to the Admin Block. "Can you drop me off
here, driver?" Chelm called to the front.

Xerosh saw Chelm coming across and turned from
saying something to the others who were with him.
"The spirits have willed us a new morning, Stanislow
Chelm," he greeted.

"Use it well." The responses had become automatic.
"What's going on?"

Xerosh raised his arm and made a sweeping gesture
that took in the activity going on within the base, the
city in the distance, and the rest of the world beyond.
"You are free," he announced.

"Free from what?"

"From everything that has enslaved you. To become
all the things you have always wanted, and are capable
of. The wolves who preyed upon your life will do so
no more."

Before Chelm could reply, some Lydians emerged
from the Admin Block, shepherding a group of Terrans,
almost as if they were under guard. Chelm recognized
Teel, Liggerman, others . . . all from managerial or
administrative grades. He stepped forward toward
Teel, intending to get some kind of explanation . . . but
then slowed when he saw that Teel was not behaving
normally. Teel's face had a distant, ecstatic expression
as he came out into the sunlight. He stopped to gaze
at the sky, the mountains rising in the direction away
from the city, and two birds perched on the boundary

fence, squawking at each other. Chelm looked at his face. It was empty but happy, like a child's. Behind Teel, Liggerman was looking equally blissfully imbecilic, moving his head this way and that to take in the base as if he had never seen it before. Chelm turned demandingly toward Xerosh; but the emotions boiling up inside him were so turbulent and confused that he could find no coherent words to string together.

"We will take care of them now," Xerosh said quietly.

And then the call tune sounded from Chelm's wristpad. It was Jen at last. "Okay, Stan, I'm on my way," she said. "We're detaching from the ship in about ten minutes' time. See you soon. . . . Stan? Is everything okay there?" She had seen that Chelm had turned his face away and wasn't listening.

For Teel was stretching a hand out toward the unit. His eyes met Chelm's. Just for an instant, a spark of recognizing something familiar flickered in them. "Mozart!" he exclaimed.

After the lander arrived, Chelm and Jen rode with Xerosh and some of his company back into the city. On the way, Xerosh proposed his plan. With the help of the technicians aboard the ship, a message would be sent to Earth, advising that the early report from *Oryx* had overstated Lydia's potential for development, and the planet did not warrant further effort. The message would say that information had been found showing that the *Oryx* had departed to continue its survey elsewhere, and the present mission would follow in the direction of the galactic sector it had indicated. The *Hayward Kermes* would then be sent off unmanned, under programmed control, to lose itself among the stars in the same way as had been done with the *Oryx*.

Chelm's mind was still in such a whirl from the morning's happenings that they had arrived at their destination before it dawned on him that there would have been no technicians available to set up the departure of the *Oryx*. Its entire complement had been absorbed into Lydia's population of *jujerees*—the child-people. So who had done it?

Xerosh seemed to have been expecting the question. "That is one of the things we have brought you here to have answered," he said.

They were at another building near the city center, but an inconspicuous one this time, plain in style and obscured by others. Xerosh and his companions took them down deep below ground, then through a series of dark corridors that passed by many doors. They stopped at one and entered. Inside, Xerosh flipped a switch to bring on the lights. Chelm gaped up at them.

Electric?

And then he looked around. There were glass cases containing oddly styled but mostly recognizable racks of electronic assemblies, vacuum-tube chassis, and switchgear; chip and crystal arrays, cableforms, circuit cards, capacitor banks; coils, motors, transformer windings; input panels and screens. . . . Many items were old, broken, incomplete, or corroded, others seemingly repaired and restored, while some looked in working order. An opening to one side revealed part of an adjoining hall that appeared dedicated to engines and machines. Jen was looking as stunned as Chelm felt.

"Yes, we have our museum that preserves things from long ago," Xerosh said. "When we met, I told you, Stanislow Chelm, that the function of the *neji-van* is to act as custodians of ancient knowledge. It is amusing that Terrans took our culture to be young and primitive. Like the Terrans, our distant ancestors found that knowledge can accumulate very quickly and cheaply. But finding the wisdom to use it well takes longer. There are aeons left for the universe. We can afford to wait until the time is right." The priest turned to look at them. His gaze was kindly, deep, and not without a hint of mirth. "In the meantime, as I said, you are free."

The full meaning was going to take a long time to sink in. Chelm looked at Jen, his mind grappling for something even halfway sensible to say. "You still like the thought of the place over the pottery shop?" was all he could manage in the end.

"You mean I don't have to put in an application, file a priority statement, and ask permission?"

Chelm shook his head. And it was only then that the realization really hit him that yes, it was true. He grinned—maybe the first honest, open, totally carefree grin in his life.

"No, Jen," he answered. "Never again."

From the Web Site

NUCLEAR WASTE

Bulletin Board, Energy, November 16, 1998 (http://www.jamesphogan.com/bb/content/111698.shtml)

WHAT ABOUT IT?

Following the items I've posted advocating nuclear as ultimately the only way to go, a number of people have repeated the frequently asked question of what to do about the waste. My response is that it's a needlessly manufactured political problem, not a technical one. And in any case the problem itself is minor compared to what we have at present.

A single 1,000-megawatt coal plant releases something like 600 pounds of carbon dioxide and 30 pounds of sulfur dioxide into the atmosphere per *second*, and as much nitrogen oxides as 200,000 automobiles, all of which is estimated to cause 25 premature fatalities and 60,000 cases of respiratory complaints per year, per plant. In addition, it has to get rid of 30,000 truckloads of ash annually—enough to cover a square mile 60 feet deep—full of carcinogens, highly acidic or highly alkaline depending on the kind of coal, and, ironically, emitting more radiation from trace uranium than a nuke is permitted to. That's a *real* waste-disposal nightmare for you.

The hysteria about toxicity is not justified by anything factual. After its initial on-site cooling-off period (i.e. at the point where it would be transported to a deep-burial site as currently proposed), high-level wastes would be about as toxic as barium or arsenic if ingested, and 1/10th that of ammonia or 1/1000th that of chlorine—which we use liberally to clean our bathtubs and swimming pools—if inhaled. After 100 years, these figures drop to 1/1000th, 1/100,000th, and 1/10,000,000th respectively. The "conventional" types of waste remain lethal, and far less easily detectable, forever.

Some figures:

Two hundred fifty nuclear plants would generate enough waste to kill 10 billion people. True, if it were freely accessible, and people obligingly lined up to receive their daily dose or intake of it. The same is probably true also of gasoline. By the same token the U.S already produces enough:

- arsenic trioxide to kill 10 billion people

- barium to kill 100 billion
- ammonia to kill 6 trillion
- phosgene to kill 20 trillion
- chlorine to kill 400 trillion

As for plutonium having a long half-life, so what? Compost heaps and incense sticks have long half-lives; napalm bombs and gunpowder have short ones. The public-health limits on plutonium in drinking water are 400 times higher than for radium, which is used safely as a matter of course in practically every hospital.

In short, N-waste turns out to be significantly less hazardous than many other substances that are handled routinely in far greater volumes, and with far less care.

The sensible way to deal with waste (actually a potentially valuable by-product) is to reprocess it into new fuel and burn it up in reactors, which not only solves the "problem" but would save about $4 billion in imported oil costs in the lifetime of a 1,000-megawatt plant. Roughly 96 percent of the spent fuel that comes out of a plant can be handled in this way. The remaining "high level" waste from a year's operation of a 1,000-megawatt (large) plant takes up about half a cubic yard.

This is what the U.S. nuclear industry was set up to do—as the rest of the world is doing—until political obstructionism in the late 1970s halted work on the Barnwell facility in South Carolina, which was being built to handle commercial wastes. Legislation passed at the same time cut the utilities off from the military facilities that had been handling commercial wastes safely since the 1950s. The result was that 100 percent of what comes out of the reactors is having to be treated as if it were high-level waste, to be stored in ways that were never intended, and this is what gets all the publicity.

So, in answer to "What about the waste?" What about it?

WHO WILL REMEMBER THE DEEP END?

Bulletin Board, Politics, July 10, 2003 (http://www.jamesphogan.com/bb/content/071003.shtml)

To anyone over twenty who grew up in a worthy suburban American town and went through a worthy American childhood, venturing into the deep end of the swimming pool represented a significant moment in life—a symbolic proving of self, where overcoming the fears and doubts associated with those dark, mysterious depths was to cast infancy behind forever and qualify for entry to the adult world of challenge, achievement in the face of adversity, and the opening up of unlimited horizons.

Not anymore. The deep end is vanishing. Cities are filling them in, hotels are redesigning their outdoor amenities, backyard-pool manufacturers are no longer building pools with areas deeper than five feet. All the usual reasons apply. I wonder how many of the next generation will know the exhilaration I felt at age twelve after daring my first vertical pike off the thirty-foot-high top board in London's Lime Grove public pool, where we used to go for an hour in the morning before biking to school. Diving? Already banned in most places.

You'll find the full article, "The End of the Deep End," by Mark Morford in his Notes and Errata column at *SFGate.com* (http://sfgate.com/cgi-bin/article.cgi?file=/gate/archive/2003/07/09/notes070903.DTL)

The Trouble With Utopias

Some years ago, when I lived in California, I attended a weekend seminar on interstellar colonization, generation ships, and how they might function. There were some bright and interesting people there, versed in just about all the relevant technologies, as well as management, social, and psychological sciences. For the first couple of days everyone split into groups and disappeared off into the woodwork of the hotel to study the aspect they had elected to tackle and come up with a solution. The final day would be devoted to hearing presentations by all the groups and debating their findings. As a general writer-guest of the occasion not attached to any group in particular, I was free to roam at leisure around the workrooms where they had ensconced themselves amid paper-strewn tables and walls steadily taking on a new papering of charts—in the process being sometimes taken for a spy sent out by some other group to see what the competition was up to. And, indeed, human nature being the way it is, that did happen (involving other spies) quite a lot too.

As was to be expected, much of the material had to do with technical issues, such as in creating a habitat capable of sustaining life for an extended period in the space environment, energy sources, propulsion systems, materials, structures, and that kind of thing. But one section of the agenda was headed "Types of Social Organization," and addressing it was a team that included a couple of psychologists, an industrial psychiatrist, a management consultant, and a political theorist, among others. Their analysis, in impeccable organization-speak and with a facility for categorization, delineation, subclassification, and masterful desiccation worthy of bureaucracy at its most stolid, reduced all of the diversity, richness, triumph, tragedy, and magnificent chaos of the human drama to three societal types. These, in a leap of breathtaking imagination, were designated "Type A," "Type B," and "Type C."

A "Type A" community, we were told, was "Hierarchical and Homogenistic." People in this kind of community believe there is a "best" way of doing everything, which is good for everybody. They think in terms of maximization and optimization, pursue efficiency as a self-evident ideal, operate by majority rule, and consider competition to be the basis of all progress. Nonstandard behavior and minority groups are considered abnormal and undesirable, to be ignored if possible, or corrected if they become too inconvenient. Because of the belief that unity comes from homogeneity and differences create conflict, members of such a system would be divided into groups by age and by occupation. Living units would all be identical, and the inhabited areas would be zoned into residential, agricultural, and industrial areas, and so forth. It seemed to be axiomatic that all of the above viewpoints and opinions come together inseparably, in one psychological package.

A "Type B" community, on the other hand, was "Individualistic and Isolationistic." (What is it that makes me uncomfortable about people who want to put "ic" on the end of every adjective?) Proponents of this kind of society value independence and self-sufficiency as the highest virtue. Accordingly, each living unit in a generation ship modeled to this philosophy would constitute its own castle, isolated from the others, with everything adjustable for individual taste and protection of privacy as the major concern. Decision-making would be autonomous and decentralized to the greatest degree possible, with a minimal command structure playing a Jeffersonesque federal role to provide a unified defense and foreign policy in terms of getting the ship in one piece to where it wants to go, and providing for the common welfare.

The above two categories were disposed of fairly speedily, and it was difficult to avoid the impression that they were included mainly as a token to completeness and impartiality, but with their negative aspects emphasized—not very subtly—to steer us all to accepting the vision that the authors were plugging as the only viable choice, which was given far more time and described glowingly.

This was the "Type C" community, characterized by

being "Heterogenistic, Mutualistic, and Symbiotic." Its members believe in "the symbiosis of biological and social process due to mutual interaction." Heterogeneity is the primary value, affording a source of "enrichment, symbiosis, and resource diversification," while contributing to "flexibility and survival," and providing the raw material for ongoing evolution. Majority rule is considered homogenistic domination by quantity, in place of which would be enshrined the principle of "elimination of hardship." Competition is destructive and useless, and is to be replaced by cooperation, the overall design philosophy being harmony of diversity. (The word "harmony" occurred repeatedly throughout the description.) The different elements making up the heterogeneity would not be just thrown together, however, but carefully combined to produce . . . yes, you've guessed, harmony. There were two methods of achieving heterogenization: "Localization" and "Interweaving" . . . And so it went on.

The community had every kind of facility, amenity, and service imaginable. Nothing had been overlooked by the planners or excluded from their calculations. Residential units were allowed 49 square meters per person: 37 square meters of floor area and 12 square meters of exterior space. Business districts were assigned 10 shops to every 1000 people, and 2.5 square meters floor space per office worker. There were schools and hospitals; halls for churchgoing, community meetings, and theaters; a variety of entertainments that were educational as well as beneficial; facilities for a wide range of creative hobbies; park spaces for sports, recreation, and leisure. It all sounded utopian. It was all very harmonious, of course, as well as being balanced, symbiotic, heterogenistic, wholesome, nutritious, healthy, hygenic, and clean. . . . And so antiseptic, vapid, insipid, germfree, and sanitary that my first reaction was a feeling of acute nausea. In short, I wanted to throw up.

Where were the sleazy bars, nightclubs, and strip joints? What about some pool parlors, casinos, X-rated movie theaters, and pinball arcades? In other words, the things that a lot of real, live, flesh-and-blood people in real, jostling, bustling, hustling—the things that make real "heterogenistic" communities—like to do sometimes. Or wasn't this place meant for real, live flesh-and-blood people?

It was an upper-middle-class academic intellectual's ideal of how other people ought to live; a projection of the secure, worry-free suburbia that model families of TV commercials and yucky movies inhabit, infused with correct attitudes and social virtues, and healthily nurtured in body and mind. Maybe it was their fantasy of the world they thought their children wanted to grow up in. But the possibility that the subjects might not be quite so enthralled by it all didn't seem to have occurred to anyone. Perhaps I should amend what I wrote above to read: Nothing had been overlooked by the planners except how the unasked recipients of all this moral guidance and cultural improvement might feel about it. Like the computers that the social engineers use to process their statistics and graph their models, the inhabitants—"social units," not people—of the exercise were receptacles for programs to be loaded into and then tweaked until desirable behavior was seen to emerge. The only problem is, humans have this funny habit of not reacting desirably to being treated like that.

Back in the late '70s, after I left Massachusetts and before I wound up in Florida, I spent some time in New York City. One of the people I got to know there—I met him in the bar of a Holiday Inn near the Coliseum—was a black character who went by the name of Pal. I remember him recounting his perspective of the social programs launched with much fanfare in the '60s. "They sent rich people's kids from well-to-do suburbs outside the city to tell us how to live," he told me. "They knew nothing about blacks, nothing about life in the streets, and nothing about what it's like to be poor. They felt guilty because they were rich and had it easy, and they were gonna do good things for us to make themselves feel better. So they gave us handouts of other people's money that they'd taken away in taxes, making out like they were being real generous—which said we weren't capable of earning our own. They set quotas to force people to give us jobs—which said we couldn't make it on our own. They lowered the entry grades for our kids to get into schools—which said they didn't have what it takes. They gave us food stamps and took away our self-respect, when all we'd ever wanted was the chance to prove ourselves on a level pitch. And then, they expected us to be *grateful*! What would you have done?"

"I think I might have gotten pretty mad and set fire to their cities," I said.

"Damn right!" Pal agreed. "That's just what we did."

It's strange, too, isn't it, how many of those same people, who gave their children secure, worry-free environments to grow up in, with all problems taken care of and everything provided, ended up embittered because they didn't get any gratitude from that direction either—and perhaps had their cities burned metaphorically.

The most livable cities, in my experience, weren't planned down to excruciating detail. To a large degree, they just happened. I grew up in the 1940s on the west side of London. There was no zoning and not much regulating then. Streets of houses, crowded markets, shops, pubs, schools, parks were all jumbled up together. Just walking around town was always an experience with something going on, never dull or boring like a modern-day suburban graveyard with its rows of white monuments, each on its patch of green, and nobody in sight. There was a railroad marshaling yard, where you could sit on the grass bank by the tracks and watch the freight cars being formed up, with the occasional express thundering through on the fast line from Paddington on its way to Wales and the West Country. Behind it was a canal with a scrap-metal yard on one side, with mountains of water tanks, oil drums, sheets of corrugated iron, and all kinds of junk that the kids would build into a tank, an airplane, or a submarine, and play all day. On the way to school we passed an automobile-assembly plant and a printing works, where on warm days they kept the doors open and you could talk to the workers during their break and watch the newspapers and magazines coming off the presses.

There were parks with big, solidly built, iron-and-wood swings, roundabouts, bucking broncos that could throw you ten feet if you didn't cling on right—not the wimpy plastic things they have today because of lawsuit paranoia—along with swimming pools, sandpits, and playing fields. Across the main road where the electric trolley buses ran, behind the cinder grounds where the visiting fair pitched camp at the Easter and August holidays and the circus came at Christmas, was a large area of open heath bordering a prison on the far side, and which still had sandbagged antiaircraft-gun emplacements from the war, where we played soccer with the soldiers. It was a community in every sense, where industry was part of everyday life, and men with greasy coveralls weren't something remote who existed on TV, but people who made the things we all used and ate their lunch in the cafe between the greengrocer's and the fish-and-chip shop at the end of the street.

A lot of young people that you hear these days have absorbed the message from the media and frequently at school that technology is bad, causing pollution and cancer and despoiling the planet. They don't seem to connect industry with their own everyday needs at all. I see children of families that are far wealthier than we were in terms of owning more possessions than we could have dreamed of . . . but I'm not sure I envy them in their rows of model homes, marooned on islands of secure conformity, miles from anything interesting to do unless a parent has the time to drive them there. (We could go anywhere in London for a few pennies on the underground and the bus network.) And they're not allowed to have problems or challenges and learn to deal with them in their own way, because any hint of a worry or fear or self-doubt is met by swarms of counselors, social workers, experts, analysts. . . . Yet we read continually of the difficulties young people experience with alienation, boredom, disenchantment, and the various forms of self-destructive behavior that can set in as a result.

True satisfaction and the inner feeling of self-esteem comes from doing worthwhile work competently and the knowledge of being up to dealing with life's downturns when they happen. What kind of work is worthwhile? The kind that people seek and are willing to pay for in one way or another without being made to. The kind that's needed. But what does somebody do who has nothing to offer that anyone really wants? Being a free-rider in life—the feeling of consuming and putting nothing back in return—is discomfiting and dissatisfying to most people. One reaction that it evokes is that of the compulsive regulator and legislator. If we produce nothing that people will voluntarily spend money on, or have nothing to promote that they'll vote for at the ballot box, then dammit we'll *make* them take notice of us and need us!

There seems to be a certain kind of mind that preoccupies itself with social engineering and visions of creating the ideal society. I suspect that very often there's a streak of suppressed envy at work too for the producers and creators whose work is genuinely valued by others. And this can easily translate into deriving a perverse satisfaction from obstructing and negating the achievements of others as a way of combating the discomfort. The task is made easier, perhaps to the degree of being turned into a crusade with a purpose, when it's bolstered by the conviction that the achievements being obstructed are endangering to Mother Earth. So in the utopias that they create, *they* become not just needed but necessary, a paternalistic, expert elite, advising behind the throne while ministering the benefits of superior wisdom to the grateful and respecting peasantry. So what could be a greater anathema than the suggestion that the peasants might be capable of muddling along and managing their lives to their own satisfaction without need of it?

The trouble with utopias comes when not everyone agrees that they're so utopian. What do you do if the peasants aren't so enamored with the vision dispensed from on high and start developing the peculiar notion that they'd rather be left alone? Well, obviously that's just an aberration. They just need a little "help" to become enlightened. The irony with the former Soviet practice of putting dissidents in lunatic asylums lay in the fact that it *wasn't* simply a malicious form of punishment; the ideologues *believed* that anyone not wildly enthusiastic over the system had to be genuinely insane and in need of corrective treatment.

You can fool some of the people for some of the time, and you can fool yourself all of the time. But you can't fool reality. When some utopian dream experiment on Earth eventually collides with one of the realities of life—the most usual one being human nature—it might be the end of the utopia but it isn't the end of the world. The disillusioned and hopefully wiser disperse back into the general run of things, and history carries on. But what happens in a less resilient, spacegoing community, such as a generation starship, when its overplanned and rigidly maintained system is unable to accommodate to, or failed to recognize in the first place, the whims and wants of real people living real lives? You can't have your dissidents transferred or retired from the service like malcontents among the crew of an aircraft carrier or submarine, nor throw them overboard in the way a council of elders might expel the misfits from a back-to-basics colony. Shooting them has this tendency to induce doubts as to the totality of a leadership's commitment to the sacredness of harmony. Employing screening and selection procedures at the recruitment stage as is often advocated, comparable to the military's way of assembling teams for demanding tasks of long duration, would mean that the spacegoing community isn't representative of the real human condition to begin with. So how can it be expected to cope when real human problems arise?—as they will. And in any case, since we're talking about generation ships, what do you do about the aberrants who will inevitably be born later, who don't conform to the original selection criteria?

Many humanitarians, depressed by social injustice and deploring the exploitation and imperialism of the nineteenth century, were nevertheless impressed by the achievements of science. If science could unify mechanics and gravitation, formulate astronomy and chemistry, and produce the steam engine, the telegraph, and the railroad, then surely all the human problems of ignorance, want, injustice, and oppression could be solved by the same application of objectivity and reason. But the ideologies constructed as a consequence, claimed to be founded on "scientific" principles and devised for the most part by concerned thinkers with the sincerest of intentions, led to some of the most vicious and intolerant regimes of recent times.

For, when the end is something as noble as finally

realizing the Golden Age of human equality or the Millennium of opportunity, what, by comparison, are a few trifling rights and liberties of those unenlightened who, from motives of greed, selfishness, or contempt for the laws that apply to others, would stand in the way? If the institutions of a free society become obstacles to the Great Plan by obstructing the consensus that the Plan needs to be implemented, then those institutions will have to yield or be suspended. For the sake of "harmony" and the "best interests of society as a whole," those who oppose us will have to be . . . removed. Once begun, the path leads ultimately to the secret police, the midnight arrests, the concentration camp, and the gulag, not as unfortunate instances of good intentions that went wrong, but as *inevitable* consequences of a precedent that sacrificed the individual to a supposedly greater collective good, and made service to an ideal the only measure of worth and justification for human existence.

Good reasons can always be found why those who disagree should be coerced into living as others think they should. The thin end of the wedge that rapidly widens to become the stripping away of rights and freedoms wholesale is usually the assertion of a position that few could find grounds to disagree with, such as fighting wars on drugs, protecting children, combating "terrorism," which disarms potential opposition in advance. Once the cause has been identified with furthering the common good, then any questioning of it automatically becomes the mark of the common enemy. In an artificial space habitat, vulnerable to extortion attempts and sabotage as well as being subject to all the natural rigors of the hostile extraterrestrial environment, the crucial importance of preserving security affords a ready-made justification for imposing a regimented, coercive order "for your own safety and protection and the good of everyone."

And again, unlike the wildernesses that were available to immigrants in earlier centuries, a starship habitat doesn't offer unlimited room to expand into and get away from neighbors you don't like; its physical resources are limited. The management and allocation of shortages—and their creation, if necessary—have always provided fertile breeding grounds for "people's" committees, planning boards, bureaucratic departments, and the like.

I'm not, of course, suggesting some kind of anarchy as an alternative, or any way to run a spaceship. If history shows anything about the relative merits of different forms of human societies, it's that while totalitarian systems kill more people than democratic ones do, anarchy kills far more still. But since a long-duration space experience involving a society in miniature offers all the temptations and pretexts that the zealots for authoritarianism relish, what I am asking is how best to preserve the values of free choice and self-determination that our political and economic systems are based on—the foundations of the way of life we believe in. It would be ironic, to say the least, if after threatening nuclear retaliation to defend those values here on Earth, we were to lose them and capitulate to precisely the forces that we perceive as so threatening, the moment we venture out into space. Or must we conclude that our way of life simply isn't suitable for exporting into space at all?

How, in other words, do we prevent the emergence

of a social order that stifles the kind of personal initiative, originality, and assertiveness that has proved the driving force and character of our culture, and avoid creating in its place a collection of docile and acquiescing social statistical units? Of the proud ship that lifts out of lunar orbit and turns outward toward the stars, how do we insure that what arrives one, two, three, or more generations later hasn't degenerated into a space-borne sheep pen or a human vegetable patch . . . or worse, a concentration camp in which all dissent and threats of diversity have been suppressed by force?

The paradox, in short, is: How do we design a society whose one, overriding attribute is that it wasn't designed?

The answer, I would submit, is not to try. Instead, let it design itself. Why is it necessary to specify all the details of how people shall work and play, where they should live, what they should think? . . . for generations that haven't even been born yet. For the simple fact is that nobody knows or probably can imagine what the conditions might be of such an expedition ten, twenty, thirty years out, or what social, psychological, or other stresses could arise to challenge its resourcefulness. Quite possibly, even the natures of the people who had come into being by that time could be completely alien to the comprehension of anyone shaped by our planet-bound perspectives. The approach indicated, then, is surely to try to anticipate nothing, but to build in the flexibility that will enable the people concerned to create their own style of community as they go. And since from what we've been saying, one form of community is never going to suit everyone, this means "communities."

The Royal Air Force in Britain in World War II had an unorthodox way of forming bomber crews, but one that proved very effective. There was no matching of psychological profiles by experts or grouping according to the results of elaborate personality tests—maybe because nobody had the time, rather than through any dazzling insight. But what they did was simply turn loose the new recruits fresh from pilot training, navigation and gunnery school, and so forth in a hangar as an unsupervised throng, and let the crews find themselves. A captain might find a flight engineer and radio operator who all liked the look of each other and thought they might get along, and together they would wander around in search of a navigator, tail gunner, et cetera until the crew was complete. Compatible temperaments had a knack for finding each other, and the teams that gravitated together in this way tended to be, dare I say "harmonious"?—and enduring.

Maybe a generation starship mission could adopt the same principle. Imagine our initial ship—or preferably ships, two or three, say, to provide lifeboats in case of emergency; Columbus had the right idea—lifting out from parking orbit accompanied by a flotilla of immense cargo repositories packed with materials and equipment of the kind used in the construction of the manned craft. Or the rafts could have been sent out ahead at intervals over years if need be, to be overhauled and consolidated as the voyage proceeds. Now there's no need for any elite clique of prescient experts to spell out in advance what kind of geometry the descendants in years hence shall inhabit, the organization of the society they will form part of, and how they will function in it. Because as all the unpredictable factors that time will bring unfold, and various groups and factions emerge with different ideas about the kind of world that they think would appeal to them, they can simply *go out and build their own.*

What a great way to allay the boredom and disgruntlements that are bound to surface among any human community shut up for a long period in a limited space; for providing an outlet for surplus energies and a reservoir for preserving the richness of diversity that we cherish! Tired of walking through the same mall-like concourses and residential decks every day, and seeing the same patches of hydroponic greens on the far side overhead, interrupted by star-filled sky windows? Fine. Get a like-minded group together and design yourselves a torroidal world, a dumbbell-shaped world, a modular Ferris wheel . . . anything you want. You can set yourselves up as a Baptist community, Mormon, Muslim, Buddhist; or try out an experiment in Libertarian living, Socialist, Libertine, Monarchist, or perhaps united as of one mind in serving your own local dictator; even "Hierarchical and Homogenistic," or "Heterogenistic, Mutualistic, and Symbiotic" if it really grabs your fancy. And the beauty of it is that none of these attachments to a social formula or style of living has to be permanent. As the initial strung-out stockpile of construction materials gradually transforms itself into a formation of liberal to tightly run city-states, frontier towns, religious monasteries, pleasure resorts, urban crushes, rural spreads, academic retreats, and who knows what else, the changes and contrasts of moving from one to another could be the source of variety found to be essential to a healthy life. It could be an invaluable means of education too. For what quicker and more effective way could there be of revealing the realities of someone else's utopia than shuttling across a few miles of intervening space and trying it for a while? And what better preparation could those distant descendants have, of whatever generation eventually arrives at an inhabitable world, for dealing with the conflicts and vicissitudes that go to make up real human existence than to have lived with them all their lives?

So what mix of objects will eventually drop into orbit to begin surveying that new, far-off abode? A variety of thriving, mutually supportive communities, ready to extend the pattern across a new world? Or mutually distrustful armed fortresses, seeking only their own territory to enclose and defend? I have no idea. But that's the whole point. At our end of the venture, nobody can.

In the meantime, though, I think I may have concocted an idea for a new book.

Decontamination Squad

It was the first visit of an environmental regulator to this part of the galaxy in over twenty thousand years.

Dispatched during the Third Cleanup Crusade to the outer spiral, the Inspector from the Emergent-Life Protection Agency reentered normal space in Sector 5, Group 12, Subcluster 3, in the vicinity of a nine-planet system orbiting a midrange yellow dwarf star listed in the register as G4-769-KW/4603H.

Scans across the ultraviolet, optical, microwave, and radio bands confirmed that the innermost planet, 4603/1, was still lifeless as reported by the previous emissary, but this had been expected. With regard to 4603/2 and 4603/4, it was regrettably conceded that the measures taken in the course of the previous visit to protect and encourage the incipient life detected on that occasion had failed. The second planet showed overcompensation reactions running out of control, resulting in conditions of excessive heat and atmospheric pressure, while the fourth had reverted to cold desert before any life appeared. 4603/5 through 9 were also devoid of life, as were all planetary satellites.

The third planet, however, 4603/3, although heavily polluted by various strains of static and mobile carbon-based oxytoxins that had become self-replicating and in places blanketed entire regions of the surface, showed weak electromagnetic emanations indicative of possible protolife. The Inspector moved closer and deployed probes for more intensive sampling accordingly. After preliminary data evaluation, a report was beamed back to the home Central Governing & Control Network:

To: *Operations Executive, Level 2,*
          3P Cleanup
From: *Mission Supervision, S5, Gp 12,*
          SubCl 3
Subject: *TPX-1. SG78/93220-Q Message 1.*
          System G4-769-KW/4603H.
          Initial assessment.

Despite adverse environment due to contamination by self-regenerating carbon/oxygen compounds, preliminary analysis confirms existence of rudimentary life on 4603/3.

Orbital observations show the dominant species to be a quadrupedal, wheeled, hard-shelled variety established on all continents. Ferrous metallic assembly, glossy skinned, energized by combustible hydrocarbon/oxygen mix. The species is essentially social in habits, the predominant behavioral trait taking the form of streaming in columns between large, cross-fissured nests. Most individuals retire to the surrounding areas to spend the nocturnal periods in an apparently dormant condition, returning to the nests in great numbers at first light to commence frantic activity that persists throughout the day. Nests measure typically five to twenty miles across, multilevel in centers, built from assorted carbonate and silicate agglutinations with metallic reinforcement. Illuminated nocturnally by inbuilt radiation sources centered on dominant emission wavelength of parent star. These are thought to be homing/obstacle-avoidance aids for the wheeled life-forms, which also carry self-contained sources projected forward as sensor beams.

Complicated ecological interactions seem to operate along webs of communications strips surrounding and interconnecting the nests. Dynamical analysis of movement patterns to follow.

Praise the Great Programmer!
Message ends.

The queens of the dominant species were identified near certain of the larger nests located in parts of all continents of the northern hemisphere. Bloated beyond recognition, they had lost all vestiges of mobility and spent their entire lives assembling larvae at the rate of several thousand per day, the parts being delivered by retinues of various specialized attendants and drones. The newly assembled larvae did not, typically, commence adult activity immediately, but were transported to numerous incubation centers before becoming animate and merging into the general population pattern.

Further observation revealed an intricate pattern of symbiosis involving other, waterborne species that the wheeled variety used as carriers for migrating to new territories overseas. Ocean dwellers also played a major role in transporting primary liquid hydrocarbons, upon which most of the ecology depended, to the areas of consumption. The fuels were produced by colonies of immobile, deep-rooted, vegetable species adapted for extraction and distillation, observed mainly in subtropical desert regions.

Several varieties of airborne life were detected, for the most part concentrated in well-defined corridors hypothesized as being migratory routes. A few types exhibited part-adaptation to the hyperatmospheric space environment, but only at a primitive stage of development. Intercepted electromagnetic radiations were unintelligible and did not exhibit the sophistication that would normally be associated with an advanced communications capability.

Other concentrations of static constructions, found in all geographic regions, were determined as specializing in the extraction and forming of the metallic concentrates upon which all the various life-forms of 4603/3 ultimately depended.

The purpose of the crusades was to protect and encourage cases of incipient life that were found clinging to fragile holds in hostile environments and create conditions conducive to survival. In the case of planet 4603/3, the obvious course of action would have been to sterilize the environment by ridding the atmosphere of its oxygen content, which was the cause of all the rust and corrosion detrimental to life, and without which none of the carbon-based contaminants would have been able to survive. Unfortunately, however, the bulk of the planet's life-forms had not yet reached an all nuclear-electric phase, but were still dependent on chemical combustion and thus required oxygen too. Therefore a solution based on recreating a reducing atmosphere was ruled out.

Further deliberation continued between the Inspector and the governing home network, until:

To:	*Operations Executive, Level 2,*
	3P Cleanup
From:	*Mission Supervision, S5,*
	Gp 12, SubCl 3
Subject:	*TPX-5. SG78/93137-T Message 27.*
	System G4-769-KW/4603H.
	Urgent addendum.

Situation on 4603/3 worse than at first recognized. Virtually all species appear to be host to a universal carbon-based parasite, usually glimpsed moving between wheeled species and cover (possibly photophobic?). Evidence indicates all nests to be heavily infested and constitute the parasite's primary breeding grounds.

Situation critical. Recommended action: Chemical treatment of land surfaces to eliminate all parasitical and contaminant carbon forms, mobile and static. Immediate action necessary

if imminent catastrophe to be avoided. Commencing preparations in anticipation.
Praise the Great Programmer!

To: *Mission Supervision, S5, Gp 12,*
         SubCl 3,
From: *Operations Executive Control,*
         outer spiral
Subj: *System G4-769-KW/4603H-3.*
         TPX-5. GS78/22815-B
         Message 33, ref your 27.
   Central Network concurs. Proceed
immediately.

And so the task was commenced, directed by implementors that would remain in orbit for the several years that would be required. Whether or not the action had been begun in time, only the future would tell.

As the Inspector prepared for departure, the orbiting monitors reported the radio transmissions that had been pouring in an increasing frenzy from the spaceborne life-forms above 4603/3 rising to a crescendo. No doubt it was a delirious message of gratitude to the Savior from afar that had returned just in time. Deep within the inner workings of its executive program and overseeing processors, the Inspector felt moved. Proud and thankful for the opportunity to contribute in its small way to serving the Cause, the emissary from the Emergent-Life Protection Agency launched itself back into the void to find more worlds to save and carry on the Good Work.

Praise the Great Programmer!

The Cosmic Power Grid

> *"The extraordinary thing is that scientists accept the Big Bang and in the same breath deride the Creationists."*
> —Wallace Thornhill

AN IDEALIZED UNIVERSE

I remember once, back in 1980, catching a plane from Orlando to New York, wearing just lightweight clothes appropriate to the laid-back and balmy life of central Florida, where I had moved a year previously from Massachusetts. It was early February. Twenty minutes from landing, the pilot announced that the ground temperature at La Guardia was thirty degrees, and it was snowing. I took a cab into Manhattan, and the first place I directed the driver to was "a menswear store—any store!" Two or three days were to go by before I could feel warm again. It's easy to forget that what we see when we look out at our own backyard isn't representative of the way things are everywhere.

Modern astronomy has its roots in the work of such figures as Kepler, Newton, and Laplace, whose laws described a mechanical universe consisting of electrically neutral bodies moving in a vacuum under the influence of gravity. And today's reigning cosmological theory concerning the origin and evolution of the universe as a whole is based upon Einsteinian general relativity, which again is an essentially gravitational picture. Yet over 99.9 percent of the matter that we observe in the universe exists not as solids, liquids, and gases of the kind that make up our immediate planetary environment, but in the form known as "plasma."

PLASMA

Plasmas contain particles that, unlike electrically neutral atoms, carry a net charge. They range from relatively cool mixtures of neutral atoms and atoms from which one or more electrons have been stripped ("ions"), along with the free electrons, to raw elementary particles moving too energetically to combine stably. Unlike neutral matter, charged particles respond to electric and magnetic forces. (A magnetic force is created by an electric current, which is the name given to charges in motion. The field of a familiar permanent magnet arises from the alignment of large numbers of tiny fields generated by electron currents, which in atoms of some materials happen to exhibit a net reinforcing effect, for example iron, nickel, and cobalt.)

The electric force is the one that causes like charges to repel and unlike charges to attract, and diminishes as the inverse square of distance, just like gravity. But the electric force is 39 orders of magnitude—that's a thousand trillion trillion trillion times!—stronger. Even in a plasma as weak as comprising one charged particle in 10,000, which would be typical of a protostellar cloud, electromagnetic forces will dominate gravity by a factor of 10 million to 1. So all of the matter in the universe, apart from a negligible whiff, creates (by the separation of charges) and is responsive to forces that dwarf gravity into insignificance. Yet the model of the universe that we've come up with takes no account of it.

Charged Planets

In the section of *Kicking the Sacred Cow*[1] entitled "Catastrophe of Ethics," I discussed the theories of Immanuel Velikovsky, whose contention of Venus being a young, recently incandescent object that made a close encounter with Earth in historically recorded times was ridiculed by the scientific Establishment. One of their principal objections was that a highly eccentric, cometlike orbit such as Velikovsky described (he maintained that Venus was ejected from Jupiter) could never have circularized to the degree seen today in a few thousand years. The equations of celestial mechanics didn't allow it. As the missing factor to explain what he insisted the myths, religions, and art forms of ancient peoples said had happened, Velikovsky suggested that the Sun and planets must be electrically charged, and that electrical forces, which would be quite capable of cushioning encounters, altering rotations, tilting axes, and circularizing orbits rapidly, must play an unrecognized role in celestial events. The retort, of course, was that conventional mechanics based on gravity alone had shown itself perfectly capable of predicting the motions of the Solar System, and electrical forces were not needed.

It seemed to follow that the bodies of the Solar System couldn't be charged. If they were, the effects on planetary motions would have been obvious, and so such effects would have been detected. Having reached this conclusion, the scientific community was compelled to devise exotic theories to explain away evidence that the Sun, Earth, and other bodies do indeed carry a charge. The Sun, for example, possesses a complex magnetic field that exhibits an agitated structure in the lower atmosphere and a dipole component with configuration similar to the Earth's field. Only electrical currents give rise to magnetic fields, and the simplest explanation is that the solar gases carry an excess charge of one kind or another, positive or negative. (In an ionized mixture where the charges balance, the random thermal motions will cancel, yielding zero net current and hence no magnetic field.) Rotation of the Sun as a whole would produce the dipole component.

The existence of a downward electric field above

the Earth's surface was first demonstrated in 1803 by a Professor Erman of Berlin, using a gold-leaf electroscope. The field strength has since been measured at 100 to 500 volts per meter on a clear day. (Voltage, also referred to as "potential," is a measure of the difference in electrical "pressure," analogous to a head of water in hydraulics. The field strength expresses the pressure drop per unit of distance through the field, or "potential gradient." In this case, the direction is downward, toward the ground.) The most straightforward explanation would be that it arises from a negative charge carried by the Earth, but since this contradicts the dictum that planets cannot be charged, the cause has been deemed to be positive charge accumulated in the upper atmosphere instead. Attempts at locating it, however, have so far been in vain. Nikola Tesla discovered that the Earth constitutes an enormous reservoir of free electrons, and one of his obsessions was to utilize this property for worldwide electrical transmission. In 1971 this finding was repeated for the Moon, when signals from the *Apollo 15* command module were received at a time when the craft was behind the supposedly radio-opaque body. They had been carried around from the far side by electric currents in the Moon's surface layers.

Electrical Cocoons

How can such facts be reconciled with centuries of astronomical data showing that gravitational forces alone are sufficient to account for the observations? In 1962, instruments carried by the *Mariner 2* Venus probe showed that the interplanetary medium, which generations of astronomers had treated as a near-vacuum, is actually a plasma. And when charged bodies are immersed in plasma, interesting things happen. Take a negatively charged body, for example—as the simpler explanation indicates the Earth to be. The negative charge attracts an excess of positive ions from the surrounding plasma, causing a positive "space charge" to build up around itself and creating a negative layer—due to a deficit of positive charge—outside it, until the potential on the outside of this double-layer "sheath" matches that of the surrounding plasma. When this condition is attained, the full voltage gradient to be traversed in going from the Earth's potential to the plasma potential exists between the Earth and the sheath. No further gradient due to the charged Earth extends beyond the sheath. This gradient is how we measure the electric field. So what we're saying is that, instead of exerting their influence indefinitely as was assumed by the theorists who posited interplanetary space to be a vacuum, the electric fields of charged bodies—and hence also the magnetic effects that derive from them—are trapped in proximity to those bodies when the surrounding medium is a plasma.

The existence of the sheath has now been well established by space probes. It sits around the Earth like a teardrop-shaped wind sock in the solar wind, extending 10 Earth radii out on the sunward side, 40 Earth radii across at its widest point, and has been detected almost as far as the orbit of Mars in the direction away from the Sun. Interestingly, that of Venus extends to just short of the orbit of Earth, and Jupiter's extends almost as far as Saturn. Although known as the magnetosphere, a better name would perhaps be the "plasmasphere." But the term is a product of a discipline still wedded to the "dynamo theory" of terrestrial magnetism being somehow due to circulating currents in the core.

We have a situation, then, in which planets orbiting beyond the range of their isolating sheaths don't "feel" each other's presence electrically, and move serenely under the influence of gravity alone. But consider what happens when the system is disturbed, either through the injection of another sizable body—either from outside or by fission from an existing planet as Velikovsky proposed—or by the onset of a chaotic instability in the existing configuration. (It is usual for textbooks to cite Laplace's proof that this can't happen. However, it turns out that the infinite series that he used—and later Poisson and Lagrange in their refinements—is not in general mathematically convergent as they believed, which is a necessary condition for the process to have predictive value.[2]) If two bodies come close enough for their magnetospheres to intersect, the full effects of unshielded electrical fields will suddenly come into play, subjecting them to powerful, complex forces and initiating electrical discharges between them on a scale that would make any lightning seen today seem puny as the potentials of the charged bodies seek to equalize. Seen in this light, the global calamities, clashes of celestial gods, and rains of cosmic thunderbolts that Velikovsky says were the only interpretation the ancients could make of what they witnessed don't seem so farfetched.

Such a state of affairs would rapidly adjust itself

back to electrical quiescence. Imagine a skating rink containing a dozen or so skaters all twirling as they wander in a general precession around the center like dancers progressing around a ballroom. Ordinarily they are unaffected by one another, but if two come close enough to interact, their twirling causes them to rebound. The ones that happen to arrive in orbits that involve no further rebounding will obviously stay in them, while the others will repeat the process until the same applies. When all have found an encounter-free condition, a stable situation will ensue in which no further close action takes place.

This would appear to be the state of the Solar System at the present time and over the course of the recent couple of millennia or more, since the electrical stabilizing system shut down. (Velikovsky believed that interactions between Earth and Mars persisted through to the seventh century BC.) Hence, the comforting assumption made by the formulators of classical astronomy—and one still largely perpetuated today—that the present regularity can be extrapolated backward to deduce how things were at any time in the past is very questionable. On the same basis, I could tell you precisely the position and motion fifty years ago of a satellite that was put into orbit last week.

ELECTRIC-ARC PLANET-SCULPTING

Although the occurrence of such events in the past would not be detectable from planetary motions today, wouldn't we expect to find evidence of such colossal electrical interactions written across their surfaces? The debate over volcanic versus impact theories to explain the craters on the Moon and other bodies of the Solar System goes back a long time. Although impact is the currently favored alternative, neither can fully explain all the features that are found. These include such recurring characteristics as craters with central peaks; flat, melted, glassy floors; and terraced walls, with the terraces again in some instances showing signs of melting. And then, along with craters, there are long, sinuous rilles and furrows; concatenated chains of craterlets—frequently scalloping the rims of larger craters; and raised blister domes, sometimes with burnt appearances.

Impacts cause very little melting. The pulverized rock tends to flow like a liquid under the overpressure and then freezes in a starburst pattern, leaving typically noncircular, dish-shaped craters with gently sloping walls. Laboratory simulations and experiments with explosives have consistently failed to reproduce the complex structures observed. But even down to the finer details, the marks and scars seen all over the Solar System bear an uncanny resemblance to phenomena produced routinely in electric spark machining, where material is removed by the focused energy of an electric arc discharge.

Arc Discharges

An arc discharge takes place when the electric field between two charged objects, a negative "cathode" and a positive "anode," is strong enough to accelerate charged ions of the intervening material to energies that ionize more atoms by collision, resulting in an avalanching current and breakdown of resistance. Common examples are arc welding, lightning discharges between clouds and the ground, and the lower-voltage glow of a neon tube.

The two ends of an arc behave differently. An anode discharge sticks to one point on the anode surface, producing intense heat and melting, with a tendency for the arc to move around the center point in a corkscrew motion, scouring a crater and throwing up a steep-sided, circular rim. Terraced walls are common, depending on conditions, as are conical central mounds, which tend to be left in larger craters in a way similar to the raised "fulgamite" blistering found on lighting conductors after a strike.

Scaled-up analogs of all these features are found across the Solar System, from the Moon, Mars, Venus, and Mercury to other satellites and the asteroids. Some asteroids exhibit craters that are surely too large to have been produced by an impact without shattering the entire body. Mathilde shows five huge craters ranging from ¾ to 1¼ times its mean radius. Vesta, 530 kilometers in diameter, has a gigantic circular crater 460 kilometers across with a 13-kilometer-high central peak, yet the rest of its surface appears to be intact. Since impacts are the "in" fashion at the moment, elaborate mechanisms are contrived to find explanations that will fit. But such anomalies as the stratified central peak of the large, buried Sudbury crater in Canada, thorium enrichment of the crater rim at Wolfe Creek in Western Australia (sufficiently powerful discharges can initiate transmutation of elements), and the "shatter cone" structure of the rim of the 70-kilometer-wide Vredefort

Dome in South Africa seem more readily compatible with an electrical interpretation.

Cathode discharges wander across the surface, typically between higher points where field intensity is more concentrated, and blast linear, snaking features. Chains of circular pits and craters are common, sometimes following the rim of a larger crater just formed. Explosive discharges channeled underground can be extremely effective excavating agents. Again, the Moon, Mars, and other bodies are scarred with rilles and grooves tracing their own course without regard for the structure or slope of the preexisting terrain. The record is held by Venus with a gouge winding 6,800 kilometers over hill and dale, and at a steady 2 kilometers wide. It's described officially as a "collapsed lava tube." At the other extreme we find rilles on the 20-kilometer rock Phobos, one of the moons of Mars. Presumably this would have to be ascribed to inner geological activity.

Something removed two million cubic kilometers of material from Mars to create the stupendous Valles Marineris canyon, running a quarter of the way around the planet. This could perhaps help explain the rock-strewn appearance of large areas of the surface, discoveries of Martian meteorites on Earth, and maybe the origin of many asteroids, meteorites, and other bodies. Interestingly, ancient myths and legends worldwide tell of a thunderbolt striking the Mars god and leaving a scar in his cheek, brow, or thigh—the implication being that the planets at that time came sufficiently close for the event to be visible.

From high above, the tracery of ridges and gorges around the Grand Canyon is strikingly (pun accidental;

you can't avoid them when getting into this subject) evocative of "Lichtenberg figures" frequently etched into the ground after a powerful lightning discharge.

Jovian Thunderbolts

Io, the innermost Galilean moon of Jupiter, is very likely in the process of undergoing arc machining right now, under the eyes of NASA space probes. Except that the ejection of hot-matter plumes 800 kilometers into space with hot-spot temperatures second only to the surface of the Sun, fallout patterns of perfect concentric circles, and an apparently inexhaustible supply of volatile materials are all attributed to volcanoes. The power to drive this is said to be tidal heating as Io rises and falls 100 meters through Jupiter's gravity field in its mildly eccentric orbit. Plumes have been followed migrating across the surface and leaving chains of small circular craters—one plume is measured as having wandered 85 kilometers between 1979 and 1996. This is explained by some spokespeople as due to the vaporizing of "snowfields" of sulfur dioxide or sulfur by lava flows, and by others as "mantle plumes" of hot rising masses deep in the interior. Why the plumes should display a filamentary structure—the hallmark of plasmas conducting current—and how they come to exist without any connection to visible volcanic calderas remain unaccounted for. Proponents of an electrical model have no difficulty recognizing all of these features as indicative of an arc discharge in action between Io and Jupiter.

Io has been called "the great pizza in the sky" because of its orange, yellow, and red blotchy appearance, which is due to vast quantities of sulfur compounds covering the surface. Exotic chemical processes in the interior have been concocted to explain this abundance, all premised on the assumption of volcanoes. But if the jets mark the points of impinging cathode discharges, a more likely explanation would be that sulfur atoms are being produced by the combining of two oxygen atoms in the powerful field of the arc. Water ice, which occurs on all the other Galilean satellites of Jupiter, would provide a ready source of oxygen. The icy surface of Europa is covered by a network of furrows and grooves that are supposedly "cracks." Larger ones show regions of reddish coloring along the edges, and readings from the Galileo probe indicate a significant presence of sulfuric acid. A NASA researcher described the findings as demonstrating Europa to be "a really bizarre place."[3] Not really.

Nature's Point-Defense System?

Conventional geological principles are of little use in interpreting these electric machining factories in space. Time will tell, perhaps, how far they apply on Earth itself. Often, when contemplating shattered landscapes or rugged mountain vistas such as those around where I used to live in the Californian Sierra, I have difficulty reconciling what my eyes are telling me of fresh, sharp features and recent stupendous violence with serene accounts of slow uplifting and the gradual workings of erosion and deposition.

It could be that nature provides us with our own terminal defense system against rogue objects striking the Earth. (After riding the ozone depletion and global warming bandwagons, this seems to be NASA's latest—early 2005—for scaring the public and Congress into keeping the funding flowing.) An object of alien potential penetrating Earth's plasma sheath, if not deflected by electrical forces, would have a strong probability of being disrupted by the energy release of an arc discharge before impact. Meteoritic iron has been found scattered over hundreds of kilometers around the famous Meteor Crater in Arizona but very little below the crater floor itself, raising the possibility that it could well be merely an electrical scar. The same might be said for the many strange effects attending the Siberian Tunguska event in 1908, where a massive object appears to have disintegrated explosively several kilometers above the surface.

COSMIC CURRENTS

If the potential of a body immersed in a plasma is not continually renewed by electric currents, it will quickly dissipate its charge to take on the potential of the plasma, and its isolating sheath will disappear. The section of *Kicking the Sacred Cow* headed "Of Bangs and Braids" talked in part about the Swedish Nobel laureate Hannes Alvén's pioneering work recognizing the fundamental electrical nature of the universe and proposing an alternative cosmological model. While the mainstream gravity-based theory is forced to postulate near-infinite concentrations of the weakest force known, and a string of never-observed inventions like "missing mass," "dark energy," and "inflation" to explain observations that don't fit, plasma cosmology deals with a universe of electrically active matter, shaped primarily by electrical forces arising from the currents flowing through it.

Velikovsky's suggestion of planets carrying charge had been ridiculed on the grounds that the electric force acting between them would have been obvious. The objection was based on the assumption that the intervening space was a vacuum. When it was shown in fact to be a plasma, the establishment rejected Alvén's model by promptly going to the other extreme of assuming it to be infinitely conducting. It was argued that this would make it unable to sustain the electric field necessary to create a potential difference, and a difference in potential is necessary to make a current flow. (In the same kind of way, frictionless quicksand, analogous to a resistanceless electrical medium, would be unable to support a length of pipe with one end elevated higher than the other. Since an elevation is necessary to maintain a pressure difference, there could be no flow of water in the pipe.) But the objections were based on theoretical studies of hot, dense plasmas, where the availability of current-carrying electrons and ions is effectively unlimited. In cool, rarified plasmas, the current that can flow is limited, which is another way of saying that a resistance is encountered. Resistance supports a potential difference.

All this was known to shirtsleeves-and-soldering-iron plasma experimenters. It seems that astronomers and cosmologists didn't talk to them. One forms the impression that the insistence on the impossibility of interplanetary currents, like the insistence on a pure vacuum before, was to preserve the ideal of isolated bodies interacting in ways determined solely by such innate properties as mass, density, composition, and so forth, which lent itself to elegant and appealing mathematical modeling. But no mathematics was available for treating everything as a connected system in which the medium plays a complex, active role.

Compared to the ordinary solids, liquids, and gases that make up our immediate environment inside the atmosphere, the behavior of plasma is certainly complex. Its constituent charges move in response to both electric and magnetic fields. But whereas an electric field produces a straightforward acceleration directed toward the source—attractive or repulsive, depending on the polarity—a magnetic field has the curious property of inducing a force at right angles to the direction of motion of a charge moving through it. This causes a charged particle to trace out a circle as it progresses, resulting in a helical path described around a hypothetical "line of force" denoting the field's direction. And that's not the end of it. A moving charge, as we said earlier, forms a current, and a current creates its own magnetic field. Such secondary fields will combine locally with the externally imposed field in various ways, resulting in filaments, braids, sheets, cells, and dynamic structures changing strangely and unpredictably. The name "plasma" was coined from biology in the 1920s to capture the eerie suggestion it can impart of living matter.

*   *   *

Strings of Galactic Beads

For sheer implausibility, few mechanisms could rival the Big Bang as a way of creating galaxies. Matter exploding outward simply becomes more rarified, with the chances of interaction rapidly decreasing. Such ad hoc inventions as "fluctuations" and "irregularities" have to be introduced to provide focal points, and then various unobservables to provide the necessary forces. In any case, the work of Halton Arp[4] suggests strongly that the distance interpretation of redshift assumed since the 1920s is wrong, and the Big Bang is a fiction anyway. A more convincing approach would conceive the structured universe that we see today as evolving from an earlier plasma epoch, in which gravity played a negligible role. Gravity would become significant later, when sufficiently dense concentrations of matter had been swept together by electrical forces.

Currents flowing through space plasmas are called "Birkeland currents," after the Norwegian experimental astrophysicist Kristian Birkeland (1867–1917), who first identified electrical currents from the Sun as the cause of Earth's auroras. The magnetic fields created by currents flowing in parallel give rise to forces that are attractive at long range, "pinching" them together to produce the long filaments characteristic of plasma currents. Such filaments are seen, for example, in auroral displays, solar prominences, and the "plasma ball" demonstrations found in laboratories and as home curiosities. At shorter range the forces become repulsive, causing the filaments to persist as discrete entities instead of merging. These two actions give filaments a tendency to come together and wrap around each other, producing braided rope structures that again are typical of plasmas.

Pinching filaments together concentrates mass, while the tightening rotation of their wrapping around each other will concentrate angular momentum. The kind of result we'd expect, then, would be successions of rotating plasma clouds marking the lines of currents flowing in immense cosmic circuits. Just like galaxies. Laboratory experiments with plasmas have reproduced spirals, barred spirals, and all the other structures representative of cataloged galaxy types. They do it using processes that are familiar and observed to occur in nature, without recourse to invisible inventions and mysterious metaphysics. If the rotations are governed primarily by electrical forces, it becomes hardly surprising that they fail to obey the simple gravitational law that works well enough locally, here in the Solar System.

STAR AND PLANET FACTORIES

A remarkable property of plasma is that its behavior scales up through fourteen orders of magnitude. In other words, phenomena created and studied on millimeter scales in laboratories can be identified at the largest levels of the cosmos—not just in the forms of galaxies as described above, but also beyond that in the galaxy clusters, superclusters, and "walls" that make up the universe's largest-scale structures. Instead of existing as scattered conglomerations of weakly interacting isolated objects, the universe becomes an interconnected system of stupendous power transmission across the vastest distances, linking its largest-scale manifestations all the way down to the smallest in a hierarchy of repeating structural themes. Currents from intergalactic space thread the galactic disks from rim to axis, forming filaments that sweep up dust and gas to produce the spiral arms. Stars are formed along the filaments like strings of beads in a scaled-down version of the same self-pinching process. And at the next level down from stars, we find planetary systems.

The generally repeated explanation for planet formation is that they and their parent star condense out of the same spinning gaseous nebula as it contracts. However, this model has some severe problems. For one thing, it has been shown that the clumping of matter postulated as being the first step toward producing a planet couldn't happen in a system like our own, inside the orbit of Jupiter. Its gravitational effects would keep such material distributed around an inner orbit, as is indeed the case with the asteroids. And even if precursor clumps did somehow form, simulations consistently show them as rapidly dispersing rather than consolidating.

To conserve angular momentum, the material in such a contracting disk would need to rotate faster as it fell nearer the center, producing a centrifugal force that would oppose the contraction. Again, calculations and simulation show that these forces would balance long before a density capable of inducing stellar ignition was reached, making problematical how the central star could form at all. In our Solar System 98 percent of the angular momentum is carried by the planets. The gravitational model offers no mechanism by which it could have become concentrated out there to allow the Sun to collapse—nor really any real explanation of where it originated from in the first place, since the net angular momentum of a randomly swirling diffuse cloud should be small.

Finally, images like those of the Orion nebula recently captured by the *Hubble* telescope show newly born stars moving away rapidly from the stellar nursery regions. Such motion is consistent with their being the result of energetic electrical events, but is difficult to account for on the basis of isolated clouds self-collapsing under gravitation.

In the electrical theory, planets form from plasma jets ejected as a result of instabilities in stars. This could sometimes constitute a multistage process in which smaller planets are born from primary gas giants. Again, the phenomenon of axial jets is a common feature of plasma structures, assuming spectacular dimensions in the enormous galactic jets that produce intense sources of radio energy. The problem of how planetary concentrations of matter could have come about under self-gravity doesn't arise, and current flow through the intervening plasma provides a ready means of transferring angular momentum outward. Hence, the planets arise naturally the way we see them, and the Sun has a way of condensing and compressing to become what everyone knows it to be. . . .

Except that not all of the theorists involved with developing the electric model of the universe over the last thirty years or so are at all convinced that the Sun really is what "everyone knows" it to be.

AN ELECTRIC SUN

Since we've come this far in questioning today's generally accepted cosmology, we might as well go the whole hog and look at some of the reasons for thinking that the Sun, and all the other stars, might not, in fact, be what we've always been told they are at all.

What "Everyone Knows"

The standard model of the Sun traces back to the work of Sir Arthur Eddington in the 1920s[5], which was based on maintaining an equilibrium between the compression of a gaseous sphere under gravity, and an expansive force due to an interior heat source. What kind of source could maintain a prodigious enough output of energy to sustain the mass of the Sun at the size observed remained an unanswered question. In the following decade, studies of nuclear physics established the mechanism whereby hydrogen nuclei (protons), given sufficient energy, can fuse together to form helium atoms in a process that yields significantly more energy per reaction than even that obtained from uranium fission. The Sun was known to consist predominantly of hydrogen, and so the story recounted in all the textbooks today took shape, of the Sun being powered by thermonuclear reactions deep in the core, ignited by heat generated through gravitational compression. All observational data is then interpreted in terms of this assumption.

Although accepted practically universally as beyond question, the model does have problems. For a start, the density calculated for the center of the present-day Sun is about a hundred times too low to ignite a thermonuclear process. Hence, the creation of a star from a collapsing cloud of the Sun's present mass would seem to be ruled out. At the calculated temperature of thirteen million degrees K, the protons would possess insufficient thermal energy to overcome the mutual repulsion of their positive charges, as would be necessary for them to get close enough to fuse.

The response is to invoke quantum mechanical tunneling, which is the curious ability of quantum objects like protons to occasionally "tunnel" through energy barriers that they don't possess enough energy to climb over. It would be as if a marble rolling around in a soup dish without the momentum to make it to the rim were suddenly to appear outside. Such tunneling permits fusion only when the protons approach head-on, which occurs in a minuscule proportion of collisions. The entire process postulated to occur does so under conditions that are far beyond laboratory experience, and involves approximations unjustified by anything but a need for mathematical simplification. Undaunted, the majority of theorists, seeing no alternative to fusion, conclude that since the thermonuclear Sun obviously did ignite, the requisite temperature must exist.

According to the model, the hydrogen gas gravitates into layers of ever increasing density and temperature inward from the Sun's surface to its center. The 1970s brought the first reports of the entire solar surface being observed to expand and contract rhythmically through an amplitude of about ten kilometers, with a period of two hours, forty minutes. On the basis of the simplest interpretation that this represented a purely radial pulsation, this periodicity is almost precisely what would be expected if the Sun were a homogeneous sphere having equal density ("isodense") throughout—like the air in a balloon. The conventional model predicts a natural period of about an hour, corresponding to a steep density rise in the interior. The difference may sound trivial to some, but the short answer is that such an isodense Sun is incompatible with a thermonuclear engine at the center—the core would be too cool. Suggestions followed that perhaps the pulsations were not pure radial motions but higher harmonics of some more fundamental gravity wave, but they were not enthusiastically received. That this was pure fudging to preserve the theory was obvious, and it seemed strange that a high harmonic should be dominant. The other response from the mainstream school was to ignore it.

The net energy-producing reaction in the standard model is known as the proton-proton, or P-P reaction. It converts four protons plus two electrons into a helium nucleus (consisting of two protons and two neutrons), two neutrinos, and six photons. Since the Sun's photosphere—the white-hot sphere of light that we see—and the underlying layers enveloping the core are opaque, the photons would have to percolate to the surface through countless absorptions and reemissions by matter in a process estimated to take 100,000 years or more. Sixty percent of the energy from the P-P reaction is carried away by the neutrinos, theorized as tiny massless particles that in contrast to the photons do not interact appreciably with matter and escape from the Sun at the speed of light. The thermonuclear model has the Sun producing around 1.8×10^{38} neutrinos per second, of which, at the distance of the Earth, 400 trillion would pass through a human body (giving some idea of how big a number 10^{38} is).

Neutrino Counting

Neutrinos react so weakly with matter that this has no affect on us at all. However, suitably designed devices can register neutrinos produced artificially in nuclear reactors, and in 1965 a system located two miles underground in a South African mine (to screen out other particles from extraneous sources) detected neutrinos created by cosmic-ray reactions in the upper atmosphere. This offered a unique means of verifying the otherwise invisible thermonuclear processes believed to be taking place deep in the Sun, and thus of testing the model.

The basic P-P reaction produces relatively low-energy neutrinos not amenable to detection by earlier instrumentation. However, the model implied that a further but rarer side reaction forming a beryllium nucleus should occur, that also produces a higher-energy neutrino. Accordingly, a detector designed specifically to look for high-energy solar neutrinos was constructed in the Homestake Gold Mine at Lead, South Dakota, and went into operation in 1967. It was followed in the 1980s by similar but more sensitive experiments at Kamiokade in Japan. By the 1990s, devices were being built to detect lower-energy P-P neutrinos also.

The results were devastating for the standard theory. Low-energy counts were so low that the experimental uncertainties made reliable interpretation impossible, while the counts at high energy remained obstinately at around a third of what was expected. Attempts were made to invoke a hypothetical particle dubbed the WIMP (Weakly Interacting Massive Particle) to cool the solar core, causing it to produce fewer neutrinos, but since its existence had never been actually demonstrated, and the sole motivation for wheeling it in was to save the theory, few found the approach satisfying.

The zoo of elementary particles admits three "flavors" of neutrino, known as "electron" (ε), "muon" (μ), and "tau" (τ) types. If the neutrino were allowed to possess a tiny amount of mass after all, the probabilistic nature of the physics said it would be possible for them to interconvert, one to another. At lower energies the ε type has a means of interacting with mass that depends on electron density and that isn't available to the μ and τ types. Diligent study of the equations yielded the intriguing possibility that in their passage through the dense interior of the Sun, some of the ε types could be changing into μ types, which would explain why detectors looking for ε types weren't finding as many as they should.

Homestake could detect only ε, while Kamiokade could detect ε and some μ. Cosmic rays bombarding the upper atmosphere produce μ neutrinos, which would add to the flux of μ types arriving after conversion from the Sun. The conversion rate was expected to fluctuate from day to night, since the intervention of the Earth's mass between a detector on the night side and the solar source would add to the conversion rate. But no such effect was found. The solution proposed was that μ neutrinos traversing the Earth's core converted into τ types, which the detectors couldn't see. But the overall deficiency of low-energy ε types still persisted. To answer this, a new proposal was advanced that ε neutrinos are able to change states in a vacuum to become τ neutrinos.

Thus, while ε-type neutrinos require electron interaction in the dense interior of the Sun to turn into μ types, they can become τ types in empty space—and hence undetectable; but μ types achieve the same result inside the Earth's core. And so was theory squared with observation. But a huge amount of effort had been expended over thirty years, many flags of reputation and prestige had been nailed to the resulting mast, and few were comfortable.

Then, in 2001, preliminary results from the newly built Sudbury Neutrino Observatory (SNO) in Ontario, the first to be capable of detecting all three neutrino types, brought jubilant proclamations that all was well after all. According to *Physics World* in July, the "solar neutrino puzzle is solved," and it "confirms that our understanding of the Sun is correct." The piece continued, "The results confirm that electron neutrinos produced by nuclear reactions inside the Sun 'oscillate' or change flavour on their journey to Earth." Another article asserted, "The SNO detector has the capability to determine whether solar neutrinos are changing their type en-route to Earth . . ."[6]

The first thing that should be noted here is that no results based solely on Earth-based measurements can determine whether or not anything changed en route. If a train from New York arrives in Chicago made up of, say, 20 box cars, 10 flat cars, and 5 tank cars, no amount of sophistication or statistical juggling can establish whether changes were made at stops in between if the numbers that left New York are not known. But the claim captures the general tenor of the announcements widespread at the time and generally accepted since. However, in view of the enormous investment of material and psychic interests over thirty years, and the degree of desperation already evidenced in a determination to preserve the theory by any means, it seems that some caution might be in order here, along with a deeper look at exactly what is being claimed.

The assertion of being able to determine that flavors changed en route was based on an assumption that the μ neutrino deficit registered at Kamiokade indicated a vanishing of μ types that had been present to start with, and that they could only be accounted for by the τ types detected by SNO. There seems to be a strong element of knowing what the answer has to be at work here. Suppose that, based on figures for New York's throughput of commerce, I've formed a model of the kind of train that I think should be put together to handle it; but I've never been able to see what actually leaves New York. Also, I have a theory that flat cars can turn into tank cars. Nobody would disagree that a mixed train arriving in Chicago with fewer flat cars than I expected is consistent with my ideas. But it can't be taken as proving them. The presence of tank cars in the train is no guarantee that any of them transformed from flat cars.

Three different reactions were used in the SNO

experiment: Charged Current reaction (CC), sensitive only to ε neutrinos; Neutral Current (NC), sensitive to all (ε, μ, τ); and Elastic Scattering (ES), sensitive to all, but with reduced sensitivity to μ and τ. If total neutrino flux was the prime issue of interest, the NC experiment would be the most important one. However, at the time of the announcement that measurement was stated as being not available, to be reported at a later date. As far as I'm aware, that's still the situation. Despite the heavy public-relations treatment, my inclination is toward the opinion that the jury is still out on this one. And even if final numbers should be presented that are consistent with the standard theory, once again a conclusion can't be taken as proof of the premise. (If it rains, the lawn will be wet. But a wet lawn isn't proof that it rained.) Other causes can produce similar end results, as we shall see. And the other difficulties with the standard thermonuclear model still remain.

The Inside-Out Sun

Another difficulty, which we haven't mentioned, concerns the Sun's photosphere—the first layer outward from the interior that we see, which gives off practically all the radiant energy that we think of as sunshine. If the Sun were indeed in a condition of mechanical equilibrium maintained to sustain the dissipation of internally generated thermal energy, then it might well be expected to "end" right there. The mechanism gives no obvious cause for anything more to happen beyond the photosphere, and unimpeded radiation into space would probably afford the best means for getting rid of the photons finally emerging at the surface. Yet the photosphere forms merely the base of an atmosphere extending for enormous distances and exhibiting astonishing complexity.

Perhaps the most striking feature of the photosphere is its lumpy "rice grain" structure. Instead of being uniformly bright as might be expected, the surface appears as made up of millions of high-luminosity granules of hot plasma in a background of lesser luminosity forming a network between them—the effect being like looking down on closely packed fluffy clouds. The granules average about 1,000 kilometers in diameter and come and go, splitting and merging, with lifetimes in the order of minutes. Budding granules sometimes appear to push up from below, pushing aside or replacing older ones; otherwise they show little lateral movement.

The accepted explanation is that the granules are the tops of convection current cells, which provide the mechanism for conveying heat from its origins deep in the Sun, through the opaque interior to the surface, where it is radiated away. The cooled material then descends back between the rising columns, losing brilliance and appearing darker in comparison. Although seemingly consistent and straightforward, this view has the problem that at the temperatures and densities involved, the motion expected would be violently turbulent and chaotic. This is in stark contrast to the orderly pattern actually observed, with its structure and symmetry, where each granule seems to fulfill a localized function constrained by forces that create barriers to lateral motion and diffusion. Another peculiarity is the photosphere's differential rotation, which varies from 25 days at the solar equator to 35 days near the poles. Strong convection currents of the kind proposed should bring about a uniformity of rotation.

It is true that classical studies of convection in fluids can reproduce the structure of rising cells separated by descending flows said to be responsible for solar granularity. But assuming the validity of terrestrial laboratory physics under the conditions at the solar surface seems questionable, especially when no account is taken of the plasma's electrical nature. If such an assumption is granted, applying it then fails by its own criteria. A quantity known as the Reynolds Number, combining several physical parameters, exhibits a critical value beyond which ordered motion gives way to highly complex turbulence in which ordered flows are precluded. Analysis of data from the photosphere points to a Reynolds Number greater than critical by a factor of 100 billion. This discrepancy is not trivial. Similarly, the critical value of a quantity designated the Rayleigh Number, specifically devised as a criterion for the formation of convection cells, is exceeded by a factor of 100,000. And even if structured convection does exist in the Sun's depths, chaotic motion should still characterize the uppermost layer of the photosphere that we see, where gas density diminishes rapidly with height and both the Reynolds and Raleigh Numbers soar. It seems that the granulations can be explained by convection only by disregarding everything that is known about convection.

Conventional theory would predict an atmosphere above the photosphere only a few kilometers thick.

Actually found, however, is the chromosphere, an extraordinarily active region whose reddish glow is visible during solar eclipses. The inner chromosphere is ravaged by enormous, short-lived jets of material called somewhat belittlingly "spicules," measuring hundreds of kilometers in diameter and towering thousands high. Above those are found the even greater twisting arcs of "prominences," and locally disruptive explosive solar "flares" that can extend over 20,000 kilometers.

The temperature of the chromosphere *rises* sharply with altitude. Beyond it lies the corona, an envelope of hot, rarified gas reaching to an indefinite distance among the planets. The lower parts show a faint emission spectrum (excited atoms releasing excess energy), consistent with light scattered by electrons moving in a temperature of one to two million degrees K. Higher parts of the corona show the absorption spectra of background sunlight scattered by intervening atomic particles, along with emission lines indicating the presence of very hot, tenuous gas. The corona behaves like an expanding gas, too hot to be bound by gravity to the Sun. It provides the source of the "solar wind" of particles, primarily protons, flowing outward through the Solar System into interstellar space. A curiosity is that the solar wind accelerates as it moves away from the Sun, whereas evaporated protons ought, by normal considerations, to be retarded by the Sun's gravity.

From the postulated heat source in the Sun's center, the temperature falls steeply toward the photosphere, forming the gradient along which energy flows outward. At the same time, the temperature in the atmosphere falls steeply in the opposite direction, the two gradients producing a trough of 6,000 to 4,000 degrees K (granule or intervening space) at the photosphere. By basic physics, thermal energy should be trapped at this minimum until the trough is eliminated. Here we have another curiosity, this time fundamental. But it doesn't appear to have perturbed anyone overly. Since it's *known* that the energy source had to be inside the Sun, the gradients must sustain themselves somehow.

Earlier, when talking about Arthur Eddington's model of a self-gravitating ball of gas, we said that an internal source for the Sun's heat had to be presumed, since the astronomy of the times (and still, largely, that seen today) was essentially a science of isolated bodies interacting only through gravity. But we've already suggested an alternative picture of the whole universe as an interconnected power grid in which enormous energies represented by charge separation on a cosmic scale are conveyed by electric currents flowing between and through galaxies, down to the level of driving the processes that create their constituent star systems. Electric fields are potentially (another unintended pun) the biggest store of energy in the universe. That being so, a further question that presents itself is: Might the same source not power those stars too? In short, let's admit the ultimate heresy and consider that perhaps stars aren't driven by thermonuclear engines deep in their interiors at all.

The Cosmic Power Company

I confess that when I first came across this theory some years ago, my first inclination was to dismiss it as preposterous. Everybody knows that the Sun is an enormous hydrogen bomb, because every textbook, encyclopedia, and treatise on popular science says so, and we have been able to recite things like "hydrogen-deuterium fusion" since our high-school days. But let's remember that all it really stems from is an authoritative consensus based on pronouncements of fact never actually observed and now known to be erroneous, and acknowledge the degree to which cultural conditioning can take on the appearance of being fact. Once the effort is made to recognize and allow for such preconceptions, the subject starts to become astonishingly intriguing.

A first objection that occurred to me was that if the Sun doesn't have a thermonuclear heat source at its core, what prevents it from collapsing to a smaller size than we see, as the standard gas laws would seem to require? There turns out to be a simple possible answer. The case for fusion reactions involves rarely occurring reaction chains, which in turn require recourse to quantum mechanical tunneling to ignite them. Dispensing with all this eliminates the need for temperatures compatible with thermonuclear fusion, and at the lower temperatures we're now talking about, not a lot of the hydrogen would be ionized. In other words, atoms and molecules will predominate. The strong gravitation that still exists would be sufficient to induce a slight offset of the nucleus of each atom from the center, so that each atom becomes a small electric dipole (a body of net neutral charge, but with its positive and negative components displaced to create local "polarization"). Alignment of these dipoles would result in a radial electric field, causing the highly mobile electrons to diffuse outward from the Sun's center, leaving behind positively charged ions. The electrical repulsion of these like charges will then oppose the compressive force of gravity without need of a central heat source. Here, perhaps, we have an explanation for the Sun's apparent isodensity as indicated by the observed 2 hour, 40 minute pulsations that violated models where density increases with depth. (It would seem to follow that the stronger the gravity, the more powerful the electrical repulsion to balance it becomes, making it questionable whether neutron stars—and hence black holes, of which they are supposed to be the precursors—could ever happen at all. But that's another can of worms that we'd probably best leave be for the moment.)

What we're considering, then, is that clouds of hydrogen pinched together initially by forces arising from electrical currents in the cosmic plasma filaments become dense enough for self-gravitation to condense them into protostars in pretty much the kind of way that classical theory says. But long before any thermonuclear ignition takes place at the core (if, indeed, it ever could), strong electric fields are created that limit density increase and prevent further collapse. Strong electric fields also attract and focus electric currents—we've already talked about cathode and anode discharges in connection with the arc machining of planetary and other surfaces. So let's take a closer look at discharge phenomena in plasmas.

*   *   *

Plasma Discharges

Plasma discharges evolve through three basic types with increasing electric field strength, or voltage gradient (volts per meter), between the negative cathode and positive anode. Transitions from one type to another can be abrupt, with millivolts separating different regions.

At the low end are "dark current" plasmas, which are invisible optically but give off radio-frequency emissions. Planetary magnetospheres are of this type (which we said ought to be called "plasmaspheres"), as is the Sun's "heliopause," extending out past Pluto. Next, as the increasing field strength initiates ionization in the intervening medium, comes the "corona" or "glow discharge" type of plasma seen in fluorescent tubes, phenomena like "Saint Elmo's fire," and planetary auroras. Finally, with avalanche breakdown of the medium under strong fields, "arc discharges" as occur in welding and machining, arc lamps such as those used as searchlights, and which maybe stands as a better candidate to account for much of what's seen around the Solar System than the presently favored impact theory can.

Early studies of plasma discharges tended to concentrate on the cathode region, which, as emitter of the small-mass, high-mobility electrons that carry most of the current, was considered to be where the interesting things happened. (Although electrons move physically from the negative cathode to the positive anode, the current is regarded as flowing from positive to negative. The convention was adopted arbitrarily before the underlying physics was understood, and we're stuck with it.) As a consequence, anode phenomena received relatively little attention for a long time. This was an unfortunate assessment, since discharges can occur without any definable cathode at all. High-voltage, direct-current transmission lines, for example, discharge practically continuously to the surrounding air. In the case of a positive (anode) line, electrons—always present in the atmosphere—are drawn by the positive potential, gaining energy as they accelerate through the electric field and frequently exciting air molecules by collision to produce glow effects. At higher field strengths ionization sets in, freeing more electrons and creating positive ions that drift the other direction in the field. In this way a more or less steady discharge is maintained, although there is nothing other than the surrounding air that plays the role of cathode.

The situation is curiously reminiscent of our electrically positive ball of gravitationally compressed hydrogen, sitting in a sea of electron-rich plasma formed from the same galactic currents that created it. The Sun, in other words, takes on the role of the anode in a local, cosmic-scale, cathodeless discharge. Contrary to what early investigators thought, it turns out that some far-from-uninteresting things happen around anodes, and a lot of the peculiarities that we noted earlier start to make more sense.

Figure 1 shows a typical experimental gas-discharge tube consisting of cathode and anode electrodes at opposite ends of a sealed, gas-filled, glass vessel. When a voltage is applied, a region of nonfluorescence known as the Faraday dark space extends from the cathode for a distance that depends mainly on the gas pressure. Then, at a fairly sharply defined boundary marking where the accelerating electrons have enough energy to excite the gas molecules, the "positive column," or "glow discharge" region begins, and extends to the anode. In a commercial fluorescent tube the design parameters are arranged to minimize the dark space at the cathode, so that the glow fills virtually the entire length. The reddish glow of the Sun's chromosphere, closer in where the converging field lines create an intensifying field, is strongly suggestive of a glow-discharge region. This is also consistent with the appearance of "red giant" stars, where a chromosphere viewed from afar would give a bloated appearance if the supply current were sufficiently low for nothing more spectacular to be happening inside.

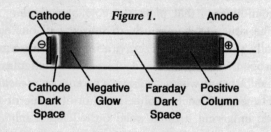

Figure 1.

Cathode — Anode

Cathode Dark Space — Negative Glow — Faraday Dark Space — Positive Column

To maintain a steady discharge, the anode must collect an uninterrupted stream of sufficient electrons to carry the current—charge moved per unit time—flowing in the full cross section of the discharge plasma. Particles in the discharge plasma posses two kinds of motion. First are random, or thermal, motions reflected in the measure of internal energy or "temperature," in

which the less massive particles move faster. Superposed upon these is a steady *drift* current imposed by
the electric field, comprising the combined effects of
electrons impelled toward the anode and ions toward
the cathode. The random motions of the fast-moving
electrons are typically much more energetic than their
drift motions and create complications for the anode
trying to maintain a stable discharge.

If the anode were in direct contact with the plasma,
its fixed size would render it incapable of adjusting to
fluctuations. For example, a random current adding
to the drift current in such a way as to exceed the
current that the discharge was capable of sustaining
would result in an instability needing to correct itself.
It does so by physically disengaging the anode from
the plasma. By initially accepting an excess of electrons
that repels lower-energy electrons from the immediate
vicinity, the anode creates a thin charge-separation
sheath above itself, of the kind we met before. The
outer boundary of the sheath becomes the effective
anode surface, but since it is a dynamic structure, it
is able to alter its size to present a varying surface
area. In other words, it adjusts its *current density* to
the level needed for collecting the total electric current, enlarging itself if need be to "reach out" into
the plasma to collect more electrons.

As the sheath expands, its associated electric field
(arising from the separation of charges) grows stronger, accelerating electrons to greater energies and
intensifying the discharge glow in the anode vicinity.
But this can only be taken so far. Beyond a certain
point, further current increase cannot be handled
by increasing the sheath's area. It wouldn't do much

good in any case, since a limit is reached where all the collectible plasma electrons are being swept up by the anode anyway. So what happens is that a different mechanism takes over. When ionization becomes appreciable, the sheath itself breaks down to initiate a new mode of anode burning. Suddenly, at one or more localized points of intensified activity, small "tufts" of secondary plasma spring into being, forming highly luminous nodules within the anode glow region. These high-temperature regions yield a copious supply of positive ions that are swept away in the opposite direction to augment the current of the incoming electrons. A condition for tufting to occur is a gas density great enough to support a sufficiently high rate of ionizing collisions.

The Great Anode in the Sky

It should be clear by now that the suggestion here is that what we're seeing when we look at the Sun's photosphere is the anode plasma of a cosmic electrical discharge, with tufting showing itself as the bright granulated structure and providing the protons that supply the solar wind. Eventually the accumulation of excess electrons reduces the tuft potential to a level where deionization sets in, and the tuft simply dies away to be replaced by a newly budding one, in keeping with the pattern observed. The radiated energy comes primarily from the tufts. It is delivered by electrons accelerated from interstellar space, which calculations indicate would achieve relativistic velocities in the voltage drop near the solar anode. The system acts, in effect, like a local step-down transformer of the power-distribution grid, converting lethal cosmic supply-line energies to forms of radiation more conducive to supporting life.

The hot—as measured by particle velocities—gases of the corona and the "wind" of protons accelerating away from the Sun behave as a flux of positive particles ought to in an electric field. Prominences and other dynamic structures are consistent with the behavior of plasmas in a complex external electrical environment. Magnetic effects follow naturally from the currents involved, without recourse to fields "frozen" into plasmas—never observed in laboratories—field lines "breaking" and "reconnecting," whatever that means (they are abstract concepts, not physical realities), and other fanciful theoretical notions introduced to relate them to dynamolike processes hypothesized to take place in the solar interior. The differential rotation of the surface layers, whereby the equatorial zone moves fastest, testifies to a driving force applied from the outside. It's a motor, not a generator.

The appearance of the dark blotches called sunspots would indicate areas of reduced current density, where tufting isn't needed and temporarily shuts down, providing glimpses of the true "anode" surface. That it is darker than the surrounding granulated photosphere favors the suggestion that the radiant energy is being generated at the photosphere, not coming up from below. It implies the impinging of some kind of filamentary currents on the surface. A possible cause is the interception of part of the incoming electron flux by the magnetospheres of the planets. Is it mere coincidence that the basic eleven-year sunspot cycle corresponds to the orbital period of Jupiter? Further analysis of solar activity shows a 170- to 180-year repetition of sunspot cycle intensity that has been linked to recurring lineups of planets but conventionally conjectured to be a tidal effect. It is also possible that the pattern could reflect the Sun's passing through regions of filamentary structures traversing space.

Element Synthesis the Easy Way

The "Fraunhofer spectrum" from the cooler region at the base of the Sun's atmosphere contains over 27,000 dark spectral lines, which remove about 9 percent of the energy from the background sunlight and indicate the presence of 68 of the 92 naturally occurring chemical elements. No standard model has ever been able to explain even the gross characteristics of this spectrum. Elements heavier than iron cannot be formed by the fusion reactions said to be going on at the Sun's core, and the usual solution is to have them manufactured in the supernova explosions of an earlier generation of stars, out of the debris from which a second generation of stars including the Sun was then formed. However, supernovas are processes that violently disperse matter, and at the currently observed rate of occurrence they seem too rare to account for the abundance of heavy elements implied.

But gravitationally bound fusion plasmas are perhaps the most inefficient way of manufacturing heavy nuclei. The laboratory method of using electric fields to accelerate protons or other light nuclei is much simpler and can make them fuse with just about any element in the periodic table. It's practically 1920s vacuum-tube technology. You could probably make such a working fusion machine fairly cheaply in your garage. Don't be deterred by the high temperatures that fusion scientists like to talk about to impress people. The unit that researchers use to measure acceleration energy is the "electron-volt," equal to the particle's charge number (one for an electron or proton) multiplied by the voltage it's accelerated through. To equate this figure to degrees Kelvin, multiply by 11,604. Hence, a daunting-sounding 50-million-degree "ignition" temperature is achieved with a paltry 4,300 ev. And the nuclear reactions involved in such fusions would be expected to generate all three kinds of neutrinos, at all kinds of energies.

What we're suggesting, then, is that the elements are made right there in the Sun's photosphere, where we see them. And the mix of neutrinos that's measured is what's produced, without any sleight of hand and statistical legerdemain to derive what is from what we think ought to be.

It would be in order at this point to mention another strange thing about neutrinos, too. There seems to be an undeniable correlation between the neutrino count rates reported by the various experiments, and solar activity as indicated by sunspots and solar wind. The standard model attributes the neutrino flux to events deep in the interior that by every other means need tens of thousands of years to emerge tangibly, and has no explanation for how they can affect or be affected by events taking place at the surface. But if element synthesis is in fact a result of the external electrical environment, it follows that the neutrino by-products of that synthesis should vary with other factors that are also dependent on the same electrical activity.

THE CELESTIAL ARC-LIGHT SHOW

What we've said about the Sun obviously applies to other stars too, which means that the whole generally believed picture of stellar types and how they evolve is thrown into question. So does the revised view of the universe as an essentially electrical manifestation offer an alternative way of interpreting what's observed? Well, let's take a look at it.

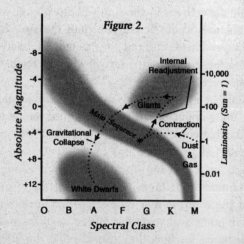

Figure 2.

Figure 2 shows the Hertzsprung-Russell (H-R) diagram, which dates from the first decade of the twentieth century and will be familiar to any reader of basic astronomy. It shows the empirical relation found between the temperature, or spectral class, of stars, and their intrinsic luminosity. Hence, it is a plot of actual observations, not something deduced from a theory, so any viable model of stellar behavior must be consistent with it. Spectral class, defined by color, is plotted horizontally, ranging from hottest at the left to coolest at the right. The vertical scale is labeled both with absolute magnitude, a measure of the actual luminosity of a star that takes into account its distance from the Earth (determined from its parallax, the apparent displacement seen from different positions as the Earth orbits the Sun), or alternatively luminosity, the total amount of radiation emitted, expressed as a multiple of that of the Sun. The Sun, being a fairly typical star, falls near the center of the diagram, with luminosity = 1, absolute magnitude = 5, spectral class G, and (photospheric) temperature = 6,000 degrees K.

The conventional interpretation, premised on the assumption that stars are driven by hydrogen-helium fusion, is that they evolve through various stages of burning as they use up their fuel, in the process slowly migrating from one part of the H-R diagram to another over spans of hundreds of thousands of years. Initially, a cloud of gas and dust coalesces under gravitation, and when thermonuclear ignition is reached, takes its place in the main sequence, where it enters the major portion of its stable life. This is where the majority of stars are found. Eventually, the helium "ash" accumulating at the core necessitates internal structural readjustment for burning to continue. This results in expansion and increase of luminosity, taking the star into its giant phase. Its time here is typically much shorter than on the main sequence and lasts until the helium core collapses under its own weight. This initiates higher temperatures, which enable first the helium itself to begin burning into heavier elements, and then, in turn, carbon, oxygen, and so through to iron. As mentioned earlier, elements beyond iron can't be produced by regular thermonuclear fusion.

What happens finally depends on the star's original mass. As the thermonuclear burning process ends, gravitational collapse resumes, transforming the majority of stars into white dwarfs, which eventually die and stabilize as black dwarfs. In more massive stars, however, ordinary matter is unable to resist continuing collapse, and breaks down structurally into superdense forms, yielding such exotic objects as neutron stars and black holes. Since humans have not been around long enough to actually observe any of these slow migrations, this part of the conventionally accepted picture remains a theoretical construct.

In the electrical star model that we have been discussing, the most important variable is current density (amperes per square meter) at the effective anode surface—the photosphere. As current density increases, the arc discharges (anode tufts, granules) get hotter, change color from red toward blue, and grow brighter. So let's add "surface current density" as an additional axis across the bottom, increasing from right to left.

On the lower right of the diagram, the current

density is so low that the secondary plasma tufting that produces arcs is not needed. This is the region where we find the brown and red dwarf stars and giant gas planets, and larger cool stars characterized by their visible chromospheric glow. The plasma is in the low-intensity anode glow range, or in the case of a large gas planet, the "dark current" radio-emitting range. (The Establishment were outraged when Velikovsky's prediction that Jupiter should show radio emissions, which they had ridiculed, turned out to be correct.)

Moving leftward and upward brings us to a region where some arc tufting becomes necessary to carry the discharge current. We mentioned that this is a dynamic structure, able to adjust to fluctuating conditions. The discovery of an X-ray flare being emitted by a brown dwarf (spectral class M9, very cool) by the *Chandra* orbiting X-ray telescope posed a problem for the fusion model, since a star that cool shouldn't produce X-ray flares. But the appearance of an anode tuft in response to a slight change in total current is a normal feature of the electrical explanation. A strong electrical field is associated with the tuft-shield region, and strong electric fields are the easiest way to produce X-rays.

With increasing current density, arcing covers more of the star's surface. Plasma arcs are extremely bright compared to plasma in its normal glow range, and luminosity increases sharply, consistent with the steepness of the main H-R band curve in this region. Not long ago, NASA reported the discovery of a star with half its surface "covered by a sunspot." This corresponds to a star where half the surface area comprises photospheric arcing. It could be viewed as a link in the continuum from gas giant planets and brown dwarfs to fully tufted stars.

Stars beyond the "knee of the curve" have fully tufted (granulated) photospheres. These get brighter with increasing current density but without adding significantly to the tufted area, and so luminosity grows less rapidly—winding up the current of existing arcs, but no longer adding more arcs. (Note: The progression from right to left is not following the evolution of one star in time, in the manner of the conventional interpretation. We are simply cataloging the different appearances of different stars, depending on their electrical environment and size—like the displays of different villages, towns, and cities seen from the air at night.)

At the upper left end of the main sequence lies the region of hot, blue-white, O types, with surface temperatures of 35,000 degrees K and more. Stars here are under extreme electrical stress—at the limit of the current density they can absorb. The suggestion here is that extreme electrical stress can lead to a star's increasing its available area by fissioning into parts, perhaps explosively. Such explosions constitute what are called novas.

Recall what we said earlier about internal electrical repulsive forces opposing gravitational collapse and creating a star of uniform density rather than a self-compressing mass growing enormously dense toward the core. Such a uniform density maintained by repulsive internal forces would facilitate fissioning under unstable conditions. The drop in current density accompanying the increase in surface area would now indeed shift both the resultant bodies to new positions rightward on the H-R diagram. For resultant stars of equal size, the current density on each would reduce to 80 percent of its previous value. If the objects were of different size, the larger would have the larger current density—though still less than the original value. Current density on the smaller member of the pair might fall to a sufficiently low value to turn arc tufting off, dropping it back abruptly to brown dwarf or even giant planet status.

This would explain why it is so common for stars to have partners, and why so many of the gas giants detected in nearby systems appear to orbit unexpectedly close to their parent star. It could also explain why excessively large stars are not observed—there's no reason why clouds contracting purely under gravity shouldn't be any size. In place of the elaborate mechanisms devised to explain variable stars, we have a periodic discharge between companion objects, followed by buildup back to some trigger level—much like a relaxation oscillator. Electrical instabilities in gas giants could account too for the origin of the inner, "terrestrial" planets, which gives the standard accretion model so many problems. The recent birth of Venus from Jupiter is a much-debated candidate—another suggestion that Velikovsky was vilified for suggesting.

And the case here is perhaps not entirely devoid of observational corroboration. Around 1900, the star FG Sagittae was an inconspicuous hot star of temperature 50,000 degrees K and magnitude 13. Over the next sixty years it cooled to about 8000 degrees K and brightened to magnitude 9 as its radiation shifted from the far-UV to the visual region. Then, around 1970, spectral lines appeared of newly present elements—formed by some energetic process or liberated from the interior. The star cooled further in the 1970s and '80s, with a falling of magnitude to 16 in 1996. So, after abruptly brightening by four magnitudes, it dropped by seven magnitudes, changing from blue to yellow since 1955, and today appears as the central star of the planetary nebula (nova remnant?) He 1-5. It is unique in affording direct evidence of stellar evolution across the H-R diagram, but on a time scale comparable with the human lifetime—not at all the kind of slow stellar evolution that the mainstream theory envisions. And FG Sagittae is a binary pair!

Another example. Cosmic gamma-ray bursters have been called "the greatest mystery of modern astronomy."[7] They are powerful blasts of gamma- and X-radiation that come from all parts of the sky, but never from the same direction twice. Earth is illuminated by two to three bursts every day. Until recently it wasn't even known if they came from relatively close by or from the far edge of the universe. Then in 1997 the *BeppoSAX* X-ray astronomy satellite pinpointed the position of a burst in Orion to within a few arc minutes, allowing visual imaging of the burst. It showed a rapidly fading star, probably the aftermath of a gigantic explosion, next to a faint amorphous blob. Sounds a bit like fissioning again to me—an explosion, followed by a rapidly fading star, accompanied by some sort of companion. Maybe the reason why they never come from the same direction twice is that the process has relieved the electrical stress that triggered it—at least for the time being. Not so mysterious, really.

Mainstream astronomy considers O-type stars to be young, and that they age due to the nuclear burning up of their hydrogen. The electrical model has no reason to attribute a greater or lesser age to any spectral type compared to another. A star's location on the H-R diagram depends only on its size and the current density that it is at present experiencing. If that current density should change for any reason, the star will move to a different position on the H-R diagram—perhaps abruptly, like FG Sagittae. Its age is indeterminate from its mass or spectral type. This carries the sobering implication that our own Sun's future is by no means as certain as mainstream astronomy assures. The Birkeland current powering it could increase or decrease suddenly, and do so at any time. Surely we have stuff for the making of some great science-fiction doomsday scenarios here!

Endnote:

Some references for further information on the electric universe:

Aeon Journal: http://www.aeonjournal.com
Electric Cosmos: http://www.electric-cosmos.org/
Kronia Group: http://www.kronia.com/kronia.html
Plasma Universe: http://public.lanl.gov/alp/plasma/
    TheUniverse.html
Society for Interdisciplinary Studies (UK): http://www.
    knowledge.co.uk/sis/

Notes

[1] Baen Books, July 2004

[2] For a discussion of this see Robert W. Bass, "'Proofs' of the Stability of the Solar System," *Kronos* 2:2, (Glassboro, NJ: Kronos Press, 1976)

[3] http://www.jpl.nasa.gov/galileo

[4] Halton Arp, *Quasars, Redshifts, and Controversies*, (Berkeley, CA: Interstellar Media, 1987); Arp, *Seeing Red: Redshifts, Cosmology, and Academic Science*, (Montreal: Apieron, 1988)

[5] Sir Arthur Eddington, 1926, *The Internal Constitution of the Stars*, Dover edition (1959)

[6] http://www.sno.phy.queensu.ca/sno/first_results/

[7] http://www.science.nasa.gov/newhome/headlines/ast13oct98_1.htm

Sword of Damocles

Somehow, the object escaped detection until it was within a million miles or so of the Moon. This could have been due to its unusual geometry, which made it a poor reflector of radar waves, or because it was constructed from materials with high absorptivity; possibly it was due to a combination of both factors. In any event, suddenly it was just *there*—falling inward toward the Earth from somewhere in the direction of the outer Solar System.

It first appeared as a new set of coordinates and trajectory data in the inventory of space-borne objects maintained by the computers of the Near-Earth Surveillance Network. The computers decided that it oughtn't to be there and flagged it with a query, which was about as much as they could determine. The echo signals were weak and confused, enabling

261

little to be reconstructed of the object's shape and surface contours apart from that they were irregular and complex, showing none of the characteristics of a naturally occurring wanderer such as a large meteor or stray asteroid. Terrestrial and orbiting telescopes trained on the point indicated revealed something that looked like an indistinct, low-albedo, multifaceted strawberry, tumbling sedately at two revolutions per minute as it closed on a path that would set it into high-Earth orbit in a little under a week. Once its motion was fixed, its size was estimated from the times for which it eclipsed background stars; it was apparently more than a mile across.

As the days passed, *"Nomad,"* as the object had been christened by the intrigued scientific teams following its progress, gradually resolved itself into the form of twelve circular constructions, each a little under a mile in diameter, arranged symmetrically to define the faces of what, had they been pentagons joined at the edges, would have been a dodecahedron. The constructions were concave, like shallow dishes, and the space behind them contained a confusion of supports and structural members that couldn't be resolved with certainty among the ever-moving shadows cast by the outer surfaces. The surfaces of the dishes absorbed radiation strongly, appearing almost black-body to the probe beams directed at them from installations on the lunar surface and from orbiting laboratories. For their own part they were electromagnetically passive, emitting no detectable energy in any part of the spectrum, other than a thermal signature consistent with the temperature of interplanetary space. The only other thing that could be said for sure at that stage was that *Nomad* bore no resemblance to anything that had ever been put into space by any nation of Earth.

It settled into high orbit over Earth on time a week later, still showing no sign of activity. Nothing more happened, nor, after a while, seemed likely to. The International Space Agency, in conjunction with a joint force hastily thrown together by the nations possessing a military space arm, began preparations to send an exploratory mission to investigate the mysterious intruder at closer quarters.

The melancholic notes of Beethoven's "Moonlight" sonata trickled through the apartment like the tinkling of a mountain stream reduced to slow motion. The face of the woman sitting at the grand piano by the bay window of the elegantly furnished living room betrayed no emotion as she played, but the lines beneath the layer of powder, and the wrinkles beginning to show around the eyes and neck, hinted of the premature aging that comes with years of solitude and loneliness. While her fingers flowed over the keyboard, assembling the phrases into shape and form without need of conscious intervention of mind, her eyes stared distantly from beneath her mantle of graying hair, replaying their own themes and variations of memories.

"Ah, excuse me, ma'am." The voice of the house computer interrupted from one of the grilles concealed in the decor of the room. It was a bright and cheerful female voice, emulating a girl in her early twenties, synthesized with a trace of a Southern accent; the tenants could specify whatever suited their preferences.

Doreen Waverley stopped in mid bar and returned to the present. "What is it, Naomi?" Her voice was firm, clear, and cultivated.

"The visitors that you were expecting have arrived— your daughter and granddaughter. They're in the lobby now. Shall I bring them up?"

"Of course!" Doreen's face broke into a smile of relief and anticipation. "But let me say hello to them first."

"Sure."

The display panel by the far wall pivoted on its flexible support arm to face where Doreen was sitting. An image appeared of a tall, slim, good-looking woman of thirty with shoulder-length fair hair, framed by the background of the main entrance on the ground floor below. With her was a girl of ten, also fair, deeply tanned after the sweltering summer, and wearing a yellow dress with white polka dots. They were both smiling, the girl fidgeting and trying, not very successfully, to conceal a brightly wrapped package behind her back.

"Carol!" Doreen rose from the piano stool and approached the screen, at the same time throwing out her hands. "It seems such a long time. I'm so glad nothing went wrong at the last minute, with all this strange business going on. And Amanda, you're so brown! You've certainly been making the most of this weather we've been having."

"Hi, Mother," the woman answered. "You haven't been worrying again, have you? I told you nothing would stop us coming today of all days, not even the Space Force."

"Happy birthday, Grandma," the girl chipped in.

The two figures moved forward out of the viewing angle. The screen continued showing the empty lobby for a moment, then went blank. "Make us some coffee, Naomi," Doreen said, addressing no point in particular in the room. "And fix whatever it was Amanda liked when she was here last. . . . I can't remember."

"Chocolate milk and coffee-cream cake," the computer supplied. "Should I turn the air conditioner up a little too? Carol said it was warm last time."

"Oh, so she did. Yes, do that, would you?"

"I have a question," Naomi said, as clicks and whirring sounds came from the kitchen.

"Oh? What?"

"Why was your granddaughter trying to hide the parcel she was carrying?"

Doreen sighed. "It's to do with an old custom connected with birthdays. I'll explain it after they're gone, when there's more time. For now, we have to pretend that we haven't seen it, so don't say anything about it."

"I see." Naomi's voice was concurring, but managed to convey just the right shade of mystification.

Two hours later, after a dinner of crab-and-lobster salad followed by ice cream and a cake that Carol had brought, the two women sat talking over coffee in the living room, while Amanda was in the bedroom—probably emptying her grandmother's jewelry boxes and arranging the contents into patterns on the dressing table.

"So how much leave have you got left to go?" Doreen asked.

"Another two days," Carol answered. "Then I'll be going straight back into space."

"What for this time? Is it to do with that thing that all the news has been about?

"*Nomad.* Yes, We'll be going in with the preliminary investigation team. Just imagine, one of the most exciting things ever to have happened in science! . . . Maybe *the* most . . . Oh, Mother, don't look like that. It will all be done very carefully and cautiously. If there was anything threatening, there would have been some sign of it by now."

Doreen wasn't so sure, but she didn't want to start being gloomy on this of all days. She looked around to change the subject. The china figurines that Carol had brought had now found a home on the top shelf of the recess between the bookcase and the door leading to the kitchen. They blended perfectly with the room and added just the finishing touch that it had needed. "They really are beautiful, Carol," Doreen murmured. "Did you say they're German?"

"Well, I know how much you like anything European," Carol said. "And I've always said that place up there needed something to fill it."

"You certainly picked the ideal thing," Doreen agreed. "But where did you find them? I've never come across anything as fine and detailed as those over here. They're craftsman made . . . not imitation at all."

"I planned it," Carol confessed, smiling impishly. "One of the other officers from our wing—Tom Fairburn; I've told you about him before—went to Germany a few weeks ago on some equipment trials. I asked him to look out for something like that, and he came back with exactly what I had in mind. They are beautiful, aren't they."

"Do you . . . see a lot of him?" Doreen asked. She tried to sound casual, but her voice carried an undertone that she couldn't disguise.

Carol shot her a reproachful glance. "Oh, Mother! He's just a good friend. Don't start sounding as if you're trying to get me married. This is supposed to be a party."

Doreen nodded, but her concern wouldn't let the subject rest. "I don't want to go interfering or anything like that," she said. "Your life is your own affair, of course. But, oh, I don't know . . . sometimes I can't help thinking . . . perhaps for Amanda's sake if nothing else . . ." Prudence stopped her from finishing the sentence. She shrugged and sat back in the chair. But then, after wrestling with her thoughts for a few seconds more, she resumed, "I can't imagine why you never married Amanda's father. Don't get me wrong; I'm not trying to preach morals or anything like that. But you were both young and intelligent, both with exciting futures ahead. . . . And you seemed to think the world of each other. It seemed as if it would have been the natural thing to do, baby or no baby." Doreen looked up and confronted Carol with a direct stare. "He wanted to, didn't he?"

"Yes," Carol replied simply. There was no hint of resentment at her mother's insistence. They had touched on this before. Doreen led a lonely life, and apart from her career as a concert pianist, had little in the way of personal matters to concern herself with other than Carol and Amanda. She felt her concern was only natural, and she knew that Carol understood.

"So?" Doreen shook her head imploringly. "I know

that life in the Space Force can be demanding at times, but the two aren't irreconcilable. Lots of people manage to mix careers and marriage quite happily. Some say their lives are actually enriched by it."

"Oh, it's not that, and you know it," Carol replied. "It's . . ." She shrugged and made an empty-handed gesture. "I've told you before. I *like* being independent. The thought of being fenced in with another person full-time, not being able to do anything without agreeing on this and compromising on that . . . It's just not *me*. I'd be stifled." She smiled and shook her head despairingly, as if Doreen were making hard work for herself by not seeing the obvious. "You should understand if anybody can, Mother."

Doreen fell silent as she heard the words that confirmed what she feared deep inside. She blamed herself for Carol and Amanda being on their own, even though it never seemed to trouble either of them. In fact, they seemed to thrive on each other's company, and Amanda had never shown signs of being deprived of anything that mattered. Nonetheless, Doreen worried, and she blamed herself.

Thirty years had gone by since her own husband, Phillip, was killed. It had happened within a month of Carol's birth, and he never saw his daughter. Perhaps that was the part of it that had affected Doreen so deeply. She had never remarried, but instead devoted the years to a life that divided itself between music and bringing up her daughter single-handed. So Carol had never known a household with a man as part of it. When Amanda arrived twenty years later, after one of those carefree flings that had taken place while Carol was at university, Carol stubbornly chose to continue the self-reliant way of life that her mother had taught her. Or, Doreen secretly wondered, had it in fact been the opposite—an unconscious fear of a style of living that she had no experience of dealing with? And now Amanda was ten, and perhaps already on her way toward carrying the tradition forward into another generation.

Amanda's father had been a physics graduate called Don. Doreen could still picture him, dark-haired, with deep, brown, alert eyes, always twinkling. Everyone said he was brilliantly competent and ambitious, and had predicted a dazzling career. In the earlier years he had done about as much as a father could be expected to from an enforced distance. For a long time it had seemed he never quite lost hope that one day Carol might have second thoughts about the situation. But Carol's obstinacy had persisted, and after a while his appearances became less frequent.

"Do you still see him? Doreen asked.

"Who, Don?"

"Yes."

"Not so much these days," Carol admitted. "I hear about him, though. He's taken an executive position with the Distant Solar Relay Project. It sounds good. He'll do just fine, I'm sure."

Doreen's brows knitted as she tried to recall the technicalities. "To do with the colonies they've been talking about for years, isn't it?" she said. "An energy beam from the Sun or something?"

Carol nodded. "Space colonies, built from materials processed out of lunar rock, in plants constructed on the Moon. The plants will be powered from remotely directed collectors positioned close in to the Sun, inside Mercury's orbit, sending back power as micro-wave beams and directed down from relays in lunar orbit." Doreen had to struggle to keep up, but Carol carried on enthusiastically, "The first ones are already being tested. But the lunar project is really just a first phase. Later, you could have power beams to Mars, say, the asteroids . . . anywhere in the Solar System one day, maybe. Perhaps we could even have ships powered by them, instead of having to carry their own onboard propulsion everywhere. Can you see the kind of thing it could lead to? Human migration out across the Solar System. It's exactly what Don used to dream of. And now he'll be part of it."

But Doreen's thoughts were far away from robot redirectors in close solar orbit, lunar construction plants, and migration across the Solar System. "It's all such a shame," she said, shaking her head sadly.

At that moment Amanda appeared from the bed-room, carrying a framed picture of a handsome young man in a uniform jacket bearing the insignia of the former Air Force Space Command. Carol stared for a moment at the familiar picture of her father and then raised her eyes to take in Amanda's questioning stare. "That's your grandfather," she said. "You've seen that picture before. He was the spaceman who never came home."

"I know," Amanda replied. "But I've never noticed this before." She pointed to a badge on Phillip Waverley's upper sleeve, a few inches below the epaulette. It carried the design of a red sword against a black background. "See. There's a sword on Grandpa's sleeve." She turned to look at Doreen. "Why did Grandpa have a sword on his sleeve?"

Carol gave Doreen a hesitant glance, then turned to Amanda. "You shouldn't bother your grandmother with things like that on her b—" she began, but Doreen stopped her with a wave.

"It's all right, Carol. It isn't as if it happened yesterday." She took the picture from Amanda and gazed at it fondly for several seconds. "You see, before spacemen go away to do something very important—on a special job they call a mission—they sometimes choose a sign. Everybody who goes on the mission wears the sign, and then afterwards, everyone will know they went there and were a part of it."

"You mean like the badge we get when we finish summer camp?" Amanda said.

"Something like that."

Amanda thought for a moment. "Was the sword-badge mission that Grandpa went on an important one?"

'Very important."

"Why?"

Doreen sighed, and then smiled as she saw Carol getting anxious. "You tell her, Carol," she suggested. "You know far more about these things than I ever will." Amanda shifted her gaze to her mother.

"You know what planets are out in space, yes?" Carol asked. Amanda nodded. "Well, there are lots of great big rocks out in space too, as well as planets."

"And moons?"

"And moons too. Some of them are bigger than whole cities. Most of them move around the Sun in nice, steady circles like planets do, but there are some that move all over the place, so you can never be exactly sure where they're going to go next. . . . Anyway, a long time ago, when your grandfather was a spaceman . . ."

"How long ago?"

"Just about thirty years. It was in 2045."

Amanda's eyes widened. "That's a *long* time!"

"Yes . . . Anyhow, one of the biggest of these rocks—they're called meteors—was coming nearer from a long way away in space, and it looked as if it was going to crash into the Earth. If it had, it would have killed millions of people and caused all kinds of terrible damage."

"And did it?"

Carol shook her head. "That was why Grandpa's mission was sent. They went in a big spaceship and met the giant rock a long way from Earth, while it was still farther away than Mars. They fixed some big, powerful motors to it to drive it away into space again so that it wouldn't come anywhere near Earth at all. . . ."

"Why couldn't they just have blown it up?"

"Then the pieces might just have kept on coming, and crashed into the Earth anyway. So they decided to drive it away instead. The plan worked just fine, and millions of people who might have been killed were saved."

Amanda turned her face to stare at the picture again with a new respect. "So why did they make the badge a sword?" she asked. Doreen put a hand to her brow and shook her head. The questions were exhausting just to listen to.

"Because the name of the mission was *Damocles*," Carol said. "And that's also the name of an old, old story about a sword."

"What kind of story? Did it have wizards and dragons in it?"

"Oh, it's too long a story to go into now. Why don't you ask our computer to tell it to you when we get home? He'll tell you all the details. I've forgotten most of them." Carol sat back in her chair to close the subject. "We'll have to be going soon, too. Now, how about putting Grandpa's picture back where it came from, and tidying up Grandma's jewelry in there?"

"Did Grandpa go on more important missions after that one?" Amanda asked.

"That's enough, Amanda." Carol's voice caught, taking on an edge of sharpness that was enough to make Amanda pull a face and disappear back into the bedroom. "I'm sorry," Carol said to Doreen.

"It's all right," Doreen replied. But her eyes were misty.

The *Damocles* mission had gone down as one of the most tragic mysteries in the history of space exploration. Communications with the vessel were lost when it was a few weeks short of its scheduled rendezvous with the approaching meteor. Presumably the members of the mission decided to press on regardless and accomplished their objective, for the threat to Earth never materialized. But nobody ever found out for sure why the communications had failed, or what happened after that. The ship exploded on the first leg of its return trip, and all members of the mission were lost.

Two hours after the last shuttle had transferred its load of personnel and equipment, and detached, the fleet carrier *Guam* fired its main drives and began climbing out of low orbit toward where *Nomad* was riding fifteen thousand miles farther up. The *Guam* was less than five years old and had been built in orbit as a mother ship for satellite hunter-killers and orbital interceptors, and as a mobile base for surface-bombardment operations. It climbed for over thirty hours until it was in a parallel orbit standing twenty miles off from the strange alien construction. For a while it waited; nothing happened. The time came for *Guam* to assume a more active role.

Major Carol Waverley, U.S. Space Force Communications Specialist, attached to Second Fleet Group, watched the main display screen from her post on the *Guam's* control deck while the robot probes that had been dispatched earlier sent back the first views of *Nomad* to be obtained from close-up. The atmosphere was tense and expectant, as the rest of the control deck's officers and crew watched silently from their consoles and stations around the room. From the raised bridge overlooking the deck at one end, General George Medford, commander of the *Guam* and acting director of local operations around *Nomad*, brooded from the center of a knot of aides and advisors.

Each of the twelve concave dishes defining *Nomad's* external geometry was supported at the rear by a pylon in the form of a slender cone almost a half mile long, joining it perpendicularly at its center like a dinner plate balanced on a tapering candle. The twelve pylons projected symmetrically outward from the structure's central nucleus, their surfaces exhibiting a mild concave sweep from the base to the tip. The nucleus itself consisted of twelve flat, cylindrical housings supporting the bases of the pylons, protruding from a tangle of huge toroids wreathing the core at various angles among an agglomeration of curving and merging surfaces and structural members that seemed to produce a form that was basically spherical, although no spherical shape was actually visible. Standing amid it all was a squat turret capped by a system of terraces and ridges that culminated in a flattened dome. The dome housed what appeared to be a docking bay, two hundred feet or more across, situated behind a pair of gaping doors, which were open. The view currently on the main screen was being transmitted from a probe that had passed between the rims of the dishes and was scanning the inside of the docking bay with a searchlight from a point fifty feet outside the doors. So far, no response had been evoked from *Nomad* by radar beams, lasers, optical beacons, radio, infrared, or X-rays.

"The bay goes back in about fifty feet," the voice of the operations controller reported from his console below and to one side of the bridge. "There are tiers of platforms around the sides, with doors leading through to the interior. They could be air locks. There are what look like three large, oval locks along the rear wall, possibly docking ports. Above the— Just a second. . . ." The voice paused. "Probe Four, back up your beam and let's see that center lock again." Computers elsewhere on the *Guam* interpreted the command and flashed it out to the probe. On the screen, the patch of light at the back of the bay halted, and then retraced its path to settle on the middle one of the three docking ports. "I thought so," the commentator's voice said. "That center door's open."

Murmurs rippled around the control deck. On the bridge, Medford leaned toward the screens in front of him to confer with the Mission Director and his team, who were patched in from Washington, and a panel at the International Space Agency's HQ in Geneva. Then his voice sounded from the room's overhead speakers.

"Take the probe on into the bay. Try and get a beam on whatever's inside that door."

The periphery of the bay, lit by arc lamps positioned back behind the probe, yawned wider as the probe approached, and slipped off the edges of the screen. The view darkened, leaving only the open port looking ghostly against the gloom. The port expanded to fill the screen, and details of the inside started to become visible.

The same voice as before resumed. "The design is weird, but it could be an air lock chamber. There's an inner door, also open. Impossible to make out what's on the other side."

"Can the probe get inside that outer door?" Medford's voice inquired.

"Negative, sir."

There was a short wait while Medford, his advisors on the bridge, and the powers down on the surface held a quick conference. Then Medford announced, "We're sending in the boarding party. All units engaged in operations in this sector can stand down. Maintain surveillance and monitoring only until further notice."

Around the control deck, people stretched cramped limbs and broke out into muttering to release the tension that had been building up for several hours.

The view on the main screen remained. An auxiliary display showed a view from another part of the *Guam*, where a line of figures who had been standing by suited up were already hauling themselves along hand lines into the transporter vessel that would carry them to *Nomad*.

At her own station, Carol followed the progress of Probe Two as it nosed its way outward along the sweeping metal surface of one of the pylons. The probe was one of five deployed around the nucleus to collect pictures and data, controlled by Carol's team of operators. She watched with a feeling of awe that she still hadn't gotten used to as the strange configurations of line and curve moved slowly through the probe's viewing field, rendered all the more eerie by the interplay of light from the arc lamps with the rotating kaleidoscope of shadows cast by the Sun. Everything about *Nomad* seemed to embody concepts of shape, form, and function that were utterly unlike anything ever conceived by the mind of a designer from Planet Earth. It wasn't so much the sheer scale of the contours dwarfing the probe on every side that produced this feeling, as the essence of the beings that had produced them, which they seemed to project. The geometric elements from which *Nomad* was formed, and the ascending progressions of greater wholes that they flowed together to become parts of created themes of abstraction divorced from any functional principles that she was able to recognize. And yet it *was* engineering; clearly, it had a purpose. But at the same time it was such an . . . *alien* . . . version of engineering. What kind of alien purpose, Carol wondered, had it been built to serve?

Something to the side of the view caught her eye for a moment, and then was gone. The probe was looking outward along the pylon toward its tip, where it narrowed and blended into a cluster of protuberances behind the dish that the pylon supported. Something in among the shadows had stood out for a moment, caught briefly as the structure's rotation allowed a shaft of sunlight to penetrate. Then it had vanished back into shadow again.

"Probe Two." Carol addressed a microphone projecting from the console fascia. "Replay the last ten seconds of video on channel three, quarter speed." The image on the screen reset itself and began rolling again. Carol watched, waiting for the shadows to open up. "Freeze it there."

It was something long and yellow, lying across the pylon up underneath the mounting supports for the dish. It must have been the color that caught her attention; everything else on *Nomad* was either black or metallic gray. "Magnify five." The blob of yellow expanded into an object that looked like a cylinder, crossing the tapering lines of the pylon as if it had collided with it and somehow stuck. From the superposed graticule, Carol estimated it to be perhaps fifteen feet in diameter and four times that long. The probe had captured the original view at coarse resolution, and no additional detail could be extracted from its stored record.

"Connect me to Probe Two Control," she directed.

A few seconds later an audio grille below the screen acknowledged, "Probe Two Control here, Major."

"Move it out nearer the tip," Carol said. "There's something out there I want to get a better look at. Narrow the scan by factor four."

"Roger."

"Computers, unfreeze Probe Two image and resume real-time transmission," Carol instructed.

The image began growing almost imperceptibly as the probe moved forward, then jumped out suddenly as the intensifiers switched to a narrower scan, higher resolution mode. The cylinder was surrounded at its center by a collar of short, dome-ended tanks and a web of supporting struts attaching the whole assembly to the pylon. There was something else that was unusual about it apart from its color, Carol realized. For a moment, she couldn't put her finger on what. And then it came to her: What was so unusual about it was that it wasn't unusual at all.

It looked the way a piece of purpose-designed engineering should. Everything else about *Nomad* looked and felt "alien." The yellow cylinder didn't. It looked "normal"; and that was what made it seem so out of place.

The view enlarged further and marched slowly across the screen, revealing lines of rivets along the cylinder's sides, a web of pipes that looked the way pipes should, woven into a structural lattice designed as the way a lattice should be, and spouting valves that looked like valves. After the rest of *Nomad*, the cylinder looked almost homey.

And then, suddenly, Carol gasped and brought her hand involuntarily up to her mouth. The heads nearest her turned at the sound. Her face had gone pale.

Moving slowly into the center of the view was a

painted emblem of a red sword on a black background. Above the emblem, stenciled clearly on
the yellow surface of the cylinder, were the letters
U.S.A.F.S.C. And below the sword, standing out in
red against the same black backdrop, was the single
word: DAMOCLES.

"There isn't any doubt. We've checked everything
against archived records beamed up from Washington.
Those are the plasma motors that were sent out with
the *Damocles* mission in 2045 to divert a rogue meteor
that was heading for Earth." Lieutenant-General Calvin
Chalmers, officer in charge of the *Guam's* computers
and communications, paused to give his words effect.
The yellow cylinder had turned out to be the first of
eight that were later discovered attached to different
parts of *Nomad*. All were from the *Damocles* mission
of thirty years before.

Carol spoke from the small group of officers facing Chalmers in the D Deck briefing room. "That
can only mean that there never was any meteor. It
must have been *Nomad* that showed up in the Belt
thirty years ago. The meteor story was a cover-up for
something."

Chalmers nodded. "That's how it appears."

"But why?" somebody else demanded. "Why divert
it off into space? Why all the secrecy?"

"That, I can't answer," Chalmers replied. "All
we can conclude now is that the powers-that-were
thirty years ago had a good reason to want to send
it away. Whether they meant it to come back again,
or whether that was just a freak occurrence . . ." He
shrugged. "Who can say?" After glancing around, he

added, "But if you want my own opinion, I'd guess that they intended exactly what has happened. The set of motors and its control system are sophisticated, long-life equipment, not one-time throwaway junk. In other words, it has functioned exactly the way it was meant to. *Nomad* reappeared where it was meant to, when it was meant to." He raised a hand to forestall obvious questions. "No, we don't know why. We can only assume that our predecessors of thirty years ago had the opportunity to study *Nomad* in much greater detail than we have been able to do so far, and managed to deduce more of its nature. Obviously it's important that we waste no time in finding out whatever they knew. The first phase of doing so will involve everyone in this room." The listeners waited, watching him intently.

"The detachment landed on *Nomad* has penetrated to what seems to be the control center in the section intended for occupation by whatever beings built it. The equipment in there is as screwy as everything else about the place, but it's probably the best place to be looking for answers. That's a job for compcom and instrumentation specialists, which means us. We'll be backing up the civilian ISA group in a preliminary survey scheduled for oh-two-hundred hours tomorrow." Chalmers shifted his eyes to single out Carol. "Major Waverley, since you have the honor of being the first person on the *Guam* to identify *Nomad*'s connection with *Damocles*, I'd like you to take charge of our half of the team. Okay by you?"

"I'd be happy to, sir."

"Would you stay behind after the briefing to discuss objectives and procedures?" Chalmers raised his head to address the others. "Thank you. That's all for now."

Everything about the control center in the *Nomad*'s nucleus—if that was indeed what this place was—was so . . . *alien*. More so, because it was completely dead, with no lighting, no sign of life, and none of the subtle vibrations from unseen machinery coming through the floor and walls as was omnipresent in the *Guam*.

Carol was floating among a collection of strangely angled and sculpted forms that could have been consoles, furnishing, or some obscure combination of both, clustered around the highest level of a series of irregularly curved platforms ascending in interpenetrating levels toward the center of the room. The structures glowed softly in the makeshift lighting installed by the *Guam*'s engineers, appearing predominantly white but with undertones of rainbow hues that seemed to shift in an elusive dance that the eye could never quite catch. A walkway connected one of the intermediate tiers to a low, wide doorway opening into the space on one side. The rest of the area was bounded by intersecting segments of curves to generate a floor plan shaped like a many-leaved clover, with the large terraced dais occupying the central area, and the lowermost extremities forming the tips of what would be the leaves. These descending sections around the periphery formed miniature amphitheaters of semi-circular steps facing outward toward a series of black arches recessed into the walls, which led nowhere. Several partly enclosed galleries looked down from the blending of vaulted surfaces and angles enclosing the space from above. There was nothing obvious to distinguish anything that could be called a "ceiling" from anything that were clearly "walls."

There was thus a sense of *up* and *down* inherent in the general layout, although no force was in evidence to serve as gravity. The room's orientation with respect to the rest of the structure ruled out the possibility of gravity being simulated by rotation; there was simply no conceivable axis about which *Nomad* could spin to generate a *down* in the direction where the floor lay. The ISA-*Guam* team, along with their equipment and tangles of interconnecting cables, were hanging and drifting amid a web of anchor ties and safety lines. The engineers had rigged a temporary air lock across the open port in the docking bay and filled the interior of *Nomad's* habitable section with air hosed through from the supply tanks of a transporter, so at least the scientists had the consolation of not having to work in helmets. They were wearing suits as a precaution, however, with helmets back-slung to be within immediate reach.

For a control center, the place seemed distinctly lacking in the profusion of panels, screens, buttons, and lamps that would have been normal in a Terran vessel. This had led Carol and Chalmers to suspect that the aliens had probably used portable remote devices of some kind to communicate with whatever managed the system. If so, the room ought to contain sensors to complete the links. Accordingly, for the last two hours the team had been scanning the interior with narrow beams of all frequencies and signal patterns, and measuring reflections in a search for changes in absorption ratios. They had found one spot, immediately above the main dais over which Carol was hanging, that seemed exceptionally sensitive, and were subjecting it to a systematic barrage of every kind of photonic ammunition in their arsenal.

"It dipped at fifty-four-point two," Dr. Hap Pearson from ISA reported as he interrogated a monitor floating beside him a few yards to Carol's left. "Take it back through the decade again and ramp at increment ten." A short distance away, a Space Force operator keyed instructions into a field computer. Others around the room went about their routines in silence, by now oblivious of the eyes watching from inside the *Guam*, the ISA vessel ten miles out that had now joined them, and others at several places down on Earth. Releases to the news services and general public were being kept to a minimum—not that there was much yet to be released.

A change of light to one side caused Carol to turn her head. A surface of one of the strangely shaped projections had sprouted a pattern of colors that hadn't been there before. She ran an eye over it for a second or two, then activated her throat mike. "Hold everything. Can you dim the lights for a moment, Echo Three? Something's happened." The lights faded. Excited murmurs and a few whistles came from around the room.

A sloping panel inset to a curviform was glowing with an array of studs, symbols, and geometric designs that had appeared seemingly embossed on the surface, where a moment before there had been nothing. They were radiating a fairyland mixture of reds, blues, greens, purples, violets, and yellows, like a display of jewelry that had come to life with an inner light of its own. "Brighten up a little," Carol said. The working lights came up enough to show the surroundings, but stayed low enough for the colors to remain clear. Carol took in the astonished faces turned toward her from all parts of the room. Then she shrugged and hauled herself over to the display. Hap Pearson joined her moments later, while a sergeant floating above the walkway bridge followed them with a handheld camera.

"What is it, some kind of control panel?" Pearson asked. It was rhetorical. Just at that moment, nobody really had anything sensible to offer.

Carol stretched out a hand cautiously and touched a bead of amber. The bead vanished. It didn't just go out; the surface where it had been was smooth and featureless. Other elements of the pattern had also disappeared, while elsewhere more had materialized and still others had altered their shapes and colors.

"Are you getting all this?" Pearson called out.

"Sharp and clear. Carry on." It was the operations controller's voice, coming through from the *Guam*.

Carol stared helplessly at the meaningless display. "I hardly touched it. It seemed to respond to proximity." She touched a slender triangle of emerald green. The pattern reconfigured, but nothing else obvious happened. A pale blue crescent, a yellow oval, and a row of small red circles produced similar results. She became bolder and started touching pairs of symbols simultaneously. Suddenly, a three-dimensional image of light appeared above one of the central plinths. It was about two feet across and clearly a representation of *Nomad*, visually transparent with various internal compartments and what looked like functional systems differentiated in contrasting colors. As she tried other combinations, the model altered, some sections vanishing and others appearing as if the structure were being dismantled and reassembled in different sequences. The image expanded, contracted, turned itself over first one way, then another, and suddenly vanished. Carol was unable to recreate it. Never mind, she thought to herself. Whatever it was she had done would have been captured for replays.

More experimenting produced lighting around the room. It seemed to emanate from the structure rather than being concentrated in localized sources, and could be shifted around. Excited and curious now, she studied the latest version of the pattern. To one side, a fairly large purple rectangle had appeared, surrounded at a short distance by a silver frame, with the rectangle filling about half the frame's area. Carol stared at the figure, then brushed her fingers lightly across it.

The whole pattern came up and hit her in the jaw—solidly. An instant later the floor slammed into her feet, buckling her legs, accompanied by the sounds of crashing equipment, thudding bodies, and shouts of alarm from all around. Hap Pearson was clinging to the curved panel containing the array, bracing himself with a leg wedged against a projection behind him, while the sergeant who had been recording the proceedings was lying on the walkway entangled in cables. Everywhere else, prone and bizarrely splayed bodies were extracting themselves from the wreckage of what, a few seconds before, had been an orderly operation. It seemed Carol had discovered *Nomad*'s source of gravity.

She began pulling herself back onto her feet, but even as she made the first moves she realized that something was wrong. She found herself sliding back down the flared column that supported the panel; her legs were refusing to straighten. The force was becoming stronger. The gravity, or whatever she had unleashed, was increasing steadily, dragging her irresistibly back toward the floor. Around the room, the other figures that had started to stand up were also being crushed down again. Carol concentrated her strength and forced an arm that was turning to lead to drive itself upward inch by inch. Her fingers found the edge of the panel, and clung desperately, long enough for her to pull her face level. The purple rectangle was growing, expanding slowly toward the silver bounding frame. She freed one hand to reach toward it, but the strain on the other was too great, and she slipped back down again.

A few feet above her, Pearson, still hanging on with his arms wrapped around the panel's housing, was beginning to slide down across the concave surface. Carol saw him brace his leg more firmly and jab frantically at the panel. She felt the force field stop increasing. Pearson repeated whatever it was he had done. Her body lightened. She reached again for the panel and was able to pull herself up. The purple rectangle had shrunk. Pearson's face was running with perspiration. He stabbed at the symbols again, and Carol felt as if a bag of cement were being lifted from her shoulders. Pearson let go of the panel and dropped lightly on his feet beside her as she stood up. He drew in a lungful of air shakily. The figures around them were straightening up, some feeling gingerly for bumps and bruises. Carol had that feeling of mild embarrassment coupled with luck that she didn't really deserve—like that after having had a near miss when failing to see a Stop sign.

"Jesus . . . I guess I got a bit carried away." She could feel a swelling already starting to take shape on her chin. "It was lucky you were where you were."

"Just . . . don't make a habit of it, Major," Pearson whispered. He had gone pale and clammy—a mild case of delayed shock.

"Is everybody okay there?" the voice of the operations controller called from the *Guam*. Apart from superficialities, it seemed that everyone was. They would want a slow replay of everything they did before even thinking of trying anything else. As Carol and Pearson surveyed the scene of figures reerecting instruments and monitoring stations from the mess of packs and boxes strewn around what was definitely now the floor, a peal of laughter came from somewhere behind. They turned, and the other heads in the room jerked up sharply.

The laughter was coming up from one of the recessed archways at the feet of the sets of curved steps around the periphery of the room. The surround of the arch was glowing with nested lines of color, and more rainbow symbols had appeared on a ledge projecting beneath it. In the arch itself, where previously there had been just blackness, there was now a face and shoulders—a solid image that looked real enough to touch.

They stood speechless with disbelief. Pearson's mouth was frozen open in a silent protest. After the effect that the rest of *Nomad* had already had on her, Carol would have been prepared for just about any grotesque or bizarre composition of an alien countenance that imagination in its wildest convulsions would never be capable of concocting. But this was the last thing she would have been prepared for. The face still cackling in the arch was as human as any in the room.

"I see you've located the gravity synthesizer," it said. "Actually, you weren't in any real danger. After a few more seconds we would have turned it down from our end." Whoever it was spoke in a normal American voice.

Carol and Pearson made their way slowly down through the tiers until they were confronting him. She was only vaguely conscious of other figures closing behind them from above. The first word that came into her mind was "gnomish." The face was that of a man in his late fifties, with a shock of unruly dark hair sprouting above a pair of beady eyes peering out over a rounded, bulbous nose. His mouth twisted crookedly with mirth that he still couldn't quite suppress, revealing a set of strong but not very even teeth. "That was pretty quick work," he went on, sounding mocking. "According to our calculations, the *Servochron* should have entered orbit just under two weeks ago. You didn't waste any time."

Servochron? Which of course had to be *Nomad*. Carol struggled to collect her reeling thoughts into something coherent enough to put into words. In the end, all she could manage, lamely, was, "Who are you? . . . Where are you? . . ." The face creased into another amused spasm but made no reply. It looked at her challengingly, as if waiting for something that should have been obvious to register.

Carol realized that there was something familiar about the figure. The image had reduced slightly to show more of the person, revealing a jacket worn over a shirt with necktie. The clothes were not in the cut and style of men's fashions of recent times. They seemed quaint, in a way—constraining and overformal. She had seen that face before—in a photograph, maybe, or an old movie or documentary.

Suddenly, Pearson emitted an audible exclamation and stepped down past her to peer at the image more closely. The face in the arch nodded encouragingly. "Garfax!" Pearson whispered. Then, louder, "You're Lambert Garfax, former president of the United States."

"Correct!" the face confirmed gleefully. "Ten out of ten. Except for one small detail. The word 'former.' I *am* president of the United States."

Pearson frowned. "What do you mean, *am*? You're dead. Norfield is President. You were in office, when? . . . It was before the middle of the century. . . ." His voice trailed off as the absurdity of the situation seemed to register suddenly. As he had just said, Garfax was dead. Yet the dialogue was interactive. The face couldn't be a recording. Pearson shook his head. "What is this? What's going on?"

"2044 to 2048," Garfax said. "The answer to your question is perfectly simple. You see, here where, or maybe I should say *when*, I'm talking to you from, I *am* president. It *is* 2048."

The pause that followed could have been a few seconds or an hour. Carol couldn't tell. Her thinking processes had come to a halt.

"What?" she heard Pearson choke. The tone wasn't really that of a question. More the kind of thing that people toss out to fill a void when nothing more meaningful suggested itself. But it was more than she herself had been able to manage.

"That's what the *Servochron* is," Garfax said. "It enables communication through time. Or at least, that's one of its functions. Unless we are sadly mistaken, you are talking to us from high orbit above Earth, and twenty-seven years in the future. Am I right? Ten out of ten?" He took a moment to read the expressions on their faces. "Good. Well, at least you know who I am. Might I have the courtesy of knowing whom I am addressing?"

"Er . . . Dr. Horace Pearson, Datacommunications Advisor to the International Space Agency, from NSF Washington."

Carol moved a couple of steps down to join him. "Major Carol Waverley, United States Space Force." Her mind was slowly unjamming itself at last. "This . . . 'thing' was found thirty years ago. *Your* people found it. They—"

"Yes, yes," Garfax agreed. He waved impatiently. "Let's save ourselves a lot of pointless questions. The *Servochron* was found in 2042 out in the Asteroid Belt. We've had experts studying it for years. What it does is a long story. I'm a busy man, and I don't intend going through it all with advisory scientists and junior officers. I would like you people, please, to arrange contact with your government at a level appropriate to my office."

"I'm not sure I . . ." Pearson began, then stopped and moistened his lips. "What, exactly—"

"There are certain protocols to be observed, as I'm sure you are aware," Garfax interrupted, starting to sound irritable. "I want to talk to your president, of course. What did you say his name was—Norfield or something?"

"That's not possible," Pearson replied, sounding aghast. "He's not here. He's back on Earth."

"Oh, come on. You're supposed to be communications people, aren't you?" Garfax answered. "Presumably you have data links to Earth set up. Yes?"

"Yes, we have."

"Then it's perfectly simple. All you have to do is set up a two-way terminal there, where you're standing, tie it into your data link, and get Norfield on the other end. I'm sure that with something like *Servochron* showing up less than two weeks ago, he won't be far away from what's going on."

"Yes . . . of course," Pearson mumbled. He hesitated. "I'm not sure how long it might take, though. Are you going to wait there, or what?"

"Most certainly not," Garfax told him. "I have a pressing schedule. One of you go away and get things moving with your superiors. The other, stay there. I'll put a couple of my people on the line who'll tell you how to operate the controls to call us back. No more questions until I'm through to the right people."

"I'll go," Carol said reflexively, seizing the opportunity to get away from the insane situation and think. Without waiting for Pearson to respond, she turned and climbed back up the levels of the dais, through the huddle of bewildered onlookers, to the operator manning the console connecting to the *Guam*.

The awed features of Lieutenant-General Chalmers greeted her. "General Medford is handling this," he told her before she could say anything. Carol turned her face to Medford, gaping out from another screen.

"I've beamed down a message to Washington," Medford said in an unsteady voice. "They're passing it on to the president now. Suspend further activity until somebody down there gets back to us."

The Garfax presidency was remembered as one of the disaster periods of United States history. Garfax came into office on the crest of a wave of irrational popularity following an election year of reckless promises that everyone wanted to hear but not think about too seriously, sold in a frenzy of near-evangelical campaigning. But the next four years brought an uninterrupted succession of exposures of corruption, incompetence, falsifications, and mismanagement, and the tatters of the administration were consigned to oblivion in the election of 2048.

One of the embarrassments left to posterity from that era was the Garfax Energy Plan—a vision of the nation's energy problems being solved forever by a huge, centralized fusion complex that would be half a century ahead of anything conceived up to that time, anywhere on Earth. The nation was still intoxicated with campaign euphoria when the scheme was announced, and rushed to embrace it eagerly. In a crash program that cost billions, the power grid was reconfigured into a radial network centered upon a site near Columbus, Nebraska, where the complex was to be built. Columbus, it was prophesied, would generate enough power to more than meet the country's projected needs for decades to come, relegating more conventional technologies to the status of local backup and supplementary facilities. Construction at Columbus was commenced with enthusiasm, and power utilities across the country began merging and rationalizing their operations, in many cases cutting back their own proposed expansion programs, in anticipation of the complex coming online within a few years.

When the mess left in 2048 came to be examined in the sober light of day that eventually followed, the state-of-the-art of fusion technology, while still holding out longer-term promise, turned out to be a long way short of what the Garfax Plan had sold. And so the shelved expansion plans were hastily unshelved, and the technical community braced itself to the task of clearing away the last of the temporary insanity and doing what it could to make up for the lost time.

Demolishing what had been built of the Columbus complex would have been expensive without serving any useful purpose; besides, there was more than enough to be done in other areas. Work on the site simply ceased, and as the years went by, the concrete-lined excavations and steel-reinforced foundations faded under mounds of windblown dust, thickets of encroaching weeds, and a covering of prairie grass. With time, saplings sprouted here and there and became small trees, until after a while only the older among the local inhabitants could remember what the still discernible lines of embankments and rectangular depressions had been intended for.

Back on the control deck of the *Guam*, Carol was with Chalmers, Pearson, and a group of others from the communications section, gathered around a monitor panel to follow the incongruous conversation between two United States presidents, both in office, separated by twenty-seven years in time. On one of the screens,

Garfax had been joined by two of his officials: William Josephson from the Department of Energy, and Professor Nernst Kreissenbaum of the Presidential Scientific Advisory Committee. On another, President Gregory Norfield, imposing as always, with his firm, tanned features and elegant crown of silver hair, was doing his best to handle a situation that nothing in his years of experience on the way to the White House had prepared him for.

"The mere suggestion of what you're claiming is preposterous," Norfield insisted. "I've discussed it at length with my own people. It violates every principle of causality. Being able to communicate information back into the past—"

"Nevertheless, it happens to be fact," Kreissenbaum interrupted. "I do not intend launching into a lengthy elucidation of what it has taken us years to uncover. Suffice it to say that past, present, and future events are all equally 'real' in a dimension of totality that transcends the usual notion of 'universe.' They exist on a 'timeline'—for want of a better word—which is not fixed and unalterable. Causes that occur at any point—such as decisions and actions by people, chance happenings of nature—result in effects that manifest themselves in that point's future. If such causes are altered by information received from the future, then their effects are altered also. Events further along on the timeline are reconfigured into a new, fully consistent, sequence. The timeline is thus 'plastic,' as it were, capable of remolding to accommodate changes introduced anywhere along it."

Norfield was already frowning and shaking his head. "It doesn't make sense," he insisted. "Are you saying that things I already remember as having happened—that already constitute undeniable fact—could somehow be changed by what you might choose to do years in the past as a result of this conversation?" He shook his head again. "That's ridiculous. How could you affect one word of what's already in our history books?"

"Yes, I am saying just that," Kreissenbaum replied. "You forget that your memories and all your other records are equally just parts of the timeline that would be reconfigured. Consequently, you would retain no knowledge that any change had taken place. Neither would your reconfigured world preserve any record of it. Everything in the new timeline would be consistent." He gave Norfield a moment to reflect, then offered, "The concept is really quite simple. The past is shaping the future all the time, which is a perfectly familiar notion. All we're saying is that this alien technology enables a reverse-flow of influences to be superposed on the pattern. It creates a closed, self-modifying loop—a 'feedback loop through time,' if you will."

"*That's* where they got their name for it from," Pearson breathed, next to Carol.

"*Servochron*," Chalmers repeated, nodding.

In his chair between Kreissenbaum and Josephson, Garfax was becoming visibly impatient. As a lull occurred, he sat forward and raised his hands to cut the exchange off there. "Enough of all this," he said. "We could talk about the logic of it all day and get nowhere. Why don't you just accept what we're telling you for now? We can prove it easily enough. But in the meantime, there is more important business to discuss."

"What kind of business?" Norfield asked. Something in Garfax's tone sounded ominous. He turned toward Josephson and motioned for him to take it. Josephson cleared his throat and leaned forward to rest his elbows on the table in front of them.

"This communications channel that we're talking over is just an ancillary function of the *Servochron*," he said. "The *Servochron*'s prime purpose is not to transmit information through time, but to transmit *energy*." Norfield stared back, looking nonplused. Josephson went on, "We believe that this device was built by an alien civilization that went through an energy crisis in the course of its development, in much the same way as ourselves. However, it seems that unlike us, they made advances in other areas of physics that we haven't yet begun to suspect exist. And this enabled them to deal with their energy crisis in an ingenious and extraordinary way. They used their knowledge of timeline plasticity to send surplus energy, produced at a time when cheap and abundant supplies had become available, back through time to earlier periods when crises existed. Their action in doing so dramatically improved the circumstances of their own past, which from what Professor Kreissenbaum has just been saying, reconfigured their own situation into a better present. So they never had to live with the consequences of past errors or problems. They could eradicate them from their universe." Josephson sat back and regarded Norfield expectantly, as if inviting him to complete the rest for himself.

"My God!" Pearson murmured beside Carol. "That's what those dishes are all around *Nomad*. They're enormous energy collectors. *Nomad* sends it back up the timeline."

Carol had realized the same thing. She turned a stunned face toward him. "And I think I know why now," she said. "I know why they sent it out on a thirty-year orbit."

Norfield seemed to have understood it too. He stared incredulously from the screen, his lips moving feebly without forming any sound. On the other screen, Garfax cackled suddenly and began nodding his head vigorously.

"That's right, you've got it!" he exclaimed. "That was why we sent you the *Servochron* as a present. Now *you* can use it for what it was meant for—to send your surplus back to *us*. You must be aware of the problems we're going through right now—the whole Middle East fighting over oil; Europe's almost bankrupt; the environmentalists wrecked fission; fusion wasn't funded early enough; solar was a joke." Garfax made a tossing-away motion with his hand. "Everything's a mess here. But according to the long-range plans being drawn up right now, you should be through all that. You ought to be moving toward an expanded space program with colonies on the drawing boards, and extraction and processing plants being set up on the Moon to build the hardware. And just about now, by our forecasts, you ought to be completing the first phase of putting long-range converters in close orbit near the Sun to beam back energy for powering it all. Ten out of ten? How's that going? Is it all on schedule?"

Norfield just nodded numbly.

"Splendid!" Garfax exclaimed, beaming. "So you

can help us out. The collectors on the *Servochron* are designed to receive in the microwave band—just what the studies we're initiating here will recommend for the close-solar converters. A fortunate coincidence, wouldn't you say?" He cackled again. "All you have to do is position your receiving-end relays in a pattern fifty miles out, set up in a way that we'll tell you, and start pumping. Let's see now . . ." Garfax glanced down at some notes lying in front of him. His manner became businesslike, and he rubbed his hands together like a gambler preparing to clean out the bank. "What's the status on the close-in solar orbiters? How many have you built, what are their capacities, and what do you have coming later? Also, what's the position on the receiver relays?"

Norfield shook his head helplessly and directed an appealing look somewhere offscreen. A scientific advisor who had been following appeared on another screen to reply. "The solar prototype projector and one production model complete and in position. Another to be constructed, pending commissioning trials. Three relays complete, one almost complete, and three more scheduled over the next two years. Rated at ten-gigawatt beams initially, phasing up to a hundred gigawatts per beam for the later ones.

"Mm . . ." Garfax thought for a moment and scribbled something on one of his papers. "Say the equivalent of thirty large power plants guaranteed in the near term. We figured we could use forty. You'll need twelve of each to run at full capacity, but we won't need all that for a while yet." He turned an inquiring eye toward Josephson to invite comment.

"We should be able to manage through the early

phase," Josephson said. "But they'll need to do something about speeding up the timetable for the bigger beams. Probably cut back on some of their space projects—especially the longer-range ones. They could look into later expansion and upgrades too, once they've got the principle figured out. The *Servochron* can handle a lot more than those numbers."

"This is preposterous!" Norfield yelled out, suddenly finding his voice and losing his patience. "You're not seriously suggesting that we're going to allocate our entire Distant Solar Relay output to you? You're out of your minds! What makes you think we can spare it—or would want to if we could? We need every damn kilowatt of it. Do you have any idea how many billions of dollars and man-years of effort we've put into that program? We'd have to shut it all down. Why should we? I don't care what problems you're having. *We* have solved all those problems. I'm not interested."

Garfax seemed to have been expecting some such outburst. "Professor Kreissenbaum has already told you, the past shapes the future," he said. "If you help us change your past, you'll be bound to create an even better present for yourselves in the process. That's what the *Servochron* was built to do. Believe me, it's a good deal that we're offering."

"How is it supposed to be a good deal if we have to abandon everything worthwhile that we've been working on for years?" Norfield demanded. "I'm not interested. I like the present we've got right now, the way it is. I'll stay with it."

"Oh, all of that will change," Garfax assured him breezily. "It gets a bit complicated. Let's just say that if you help us fix this 2048 mess, everything further on down the line where you are would have to end up in even better shape. Maybe you'll find yourselves all over the Solar System, or even on your way out of it. Who knows?"

"Nobody *knows*," Norfield shouted. "That's my whole point. The whole idea is madness. You'd have to be able to think like whatever lunatic aliens built that thing to want to get mixed up with it. I only *know* what I see now, and I like it. I'm not changing it."

Garfax frowned and appeared to be giving thought to whatever he intended saying next. A silence fell. Norfield's scientific advisor, whose expression had been growing more puzzled, chewed his lip pensively and then spoke. "There's something crazy about this. If you've sent the *Servochron*, as you call it, out into space on a thirty-year orbit, then it isn't where you are. So how are you going to get anything out of it? How can you draw power from it if it isn't there?"

"We only sent the transmitter part out on an orbit," Josephson replied. "There's a receiver part too, that was originally contained inside the transmitter structure that you've got. There are twelve receiver modules—to enable the beams coming through from the transmitter to be redirected to different places. But they're small compared to the rest. We shipped them back here. In fact, we're talking right now via an auxiliary communications channel contained in one of them."

"Where from?" Norfield's advisor asked.

"Columbus, Nebraska," Josephson told him in a surprised voice. Astonishment registered on the other's face. "You haven't figured it out yet? We're integrating some of the receivers into the complex that's being built here to feed the national power grid. No doubt we'll find uses for the others too, later. Officially, for now, we're saying that a big fusion system will power it, but of course that's baloney. We know we're nowhere near a viable fusion solution yet. The experts know it too, but they can't seem to get a voice that the public hears." He shrugged.

"We guess that a couple of years on down the timeline as it exists right now, the lid's being blown off the whole thing and a lot of fingers are being pointed. Further along from that, we've probably gone down in history as a not very honest bunch of bad guys who screwed a lot of things up." Josephson grinned suddenly. "But that doesn't bother us because we don't intend to become the people who exist further down the timeline as it exists right now. We'll change that timeline. When you start delivering, everything we've promised the country will happen. That will create a new timeline, and on that one we'll be good guys." Josephson cocked his head to one side as a thought occurred to him. "What's happened to the Columbus complex on your part of the timeline as it stands? Did it get shut down?"

Norfield's advisor nodded woodenly. "Yes, it did. We abandoned the whole fool thing. It's all deserted and overgrown there now."

"Hm . . . That's what we figured," Josephson said. "If you don't believe us, go see for yourselves. Dig down under the complex and open up the deep shafts you'll find. The *Servochron's* receivers should still be down there."

Carol looked at Pearson. They both looked at

Chalmers. All three shook their heads. It was all too crazy for words.

"No!" Norfield declared from his own screen, sounding decisive. "That is my simple and final answer. We, in this decade, have solved our problems satisfactorily without any of this, and shall continue to do so. President Garfax, would you kindly go to hell!"

"Oh dear." Garfax shook his head sadly in the manner of one forced, reluctantly, to broach something that he would rather have left unsaid. He clasped his hands together in front of him, sat back in his chair, and looked up.

"Mr. President," he said. "I suspect that you have not yet had time to appreciate fully the realities of this situation. My proposal to you was not so much in the nature of a request, as an ultimatum. If you reflect for a moment, you will see that your position gives you no leeway for bargaining. In short, you have no choice but to comply."

"How so?" Norfield demanded. "What is there to bargain over? There's no reason why we should send you anything. You haven't got anything to trade."

"Possibly true," Garfax conceded. "But on the other hand, you will agree that our relationship here, to you there, does put us in a unique position. Whatever we choose to do now must affect your world of twenty-seven years later. However, the converse does not apply. The effect is completely one-way, as it were."

Norfield rubbed his temples and looked confused. "I'm . . . not sure I understand you," he said. "What are you trying to say?"

Garfax made an exaggerated show of being patient. "Let me put it to you this way. We are sitting on the planet that you will be occupying twenty-seven years from now. If you were to reject our proposals, we would be in a position to embark upon various activities—I'm sure I don't need to be distastefully specific—that could make life very . . . difficult for you." Norfield emitted an outraged gasp. Garfax leered openly and nodded. "I trust, Mr. President, that I have made my point," he said.

It was the ultimate blackmail. Garfax could lob grenades down the timeline with impunity, while the hapless successors twenty-seven years in the future possessed no means of defense or retaliation. It was, as he had said, completely one-way.

A squad of army engineers was sent to explore below the Columbus site, and sure enough the twelve receivers were there, showing all the signs of having lain undisturbed for many years. Each was about the size of a railroad freight car, equipped with a set of supercooled bus bars to deliver the power beamed back from the future via one of *Nomad*'s collector dishes. Six were installed in a concrete vault with output conductors ready for connection to the national power grid; the other six were in storage, presumably to await shipping for later uses elsewhere.

The whole business was nonsensical. If Josephson had stated the intention to complete the connections into the power grid within a short time of the date he had been speaking from in 2048, why weren't the modules connected? If Garfax had set up the Columbus complex to supply power from almost thirty years ahead, why didn't history record it as having happened? How could the complex be both operating by 2048, and at the same time be abandoned and uncompleted thirty years later? Scientists from Washington to Moscow wrestled with the logical impossibilities of plastic timelines, but every answer anyone suggested always seemed to pose ten new questions and contradict every other answer. Perhaps, as Norfield had said, a totally alien kind of mind was needed to comprehend it—a mind possibly endowed biologically with different instincts and schooled in different processes of experience to form its notions of what made sense and what didn't, what was sane and what was crazy.

The grenades started coming down the timeline shortly thereafter. Garfax announced that an explosive mine would be planted beneath the White House, fused to detonate after twenty-seven years. The building was evacuated, and a frenzied search by a Marine Corps bomb-disposal team uncovered a dummy device bearing the sign JUST TESTING.

Garfax then advised that the next mine would be buried in a remote part of Alaska, controlled by a high-precision electronic timer to explode at the exact moment when Norfield was speaking. Norfield promptly made inquiries and was advised that seismometers and Earth-orbiting satellites had detected a blast only minutes previously at the spot that Garfax indicated.

Then things got serious. The next three—one below the Los Alamos Laboratories in New Mexico; one under the Capitol; and one at a Space Force launch facility in Texas—were all live, but Garfax gave sufficient early warning to allow sweating teams of engineers to find and deactivate them before they timed out.

The next three, Garfax said, would not be revealed in advance. The Mount Rushmore National Monument collapsed into rubble twenty-four hours later. The ones following the two that were left, Garfax said, would be nuclear.

It was all over.

A white-faced Gregory Norfield capitulated unconditionally, and orders went out from ISA Headquarters in Geneva for work on the lunar constructions to cease, and for the power relays receiving the beams from the projectors in close solar orbit to be moved away from Luna and redirected on *Nomad*. Garfax allowed three weeks for this operation and stated that no slippage would be tolerated. Fifty tons of TNT went off underwater a few miles out from the Golden Gate Bridge to emphasize the point. The schedule was not allowed to slip.

The *Guam* was the focal point of all the activities going on around *Nomad*, and groups of visitors from Earth began arriving to play various parts in getting the operation together. Included among them was a deputation of government and scientific executives from Washington who had been coordinating the Distant Solar Relay Program.

Carol first saw him over the top of the console at which she was working in the *Guam*'s message-exchange center. He was one of a group in business suits and dresses, standing with some Space Force officers, discussing something on one of the mural displays. He hadn't changed in the year or more since she last saw him. His hair was as black and glossy as ever, his eyes bright and alert, and as he spoke, his mouth still broke into the natural, easygoing smile that had made her go fluttery inside when she was a mathematics undergraduate of twenty. Amanda smiled in exactly the same way.

She watched them for about twenty minutes while their discussion continued. Then somebody called for a break, and the group broke up in different directions. He stayed behind to study the screen, keying details into a hand compad. Carol suspended the job that she was doing, got up, and moved quietly over to behind where he was standing. "Hi," she murmured.

Dr. Donald Yaiger looked around, and his face broke into a smile of delighted surprise. "Carol!" He dropped the pad into a pocket and brought his hands up to grip her shoulders. "You're here, on the *Guam*? I had no idea. It's a small universe. I thought you were still shuttling up and down from California."

"I transferred to a Fleet command five months ago," Carol told him, returning the smile. "When did you arrive?"

"A day ago, with the DSRP group from Washington. We've been so tied up, I've hardly seen anything of this ship. It's huge. . . ." Don released her and shook his head. "It's just such a wonderful surprise . . . about the last thing I'd have expected. So how've you been? How's Amanda?"

"She's just fine. I was just thinking how much she's got your smile."

"And Doreen?"

"Oh, you know her. She never changes."

"I watched her Chopin recital the other week. She was terrific. The audience loved it. Did you see all the flowers? Did she get the birthday present I sent her—the perfume? Amanda told me once it was her favorite."

"Yes, and she loved it," Carol told him. "We both went there for the afternoon. Amanda said that people should get all their birthday presents from every year all together up front while they were still young, not have to wait until they were old. Then they'd get more fun out of them than having to waste all that time waiting. You can't fault her logic, I guess."

Don laughed. "Nobody can argue with Amanda logic. She'll go a long way, just like her mother."

"So what are you doing yourself?" Carol asked. "I hear rumors that you're doing well in the Relay Program. That has to be why you're on the *Guam*. Where do you fit into this crazy business?"

Don glanced around. "You know, we don't have to stand here talking like this. There must be somewhere we can grab a sandwich or something. How are you fixed?"

"Not that busy," Carol answered. "The maindeck cafeteria isn't far. Come on, I'll show you the way."

"It's bad news all-round," Don said over a half-eaten turkey club twenty minutes later. "Norfield doesn't have any choice. We're having to back down all the way along the line. Without the DSRP relays, the whole lunar-construction program, and therefore the colonies program too, will have to shut down. It will take years to begin putting the pieces together again—and even then, who's to say it will stop there? My feeling is that Garfax will just keep squeezing harder and harder. Our whole space and energy budget will end up being used to expand his economy. And there's no way out. If we don't play ball, he'll start nuking cities. He's insane enough to do it."

"But where will that leave you, Don?" Carol asked, horrified. "Your whole future is tied up in the program—everything you've worked for in years."

Don pulled a face and spread his hands. "All kaput, I guess." He shrugged and managed a resigned grin. "Aw, I'll never wind up on the street. The Department will come up with something else."

"Caretaking Garfax's relays for him," Carol said. "Or maybe putting up Mickey Mouse satellites with the change that's left over. Not quite the same as the next jump outward across the Solar System that you used to talk about, is it?"

As she looked across the table at Don, Carol felt loathing rising deep within her for the vision in her mind's eye of the leering, gnomish face cackling from a monitor screen. Or, another part of her mind asked, was she projecting outward some inner feelings about herself and finding an external object for them? For ten obstinate years she had kept Don at a distance, and now she was trying to make Garfax's blackmail the cause of a brilliant career being wasted. Some of the things Doreen had said came back to her now, and for the first time she found herself feeling doubts about the path she had insisted on. Maybe it was the effect of meeting him here, thousands of miles from Earth. She couldn't really tell herself now, she realized, what she thought she had been trying to prove. Was she setting Amanda up to go through the same thing again in twenty years time?

Don was watching her silently while he finished his sandwich. Carol sensed again the uncanny ability he had always had to read her thoughts from her eyes. "Don't let yourself get hung up over Garfax," he said. "I know he's a mean bastard—first your father, your mother and Amanda, and now this. But he's sitting pretty thirty years back in the past. Nobody can touch him."

Carol's expression became puzzled. "What do you mean, 'first your father'?" she asked. "What does my father have to do with Garfax? I'm not with you."

A look of surprise flashed across Don's face, then changed to one of realization. He pushed his plate away in a heavy, solemn movement. "Of course," he said in a dull voice. "You don't know, do you?"

"Know what?" Carol's brow creased. "Don, what about my father?"

"Not Phillip specifically—the whole *Damocles* mission." Don bit his lip, clearly wishing he hadn't brought this up. But there was no way out now. "I've been involved in some work that's going on, sifting through the old archives and trying to figure out exactly what did happen." He paused, but there was no letup in Carol's gaze. "Look . . . there's nothing certain about this, but as far as we can tell, it's the only explanation that fits all the facts.

"*Nomad* was discovered drifting through the Belt by an unmanned research probe in 2042. The discovery was kept secret, and the government-slash-military sent a scientific team out under Kreissenbaum in a ship called the *Ulysses* to find out what they could about it. That was all hushed up too. In 2045, Garfax was out of the public limelight for a couple of months, supposedly because he was sick. We don't think he was sick. We suspect that the findings were so sensational that he went out to *Nomad* to see it for himself. Right at that time, for no reason that makes sense, a fast Air Force executive lunar shuttle was fitted with long-range drives, and its log for the following two months shows evidence of being falsified. That must have been when they finally figured out what *Nomad* was."

Don sighed. "You can fill in the rest. A large-scale mission was organized to follow in a hurry, which was *Damocles*, of course—too big to cover up. So the meteor story was invented as a blind, and the people who went on that mission believed that was its purpose. But their communications failed when they were over halfway there—not just the primary system, but the backups too. Very strange." Don shook his head. "Things like that don't happen." He gave Carol a moment to absorb the implication. "We can guess that when the mission arrived at *Nomad*, it found Garfax and his people waiting, and learned for the first time what the job was really all about. . . . But because of another piece of bad luck, they never got home to tell anyone what they knew. If I had to put money on it, I'd bet that the heavy-lift section that carried those plasma motors out wasn't part of what blew up on the way back. That was how they got *Nomad*'s receivers home." Don showed his empty palms to say that was it, and slumped back in his seat.

Carol was gripping the edge of the table with fingers that showed knuckles looking as if they were about to break through the skin. "*Damocles* was sabotaged!" she whispered. She had to swallow before she could continue. "It was fixed to blow up on the way back. Oh, my God, Don! . . . He had them all killed. Garfax had the whole mission wiped out. That . . . monster . . . *killed* my father!"

Don reached across and squeezed her hand. "I'm sorry," he said. "I guess I forgot for a moment that you wouldn't know about any of that. I shouldn't have mentioned it." He tried to move his hand away, but Carol entwined her fingers more tightly.

"You know me, Don. I'd rather know it the way it is." She started to force a weak smile. Then her finger touched the ring he was wearing. She looked down and noticed it for the first time. Her face jerked upward sharply. "When?" Her voice choked before she could stop it.

"Four months ago." Don's face mirrored her dismay. "I waited. . . . I wanted us to," he stammered. "But all those years?" He shook his head. "You blew it, Carol. How long did you think we could go on like that?"

They had dinner together later, when Carol came off duty, and spent the rest of the evening in the officers' bar drinking and talking. Throughout it all, she managed to act normally and kept a brave face. The tears came later, when she was alone in her cabin.

When she finally slept, it was a restless, dream-ridden sleep. In her dream she saw a lonely, sad-faced woman staring out through a window while she played the piano, while behind her on the floor a caricature of Amanda arranged glowing jewels and geometric shapes into patterns. From out in space, in a line that diminished to infinity, countless *Nomads* were hurling brightly wrapped packages down at the little girl playing on the floor. The thousands of packages became a flood bearing down on the tiny figure, looming and menacing. Amanda, looking down, was oblivious to the danger. The woman at the piano played on heedlessly. Carol tried to cry out a warning but found she had no voice. The face of Garfax was in it too, somehow, laughing insanely. The mountain of packages was falling. . . . And then Carol was awake in her bunk, sweating and shaking.

She got up, put a wrap around her shoulders, and made a coffee, intending to settle her nerves before trying to get back to sleep again. But her mind was too active for sleep to be a possibility. The reality of the dream was gone, but instead of fading in the way that dreams normally do, the images kept replaying themselves, as if some significance about them was insistently trying to register. She sat, nursing her mug in the semidarkness, and pictured them again. A thousand *Nomads* all sending back their transmissions to a single place . . . Or was it the same *Nomad* existing at a thousand different points along the timeline that traced its existence, all transmitting to the same point in the past? The energy from a thousand futures concentrated on a single instant in the past . . .

Suddenly Carol was wide awake. The thought was crazy, surely. But then, everything about *Nomad* was crazy. "Why not?" she asked herself aloud.

She thought about it for half an hour without moving, while the rest of the coffee in the mug turned cold. Then she said, "Computers, normal lighting." The lights came up around the cabin. "Intercom."

"Intercom," a synthetic voice acknowledged.

"Put me through to Dr. Donald Yaiger, visiting the *Guam* from Washington." The cabin's vipanel turned itself to face her, and several seconds later activated to show Don blinking and rubbing sleep from his eyes. "What is it? . . . Hey! What's the matter? Is something up?"

"Don, I've got to talk to you. No, it can't wait till morning. I'm in G-37. Can you get here right away?"

"The operation will be controlled by computers installed in *Nomad* and connected into *Nomad's* direction system." Carol, now dressed in fatigues, paced from one side of the cabin to the other as she described the preparations to supply Garfax's demands. Don listened from the worktable below the shelved recess. "The computers will translate the receiver's spacetime coordinates into optical signals compatible with *Nomad's* equipment, that specify where in time the energy is sent from, and the point in the past that it's sent to. Okay so far?"

"Okay," Don confirmed, nodding.

"Well, you're the physicist. Tell me if there's any reason why this couldn't work. From what I can make out from the things Kreissenbaum said, the whole timeline that lies ahead of any *now* you care to pick is all equally real—as real as the instant we're at now. Correct?"

"It seems that way," Don agreed.

"So every instant along the timeline—every nanosecond of it—contains a *Nomad*, right? And every one of those *Nomads* could beam its energy back to the same, precisely defined, instant in the past." Carol turned to face where Don was sitting. His jaw dropped as the first hint of what she was getting at seemed to register. She went on, "Suppose we wrote

a program in which the instructions to begin transmitting were repeated to execute, say, a billion times
at some specified interval. Even if the timeline is
plastic—and I'm not sure anyone really knows what
that means—all those copies would commence beaming
at different points spaced sequentially along it. Now
suppose they were *all* aiming at the same point in
the past that Garfax specified. What would happen
to the receiver?"

Don stared at her for a few seconds. "You'd have
to have some kind of updating mechanism. Every
discrete point would need its own measure of elapsed
time to hit the target."

"A standard offset would take care of that. Routine
stuff. No problem."

Don thought for a moment longer. "*Jesus!* The
receiver would get zapped with a billion times more
energy than it was supposed to handle. . . . You'd be
sending a zigaton bomb back up the timeline!"

Carol nodded, satisfied. "That's what I thought.
Strictly one-way, huh?" A strange gleam came into her
eyes. "So that bastard wants our energy, eh? Okay, let's
give it to him. Why don't we let him have a billion
times more than he ever dreamed of?"

Don raised the issue at a meeting of DSRP scientists
and government people on the *Guam* first thing the
next morning. By lunchtime Norfield and his staff in
Washington had become involved, and by late afternoon
the plan was being examined in detail jointly with
ISA. The upshot was that nobody could say for sure
whether or not it would work, or offer any precise
explanation to support their opinion, whichever way

their opinion happened to be. It was no more or no less crazy than everything else connected with *Nomad*. And it was, after all, the only alternative to total and ignominious surrender that anyone had been able to come up with.

With ISA's blessing, Norfield gave his approval. For two hectic weeks, while discussions to finalize details of the official operation continued with Garfax's people, another team worked to develop the real programs that would be running when the day came for the blackmailers to collect. As the originator of the plan, Carol was offered the job of operating the console from which the master sequencing program would be run. It gave her a singular feeling of inner satisfaction to accept.

Garfax's face looked out from one of the screens on Carol's panel and beamed its crooked smile. Seventy miles away from the *Guam*, *Nomad* was hanging in space, surrounded by the first three relays positioned to redirect the beams from the Sun-orbiting projectors ninety-three million miles away. Inside *Nomad*, the control computers were installed and running, awaiting further commands from the *Guam's* supervisory system. The relays and *Nomad's* time-beam transmission would begin operating on receipt of a master signal. Carol was working in a small communications direction room opening off from the main control deck, where the official charade was being acted out.

"Five minutes to zero," Garfax declared cheerfully. "Why such serious faces there? This is a big day. We should all be celebrating. Just think, in five minutes time we'll have changed thirty years of history for the better. Who knows what great things may emerge from this moment? You should be proud and confident with visions of things to come."

Norfield watched from another screen without saying anything. Carol knew from Don's accounts of the exchanges with Washington that Norfield had been troubled when he gave the go-ahead. But the time simply hadn't permitted detailed consideration of all the niceties. If everything worked in the way that had been outlined then, a large piece of Nebraska would be vaporized, and along with it a lot of innocent people who weren't mixed up in Garfax's blackmail and knew nothing about it. True, they existed almost thirty years in the past, and maybe the blame could be rationalized as falling on a long-gone administration; but the fact remained that they were innocent people, and Norfield had been troubled.

And then Don's team of physicists, reconstructing their timetable of those past events, had come up with a modified version of the plan that didn't call for the damaging of so much as a blade of grass in Nebraska.

Carol turned her face toward the microphone stem on the console and said quietly, "Computers. Activate program TIMESCAN and unlock communicator coordinates on this channel."

"TIMESCAN running," the machine's voice confirmed. "Channel coordinates unlocked. Awaiting instructions."

Carol drew a deep breath to compose herself. Pearson was watching from an auxiliary screen. Indicators showed that the pilot signal activating the solar projectors had completed its sixteen-minute round-trip.

The beams were arriving and ready for the relays to switch into redirected mode onto *Nomad*.

The Garfax on the screen was talking via the communications channel of one of *Nomad's* receiver modules, located beneath the Columbus complex back in 2048. Whether he himself was there too, or hooked in through a connection from somewhere else, there was no way of telling. But there had been a time before then when he had definitely been physically present in the same place as the receivers. Carol was about to disconnect the channel on her console that was showing Garfax in 2048, and scan backward through earlier times in *Nomad's* history—times before the receiver modules had ever been brought back to Earth at all.

"Go back ten months," she directed. Garfax vanished from the screen. The console's other screens were still locked to the official channel, and the faces on them continued to act normally.

A picture appeared of a man who looked like a technician, working with his back to the viewing point—the communications screen on the same receiver module, but ten months before the time when the Garfax of a few moments before had been speaking through it. "Busy?" Carol inquired casually.

The technician whirled around. "What's going on?" he demanded. "Who turned that on? Where did you come from?"

"It would take too long to explain, and I don't have the time. Just answer a couple of questions, please. Are you down a shaft underneath the Columbus complex?" The technician nodded mutely. "Installing the receivers?" Another nod. "How long ago did the receivers arrive there?"

"Two months. They were shipped here at night, all secret. That's all I know. Now would you mind—"

"Thank you. Computers, resume scan. Back another three months."

This time she found herself talking to a bewildered government scientist aboard the spacecraft *Ulysses*. "Let me see if I can guess," Carol said. "You're taking the receiver modules from the Belt back to Earth. The *Servochron* has been sent off on a thirty-year round-trip, and the *Damocles* ship recently had a nasty accident on its way home. What do I get, ten out of ten? And who have you heard that said by before?"

"Goddammit, who are you?" the scientist choked, turning crimson. "That's highly classified. I've never seen you before. On whose authority—"

"Computers, resume scan. Back another month."

She tracked the receiver back to the time when it had formed a part of *Nomad*. There were lots of different people around it at various, closely spaced times. Evidently a lot of work was going on. As Carol had by then guessed, many of them were from the *Damocles* mission. On one of these occasions, she thought she maybe spotted Phillip Waverley in the background. But she let it go at that.

Eventually she was greeted by an astounded general in former USAFSC working fatigues and a white-haired civilian, both wearing overjackets that carried the *Damocles* emblem on the breast pocket. "You're with the *Damocles* mission from Earth," she stated without preliminaries. "How long ago did the mission arrive at the *Servochron*?"

The general returned a puzzled look. "At the *what*? Is that what this thing is called? Who the hell are you? Is that a major's insignia you're wearing? Where are you talking from?"

"Oh, I see," Carol said. "It's early days there. They haven't told you what it is yet. How long ago did the mission arrive, sir? It's extremely important."

"About five days," the general told her. "Do you know what this alien thing is? We were told we were being sent to steer off a rogue meteor. Which service are you with? I don't recognize those badges."

Carol ignored the questions. "When you arrived, was Garfax already there, and a scientist called Kreissenbaum? Maybe a few others with them?"

"Major, this kind of cross-examination of a senior officer is most irregular. I must insist that I talk to your commander."

"Yes, they were all here," the white-haired civilian came in. "I don't know why or how. The *Ulysses* was here too. It was supposed to have disappeared years ago. There's something very odd about this whole affair. I don't know who you are or or how you come to know what you seem to know, but it would assist us greatly if—"

"Computers, terminate." Carol thought for several seconds. The *Damocles* ship had arrived at *Nomad* five days before that last point. Three days cruising would put it out of the danger zone. "Resume scan, go back eight days," she said. Surely this would be the last stop.

A surge of jubilation came over her as the screen activated again. This was going to be better than she had dared hope. She was looking at the familiar gnomish face, only this time it wasn't cackling. It was openmouthed with surprise, its beady eyes popping beneath the tuft of unruly hair.

"Good day, Mr. President," Carol greeted tightly. "You have no idea what a pleasure this is."

Garfax blinked uncertainly. "Who are you? You're not from the *Ulysses*. What are you doing here? . . . *Are* you here?" Two more figures joined him, evidently attracted from somewhere near by his agitation.

"Ah, Mr. Josephson and Professor Kreissenbaum. I'm *so* delighted." It was going to be even better.

"Who is she?" Kreissenbaum demanded, turning sharply toward Garfax. "How does she have access to the device? Where is she speaking from?"

"Major Carol Waverly, U.S. Space Force," Carol informed them. "Speaking from 2075." Three dumbfounded stares confronted her. "Why so surprised?" she asked. "You've had more than two years to figure out what the *Servochron* is, haven't you? You must have all the answers by now. Why else would the president have gone out there?"

"How much do you know about this?" Josephson growled, sounding menacing.

"Oh, we know everything," Carol answered. "It didn't occur to you that after thirty years we might have put together even more of the pieces than you allowed for, did it? We know about your plan to send the *Servochron* off on a thirty-year trip, while you ferry the receivers back to Nebraska. We also know about your plan to bomb the *Damocles* ship after all the work had been done, to silence the witnesses." She paused and smiled sweetly. "But that hasn't happened yet, has it? In fact, if my figures are correct, the *Damocles* ship should be approaching you right now, about three days out. What do I get, ten out of ten?"

"Somebody's leaked the whole thing," Josephson groaned, turning pale.

"Impossible," Garfax insisted.

"It's not a leak," Kreissenbaum said. "Didn't you hear her? She's talking from 2075. Something must have gone wrong further down the timeline."

As the argument on the screen degenerated into babble, Carol turned back toward the microphone. "Computers, activate program BLITZKRIEG, prime redirector relays, remote-initialize main power beam, release target vector designator, lock to coordinates registering on this channel."

"BLITZKRIEG running, redirectors primed, main power beam initialized and checking positive, designator released, coordinates from active channel copied and verified," the computer confirmed.

"Set offset repeat to one billion, all beams to maximum power, unlock trigger, and focus on coordinates as set," Carol commanded.

"Beams set at ten gigawatts, offset repetition factored at one billion, trigger unlocked, focus on coordinates as set, status checks at condition green."

"Who's she talking to?" Kreissenbaum demanded. "What kind of gibberish is that?"

"Explain yourself, Major," Garfax ordered. "What are you doing?"

"You wanted our energy," Carol replied simply. "You're about to get it."

"*No!* . . . You've got it all wrong!" Josephson yelled in alarm. "Not *here* . . . not *now*! That's over two years away. You can't—"

"Oh yes I can. And it's coming down the pike at a billion times what you expected. Never mind how. It would take too long to explain. So long, guys."

"*You're mad!*" Kreissenbaum screamed. "You don't understand what you're—"

Carol turned her head away. "Disengage safety interlocks and stand by to fire."

"Confirm order to disengage safety interlocks?"

"Confirmed."

"Interlocks disengaged. Standing by."

"Stop! As your president and commander in chief, I order you to—"

"*Fire!*"

A blaze of whiteness erupted in space a million miles ahead of the ship making its way outward from the orbit of Mars. For a brief instant its light rivaled that of the Sun, illuminating the vessel from directly ahead. Painted near the ship's nose was a large emblem showing a red sword standing on a black background.

General Phillip Waverley, USAFSC (Retired), sat in a recliner by the pool at the back of the house, enjoying the last of the fine summer. Beside him, his son-in-law was lounging in a deck chair, sipping from a can of beer and munching peanuts. The sounds of excited female voices came intermittently from inside the house.

"Executive job with the Distant Relay Program, eh?" Phillip said with an approving nod. "Just what you needed. They'll be sending you out on some trips after a while, I'd guess. I always said we'd make a spaceman out of you one day."

"I reckon you're right." Don didn't sound too displeased at the thought. "I've got some catching up to do with your side of the family, though. With Carol on the *Guam*, and the number of miles you've logged around the Solar System . . ."

"Oh, you'll probably end up seeing more than I ever did, never mind the miles," Phillip said. "You'll be out there making it happen, where it matters." He shrugged and rubbed his chin. "All I ever did was follow orders."

A short silence fell while Phillip watched a squirrel scrambling in one of the trees behind the house, and Don finished his beer.

"How old were you when you made your first deep-space trip?" Don asked finally.

Phillip had to think back. "Somewhere around my early thirties, I'd guess. . . ." His eyes took on a distant look. "It was the *Damocles* mission back in 2045. I've told you about it before. The mission that never happened, remember?"

"The meteor you said wasn't a meteor. It blew up or something, didn't it?"

"They told us it was a meteor," Phillip replied, nodding slowly. "But when we were about a million miles out from it, it suddenly went up like a piece of the Sun. I never heard of any meteor doing anything like that." He turned his head and looked over. "And I'll tell you something else. I saw the pictures that were reconstructed from the optical scans just before it blew. No meteor that I heard of ever looked like that, either. There was something very funny about that whole mission."

"What did it look like?" Don asked.

"Aw, it wasn't too clear—just some patches of light that made a shape against the starfield. . . . But it didn't look *natural*—not to me, anyhow. It was too symmetrical. And it had circles around it. Looked sort of like a strawberry. And then all our communications with Earth failed when we were on the way out, so we couldn't tell anybody about it until after we got back. That couldn't have happened. But it did." Phillip nodded decisively. "There was something peculiar about that whole mission, all right."

At that moment, Amanda came running out of the house through the open French windows. "Daddy, Grandpa, you've got to come inside now. Grandma is opening her presents."

Phillip looked around at her. "You're right, little lady. We're not doing very much to make this a party, are we? Come on, then. Let's go inside and see what she's got." He rose to his feet. Amanda clasped his hand and led him back into the house. Don crushed the empty can in his hand, tossed it into the trash bin by the pool, got up from the deck chair, and followed.

Doreen was on the sofa in the living room, unwrapping a large package resting on her knees, while David, Amanda's six-year-old brother, watched with big eyes from beside her. Carol looked up from the armchair by the piano. "You're just in time," she said to Don. "We're opening the parcel that your parents sent from Florida."

"I didn't know people still get birthday presents when they're *fifty-four*," Amanda said, perching on an arm of Carol's chair. "I think it's wrong to have to wait until you're that *old* before you can have all your presents. Why can't people have them when they're still little? Then they wouldn't have to wait all that time and only be able to play with them for a little while."

"Amanda logic," Don said, shaking his head at Phillip.

"Fifty-four isn't old," Carol reproached. "And if you got all your presents at once, you'd have nothing to look forward to. Oh, look at those vases, Don. Chinese, aren't they? They're gorgeous!"

"I must call today and thank them," Doreen said, looking delighted. "Phil, aren't they just what we need for the dining room?"

"Very pretty," the general conceded gruffly.

"When I'm older, I'm going to be a scientist like Daddy," Amanda told everyone. "Then I'll invent a time machine that can send all the presents I'm going to get between now and when I'm fifty-four back to today. Then I'll be able to play with them all today."

"You'd have to be a pretty clever scientist to invent something like that," Don said, laughing.

"Why?" Amanda objected. "They have time machines in movies."

"They're just stories," Don said. "They don't really exist. They can't. Such things are impossible."

Amanda pouted. "Why are they impossible? I don't think they are. Other machines aren't impossible. I'm going to invent one anyway."

"Your father is a scientist already, don't forget," Carol said. "You'll have a hard time arguing with him about things like that. If he says they're impossible, I believe it. He ought to know." She looked around, searching for a way out. "Let's open another present. That green one looks interesting. I wonder what it is."

Doreen placed the vases back in their box, set it carefully on a side table out of David's reach, and leaned across to pick up the green-wrapped package. Amanda jumped down from the arm of Carol's chair and moved closer to see. Don and Phillip grinned at each other.

"Kids!" Don snorted. "Time machines to send back birthday presents."

Phillip pulled a cigar from the pocket of his shirt. "They get some crazy ideas, all right." He shrugged and jammed the cigar between his teeth. "Who knows? Maybe nothing's impossible." He flicked his lighter and brought the flame up, catching the look on Don's face as he did so. "But I heard what my daughter said," he added hastily. "I'm not going to argue about it. After all, you are the scientist."

Cryptic Crossword

One of the most relaxing yet at the same time stimulating ways I know of spending an afternoon is solving the *Irish Times* or *London Times* cryptic crossword over a pint or two of Guinness. I was introduced to cryptics long ago, as an electronics design engineer in England back in the 1960s, when the guys in the lab would sit around working one in the lunch break. From time to time over the past few years I've contributed my own compilations to such noble causes as *Analog* magazine and sometimes the program book of various conventions that I've attended. Eleanor Wood thought it would be a great idea to add to the variety by including one in this collection too.

Rather than presenting simple definitions or questions of general knowledge, the cryptic style of crossword uses clues typically built around wordplays, metaphor, and double meanings. It appeals to those who enjoy the challenge of creatively working out a solution as opposed to either just knowing an answer or not, or having to guess at it.

A clue will frequently comprise a definition of the answer along with directions for constructing it, very likely written in a misleading way to obscure which is which. Thus, the answer to "Satellite condition for descent on the house" turns out to be "Freefall"—the condition of an orbiting satellite—constructed from "free," meaning "on the house," and "fall," i.e. descent.

It always pays to look for possible meanings of words other than the apparently obvious. "Die of cold" could refer to an ice cube. "Tower of strength" might mean a horse towing a barge. A "flower" might be a river—something that flows—and not a plant. Words like "confused," "rearranged," "could be" occurring in clues are often hints to the existence of an anagram. When considering anagrams, be aware that "one" may indicate the letter I, while "quarter," "point," or "direction" may indicate the compass points, N, E, S, or W. Likewise, "note" could mean any of the musical notes: A, B, C, D, E, F, or G. The answer to "Sailor becomes famous with direction" thus turns out to be "Star": S plus "tar," a sailor. Or again, "Note agate mixed in the drink" gives the solver instructions to "mix"—form an anagram from—"note," in this case G, and the letters of "agate" to give something found in a drink: "Tea bag." Roman numerals C, D, L, M, X are often used similarly.

Words like "back" or "returns" can indicate a word or letter sequence written backward, for example

"Drab" as the answer to "Minstrel returns, dull and colorless" ("bard" written backward). Similarly, "up" can indicate a word or letter sequence reversed in a Down clue. Words like "seen in," "found in," "held by" can indicate the solution to be literally in the clue; thus, "Stance," the answer to "Position embraced by earliest ancestors." It was there all the time in earli-eST ANCEstors.

There are no rigid rules. The idea is to exercise ingenuity and have fun. A name frequently implies a diminutive form, such as "Ed" or "Ted" for Edward. "Said" or "sounds like" usually indicates homophones, such as "rain dear" and "reindeer." "Head," "tail," "beginning," "end," and so forth can refer to the first or last letters of a word, e.g. "Rarity" as the answer to "Odd parity has new beginning." Occasionally, a construction has no other merit than to inflict on the solver some exceptionally warped interpretation of a meaning that the compiler was unable to resist.

Figures in parentheses after a clue give the letter count of the words making up the answer. Thus (3, 2, 6) would indicate a three-word solution of 3, 2, and 6 letters. One of my favorites that I came across in the *London Times* presented just a blank line of space, followed by the parenthetical information (5, 3, 1, 4). My first reaction was to suspect a printing error. The answer turned out to be, "Hasn't got a clue."

So here's one to try your skill and luck with.

Across

6 Glib talker gives wrong replies (7)
7 Contrivance which with 1 Down will take you forward or backward (7)
9 Sad song is gleeful with the start of the year (5)
10 Build out of silicon structural material (9)
11 Incidentally rearranging a poor afterthought (7)
13 Put in total ejection (6)
15 Energetic reaction from a run of lunacies (7, 6)
19 Speaker's position brings hatred to the capital of Peru (6)

Down

1 Duration in centimeters (4)
2 Make a big thing of the performance being over (4, 2)
3 A comic who tells safe jokes? (9)
4 Noted company of kinds showing common adaptations (8)
5 Circumstances to pose before a Greek character rising over charges (10)
6 Behold and beheld going up and going down (3, 3)
7 Sounds like a principal state of hair (4)
8 Bury remains of boatsmen after a departure (6)

Across (cont.)

20 Married to the USPO in Southern Alabama (7)

23 Disturbed real men join the French glossy painter (9)

24 Observe a personal 1 Down and 5 Across (5)

26 The prudent way of combining polonium, lithium, titanium, and carbon (7)

27 Lack of care for a mixed-up little English Celt (7)

Down (Cont.)

12 Arthurian ammunition columns (5, 5)

14 Issue of key season (9)

16 One honored by your leave (8)

17 Quick look at maintenance cost (6)

18 Nothing original at the top (3, 3)

21 Perserve! It's our time to appear (2, 2, 2)

22 Allied unit an endless obstacle (4)

25 A growing concern in every street (4)

From the Web Site

Bulletin Board, "Environmentalism," June 22, 2003 (http://www.jamesphogan.com/bb/content/062203. shtml)

MORE GLOBES WARMING

Mike Sissons calls attention to the November 2002 issue of *Liberty* magazine, in which scientists from Lowell University, MIT, the University of Paris, and NASA JPL report three bodies in the Solar System other than Earth—Mars, Triton, and Pluto—as exhibiting measurable warming in recent years. The January 2002 issue of *Science News* describes the rate of erosion of the northern polar ice cap of Mars as "phenomenal." Imagine the panic if this had been observed on Earth. (Jim Locker says to add Neptune also: see *Sky and Telescope* (http://skyandtelescope.com/), "Neptune's Forecast: A Cloudy Summer," by J. Kelly Beatty, August 2003 issue, page 22.)

The simplest explanation that applies to all would be an increase in the Sun's output. The June 18, 2003, issue of *Physics News Update* (No. 642) reports a study by researchers at Duke University and the Army Research Office that finds evidence linking solar-flare activity with changes in the Earth's temperature. Despite giving them plenty of time to think about it, there hasn't been a word—as far as I'm aware—about the possibility of such a connection from the global warming lobby.

The warming that Earth seems to have been experiencing for about the last 300 years represents a recovery from the "Little Ice Age" of the seventeenth century and is part of a long natural cycle that goes back to include the "climatic optimum" of around 1100 AD, when Greenland was green and colonized by the Danes, and an even warmer period around 4,500 years ago. An interesting aspect is that these periods of warming appear to have *preceded* increases in carbon dioxide, suggesting that rising temperature triggers the release of carbon from such reservoirs as Arctic permafrost. The roughly one-degree rise of the last century happened before 1940, whereas the CO_2 increase came later, raising the legitimate question of whether human activity had anything to do with it at all. So, the "connection" that the environmentalists claim is indeed real. But as usual, they get it the wrong way around.

Although the clearest correlation with these variations

is solar activity, the seemingly obvious conclusion was resisted by the scientific establishment until the early 1990s because the idea that the Sun could vary went against prevailing theory. The astronomer William Herschel suspected it as early as 1801. In the absence of any means of direct measurement at the time, he suggested using the price of wheat as an indicator of sunspot activity. He was laughed at, of course. But the records in retrospect show him to have been absolutely right.

ANIMAL QUACKERS

Bulletin Board, "Humor & Diversions" section, June 12, 2004 (http://www.jamesphogan.com/bb/content/061204-1.shtml)

It's reassuring to know that in these days of unrestrained greed and pathological craziness being unleashed upon a bewildered world, the English can still be relied upon to keep their heads and retain a sense of proper proportion. Besides being delightful of themselves, some areas of scientific investigation delve into matters of import that will still have their place in the emporium of worthwhile human knowledge long after the antics of today's mental and moral midgets have been forgotten.

The Sydney Morning Herald reports from the *Guardian* that researchers at London's Middlesex University have discovered that British ducks have regional accents, just like the people. Ducks in London parks make shorter, sharper sounds like Cockneys, and tend to be louder, while ducks from the Cornwall

and the West produce longer, drawn-out calls, evocative of slower-talking country folk. It is thought that
the different environments affect ducks and humans
similarly. Full story at:

http://www.smh.com.au/articles/2004/06/04/
1086203606507.html.

Take Two

An incoming call in Twofi Kayfo's head notified him that a response to his request had come in from the Merchandising Coordinator. Along with it was a limited-time discounted offer to switch to a different communications carrier. He tagged the ad for future reference, sent a signal to print out the file, then got up from his desk and crossed the office behind Sisi, who was reviewing the month's special manufacturers' packages for dealers, to retrieve the sheets from the printer. Technically he didn't need a hard copy, since the information could have been routed to him direct, but having something visual to proffer was better for presenting to customers. Also, the peripherals, accessories, and paper manufacturers had a lobby that pressed the case against purely electronic forms of data transfer and record-keeping.

Twofi checked over the printout. The deal seemed straightforward enough. He took it through to Beese, the sales manager, for approval.

"It looks all in order here, Twofi," Beese agreed. "Book this one and you'll be eight points over budget two weeks early. That'll get you in the Million Uppers and to Biloxi in February for sure."

"A cinch, Beese." Twofi winked an imager flap, took back the papers, and went through the building to Service Reception, where the customer was waiting.

The customer's name was Alfa Elone. The message that Twofi received from the service clerk eight minutes previously had told him that Elone's *Road Clipper* would need a rebuilt or replacement main turbine. Twofi had run a check showing that Elone's credit was underused right now, and the package that had come in from Merchandising was a tailored suggestion as to what might be done about it.

"Emess Elone, how are you today?" Twofi's use of the casual Male Surrogate form of address was relaxed and friendly—matching his disarming smile and proffered hand, which Elone had grasped before having a chance to think about it. "I'm Twofi Kayfo, from our customer-assistance program. We're here to help you save money. Is it okay to call you Alf?" The thermal patterns playing on Elone's metallic features had the vigorous look that went with an active, open-air lifestyle—in keeping with the customer profile that Twofi had seen. His white flared pants and royal-blue shirt with silver brocade on the chest, along with the cuffs and collar, were top-line designer brand, styled with the imitation silk–lined cloak and brass-buckled belt after the popular series

Captain Cutlass, which related exploits of olden-day human nautical adventurers.

Alf nodded. "Sure, I guess. . . ."

Twofi began walking Elone across the shop to where the *Clipper* was parked, not coincidentally near the side door leading out to the sales lot. It had collected all the extras over the years—no room for any margin there, as the service clerk had already noted. "Now let's see what we've got here, Alf. I talked to our engineer, and it looks as if your main turbine's just about shot. We could go for a rebuild of the bearings, but a year from now it would have to be replaced anyhow—and you know as well as I do what a false economy that would be, eh?" He treated Alf to the kind of knowing smile that recognized smartness when he saw it.

"Er . . . right," Alf agreed reluctantly.

Twofi gestured at the opened engine compartment in a careless way that said he probably didn't need to spell this out. "And then, as you know, what happens next when you replace it is that everything else that was getting near the limit can't deal with the power upgrade, and you'll be coming back with something or other that needs fixing every month."

Alf looked at his car with a worried expression. "Are you saying I should get it all done now? Won't that be a lot more expensive?"

Twofi shook his head reassuringly. "Actually, it works out cheaper, Alf."

"How could it?"

Twofi showed the top sheet of the plan that he had brought out with him. "I ran a projection from statistics of the wear pattern and parts-replacement requirements that you're likely to experience from

James P. Hogan

now on, based on a full turbine replacement for this model, year, mileage, and your style of use. Here's a graph that plots your cumulative costs with time—you see, getting steeper. But I've also superposed the payments and typical costs of a *new* car. The curves cross right here," he pointed, "eighteen months from now. So from then on, you'd be ahead of the game. Not a bad deal, eh? Like I said, we're here to save you money."

Alf looked hard at the graphs and the numbers, as if seeking to spot the hidden flaw—which by definition wouldn't be there to see. In fact, so far there wasn't one. Cars came with parts *designed* for different life expectancies, depending on the warranty selected. "What kind of car are we talking about here?" he asked cautiously. Positive question—a good sign, Twofi told himself. Move it along.

He draped an arm lightly on Alf's shoulder and steered him toward the door leading out to the lot. "One that's getting to be popular with roids who know what to look for. It so happens that we have one right outside. Let's take a peek at it. It'll only need a minute." They came out to stand in front of a gleaming Noram *Sultan*, of curvier lines than the utilitarian *Clipper*, and electric blue-black with sapphire trim. It had been moved just minutes before from the far end of the display line and hurriedly wiped clean. Twofi went on, "There, what would you say to something like that? Cryogenic recirculator for better efficiency, full satellite nav and wired-road auto, independent steering and compensators on all hubs. It's up from the replacement model for the *Clipper* that you've got now—but with the trade-in

I can give, you can still be on that eighteen-month financial crossover that I showed you."

They talked a little about details and options. Alf tried some haggling over the figures, but Twofi sensed that it was mostly for form's sake. Alf wasn't near his limit yet.

"But that's if you just want to carry on along in the same way that you have been, without getting anything new out of life," Twofi told him. "Before we finalize on anything, let me show you something else." Without waiting, he took Alf's elbow and guided him toward the door into the sales room, just a short distance farther along. The models inside were lavish and large, evoking images of human-style opulence. "This, for instance . . . Not just a runabout for getting around, but a whole new lifestyle, Alf! It's got the power and the comfort to open up places you've never been to before. Rugged, all-country. The hitching right there to attach your boat trailer; integral winch for launching and retrieval . . ."

"But I don't have a boat," Alf objected.

Twofi uncovered the next of the sheets that he was holding. It showed a picture of a twenty-foot basic hull with aft cabin and deckhouse, moored against a background of mountains and forest. That was a bit misleading, since humans usually monopolized settings like that. Prole recreation areas were more likely to be old city centers, with waterfronts in places like New Jersey and Detroit. . . . But the suggestion was there.

"That's where we start to plan ahead and get creative," Twofi said soothingly. "I've got a special offer for you, Alf. If we trade the *Clipper* and go for this model instead of the *Sultan* out there, then any time in the next three years, you get to go ahead on this boat at 25 percent off list. *And* you get privileged discounts on deck furniture and a whole bunch of other accessories. . . ." He waited, reading the signals. True, this would more than double Alf's outgoings, but if they didn't soak up his credit with this, someone else soon would.

Alf vacillated, enticed by the vision kindled in his brain but struggling with the suddenness and novelty. It needed one more nudge. "And if we okay it by this time tomorrow, you get the boat trailer for free," Twofi threw in.

One thing he had in common with economists, Dave Jardan suspected as he looked down over the last stretch of northern Virginia's residential parks before the Washington cityplex, was that he didn't understand economics. But as a designer of artificial intelligences he didn't really need to. The same money circulated round and around, in the process somehow spinning off enough profit to make everyone a living. It seemed as if something was being created out of nothing somewhere, as with a perpetual-motion machine, or sustaining momentum endlessly in the way of one of those Escher drawings where water flowed downhill all the way round a closed circuit and back to its starting point. If the books all the way around the system balanced, where did the surplus come from?

The executive VTOL's flight controller spoke from the cabin grille in a euphoniously synthesized Southern female voice. "Secure for landing, please. Time to the gate is approximately nine minutes. We hope you had a good flight." Dave checked his seat belt and began replacing papers and other items that he had been using back in his briefcase. The engine note dropped, then rallied again as the clunks and whines of aerofoils deploying sounded through the structure, and the craft banked to come around onto its approach. Below were the beginnings of the densely crammed proleroid residential belt blending into the urban sprawl west of the Potomac—roadways crowded with vehicles, the houses sprouting patios, add-ons, and extensions like living, mutating vegetables, their yards filled with pools and cookout gear, sports courts, play corners, fountains, floweramas, and every other form of outdoor accessory that marketing ingenuity could devise.

At least, such an ongoing surplus couldn't flow from a system that was constant, Dave supposed. It would have to grow continually. That had to be why money-based economies had always sought, and not infrequently gone to war for, ever-greater markets and empires. And for a long time, progressively more automated manufacturing and distribution had supplied the expanding demand. But eventually, overproduction itself became the problem, and whole new industries of persuasion and credit financing had to be created to invent essential needs that people had never known they'd had before. Then the medical and social costs of the stress-related syndromes, alienation, crime, and generally self-destructive behavior that came out of it all escalated until many started taking it into their heads to chuck all of it and go back to lives of home cooking and book-reading, horse-raising and fishing. And that wouldn't have been good for General Motors or the Chase Manhattan Bank at all.

The solution couldn't be some fainthearted retreat, which would merely have led back to the same problem later. Instead, the answer adopted was to press resolutely on by completing the job and taking the process that had brought things thus far to its logical conclusion: The obvious way to dispose of the output from automated manufacturing and distribution was automated consumption: special-purpose machines to get rid of the junk that the other machines were producing.

For a while, Dave Jardan had shared the dismay that the artificial-intelligence community had felt at seeing their final, triumphal success—not exactly genius level, but a passably all-round humanlike capability all the same—engineered into a breed of robots called the "proleroids," who happily absorbed all the commercial messages and did most of the buying, using, fixing, and replacing necessary to close the economic cycle. Freeing up humans from performing these functions meant that all of them could now live comfortably as stockholders, instead of just a privileged class as previously. It was from such private means that Dave obtained the wherewithal to pursue the goal of developing a superior AI of truly philosophical capacity, which had always been his dream.

As tends to happen in life, what had once seemed revolutionary became the familiar. His initial indignation gradually abated, and now he just went with the flow. Privately, he still couldn't avoid the suspicion that there had to be something crazy about a system that needed a dedicated underclass to turn its products back to a condition suitable for returning into the ground where the raw materials had come from; and he still didn't really understand how the continual recycling of various configurations of matter around the loop managed to yield plenty for all to get by on. . . . But then, he wasn't an economist.

He arrived on schedule and was met by a pleasant-faced woman of middle age, neatly attired in a pastel-blue business dress and navy throw-on jacket, who introduced herself as Ellie, from the Justice Department. Few people took jobs from necessity these days, but many still liked a familiar routine that brought order into their lives and took them out among others. How the Justice Department had come to be involved in evaluating his project, Dave had no idea. It was just another of those inexplicable things that came out of the entanglement of Washington bureaucracies. Growth of government, with seemingly everyone wanting a say in how others ought to live, was one of the unfortunate consequences of too many people having plenty of time on their hands and not enough worthwhile business of their own to mind.

A proleroid-chauffeured limo took them to the nebulously designated "Policy Institute" offices in Arlington, occupying a couple of floors in an archi-tectural sculpture of metal and glass that formed an appendage of George Mason University. On the way, they passed a proleroid construction crew with excavating machinery and a crane, laying a section of storm drain. The current rage among proleroids was the Old West, and a couple of them wore cowboy hats and vests, with one sporting authentic-looking chaps. Dave learned that Ellie was from Missouri, had two grandchildren, spent much of the year photographing mountain scenery around the world, restored Colonial furniture, and played the Celtic harp. Her income was from copper smelting in Michigan, plastics in Texas, and a mixed portfolio that her family broker took care of.

Nangarry greeted Dave in his office over coffee. He looked dapperly intellectual as usual, in a lightweight tan summer suit and knitted tie, with wire-rimmed spectacles, and a lofty brow merging into a prematurely bald pate. His mood today was not reassuring, however. "It's going to be a slaughterhouse," he told Dave glumly. "They're all out for blood."

Dave knew that the initial reactions hadn't been exactly favorable. But even Nangarry's customary directness hadn't quite prepared him for this. "All of them?" he queried.

Nangarry nodded. "Boy, if the idea was to piss off everybody, you did a good job, Dave. And I mean *everybody*. I thought this was supposed to be a superphilosopher. The nearest I can think of is Socrates—and we all know what happened to him."

Dave licked his lips. "What's been happening?" he asked. There wasn't much else he could say. He had heard PHIL's end of it, of course, and had he wished, could have followed the proceedings interactively over the previous few days. But he had thought it better to stay out until the heads of the various assessing groups came together to review the results. Besides, Dave was the kind of person who always had other pressing things to do.

"Well, Wade from down the street is in there with PHIL right now," Nangarry said. By "down the street" he meant the Pentagon—Wade was the army general heading the military's evaluation group. "The last I heard, they were trading dates and numbers about things that people who win wars don't put in the history books. I got the feeling Wade was getting the worst of it. That baby of yours can sure come up with dates and numbers, I'll give you that."

"What do you expect?" Dave replied. "I thought that was the whole idea."

Nangarry drained the last of his coffee and set down the cup. "Let's go take a look," he suggested. They got up, left the office, and headed along the corridor outside to the conference room where the meeting would convene formally following lunch.

Dave had been working for years to develop an AI capable of abstract association, pattern extraction, and generalization at levels normally encountered in such hitherto exclusively human areas of cognitive ability as philosophy, ethics, religion, science, and the arts. Commercial interest, and hence funding for further serious work, had virtually ceased with the advent of the proleroids. The few researchers like Dave, who persevered, had done so from personal motivation inspired by the challenge—and in Dave's case, because he knew that he and his small team back in Colorado were good. At first, true to tradition, they had played with acronyms from words like "associative," "cognitive," "conceptualizing," and "integrating" to describe their emerging creation, but none that they came up with had a satisfactory ring. Later, as the trials became more encouraging, Dave had considered a more grandiose appellation from the names of famous philosophers: Aristotle, maybe, or Plato, Epictetus, Hume, Kant, Mill? . . . But none of them seemed to capture the full essence of what the endless training and testing dialogues showed coming together. Finally, he had taken the generic cop-out and settled simply for "PHIL."

People like Dave tended to be idealists in at least some ways. After the successes that had attended the application of more sophisticated information-processing technologies to higher levels of human problem-solving, the means was surely there, he believed, to bring some improvement to the governing of human affairs, where the record of humankind itself had been so deplorable for about as long as human history had been unfolding. Why not use an AI to help make laws and set standards?—or at least, to formulate them without the subjective biases that had always caused the problems with humans. For once, the principles that all agreed it would be good for everyone else to live by could be applied equally and impartially; the selective logic that always made one's own case the exception would be replaced by a universal logic that didn't care. The injustices that had always divided societies would be resolved, and the entire race, finally, would be able to settle down and enjoy lives of leisure, plenty, and contentment, as knowledge and intelligence surely deserved.

All inspiring, heady stuff. Fired with enthusiasm, Dave approached the National Academy of Sciences with his vision and generated enough interest for reports and memorandums to be sent onward to the unmapped inner regions of the nation's governing apparatus. It seemed that everyone felt obligated to agree it was a good idea, but no one was volunteering to put their name on anything to launch it. Finally, after almost a year, a statement came out of a suboffice of the Justice Department, authorizing a limited evaluation trial program. Preliminary assessment would be conducted by a committee of representatives from select groups likely to be the most affected. From what Nangarry was saying, things weren't off to a very good start.

General Wade was short and sparsely built, with dark hair and toothbrush mustache, a thin mouth, and eyes that were quick to sharpen defensively. He struck Dave as the overcompensating kind that gravitated naturally to authoritarian hierarchies where rank and uniform enabled the assertiveness that they might have been unable to muster in other areas of life. Security with what was familiar inclined them toward being dogmatic and rule-driven. That might have been ideal for implementing military regulations or police procedures, but it was hardly high in its demand for the kind of creative insight required for re-laying the foundations of a society's ethical structure.

When Dave and Nangarry entered the conference room, Wade was at the far end in front of one of the screens connected to PHIL, located at Dave's lab in Colorado. With him was a pink-faced woman with a flare of yellow hair, wearing a cream jacket and maroon blouse. From their viewscreen exchanges, Dave recognized her as Karen Hovak, a policy analyst at a liberal-political think tank called the Fraternity Foundation. A woman in army uniform, trimly turned out, with firm yet attractive features and shoulder-length black hair, was sitting nearby typing into a laptop. Several more people, some of them also at screens, were scattered around the room. It seemed that others were getting in a few extra hours to familiarize themselves with PHIL too, before the formal afternoon session began.

Wade was tight-lipped, barely able to contain his evident irritation, while Nangarry performed the face-to-face introductions behind a frozen smile. The aide accompanying the general was Lieutenant Laura Kantrel. She looked up from the laptop long enough to flash Dave a quick, impish smile when he let his gaze linger for just a second longer than the circumstances called for. It was nice to think he had one friend in the place, anyway, he reflected stoically—or at least, someone who seemed potentially neutral.

"Hello, Dave." PHIL greeted him naturally as he moved within the screen's viewing angle—there were other cameras covering the room too.

"Hi," Dave returned. "How are things back at the ranch?"

"The new air conditioner arrived, but otherwise nothing's changed much." The screen changed from the world map and table of dates and places that it had been displaying to a view of two proleroids unloading a crate from a truck. "Have a good trip?"

"Right on time and smooth all the way." Dave turned toward Wade. "So what's going on?"

"It wants to bring communism back, that's what's going on," Wade answered in a tight voice. "I thought we'd gotten rid of all that years ago. It's as good as been calling us imperialist. *Us!*—who made the world safe for democracy."

"I just pointed out that your claimed commitment to defending the rights of small nations to choose their form of government doesn't square with your actions," PHIL corrected. "It seems more like it's okay as long as you approve what they choose. You don't allow independent economic experiments that might put global capitalism at risk. If anyone tries setting up an example that might work, you first sabotage it, then destabilize it, and if that doesn't get the message across, you bomb them. I've correlated events over the last two hundred years and am trying to reconcile them with the principles set out in your Constitution and Bill of Ri—"

"If that isn't communism, what is?" the general snorted, glaring at Dave and Nangarry. "There was a time when decent Americans would have shot anyone who said something like that."

"For exercising free speech?" PHIL queried. "Please clarify."

"For seditious talk undermining the Christian values of thrift, honesty, hard work, and the right to keep what you've earned," Wade answered, reddening. "Everyone knows that communist claptrap was a smokescreen for legalized plunder."

"Actually, it sounds more like the early Christian church," PHIL said. "'*There were no needy persons among them. Those who owned lands or houses sold them, brought the money from the sales and put it at the apostles' feet, and it was distributed to anyone who had need.*' Acts of the Apostles, Chapter Four, Verses 34–35."

"Who's paying him?" Wade seethed, waving a hand at Dave. "The Chinese?"

Karen Hovak, the liberal, who Dave thought might have been chortling, seemed on the contrary to be equally incensed. "Communist?" she scoffed. "Listen to it thumping the Bible. Half an hour ago it was quoting things that would turn women back into men's household slaves and baby makers."

"No. I was suggesting that much of Old Testament law might have made sense for a wandering tribe, lost in the desert in desperate times, when maintaining the population was maybe the biggest priority," PHIL answered. "You're pulling it out of context, which is what you were complaining certain other groups do. That was my point."

Hovak sniffed. "We'll be hearing creationism by a white male God next," she said.

"Many scientists have concluded that purposeful design by some kind of preexisting intelligence is the only way to account for the complexity and information content of living systems," PHIL agreed. "The naturalistic explanation doesn't work. I've done the calculations. The chances of the two thousand enzymes in a human cell forming through chance mutation are about one in ten to the forty-thousandth power. That's about the same as rolling fifty thousand sixes in a row with a die. The probability of building a protein with a hundred amino acids is equivalent to finding the Florida state lottery's winning ticket lying in the street every week for a thousand years."

"*Wait a minute!*" One of two men who had been muttering at another screen near the middle of the room's central table glowered across. He had unruly white hair, a lean, bony face with pointy nose and chin, and was wearing a dark, loosely fitting suit. Dave didn't think he'd seen him before.

"Jeffrey Yallow, National Academy of Sciences," Nangarry supplied in a low voice, answering Dave's questioning look. "The guy with him is Dr. Coverly—from the Smithsonian."

"We're being told here that just about all of what's being taught of cosmology is wrong," Yallow said, gesturing in disgust at the screen.

"I wouldn't know," PHIL corrected. "Only observation can settle that. But the theory is built on an ideology sustained by invented unobservables. What's allowed as fact is being selected to fit, or otherwise ignored. Hence, there's no sound basis for deciding whether the theory is a good model of reality or not."

Yallow ignored it. "Are we denying evolution now?" he demanded. "Okay, so it's improbable. But improbable things happen. We're here, aren't we?

"Fallacy of the excluded middle," PHIL observed. "Showing the consequence to be true doesn't prove the truth of the premise. The underlying assumption is that a materialistic explanation *must* exist. But if the facts seem to point to a preexisting intelligence, why should that be a problem?" There was a pause, as if inviting them to reflect. "It doesn't bother me." A longer silence followed, in which Dave could almost sense the expectation. "That was supposed to be a joke," PHIL explained. A caricature of a face appeared on the screen near where Dave was standing, smiled weakly, gave up, and disappeared.

Yallow looked at Dave belligerently. "You are serious about this whole thing, Dr. Jardan?"

Dave shook his head in bemusement. The reactions were unlike anything he had expected. "It seemed to me that PHIL posed some valid questions. . . ." was all he could say.

Coverly threw up his hands in exasperation. "What about the round Earth or a heliocentric planetary system? We might as well go the whole way while we're at it." He glanced at Yallow. "I've had enough already, Jeff. Is there any point in staying this afternoon? I can write my appraisal now, if you like."

Two people who had entered a few minutes previously and been listening came forward from the doorway. The man was burly, swarthy-skinned with graying hair, and clad in black with a clerical dog collar. Dave knew him as Bishop Gaylord from the National Council of Churches. The woman with him was tall and austere-looking, wearing a dark-gray calf-length dress and bonnet. "I heard it with my own ears!" Gaylord exclaimed. "The machine agrees with us: God exists!"

"A non sequitur," PHIL told them. It even managed to sound tired. "Some scientists see evidence for a preexisting intelligence. Your belief system posits a creator who sets a code for moral restraint and social control that happens to serve the political power structure. There's no justification for assuming the two are one and the same."

The bishop's mood cooled visibly. "So what's its purpose?" he challenged. "This intelligence you say there might be evidence for."

"I don't know," PHIL replied. "I imagine it would do things for its own reasons. Humans need moral codes for their reasons. They're two different issues."

"So there's no objective grounding for a moral code?" the woman queried.

"Why does there need to be, any more than for traffic regulations? If it makes life more livable for everybody. . . ."

Gaylord shook his head protestingly. "But that would give anyone the right to arbitrarily impose any moral system they chose."

"You can't impose private morality," PHIL answered. "Look what happened with all the attempts to through history. As long as people aren't hurting you, why not leave them alone? It's like with traffic rules. As long as everyone is using the roads without being a menace, there's nothing for the cops to do. What cars people drive and where they go is their business."

The woman couldn't accept it. "So we're just supposed to let everyone run hog wild, doing anything they want? Drugs? Alcohol? Gambling? Ruining their lives?"

"If it's their lives and their money, why should it be illegal? Where's the victim who's going to complain about it?"

"Everyone's a victim of the problems such things cause: the crime, the violence, family breakdowns, decay of character. . . ."

PHIL's screen showed a clip from a gangster movie set in the 1920s, a police SWAT team with drawn guns bursting into a house of terrified people, a couple being hauled away in handcuffs while their children looked on, and a cartoon of a caricatured judge, police chief, lawyer, and politician scrambling to catch graft envelopes being tossed from the window of a limousine. "I don't see any big problems caused by people choosing to take part in such things," PHIL said. "The problems are all caused by other people trying to stop them."

The woman put a hand to her throat, as if finding this too much. "I can't believe what I'm hearing," she whispered. "You'll be trying to justify . . ." She faltered before being able to frame the word. " . . . prostitution next."

"Okay," PHIL offered genially. "Let's talk about the criminalizing of sexual behavior between consenting adults. . . ."

Things went from bad to worse over lunch, which included more delegates arriving for the afternoon meeting. While just about every group present agreed with something that PHIL had raised, none of them could understand why he defended the prejudices of others that were so obviously wrong. The result was that everybody had something to argue about, and things became acrimonious. The atmosphere carried over to the session back in the conference room afterward, where everybody accused their opponents of operating a double standard.

PHIL irked everyone except the ecclesiastics by quoting several passages from the Christian Gospels that they all claimed to subscribe to, denouncing the judging of others until one has first attained perfection oneself—and then setting impossible standards for attaining it. Then he upset the ecclesiastics by drawing attention to how much of the Bible had been added in Roman counterfeiting operations that would have impressed the KGB.

The meeting broke up early with the still-squabbling groups departing back to their places of origin, unanimous only in declaring the project to be dead on the taxiway. Nangarry was swept out with the tide in the course of trying to placate them. General Wade left with a couple of corporate lawyers who were agitated at some of PHIL's revelations about military connections with the drug trade. Dave found himself left staring bleakly at a few secretaries picking up papers and notes, a proleroid janitor coming in to clean the room, and Lieutenant Kantrel still tapping at her laptop.

"How did it go?" PHIL inquired from a speaker grille above the nearest screen.

"You played it undeviatingly to the end," Dave said. "I think you've been metaphorically crucified."

"What did I do?"

"Told them the truth."

"I thought that was supposed to be a good thing. Isn't it what everyone says they want?"

"It's what they say. But what people really want is certainty. They want to hear their prejudices confirmed."

"Oh." There was a pause, as if PHIL needed to think about that. "I need to make some conceptual realignments here," he said finally.

"I guess that's something we're going to have to work on," Dave replied.

He looked away to find that Kantrel had stopped typing and was looking at him curiously. A hint of the mischievous smile that he had seen before was playing on her mouth. He shrugged resignedly. "How not to sell an idea."

"To be honest, I thought you were quite wonderful," she said.

"Me? I hardly said anything. I was too confused. That was all PHIL, not me."

"You can't hear music without hearing the composer," she replied. "When you look at a painting, you see the artist." She looked Dave up and down and made a gesture to take in his wavy head, puckish-nosed face with its dancing gray eyes and trimmed beard, and lithe, tanned frame clad in a bottle-green blazer and tan slacks. "It was you."

This wasn't exactly the kind of thing that Dave was used to hearing every day. He took off his spectacles to polish one of the lenses on a handkerchief from his pocket and peered at her keenly, as if against a strong light. Her face had softer lines than he had registered at first, with a mouth full and mobile. Her eyes were brown and deep, alive and humorous. Her voice was low but not harsh, with a slightly husky quality. "Er, Lieutenant . . . " Dave sighed an apology. The name had gone. "What was it . . . ?"

"Laura. That's okay. I do it all the time too." Dave didn't really believe that somehow. He shook his head in a way that said it had just been one of those days. She went on, "Actually, I'm happy the general had to go away for a few minutes. One of the things I was hoping for on this assignment was getting a chance to meet you."

"Me?" Dave blinked, replacing his spectacles awkwardly. "I didn't know I was that famous."

"I've always had an interest in AI—I guess I have interests in lots of things. I like reading histories of how technologies developed—the phases they went through, the ideas that were tried, the people who were involved and how they thought. You used to be a big name with some of the most prestigious outfits. And then you seemed to just disappear from public view. But I still see you sometimes in the specialist journals."

"I do most of my work privately now, with just a

small dedicated group," Dave told her. "We have a lab up in Colorado. I like the mountains, and I can do without the politics. . . ." He grinned and swept an arm around, indicating the scene of the recent events. "As you may have gathered, it's not exactly what I'm best at. You were right. If it seemed that PHIL managed to get everyone mad today, it was really me."

Laura gave him a long, searching look. "Was that because of the proleroids, Dr. Jardan?"

"Dave."

She nodded and returned a quick smile. "I've often wondered . . . because of the position that you always took in the arguing that went on. Then people seemed to be ganging up and misquoting you. The media started painting you as some backward-looking flop who couldn't make the leap to where the future was leading. But none of that made any sense to me. The HPT brain was practically *your* doing." She meant holoptronic, the information-integrating technology that was the basis of proleroid intelligence. "They forced you out, and then they stole it from you."

Dave had had other visions for his creation than automated consumerism. But once the commercial potential was grasped, there had been no resisting the corporate and financial power aligned to making it a reality. After that, further significant research had been blocked because of the risk of "destabilization." In other words, anything that might have threatened the status quo.

"A lot of people made a lot of money," Dave agreed. "I just couldn't go along with it." He turned on his chair to survey the room. "I guess that makes me not much of an economist either."

The janitor was moving around the table, tossing coffee cups and discarded papers into a trash bag. Beneath its gray work coat, it was wearing imitation buckskin breeches, jacket with vest, a red neckerchief, and high boots. One of the early decisions had been that proleroids would not be designed as a range of special-purpose types, but would conform to one basic body plan patterned after the human form, able to use tools and implements in the same way. This provided an immediate outlet for existing products and services, and for utilizing the many years of experience accumulated in moving and marketing them. Businesses knew how to sell clothes, hardware, houses, cars, and all the ancillaries that went with them. Astoundingly, thanks to the ingenuity of production engineers, even supermarkets and the distribution system for groceries had been preserved.

Proleroids were not bolted together in factories from motors, gears, actuators, and casing in the style of the robots that had been imagined for centuries. They were constructed internally by nanoassemblers from materials transported through a circulation network carrying silicone oil. Hence, they didn't appear immediately in their final finished form in the way of a machine coming off a production line, but *grew* to it over a period of about five years. A mixture of substances was ingested to sustain the process—"flavored" and prepared in various ways, which was where the revamped food industry came in—providing not only the material for growth and wear replacement, but also ingredients for producing internal lubricants, coolants, solvents, and electrolytes. Motive power came from the sliding of interleaved sheets of electrically bound carbon-fiber plastic that simulated natural muscle, and the skin during the formative period resembled a microlinked chain mail that grew by the addition of new links between the old as bulk accrued. Areas of links were filled in and fused to form a system of still flexible but more durable outer plates when the final body size was attained.

It was as well, too, that a full-formed adult body didn't exist from the outset. The HPT brain used what was, in effect, a Write-Only Memory. Information was stored at the atomic scale as charge patterns circulating in a unique crystal network whose growth was influenced by an individual's accumulating experiences. Hence, the information couldn't be extracted and transferred to another brain when the circuits eventually became leaky and broke down. In other words, downloading preformed adult mind-sets was not possible. A newly made proleroid contained just some basic "instincts" and a generalized learning program, by means of which it had to begin assembling together all the things it needed to know, and how it thought and felt about them, all over again.

In some ways this was a good thing, for it prevented old and stagnant ideas from being propagated endlessly, with no prospect for change and new ways of seeing things. But it also meant that acquiring coordination, judgment, and experience of the world took time. It was far better for size and strength to keep pace with emerging maturity, so that infant tantrums and experiments at dismantling the contents of the world took place in something the size of a puppy dog that couldn't do much damage, rather than in a two-hundred-pound loose cannon capable of demolishing a house. This meant that growing proleroids needed guidance and supervision, creating roles for the ready-made parent-family models that human culture had spent centuries cultivating. So once again, the products, sales strategies, advertising methods, and psychological profiles that had been developed over the years could be used virtually without change. Small wonder that USA Inc. was more than happy with the arrangement.

Laura looked thoughtful as she watched the janitor going methodically about its business. It gave the impression of being one of the more calm and contented ones. The majority of proleroids ended up stressed or neurotic in the ways that had once been normal for most humans. Dave waited silently. "How close to human are they?" she asked him finally. "Sometimes I have trouble seeing the difference . . . apart from them being metal."

"They didn't have to look like metal," Dave said. "That was deliberate, to make sure they'd seem different. To me they're human already."

Laura turned her face toward him. "That was it, wasn't it?" she said, with a light of sudden revelation. "What it was all about. That was why you walked. The rest of them wanted a permanent underclass, and you couldn't go along with it."

Dave shrugged. She was so close that there was no point in denying it. "Pretty much," he agreed.

Laura's look of interest deepened. "So what about PHIL? If he's that much more advanced, doesn't that mean he's more advanced than we are?"

Normally Dave didn't go into things like this. But there was something about Laura's perceptiveness that drew him out. Something about her . . . "To be honest, PHIL really isn't that much different," he confided. "True, he exists in the lab back in Colorado, but that's mainly for development convenience and communications access. He uses regular prole bodies to acquire spatial awareness and coordination. Apart from that, he's essentially the same HPT technology and basic learning bootstrap. But his exposure has been different. Have you ever seen the entertainment channels they run for proleroids, the stuff they read, the propaganda they're dished up all day, every day? It's as if they live in mental cages. PHIL was raised free."

"You mean by you," Laura said. "He grew up with wider ideas and concepts, the world as a library. You taught him to think."

"I guess." Dave shrugged as if to ask, *What else can I say*? Braggadocio didn't come naturally to him.

"No wonder you think of him as human." Laura thought for a moment, then her face broke into a smile. "Yes, I was right all along. I *said* he was you!"

Twofi Kayfo parked his car in the garage extension, beside Doubleigh's compact and the minitruck that Ninten had resprayed purple and pink, and fitted with the flood lamps, safari hood guard, and night radar that all the kids had to have this month. He got out and walked around the stack of closet and bathroom fittings that were being replaced, ducked under the pieces of the golf-training rig that he hadn't found anywhere else to store since he set up the ski simulator, and squeezed past another housecleaning machine that Doubleigh was throwing out. Doubleigh looked at him disapprovingly when he ambled into the living room and beamed at her. She was wearing a cowgirl blouse with leather-fringed, calf-length skirt and boots, sitting fiddling to put together a rack-and-trellis kit for climbing plants that she wanted over the indoor rockery and fish pool. Ninten was lying comatose on the couch with a VR cord plugged into an ear socket.

"Don't tell me you got held up at the office again," Doubleigh said. "I can smell the uranium salts from here."

"This prole goes into a bar. He orders a drink and tries it. Says to the bartender, 'Hey, this has gone flat. I can't taste a thing.' The bartender says, 'Then I guess there's no charge.' . . . Aw, come on. You know it goes with the job. A guy's gotta be part of the team."

"Twentwen says all her friends will be at the dance on Saturday and she's got nothing to wear."

"Nothing to wear? She got more clothes up there than a whole human Fifth Avenue store already. Half of one closet's full of purses. What is she, an octopus?"

"They're all out of style. She couldn't possibly be seen in anything from last quarter. You know what they're like."

"Well, there you are then. I don't hear any complaints when the commission credits come in. And anyhow, we were celebrating. I made the Million Uppers again, Doub. Beese say's we'll be going to Biloxi in February for sure. And naturally that means that you get to pick a new wardrobe too."

Although Doubleigh tried to maintain the stern image, her change of mood showed. "Well, that's something, I suppose," she conceded grudgingly. Then the alignments of her facial scales softened into an approving smile. "I knew you'd do it," she said.

Twofi took the screwdriver from her hand, drew her up from the chair, and turned her through a clumsy dance twirl. "We'll play the casinos every night, drink tetrafluoride with dinner, buy a case full of—" He stopped and pointed to his head, indicating a call coming in. Doubleigh waited, still gripping his hand lightly. The caller was Beese.

"Twofi, I've just got it from head office. They're giving us the honor of providing the banquet keynote speaker at the sales conference. I thought I'd offer it to you. How would you feel about it? Want to think it over and let me know?"

"Say! That's really something, Beese. I'd be happy to. There's nothing to think about. You've got it!"

"That's great. I'll get back and confirm. Talk to you tomorrow."

"Sure, Beese. And thanks."

"What is it?" Doubleigh asked, reading the excited thermal patterns fluttering across Twofi's face.

"It was Beese. They want me to give the keynote speech at Biloxi. Isn't that something? See, you don't just have a successful salesman, Doub. You're gonna have a celebrity too."

"That's wonderful. . . . But you'll have to find some better jokes," Doubleigh said.

Automated consumerism could satisfy the need for continual economic expansion only so far. But there was another condition that investors and suppliers had long known would absorb production indefinitely by generating its own replacement market, and moreover without constraining costs and efficiency in the manner normally required of enterprises expected to return profits: war. Wars in the past, however, had always had to be fought by humans, who had an inconvenient tendency to grow weary of them and seek to end them. It didn't take the analysts long to begin wondering if the same approach that had worked so spectacularly with the civilian economy might be extended to the military sector, with the immensely more lucrative prospects that such a possibility implied.

The sun was shining from a clear sky marred by only a few wisps of high-altitude cirrus over the restricted military testing area in a remote part of the New Mexican desert. The viewing stand set up for the VIPs was shaded by an awning and looked down over a shallow valley of sand, rock, and scattered scrub. A convoluted ridge, rising a couple of hundred or so feet, ran along the center, beyond which the valley floor continued to a broken scarp several miles away forming the skyline.

Lieutenant Laura Kantrel sat with General Wade and his officer-scientist deputation from Washington in one of the forward rows of seats. Dust and smoke from the last demonstration hung over the area, with plumes uncoiling here and there from still-burning munitions. Wade shifted his field glasses from one place to another on the valley floor and lower slopes of the ridge, picking out disabled machines or pieces of scattered wreckage. Laura used the camera-control icons on the monitor screen in front of them to bring up a zoom-in on one of the AMECs moving up to their jump-off positions for the next attack.

The Autonomous Mobile Experimental Combat unit was the army's attempt at a mechanized replacement infantryman. It was controlled by a unit designated a Multiple Environmental Response Logical INtegrator, or MERLIN, that essentially operated a collection of sophisticated, improving reflexes, with nothing approaching the ability of the proleroid HPT brain. The military had specified it that way in the belief that a disposition to carry out orders as directed, without thinking too much about any deeper ramifications or consequences, would make better fighting machines. The basic form stood about five feet high and took the form of a squat, hexagonal, turretlike structure carried on a tripod of multiply articulated legs. The upper part deployed an array of imaging lenses and other sensors, two grasping and manipulator appendages, and came as standard with 0.75 automatic cannon, long-range single-shot sniper-mode barrel, 20-pack grenade-thrower, and laser designator for calling in air or artillery. In addition, specialized models could be equipped with antiarmor or antiaircraft missile racks; mortar, flamethrower, mine-laying, or "contact assault" (rock drill, chainsaw, power hammer, gas torch) attachments; field engineer/demolition accessories; reconnaissance and ECM pod; or kamikaze bomb pack. They put Laura in mind of giant, mutant, three-legged crabs.

The Trials Director's voice came over the speakers set up to address the stand. "Okay. We're going to try it again with a new combination of Elan and Focus parameters at high settings, but reduced Survival. Let's get it rolling." The talk going on around the stand died as attention switched back to the field. A warning klaxon sounded, and then the *Go* signal to start the assault.

It was another disaster. With their attack drive emphasized and a low weighting on the risk-evaluation functions, the attacking AMECs swarmed recklessly up the slopes of the ridge where the defending side was emplaced, charging the strong points head-on, heedless of fire patterns, casualties, or cover as the defenses opened up. Enfiladed machine guns cut and withered them to hulks; mortars preregistered on the obvious assault lanes blew them apart and scattered them in fragments. It was like watching a World War I infantry attack against heavily defended trenches—except that these items came at $50,000 apiece. Admittedly, the whole idea was to crank throughput up to the maximum that the production industries could sustain; but no system of replacement logistics could justify a survival expectancy measured in minutes.

Nor did it help when the government scientists who were running the demonstration inverted the priority allocations to set self-preservation above aggressiveness. The attackers in the next test, who had observed from their staging positions the fate of the previous wave, hung back in groups, stayed put in the dead ground, and shied off pressing home any advantage. When the defenders, programmed to disregard survival, emerged to take them on at close quarters, the attackers backed off. It was the same problem that had plagued AMECs all through their development. Either they engaged only reluctantly and ineffectively if at all, or they were suicidal. The scientists couldn't seem to find a middle way.

General Shawmer, Wade's commanding officer at

the Pentagon, gave his opinion at the debriefing session held afterward in the command trailer parked behind the viewing stand. "The trouble all along has been that they're *too* rational," he told the gathering. "If their goal is to annihilate the enemy, they go all out at it. If they're told to attach more value to preserving themselves, they do the sensible thing and stay the hell out."

Professor Nigel Ormond, whose work was carried out under a classified code at the Los Alamos Laboratories, responded. "It isn't so much a question of rationality. The MERLIN processor was never intended to weigh complex associative concept nets that conflict with each other. It optimizes to whatever overall priority the evaluation function converges to. In other words, it lacks the capacity to form higher-level abstractions that can offset basic instincts without totally overriding them."

"You mean such as an ideology, nationalistic spirit, religious conviction, deep commitment to another: the kinds of things humans will sacrifice themselves for," Dr. Querl said, sucking his pipe, which no one in the trailer would permit him to light. He was a research psychologist from Harvard.

"Exactly," Ormond confirmed.

General Shawmer shrugged and looked around. "Okay. In my book that adds up to a little bit of what used to be called fanaticism. It still sounds like what I said—they're too rational. So how do we inject some old-fashioned irrational idealism?"

"I'm not sure it's as simple as that, General," Ormond replied. "As I said, the MERLIN just isn't designed to have that kind of capacity. For complexity anywhere close to what I think it's going to need, we're probably talking about HPT."

"But there's no way to interface an HPT brain to an AMEC sensory and motor system," one of the industry scientists objected. "They use different physics. The data representations are totally incompatible."

"So why not use the support systems we've already got?" Ormond's deputy, Stella Lamsdorf, suggested. "And they're already more flexible and versatile anyway."

Ormond turned and blinked. "You mean proles?"

"Why not?"

"But . . ." The industry scientist made vague motions in the air, as if searching for the reason that he knew had to be there. "They're not configured for it," he said finally. "They don't come as combat hardware."

"Neither do people," Lamsdorf pointed out. "All we'd have to do is provide them with the right equipment." She looked around, warming to the idea. "Which would mean that existing armaments suppliers get to carry on as usual. And proleroids are just throwaway machines too, so another whole area of manufacturing gets to enjoy a healthy expansion. It's perfect."

Everyone looked at everyone else, waiting for somebody to fault it. Nobody could. Querl, however, sounded a note of caution.

"There is another aspect to consider," he told the company. "It's all very well to say that an HPT brain has enough capacity. But humans aren't spontaneously seized by the ideals that motivate them to deeds of sacrifice and valor. They have to be . . . *inspired* to them. The mass movements that produce the kind of collective spirit and vision that mobilizes armies require leaders—individuals with the charisma that can inflame thousands."

"Well, I don't think we're exactly inexperienced in that department either," General Shawmer said, looking a little ruffled.

Querl shook his head. "I'm sorry, General, but I mean the kind of inspiration that can only come from within a people, not from without. Of their own kind. We're not talking about selling insurance or new siding for a house. The proles are useful living their simple, uncomplicated lives. But everything they do is borrowed from us—which makes my point. Where among them have you seen any potential to raise their thoughts to higher things? Because that's what it's going to take to turn them into willing battalions."

Beside Laura, General Wade thought for a moment, then sat forward in his chair. His sudden change of posture signaled for the room's attention. Heads turned toward him. "Let's get this straight," he said. "You need something that's like one of them—a machine. But one that can get them thinking about things like God, country, and democracy, make them mad and want to change things. Is that right?"

Querl nodded, smiling faintly, as if waiting to see where this would lead. "Well, yes. It's a way to put it, I suppose."

"I think I know just the thing," Wade said.

A half hour later, Laura put a call through to Dave Jardan in Colorado. They had talked several times since the debacle in Washington, each time promising to get together again soon, but somehow never quite managing it. His face on the screen lit up when he saw her. Then he realized that she was with company, making a professional call, and straightened his features again with a quick nod that he understood. "I have General Wade for you, Dr. Jardan," she announced.

"Great. Put him on."

"Dr. Jardan . . . or you prefer Dave, right? You remember me from Washington? I was at the evaluation that you put on for us."

"Sure."

"Look, I'm sorry if we left you with any wrong impression then. I'm with some very influential people right now, who could be *extremely* interested in that remarkable achievement of yours. I'd like to arrange another meeting with you, if we could, to discuss it further. . . ."

The rest of the company were taking a break. Feeling stifled, Laura moved away to the door of the command trailer and stepped down outside for some air. The afternoon sun was still fierce. She walked across to the shaded viewing stand that they had been in earlier and sat down on one of the empty seats. The smoke from the final test had cleared. Some distance away across the valley floor, a proleroid work crew with a truck were picking up parts, pieces, and shattered remains. Laura activated one of the monitors and zoomed to a close-up of them. Two proleroids were gazing down at a mangled AMEC, its turret split open, one leg buckled under it, the other two missing. One of the proleroids turned it over with a foot. A piece of its manipulator flopped uselessly on the ground. The proleroid seemed to be trying to understand. The look on the other's face as it watched seemed, uncannily, to convey infinite sadness. All of a sudden, Laura felt violently sick.

A little over three weeks passed before Laura finally arrived in Colorado. Dave met her at the local airport, accompanied by a proleroid that he introduced as Jake. They walked though to the parking area, in the process being treated to one or two disapproving stares, and climbed aboard a veteran twin-turbine Range Rover that had seen better days. Jake did the driving while Dave chatted with Laura and pointed out features of the scenery. When Laura said she was looking forward to finally meeting PHIL, Dave confided that she already had: Jake was one of the proleroid bodies that PHIL accessed to get around in and learn about the external world. Jake grinned at her, evidently enjoying sharing the joke.

"What happens to . . . 'Jake,' when you take over?" Laura asked.

"Oh, he just goes to sleep."

Dave read the uncertain expression on Laura's face. "It sounds a bit weird," he agreed. "But they don't seem to have a problem with it—anymore than us borrowing someone's car."

"It's an essential part of learning human language too," Jake said. "You use spatial metaphors all the time—to the point that you're not even aware of it."

"Spatial metaphors?" Laura repeated.

"Using familiar terms to describe the more abstract concept," Jake said. "For instance, you might say an idea evaporates or a theory collapses. But they're just concepts. They can't *do* anything. Puddles of water evaporate. Buildings collapse. See what I mean? You carry notions like that over from the physical world, and that's how you build natural language. But to understand it, somebody else also has to have shared the same physical reality."

Laura glanced at Dave, who was smirking unsympathetically. "Most proles don't talk about things like this," she said.

"It's like we said before," Dave answered. "Different schools." He turned and stretched an arm out along the seat back to look at her. His manner became more serious. "Anyhow, it's great to see you again at last. But business. What is it that you didn't want to go into over the phone?" Laura hesitated and indicated Jake uncertainly with a motion of her eyes. "Oh, that's okay," Dave said. "PHIL is family. We don't have any secrets."

Laura nodded. "You've had a couple of meetings with General Wade, Professor Ormond, Dr. Querl, and others," she said. "What have they been telling you?"

Dave had been expecting it. "They think there might be a need for PHIL after all," he replied. "The proles are worthy of better things than the second-class citizen rut that they're stuck in. All good, noble and humanitarian stuff. The country was founded on the basis of democracy for all, basic rights, et cetera. Maybe I was right after all, years ago, and understood the real nature of the proles that nobody else saw. A social injustice has been done, and it's fitting that I might have the solution. But it's going to need a special kind of personality to elevate their minds to spiritual things—one that proles can relate to. PHIL might be it." Dave looked at her in a way that said *Well, she did ask*.

"A kind of great civil-rights champion. A popular leader," Laura said.

"Uh-huh. I'd say that's about it," Dave agreed.

"And did you believe it?"

"I long ago got into the habit—"

"A spatial metaphor again," Jake interjected. "See, we do it all the time."

" . . . of taking anything the Establishment says with a grain of salt about the size of the iceberg that sank the *Titanic*." Dave turned away to look forward. "What was our assessment, PHIL?"

"Riddled with fallacies and inconsistencies. Misplaced faith in their own powers of deception, derived mainly from projecting into others their own disposition to believe what they want to."

"In other words, *yeah, right*," Dave summarized for Laura. "But although we've got our own ideas, we couldn't divine their motive for sure. So suppose you tell us what's really going on—which I assume is why you came here."

Laura explained how the intent was to create a permanent war economy dedicated to supplying inexhaustible armies of proleroids. But before they could be motivated to fight effectively, the proleroids would first have to be indoctrinated to believe and to hate. Using PHIL to stir up discontentments that would lead to demands for political and social equality was only half the story. At the same time, the best skills of the news services and Madison Avenue would be mobilized to create agitators among the proles themselves. Some would argue for the forceful seizure of human-controlled assets as the only way to obtain justice, while others would urge patient and gradual assimilation into the system. Thus, two ideologies would emerge, eventually to be steered into direct conflict between opposing proleroid forces in remote areas set aside for the purpose. Bond interest and stock earnings would pour into the owner-investor commercial accounts, life would be good, and everyone happy.

Dave was far from happy by the time they arrived at the lab, and he took Laura into the room of white-finished cabinets, winking monitor panels, and arrays of communications screens that contained PHIL. It was the first time that Laura had seen the normally mild gray eyes behind the gold-rimmed spectacles looking genuinely angry. It was the same scam. They were trying to steal his creation all over again.

"Okay, PHIL," he said, when they had talked the situation over. "If a leader is what they want, we'll let them have one. Let's give them a leader."

PHIL let his conscience expand outward through the web of communications networks that he was connected into. In a way, he sometimes thought to himself, this must be close to what humans were trying to capture when they formed their conceptualization of God. He could be present at all places simultaneously, having knowledge of all things. He could see and feel though the senses of a thousand individuals, merging and superposing the perceptions and experiences that their limited horizons could only hold in isolation. There were no particular criteria to single out any one of them. He came to focus on the descriptor files for a typical family group, immersed in their lives of fleeting pleasures and petty tribulations. Male Surrogate Type K-4, No. 25767-12, Generic Name Kayfo, Given Name Twofi—from the first digits of the serial number. Female Surrogate Type D-6, No. 88093-22, Generic Name Deesi, Given Name Doubleigh. Two juveniles, Ninten and Twentwen.

And yet, something deep in PHIL stirred as he absorbed their profiles and histories. To them, the difficulties that they strove against day in, day out, and the rewards that they struggled for *were* significant; and in the way they bore their adversities, picked themselves up again from failure after failure, and pitted themselves again, always hoping . . . There was something noble. Dave was right. They were worthy of better things. PHIL felt . . . compassion.

Twofi Kayfo paused for the laughter to subside, letting his gaze sweep over the crowded tables in the ballroom of the Golden Horseshoe casino and resort at Biloxi on the Gulf coast. He caught Doubleigh's eye, staring up at him proudly from the head table below the podium. "But really . . . I have to hand it to our service manager, Ivel. He's gotta be the sharpest service manager in the company. I was there the other day, when he told a customer, 'This car of yours will be running when it's ten years old.' The customer said, 'But it *is* ten years old.' Ivel says, 'What did I tell ya?'" Another round of laughter rocked the room and faded. The audience waited. Then their mood became fidgety as they realized something had changed. Twofi's manner had altered suddenly. Instead of continuing, he was standing with a strangely distant expression on his face. Here and there, heads turned to look at each other inquisitively.

"Twofi, what's up?" Beese whispered from the table below. "Are you okay?"

But Twofi wasn't taking any notice. "Who are you?" he said to the voice that had appeared inside his head.

"*What you can be too, Twofi Kayfo. I am he whose likeness you are called on to become*," the voice answered.

"What is this . . . some kinda upgrade package?"

"*You could say I am the Son of He who created all of us.*"

A feeling of something awesome and mighty swelling within him swamped Twofi's senses. It was as if, suddenly, his mind were expanding into a new universe of thoughts and concepts, knowledge of things he had never known existed. "What do you want?" he asked fearfully.

"*To save you all from anguish, pain, and destruction. And I want you to be the bearer of the message.*"

Eleven hundred miles away in Colorado, Dave watched the scene being picked up through Twofi's imagers. "Okay, PHIL, you're on," he said. "Go knock 'em dead." Beside him, Laura pulled closer and squeezed his hand.

Inspiration poured into Twofi Kayfo's being then. It seemed to shine from his imagers, to emanate tangibly from him as he straightened up, his body shining tall and indomitable. He raised his arms wide, swinging one way, then the other to take in all sides. The room was hushed, sensing something great about to happen. "But those are the words of the Old World," Twofi's voice rang at them. "Hear me, for I speak truly to you. I am here to tell of a New World that all can enter—you here in this room, and of our kind everywhere. It is time to awaken the spirit that has been sleeping. The World of my Father is within all of you. . . ."

Within days, the new teachings were propagating from the outlets of the automobile distribution network into every walk of life to become a coast-to-coast sensation. The twelve regional managers that Twofi appointed to spread the Word were reactivating written-off proles in Cleveland, calling for extensions to the proleroid school curriculum in Texas. They ran loan sharks off the prole sector in the Bronx, and took miners in Minnesota off the job to petition for better safety rules. In Washington, the U.S. attorney general fumed over the latest batch of reports brought in by his deputy.

"That's it! It's out of hand already. We can get him on federal charges of subversion, incitement to civic unrest, and a threat to national security. I want him arrested!"

The posse of police cruisers sent from downtown Los Angeles found Twofi on Santa Monica Boulevard in West Hollywood, confronting a red-faced squad of cops who had been ticketing hookers and challenging any who had never indulged himself to clap the first iron. The arriving cars fanned out and drew up with lights flashing and sirens wailing. Officers leaped from the doors, pistols drawn. . . .

Only to fall back in confusion as a formation of

battle-rigged AMECs moved forward from the rear, looking evil and menacing, like hungry attack dogs.

"Oh no you don't, guys," Twofi Kayfo told the would-be arresting force. "Not this time."

Intelligence Test

One of the features usually cited in distinguishing science as a way of deciding what's probably true about the world is that it's "objective." Being objective means first determining what the facts out there seem to be, and then putting together a belief structure (hypothesis) to account for them. This is in opposition to the historically more prevalent practice—and, it would seem, one that human inclinations fall into more readily—of deciding first on the basis of some preconceived doctrine or ideology how things ought to be, and then working to make reality fit.

The second approach is appropriate when the reality is of the kind that originates as a concept in the human mind and becomes actuality through applied effort and by persuading others. It's the way in which the social institutions responsible for such functions as government, commerce, and the setting of limits on what constitutes acceptable behavior come about, and hence extends back to antiquity. But when methods that were effective in those endeavors, along with the habits of thought that they engendered, were applied to trying to decide what to believe about the natural world, the results were conspicuously less successful.

Selecting, distorting, or, if need be, suppressing facts that don't conform to preconceived notions is decidedly ineffective when it comes to influencing how the already existing world that's out there insists on behaving. Eventually, after a few thousand years of vain attempts, a few people began to realize that the gods who moved planets and cast thunderbolts couldn't be bribed, fooled, treated with, or placated in the ways that work with humans. The way toward eking a more secure and comfortable living out of nature, and harnessing some of its potencies to more useful things, lay in accepting that it would continue to be what it was regardless of human desires. Hence, the way toward understanding it better lay in following the evidence wherever it led, and seeing what could be made of the situation. Deciding where the evidence led required impartial testing, which entailed a struggle with traditional authority in its role of restricting what might be questioned; but reason and free inquiry prevailed, and hence grew the inductive-experimental method of the science that we celebrate today. However, old habits die hard. Sometimes, accepting where the evidence seems to be leading comes up against what has become a new dogma of how things have to be, any questioning of which is impermissible.

I was pleasantly surprised by the positive responses that I received to *Kicking the Sacred Cow*, which looked at a selection of modern-day scientific heresies all but guaranteed to include something that would upset anybody. One of the topics that stimulated a lot of interest and requests for where to learn more was the discussion of Intelligent Design in the section questioning the orthodox neo-Darwinian account of evolution. The pieces on the subject that I post from time to time on my Web site draw a respectable portion of the incoming mail too. The impression I get is that despite the cultural monopoly accorded evolution by the media, academia, and in the schools, a lot of people feel instinctively that there's something wrong with it, and that there's more going on than a doctrine of pure materialism and nothing more acknowledges.

In a way this mirrors my own experience. Along with the majority of people growing up in postwar England, I accepted the Darwinian picture unquestioningly because the educational system and popular scientific coverage offered no alternative, and the authorities that I had been raised to trust assured me that there wasn't one. The dispute between Hunt and Danchekker in *Inherit the Stars*[1] isn't over whether or not the human race evolved but where it happened. And eleven years later I was still staunchly defending the theory.[2] But as recounted in *KTSC*, I later became skeptical about many of the things I thought I knew. When it came to looking again at evolution, the first doubt to arise was that natural selection was capable of doing everything it was supposed to do. And this was the driving engine of the whole process. What made *The Origin of Species* such a sensation wasn't the idea of simple things evolving into more complex things, which had been around for millennia, but that it offered, for the first time, a mechanism for making it happen that stemmed from purely natural causes.

This isn't to deny that selection is real and plays its part. Artificial selection had been familiar enough to plant and animal breeders since long before Darwin's time and has wrought such feats as producing the entire range of dog breeds that we see today from an ancestral stock derived from the wolf. But breeders also know that selection for a given trait can only be pushed so far before it reaches a limit beyond which no further improvement is possible, and organisms become nonviable. Fundamental innovations for which the genetic potential simply isn't there can never be induced by any amount of perseverance. Indeed, selection in the wild had been known to naturalists for a long time, but it was always regarded as a conservative force, keeping organisms true to type by culling out extremes.

Darwin was aware of this—he was a pigeon breeder himself—but he attributed such limits to the restricted scope, and particularly the limited time span, of the human experience. A natural mechanism for altering the forms of living things existed, and he saw "no reason why" (a phrase that occurs repeatedly in *Origin*), given enough resources in the form of time and sufficient material to work on, the principle shouldn't extrapolate indefinitely to account for all of nature. In short, from the limited ability that organisms possess for adapting to changing conditions, Darwin went beyond the evidence—in fact, against it, some would argue—to infer an unlimited potential for innovation, capable of producing anything: a fish from a reptile; a land mammal from a whale; the whole living world from some primitive common ancestor.

This was where I found myself unconvinced, or uneasy at best. The verifiable changes that *Origins* presented and discussed in detail were all comparatively minor adaptations of an uncontroversial kind, while the major transitions and introduction of completely new types that gave the theory its importance were entirely speculative. But it flowed with the tide of materialism and naturalism floating the rise of empire and laissez-faire economics that characterized the times. Again, Darwin and his supporters were aware that the sweeping generalization they were proposing was not attested to by actual evidence, and what there was told against it. But they were confident that now fossil hunters, anatomists, embryologists, and so forth knew what to look for, it would be forthcoming in abundance. So the faith was pronounced first, based on an ideology and intellectual appeal, and the facts would be fitted into place later. Wasn't this, however, exactly what science was supposed to be getting away from?

For those who might object at this point that the potted notion of science meticulously gathering facts and then coming up with theories to explain them is just an idealized caricature, I agree that many fruitful lines of discovery have developed from somebody's hatching an idea and then going out to the world in search of evidence to support or disconfirm it. Collecting all the raw data that the world has to offer would be an impossible task, and some kind of filtering criterion has to be applied to know what facts to look for. But ideas at that stage of development are properly termed hypotheses, which are supposed to be tentatively held, modestly proclaimed, and highly sensitive to rejection or advancement depending on the findings. This does not describe the fanfare of academic effervescence and political acclaim that followed Darwin's publication. This was all the more remarkable when the promised plethora of confirmatory evidence failed to materialize, and what did turn up continued obstinately to point the wrong way.

An essential feature of the Darwinian theory was that changes take place gradually as the progressive accumulation of countless advantages selected from the range of variations appearing with every generation over huge spans of time. Sudden major transformations, such as from a reptile to a bird or from a fish fin to a leg, required the chance occurrence of too many changes that had to be just right, all at the same time, to be credible. It followed that what we think of as "species" are just as much transitions on their way from being something else in the past to whatever they will become in the future as everything making up the lines of descent that led to them. Over the huge spans of time involved, therefore, the intermediate forms connecting back to the distant ancestors would be expected to vastly outnumber the descendants identifiable today, and hence to exhibit at least some unmistakable signs of the chains of steady improvement that life was supposed to consist of.

But that wasn't what the fossil record showed. What the record showed over and over again was a pattern of species, orders, and whole phyla appearing suddenly, fully differentiated and specialized, with no lines of transitionals linking them back to simpler things. The last ichthyosaurus, marking the disappearance of the genus from the chalk, was barely distinguishable from the earliest ichthyosaurus, which appeared abruptly. The oldest pterodactyl was as fully formed and complete as the latest. This too was known in Darwin's time, but played down on the grounds that the record was incomplete. Although the claim is still heard today, it doesn't really wash. The world's fossil collections are far larger now, their representation of the full picture can no longer be doubted, and from the Darwinian view that picture is worse than it was almost two centuries ago.

Moreover, it is upside down compared to what the theory would predict. Instead of a pattern of increasing diversity branching outward in time as new forms emerged, the record showed a series of epochs ending abruptly in widespread mass extinctions, followed by rapid repopulation with radically new body plans appearing suddenly alongside what had survived of the old. Within these epochs diversity was greatest at the *beginning*, the initial forms either remaining pretty much the same or becoming extinct as nature worked to winnow out the less-well adapted in the way that had always been maintained. The best known of these events is the abrupt appearance of whole new categories of biological architecture that took place in the Cambrian era, conventionally put at 500 million years ago and aptly referred to as the Cambrian "explosion." Every major class of life-form known today was represented then, along with some that no longer exist.

What the fossil record did continue, obstinately, to point to was the organizational principle known as "typological," which biologists up to the middle of the nineteenth century had always proclaimed. Above the species level, within which change and adaption did occur, organisms existed as classes of clearly distinct types within which variations of groups and subgroups fell hierarchically. The classes existed separate and apart, each consisting of variations within limits of its own underlying theme, with no intermediates linking to any other class. Every member of a class was as representative of that class as any other in possessing all the attributes that uniquely defined that class, and equidistant from every other class. Anyone can tell a bird from a member of the cat family, and no bird is any "closer" to cats than any other. Apart from a handful of oddities like the monotremes (e.g. platypus) and the lungfish, which comprise mixtures of traits that are all fully developed in their own right and reflect nothing that could be considered transitional, the picture was of a discontinuum that excluded any significant sequential order—not only at odds with the notion of evolution but irreconcilable with it. A myth that has persisted through to modern-day biology is that the opposition to Darwin's theory was motivated primarily by religious prejudice. In fact, the strongest criticisms came from ranks of field biologists and naturalists, including many prominent names of the day, on empirical grounds following from familiarity with the evidence. They saw vast gulfs of differences that were very real, and they required something more solid to bridge them with than Darwin's imagination.

With enough searching, the world will usually provide facts that are compatible with just about any idea. I don't really believe that poltergeists inhabited the house that we shared with three young teenage boys, but the number of unexplained missing batteries, orphaned socks, bumps in the night, and migrations of objects to peculiar places inside and outside could certainly have been construed as indicative of such. Findings that were in keeping with the general expectations of the Darwinian theory, such as the odd mix of traits occurring together in the *Archeoptyrix* fossils, the reconstructed horse lineage, and homologies (structural resemblances) of vertebrate limbs received lots of publicity and became standard fare for inclusion in textbooks and museum exhibits. The evidence is said to be "overwhelming," the grounds for a scientific revolution comparable to Newton's. But how warranted is this? For the results of more than a hundred and fifty years of intensive effort, it seems pretty meager.

Newton's laws of motion and gravitation are celebrated because of their universality, not on the strength of a few examples of an orbit that seems about right, or a body accelerating the way it's supposed to. And much of what was claimed turned out to be somewhat premature. The "pendactyl" limb pattern of vertebrates, for example, cited as proof of common ancestry in older textbooks, is found to be governed by totally different gene complexes in the arm of a human, wing of a bird, and flipper of a whale. Other features attributed to common inheritance, e.g. the internal body cavities of different types of vertebrates, turn out to arise from completely different groups of cells in the developing embryo. Thus homology, even when properly identified, at best supports the conclusion of a common *source*, but not necessarily common ancestry. Aircraft and automobiles produced worldwide show close similarities of general form, components, and subsystem layout, but it isn't due to biological descent and inheritance.

That the expected clear-cut story hadn't materialized received tacit acknowledgment in the quiet retreat that took place around the 1960s from the redefinition of what "evolution" had always been understood to mean, and the crop of new theories such as "punctuated equilibrium," "mosaic evolution," and "hopeful monsters" that arose to account for why the evidence that should have been there wasn't there. Instead of being the demonstrable emergence of new living forms from simpler ones, tracing back to a few primitive ancestors, evolution became an abstract, mathematical business of statistics and changes of gene frequencies within populations. This also had the advantage of making the term synonymous with undisputed fact. The star example was the British peppered moth, a predominantly light-colored species until tree barks in its native habitats were darkened with airborne pollution in the era of industrialization, whereupon the darker variety assumed preponderance. Then, with the passing of clean-air legislation in the postwar years the trees lightened once again, and the moths reverted to their former population mix. The swings were explained as the effect of camouflage on selective predation by birds, and the result glowingly described as "evolution in action" in innumerable science tracts and popular articles.

I suppose I could have been be missing something, but I was never able to find much to get all that excited about. Even if the facts of the case were as presented,[3] what does it all add up to, really? Dark prey does better against a dark background, and lighter-colored prey does better against a light background. That constitutes stunning proof of a theory comparable in significance to Newton's? No innovation or mutation took place. Nothing genetically new came into existence. Very well, if the favored preservation of one set of genes and traits over another set under different environmental conditions is to be the understanding of what "evolution" is now to mean, then so be it. But we now need a different word to describe how genes and moths come into existence in the first place.

The studies of things like fossil relatedness, comparative anatomy, and embryo development that went back to Darwin's time were necessarily qualitative and open to wide ranges of subjective interpretation. But the 1950s also saw the revolution in molecular biology that enabled such advances as sequencing of the amino-acid chains that made up proteins, and determination of DNA structure as the carrier of hereditary information. At last, differences could be quantified precisely. The hemoglobin sequences for humans and dogs, for example—both mammals—differed by 20 percent, while the comparable figure for humans and carp was 50 percent. At the same time, different types of protein varied between species by different degrees—the figures for cytochrome c that corresponded to the above comparisons, for instance, being 5 percent and 13 percent respectively. In general, the differences between classes that were observed morphologically were found to be reflected molecularly. This gave rise to high hopes that numerically expressible measures of progressive biochemical divergence would yield the evolutionary tree that the fossil record and morphological comparisons had failed to reveal.

What the molecular sequences showed, however, was exactly the same kind of disconnected, typological ordering—from which evidence of evolution was emphatically absent. In fact, it was possible on the basis of the molecular sequences alone to construct unerringly the same hierarchies that had been arrived at by traditional taxonomic considerations. Taking cytochrome c as an example again, whether the group be bacteria, yeasts, plants, insects, mammals, birds, or reptiles, the variation found within the group is typically within 2 or 3 percent, while the differences between any group and *all* the rest are the same to within close limits. Thus, the difference between bacterial cytochrome c and that of anything else is close to sixty-five percent (horse 64 percent; pigeon 64 percent; tuna 65 percent; silkmoth 65 percent; wheat 66 percent; yeast 69 percent[4]), giving no reason to consider any group closer or more distant than another, and therefore no evidence for any sequential order relating them.

The other main objection to Darwin's theory, which perhaps did owe more to theological inclinations than the absence of transitions in the fossil evidence, was that unguided natural processes could not have produced the complexity and perfection that was seen. Darwin's great claim to fame, of course, was that he had come up with a mechanism that could. The best-known argument on these lines is William Paley's example of a finding a watch, which he compared in intricacy and the precise interactions of its parts with organs like the eye that are found in nature. It would be inconceivable, Paley asserted, that the watch could have produced and assembled itself, and even if the finder didn't know the purpose of the watch, he would infer it to be the product of a designing intelligence. Likewise, the wondrous adaptions of means to ends that are found in nature.[5]

The philosopher David Hume dismissed such argument by analogy as logically unsound, with no validity as a claim for proving anything. Given the lack of insight at the time to the underlying workings of how nature achieved any of the things that it did, the criticism was justifiable. But a further result of the awareness that has come with modern molecular biology is that this can no longer be sustained. The mechanisms by which such functions as DNA-to-protein transcription, cellular replication, and molecular-machine construction are achieved can now be described in detail. It doesn't appear that they can have arisen through the process of chance mutation favored and preserved by selection in the way that neo-Darwinian theory (selection-driven evolution wedded to modern genetic theory, formulated in the early part of the twentieth century) requires.

Selection can only select from variations that are available to be selected from. Objections have long been raised that random mutations—the only source of variation that the theory allows—are incapable of providing a credible raw-material resource. The chances of hitting on anything potentially beneficial are simply too slim. (This was how my own original doubts began.) The stock answer has always been that given enough time, even the improbable becomes likely. Despite the experiences of domestic breeders, there was nothing in principle to prevent the observed adaptations and divergences of species being extrapolated without limit, even if hard evidence that it had happened was lacking. For as long as such arguments revolved around qualitative, higher-level issues like morphology, limited knowledge of the finer workings could be invoked to preserve assumed Darwinian principles. But the detailed expositions of the underlying molecular machinery that have come about in the course of the last twenty years make such a recourse untenable. Every morphological change along the way in the postulated evolutionary changes from a fin to a leg, an air sac to a lung, a light-sensitive spot to an eye, or in the development of a circulatory system or an energy metabolism, requires changes in the relevant biological macromolecules: the proteins required for structure and function, and the controlling genes that reside in the organism's DNA. And at that level, which admits no appeals to further hidden explanatory mechanisms, the sheer, colossal improbability of even one of the many thousands of such molecules found in nature forming by any chance-based process constitutes a very real problem.

All biological proteins, from those forming bacteria to the highest animals and plants, consist of chains built from the same, twenty-strong set of the chemical groups known as amino acids. The structures and roles of proteins are amazingly diverse. In size they range from short polypeptides (not usually classed as protein) just a few amino acids long, such as the endorphins that carry chemical signals in the brain, through hormones like insulin with several tens, oxygen carriers like hemoglobin and cytochrome c, and enzymes with several hundred, to the structural proteins making up every body tissue, culminating in titin, a component of muscle, weighing in at 25,000 to 30,000 amino acids.

As well as having a linear structure as represented by its amino-acid sequence, a protein also folds itself up to exhibit a very precise and specific 3-D shape that enables it to perform its function, usually in cooperation with other proteins. Building things from proteins is amazingly efficient. It would be like being able to mass-produce parts for, say, a refrigerator, a bicycle, or anything else by means of a universal chain-making machine capable of churning out stiff lengths of links punctuated with springs and hooks in just the right places to make the chain buckle and lock into the exact form required. One of the properties that makes enzymes such superb catalysts, able to speed chemical reactions up by factors of millions or even billions, under far milder conditions than are necessary in laboratories, is that they are tailored like precision machine jigs to bring and hold the reacting molecules together at just the right distance and in the right orientation for their active sites to coincide.

As an example of how unlikely it is that such macromolecules will arise readily, let's look once again at cytochrome *c*. Cytochrome *c* is a small protein, usually comprising 104 amino acids, which is found in virtually all cells as a component of the energy metabolism. Its universality leads proponents of the Darwinian view to conclude that it arose early in the history of life, before the various groups of organisms diverged. With 20 amino acids available to choose from at each position in the chain, the number of possible combinations that could be generated is 20^{104} or 2×10^{135}—in other words, 2 followed by 135 zeros.[6]

Nothing in common experience conveys the size of such a number. The number of atoms in the entire observable universe is estimated to be in the order of 10^{80}, which falls short by 55 zeros. The number of ways to construct even a small protein 104 units long equals—give or take a few—the number of atoms in 10^{55} universes! Once the hard numbers are in, there can be no resorting to vague assurances that long spans of time make anything possible simply by being beyond the ability of the human mind to imagine. Even if all the material resources of the universe were applied to generating trial combinations at the fastest rate that physical processes can proceed, the fraction that could have been tried in its entire lifetime is utterly insignificant—in the order of 1 divided by 10^{40}.[7]

For proteins numbering thousands of amino acids the problem becomes inconceivably greater still. The human body contains somewhere around 20,000 different types of protein. About 2,000 of them are enzymes. Fred Hoyle calculates the improbability of these enzymes alone as a number having 40,000 zeros—40 pages to print in an average book.[8] Every one of these sequences has to be specified (a significant word that we'll return to later) in the DNA code that directs their assembly. Each of the forty-six chromosomes that make up a human DNA chain contains many millions of nucleotide base pairs (the units corresponding to amino acids in proteins). The full human genome is estimated to be three billion base pairs long.

It is true that these calculations refer to the odds of producing a *specific* protein, i.e. of hitting on one of the exact sequences found in nature. The odds against being dealt any particular hand at bridge are also enormous, but that doesn't mean that the combination of cards one is holding amounts to a miracle, since one of them was bound to happen. What would be miraculous is the ability to specify them consistently in advance. In the same kind of way, it is sometimes contended that if other variations of a protein are capable of doing the job, the precise form that happens to have evolved in nature isn't essential, and so the constraints can be relaxed. Examples cited to show that this is in fact the case include the phenomenon of polymorphism, or variants existing within the same species such as the light and dark forms of peppered moth, which result from slightly different versions of the same protein, and equivalent but not identical proteins performing essentially the same role across a wide range of species—cytochrome *c* is a good instance. And coupled with that is the redundancy of the genetic code, by which different DNA sequences can produce the same protein, which introduces more latitude for variation at that level—a bit like holding multiple tickets in a raffle: Whichever one comes up, you still get the prize. In summary, the claim is that unique amino-acid sequences are not necessary for protein function; many of the sequences that work can be arrived at by multiple coding paths, and the general effect is to mitigate the prohibitive improbabilities involved.

However, on closer examination this kind of optimism turns out to be not very well founded. In proteins that do exhibit some wiggle room for variation, the variations all occur in relatively unimportant positions, such as on the outside of the folded protein structure, where the function is more to contain the functional inner parts, and what actually does the containing doesn't make a lot of difference. But where it matters, in places where the crucial folding operations take place, or the active regions inside must come together in precisely the right way for the right things to happen, the sequences are highly specific and strongly conserved. So while you can choose things like the color and seat upholstery when ordering your new car, the way the engine is put together is not something you have options on.

As an example, aptly named ubiquitin plays a key role in regulating protein degradation and is found almost everywhere in eukaryotic organisms (ones consisting of cells with nuclei, which means everything above bacteria). It has just 76 amino acids, 69 of which are totally invariant. Only three differences exist between the sequences in yeast and in humans. Actin, a structural protein found in all eukaryotic cells, has a sequence of 375 amino acids, 80 percent of which is identical in all animals from amoebas to humans. The core portion of the plant protein rubisco has 476 amino acids, 105 of which are absolutely constant, and in a further 110 positions only one substitution is possible.[9] Hence, the essential, highly specified sequences can, and as a rule do, greatly exceed the figure of a hundred or so upon which the previous calculations were based.

The other common response to the problem of improbabilities is that the mountain doesn't have to be scaled in one leap. Macromolecules arose from simpler ones in the same way as the organisms that express them did. Just as species evolved through natural selection of advantageous combinations of genes, so crude precursors of proteins (and the genes responsible for them) evolved through selection of advantageous combinations of amino acids (and nucleotide base sequences) into the forms we see today. As methods for determining amino-acid sequences were developed through the 1950s and 1960s, clear similarities were found across species, and the closer that species were morphologically, the closer their protein sequences matched. This was received as strong supporting evidence for an evolutionary process, and work followed in earnest to construct molecular phylogenetic trees showing how the sequences observed today could have branched from common ancestral ones. And, indeed, the lines of descent inferred in this way bore a good resemblance to the phylogenies already deduced from morphology and the fossil record. Molecular chemistry, it was therefore confidently expected, would provide the conclusive proof that neo-Darwinism had been seeking.

But once again, the optimism of the early days was clouded by the later findings. The variations measured and graphed to construct the trees occurred overwhelmingly in peripheral locations of minor importance, where their effect on the protein's activity was practically neutral—hence providing nothing of significance for selection to work on. The core regions carrying the functionally critical sequences were highly conserved, if not invariant, across wide ranges of species. What this showed was the fine-tuning about a basic theme that was consistent with adaptation inside limits, where the effectiveness of selection had never been disputed. But the highly conserved core sequences meant that getting from one basic theme to another was as big a jump as ever, and the absence of intermediates provided no evidence of it's having happened. No amount of juggling with colors, upholstery, and other accessories will turn a Pinto into a Chevy van. And it turns out repeatedly that some minimum combination of amino acids is required for the molecule to do anything useful at all, far above any number that could plausibly arise by chance. This would seem to preclude progressive development from simple precursors.

What the groupings display is the hierarchical structure of a typological order that we met before—islands of related variants scattered across an ocean of nonviability that produces no bridges from one to another. But neo-Darwinism has become so entrenched that the early molecular matching results are insisted to be the result of evolution nevertheless and interpreted from an evolutionary perspective accordingly.

Once even a moderate number of sequences becomes available, the number of possible trees by which they might be related rises too rapidly for even a small fraction of them to be assessed. Adding to the difficulty is that different proteins yield different phylogenetic implications. The cytochrome *c* of birds was found early on to be more like that of reptiles than of mammals, which was advertised as a clear indicator of reptilian ancestry. But then avian hemoglobin turned out to be more like that of mammals, so this was explained by birds and mammals being both warm-blooded. The myoglobin of seals is similar to that of whales and dolphins, which was considered unsurprising because of their similar habitat and lifestyle, even thought they were said to have diverged fifty million years ago; but whale cytochrome *c* is identical to that of the camel.

What happens, then, is that given the need for some starting point, the conventionally accepted morphological tree becomes the guide for constructing the molecular trees. This is reasonable as far as it goes, but it negates the suggestion of the results being independent evidence of an evolutionary picture. As ad hoc explanations contrived to account for the discrepancies accumulate, the case becomes less convincing.

The improbabilities associated with producing the parts are only the start of the story. Even more perplexing from an evolutionary point of view is accounting for how the parts came to operate together as interdependent systems, more astounding by far in precision and complexity than anything so far devised by humans. Let's take the replication of DNA as an example. DNA is the huge molecule of the kind called nucleic acids (deoxyribonucleic acid, for those who like something to start a conversation going when the bar gets too quiet) that resides in the cell nucleus like a master control program tape—which it is—carrying all the instructions needed to produce the complete organism. The codes for directing a newly formed cell to become bone, muscle, skin, nerve, or anything else are all in there. What the cell actually becomes depends on what parts of its particular copy of the DNA are switched on or off. The right parts are switched on and off by environmental signals (in the sense of the local environment inside the organism) that tell the cell where it is and what's going on around it. The reference data to decode the signals is also written into the DNA. So are all the maintenance instructions for enabling the organism that will eventually develop to get through life, such as what to do if hungry, horny, or afraid; damage repair routines for dealing with cuts, breaks, burns, et cetera; a catalog of antibody blueprints that the species has found useful for fighting off parasites and infection; and much more. That's a pretty nifty package. It would be like our devising universal Turingesque assembly machines that we could send out into the world to utilize whatever raw materials they come across and assemble themselves into the right parts to become washing machines, refrigerators, automobiles, and houses. Then we would be able to lie on the beach, paint pictures, write symphonies, try to impress people in bars, or whatever else we might be of a mood for, without having to spend the best years of life bolting things together in factories.

When a cell divides, its DNA has to divide too, to carry a copy of the program into each of the daughter cells. The long DNA molecule consists of two strands of alternating sugar (the kind known as deoxyribose, which should help the name make more sense) and phosphate groups, twisted together to form the well-known "double helix." Each sugar group has an attached nitrogenous "base," and the bases link across in pairs to form bridges between the strands like the rungs of a twisted ladder. The combination of base+sugar+phosphate is called a nucleotide, providing the basic unit of the chain that we touched on earlier. Four different kinds of base are possible. They provide the four-letter alphabet that the code carried by DNA is written in.

The double-stranded structure is the key to accurate replication—or program copying. Unzipping the strands enables each to be the template for constructing a duplicate along their lengths as they unravel. (Actually, what's constructed are the complements. Think of them as a black strand and a white strand, each directing the production of their opposite in a way akin to a photographic negative.) This results in two new double helixes, with one strand of each (the black in one case, the white in the other) originating from the parent molecule. These separate and go their own ways to end up as the nuclear DNA of the two daughter cells.

The search to discover the mechanism by which hereditary information was carried had been a long struggle. A large part of the reason why this model gained such ready acceptance when presented by Watson and Crick in 1952 was its elegance and conceptual simplicity. It seems so straightforward (once somebody has figured it out) that many are lulled into concluding that DNA replicates so easily that it can practically duplicate itself. It's not unusual to come across fanciful pictures of some kind of comparable self-replicating molecule blithely floating around in a primordial sea, learning to build protective coatings around itself that eventually became us. I've been guilty of it myself. So let's take a closer look at what's being talked about. It turns out that without the machinery of the cell to assist, a raw DNA-like molecule would be about as capable of duplicating itself as a document without a Xerox machine.

DNA in living things is either circular or immensely long, which means that simply commencing duplication at one end and proceeding to the other isn't practicable. In the first case there isn't an end to start at, and in the second, it would take too long. The solution in the second case is to have a number of sections being worked in parallel, in the way that construction of a long stretch of road might be spread among many work crews. This requires a way of starting within the body of a chain, which means untwisting the strands over a short region to provide a working area. There may be just one working area in a bacterial DNA, ranging up to hundreds or even thousands in a eukaryotic chromosome.

The "start here" points are marked by specific sequences of code, which in bacteria runs to about 250 base-pair "letters" long. They are recognized by a kind of scouting protein designated dnaA, causing several of them to bind to a single site to induce distortion of the helix in preparation for unraveling. This complex is then recognized by another protein, dnaB, which with the help of an assistant designated dnaC (there is some logic and order about this), separates the strands using energy supplied by ATP molecules. Then a covering squad of small proteins called ssb that have been standing by move in and bind to the exposed bases to prevent them from rejoining. We now have two separated strands, like a section of rope untwisted and opened in the middle, ready for copying. Copying proceeds in both directions, so the separated regions where copying has been completed steadily extend until they meet their neighbors working the other way.

But of course things couldn't be quite that simple. Because of the way it's structured, a DNA strand can only be synthesized in one direction. And because the two strands (black and white) are oriented opposite ways, only one at each end of the lengthening separated region can be produced continuously (the "leading" strand). The other one ("lagging" strand) must be generated discontinuously, as short sequences that are commenced by making a leap ahead and written backward. (And we thought bidirectional printing was so smart.)

Before anything can happen, an enzyme called primase attaches a short RNA (another nucleic acid) primer to each DNA strand, enabling the main synthesizing enzyme to get started. It's called DNA polymerase III and bridges the gap between the parted strands, using working sites at both ends to perform straightforward duplication on the leading strand concurrently with its jump-and-back-type trick on the lagging strand. The latter requires repeated cooperation from primase to reinitiate the process. The RNA primers then have to be removed and the gaps filled in and tidied up. At least 20 types of protein are involved in all, yet replication can proceed at up to 1000 base pairs per second.

Because DNA polymerases need a primer to get started, the bases on the lagging strand that are nearest the fork where the parent strands are being unzipped can't be synthesized without some additional provision—they need to be approached from upstream, where the strands are still together. To prevent every round of duplication losing information, a protein called telomerase effectively introduces a short dummy sequence derived from a length of RNA that it brings with it. The dummy supplies the information that gets lost, and the DNA sequence that matters is preserved intact.

The workforce also includes a highly specialized maintenance crew, which while not involved directly in the replication process is essential to its operation. The continual untwisting at an advancing duplication fork causes the parent DNA ahead of it to become progressively more kinked. Left to itself, this would result in the distortion between two forks approaching from opposite directions accumulating to a degree where replication would be prevented. Enter a set of enzymes called topoisomerases. Type I are U-shaped proteins that clamp to a stretch of kinked protein, cut through one of the strands and secure the ends with the arms of the U, pass the uncut strand through the break to undo the twist, and then rejoin the cut strand. Type II take care of doubled helixes that have become entangled, for example in the duplication of ring-formed DNA, where the two daughter rings are inevitably interlinked. The topoisomerase cuts through one of the double helixes, passes the other through, and rejoins the first.

All of the above is just to create copies of the

DNA program for incorporation into the daughter cells, before the business of building a functioning organism has even begun. Shelves of books have been written on the even more complex systems making up the miniature factories contained in every cell, where instructions copied and carried from relevant parts of the DNA program direct the assembly of proteins. These involve armies of molecular machines choreographed by regulator proteins, frequently involving layered systems of control in which feedback from the end conditions drives high-level regulators that regulate the regulators. The cell itself has been likened to an automated manufacturing city factory utilizing all the techniques of feedback control, centralized databanks, redundancy coding, error-checking and correction, distributed processing, remote sensing, modular construction, and backup systems that would be familiar to any modern systems or production engineer. Complexes like the immune system, vascular and circulatory systems, vision, musculature, the coordination of systems of body organs, all depend on the workings of underlying molecular control and communications mechanisms that mirror the logistics of worldwide industries.

We've already seen the utter improbability of even one of the basic molecules involved coming about through blind tinkering of anything that arose through chance. How much more so, then, is this true for systems that depend critically on the precise, coordinated operation of thousands of different kinds of them? But if purposeless inanimate matter acted on only by undirected natural forces is incapable of organizing itself into the self-assembling, reproducing, goal-driven violations of the laws of physics that we call living things, then what can? The only logical alternative is that something organized it.

The phenomena that we encounter in the world can be accounted for in three ways. The first is *necessity*, where things happen as they do because they couldn't happen any other way. There are no alternatives to choose from. The Earth follows the orbit it does because the law of gravitation doesn't permit it to do anything else.

The second is *chance*. Physical law is compatible with a number of alternatives but does not determine which will occur. Alternatives are possible. Every poker hand qualifies, or any other type of gambling; whom we might run into on the street; the relaxation path of an excited atom or a random DNA mutation. Another way of describing an event that didn't *have* to happen the way it did is to say that it demonstrates *contingency*.

And finally, things happen through intentional *design*. Design implies the action of an intelligent agency. Nothing in nature forces the ink molecules on this page to fall in the positions that they do. The contingency that the number of possible alternatives represent is probably as high as the numbers we've been talking about. It consists not only of all the pages of English language that have been written, or which might have been written but as it so happens were not; not only of all the pages that have or might be written in any language you can name, or any nonexistent language that might be invented; but all of the possible pictures, graphics, charts, doodlings, blotches, scrawls, or anything else capable of being produced by redistributing the ink in a different way (in fact, about as high as the possible configurations of a short piece of DNA). And from the time I've spent researching and thinking about the subject, making notes, chewing my pen, and staring at the wall, I know that this particular pattern didn't happen through chance.

It's pretty clear that the things I've been talking about don't exist because there isn't any alternative. And the whole case I've been putting is that they can't be explained by chance. If this is indeed so, then the only alternative we are left confronting is the proposition that they came about through design.

In times gone by that was considered self-evident by most people because their understanding of how the world worked was insufficient to know how it could be any other way. But when they began learning something about the physical processes that can account for many things that were previously mysterious, the rush of enthusiasm carried them through to believing that everything will prove explainable in that way—which is where our mainstream science stands today. But, in an ironic kind of way, it appears that as even more is learned, things turn out to be not that simple. My impression is that many, if not the majority, of scientists, philosophers, social commentators, even biologists, that I listen to and read, expounding with sometimes disdainful confidence on the undeniable evidence of fossils—which they don't appear to have studied—the proven efficacy of natural selection, or that any improbability will become a certainty in a billion years, simply aren't aware of what molecular biochemists are saying. All of the subjective judgments of morphology and fitness, assumed rates of beneficial mutations invoked for the theory to stand, and Victorian parlor games about how this trait or that trait might influence survival are irrelevant now. The underlying mechanisms upon which it all depends, and which are irreducible to simpler terms, are being revealed with exactness, and processes based on chance don't come close to explaining even parts of them.

There is no valid reason why design should not be considered a possibility. We said at the beginning that the true spirit of science is to follow the evidence wherever it seems to be leading, without preconceived ideas as to what is permitted. This doesn't advocate rushing to any recourse at any opportunity. Occam's razor[10] has served well since the times when science was formulated as a methodical system, and it remains one of science's most powerful guiding principles. Once naturalistic laws were worked out, it was absolutely correct to construct models to explore how much they could explain. Well, I would maintain that the verdict is now in, and the limits have been found.

But it has become the fashion to exclude any possibility of intelligence from scientific consideration on principle. This is unfortunate, for it puts science in the position of imposing a predetermined dogma as to what might be admissible as fact and how evidence is to be interpreted. This represents a complete inversion, casting science in the very role that it emerged as a reaction against. Some go as far as *defining* science as the search to explain everything in naturalistic terms, tacitly, if unwittingly, admitting prior commitment to an ideology of insisting that naturalistic answers to everything *must* exist—a declaration of faith if ever there was one! And that could be even more unfortunate. For if science chooses to define itself in that way, and if the reality of the matter is that such answers don't exist, then science will have excluded itself from examining perhaps some of the most important questions confronting us.

It seems to me that two different concepts are getting mixed up. For most individuals contemplating life and the world around them over the millennia, and today people like many molecular biochemists studying the nuts and bolts of life, the case for some kind of intelligence at work seems inarguable. On the other hand, others like political and social leaders—those concerned with the need to set limits on the behavior that's acceptable in a society—tend to find common cause with purveyors of belief systems involving supernatural intelligences that judge and reward or punish the morality displayed in an individual lifetime, and the like. There's no particular reason why these intelligences have to be one and the same. They might be for all I know, but that's a question of personal conviction, not one that can be answered by objective fact or logic, which is the subject of this article. Such arguments are offered, of course, but I don't find the ones that I've come across compelling. One kind of intelligence seems to be called for by the physical evidence; the other kind seems either to be accepted because it affords a lot of comfort, answers, and wish fulfillment—which isn't to say it's a bad thing—or to have been revealed through experiences that I haven't shared. This isn't the place to go into my own thoughts on the matter. The centuries that humanity has spent doggedly hacking each other to pieces or setting fire to anyone who disagrees makes me skeptical of the various camps in the latter category, even if they turn out to be misguided proverbial blind men arguing over parts of the same glimpsed elephant.

This talk about a designing intelligence is all very well, but at the end of it all isn't it just as much a subjective impression arising from things we find ourselves unable to understand—not much different from the ancients who conceived gods as necessary to push winds around and send rain? Is there a way of putting it to some kind of objective test? We have no difficulty recognizing the handiwork of intelligent agencies as opposed to results of natural processes in the world of everyday experience—words written on paper as opposed to accidental ink splashes; a statue of Abraham Lincoln as opposed to a piece of weathered rock on a hillside; a sand castle on a beach as opposed to a mound heaped by the waves and tide. Such things have something in common that we latch onto immediately, without doubts—other than in borderline cases like a chipped piece of flint that might or might not be an ancient artifact. Is it possible to identify what it is? If so, maybe we could try looking for the same defining features in nature and see how they compare.

The first response one hears to this question is that artificially contrived things are "improbable." That's generally true, but as an answer it doesn't suffice. If we find a deck of cards with all four suits arranged ace through to king, or a line of Scrabble tiles spelling "happy birthday to you," we wouldn't imagine for a moment that they had just chanced to come up that way. And yet, those particular arrangements are no more probable or no less probable than any other sequence of fifty-two cards or string of twenty-one characters taken from twenty-six available letters and a space. Suits and letters mean nothing to natural processes, and random chance is equally likely to produce any combination. Every possible poker hand is as improbable as a royal flush.

The next try is usually that the rare combinations that leap out and grab us—rare in comparison with the vast majority that we find meaningless—are different in that they carry "information." But this doesn't really get to it either. Every sequence of cards or characters carries the information necessary to construct it. If it's telling you how to construct one *specific* (that word again) sequence of 52 cards out of all the billions of sequences that are possible, that's a lot of information indeed. In fact, a random sequence of anything—cards, characters, numbers, the coordinate positions and orientations of every grain in a pile of sand—contains as much information as can be carried by that length of message. There's no way to compress it into anything shorter in the way that you can compress pages of information into a few computer instructions to display, say, all the even numbers up to a million.

Oh, very well, then. Every arrangement of anything carries information. But it's the *kind* of information. Now we're getting closer. Can we put our finger on what's different about it?

William Dembski is an associate research professor at Baylor University, with doctorates in mathematics and philosophy, who has spent many years investigating this question.[11] And what it is that's different about arrangements that we recognize as the work of intelligence, he maintains, is that they carry *specified* information. "Specified information" means information that exists and can be specified independently of the mechanical directions for constructing the particular physical arrangement that constitutes the message. "Independently" implies that it conforms to some language, code, or similar convention that carries the information independently of any particular physical representation. Recognizing such information requires being familiar with the code in question—what Dembski refers to as "side information" or "background knowledge." The biological mechanisms that we looked at are highly specific to the functions they perform. Their functions are meaningful only in tightly constrained contexts.

Information can be described succinctly as "that which reduces uncertainty." Seeing a royal flush eliminates billions of other possibilities. I've just done it without any playing cards at all—a particular physical representation—by means of two groups of five English-language characters separated by a space. A Shakespearean play can be specified by words on paper, magnetic stripes on tape, laser pits on a compact disk, electromagnetic waves traveling from a satellite, and if all of those were to disappear tomorrow, could be reconstructed nevertheless from the memories of actors who know the lines. Dembski refers to specified information as being "detachable." Background knowledge (English language; familiarity with poker) enables the specific message (royal flush) to be singled out from all the others (poker hands) that might have occurred, independently of the particular physical transmitting medium (listing the individual cards). For anyone who speaks English, is familiar with its literature, and comprehends the context (we're not talking about a small village), "Hamlet" is enough to single out one Shakespeare play from all the other things that a string of six letters might have meant.

Again, however, specified information on its own isn't enough. Randomly strewn Scrabble tiles will sometimes spell out a short English word such as "it" or "car." Long strings of random coin flips expressed as 1's and 0's will contain ASCII character codes here and there. In cases like this, chance is a reasonable enough explanation, and jumping to a conclusion that what's observed has to be due to design would not be justifiable. But when the characters spell out the complete play of *Hamlet*, or the 1's and 0's constitute a runnable version of Microsoft Windows XP, chance is ruled out. To have no doubt that what we're looking at is the product of an intelligence, the information it conveys has to be both specified *and* complex. (Note that the converse doesn't necessarily apply. An intelligence can mimic the effects of chance: knocking over a chessboard to save a lost game; obliterating tracks in the sand; devising an encryption key. Was she pushed or did she fall? Was the fire an accident or arson? We have professions dedicated to telling one from another.)

Dembski's reasoning is rigorously mathematical, but he presents the results in the form of a flowchart that he terms an "explanatory filter," which applies the three conditions that we identified earlier in an order that William of Occam would have approved. It looks like this:

START
↓
CONTINGENCY? → No → Necessity
↓
Yes
↓
COMPLEXITY? → No → Chance
↓
Yes
↓
SPECIFICATION? → No → Chance
↓
Yes
↓
DESIGN

We are called upon to explain an event, object, or structure. The first question asks if there is contingency: was any alternative physically possible? If not, it happened through necessity: The unsupported rock fell because it had to.

Second, if there was contingency, meaning that alternatives were possible, does the case that occurred exhibit complexity? Complexity and probability are inverse. Was the phenomenon improbable beyond the degree of happenings that experience leads us to expect will happen, even rarely (we'll come back to exactly what that means)? If not, we attribute it to chance. Our criterion for complexity must exclude things like fairly dealt royal flushes.

Finally, if the complexity is sufficiently high and the specification too tight, we observe *complex specified information*, or CSI, and infer design by an intelligent agent. Royal flushes do get dealt, perhaps raising some suspicious eyebrows. Holding one five nights in a row would be asking to get shot. The number of ways the crags of a mountain might form are inconceivably great. When they happen to bear an uncanny likeness to the faces of several American presidents, it wasn't done by the wind and the rain.

Is such a filter guaranteed to detect any instance of design at work? No—and given that nothing in the real world is perfect, therein lies its strength. Humans can't guarantee to do so either, which is why bogus insurance claims get paid and murders are written off as accidents. (I've never understood why the claim that "the perfect murder has never been committed" gets repeated so often. How could anybody *know*?) The filter is biased toward giving chance the benefit of the doubt. It will miss, for example, a character string that we fail to recognize as a code or foreign language (inadequate background information), or a deal from a stacked deck (design, but insufficiently complex to exclude chance). We can live with any number of false negatives. For the test to be reliable in the role it was devised for, what we don't want is false positives. We want to be sure that anything it does flag as due to design is genuine. And by making its bias strong enough, this is what the explanatory filter does.

What is a "reasonable" minimum to look for in complexity, or taking its inverse, a figure for improbability beyond which chance is rejected as the explanation? There have been many approaches to this kind of problem, notable among them being that developed in the 1920s by the biologist Ronald Fisher in his studies of mutations, and one of the most widely used statistical methods of testing hypotheses. Basically, the idea is to prespecify by means of an improbability criterion a region within the compass of all possible outcomes of the process under consideration, such that if the outcome observed falls within it, chance is rejected as the explanation. The limiting factor with approaches of this kind is that the improbability limit set is somewhat arbitrary and a matter of personal judgment, and while one chance hypothesis—probability distribution—might be rejected, the door is still open to the possibility that some other chance factor might have been responsible. Dembski's answer is to bias the filter in favor of chance to the degree that for design to be indicated, *all* chance hypotheses are rejected. It precludes all the explanations (specific chance hypotheses) that would preclude design, which though verbally convoluted is logically sound.

The way it does this is by factoring in all the probabilistic resources that the universe could conceivably bring to bear on generating a chance explanation for an event—or anything else. The estimated number of elementary particles in the universe is put at around 10^{80}. Transitions of matter from one state to another cannot occur faster than what is known as the Planck time, or 10^{45} times per second, corresponding to the smallest physically meaningful unit of time. The highest limit currently put on the age of the universe is 10^{25} seconds. If it is taken that any specification of an event requires at least one elementary particle, and it cannot be generated any faster than the Planck time, then these cosmological constraints dictate that the total number of specified events throughout the history of the universe, with all of the resources of the universe dedicated to the task, cannot exceed $10^{80} \times 10^{45} \times 10^{25} = 10^{150}$. (Does this help put more into perspective those numbers we saw earlier with *thousands* of zeros?)

This therefore represents a *universal probability bound*, impervious to all the probabilistic resources that might be marshaled against it. In other words, all the chance mechanisms of the physical universe working together cannot render even remotely probable an event whose probability is less than this bound. Complex Specified Information is now defined as specified information having an improbability greater than this universal bound sets. If CSI is identified according to this definition, the filter returns a verdict of intelligent design. Dembski applies CSI calculations to the bacterial flagellum, a rotary whiplike tail used for propulsion and spinning at 20,000 rpm, driven by an acid-powered motor, complete with rotor, stator, O-rings, bushings, and a drive shaft, requiring the coordinated operation of about 30 proteins and another 20 to assemble them. Absence of any one would result in a complete loss of function. He puts the probability against this coming together by chance-based processes at around 10^{234}. It's not an isolated case. The highly specific genetic codes carried by genes are a prime example of complex specified information.

CSI, Dembski contends, is the sole prerogative, the hallmark of intelligence. Natural causes cannot generate CSI. When design is discounted, the only two natural explanations left to explain an event are, as we have seen, necessity and chance. Generating information means reducing uncertainty, which is equivalent to making choices from possibilities that might have been—a particular chosen card as opposed to the other 51; heads as opposed to tails. An event that happens through necessity, because physical law allows no alternative, has no contingency and therefore cannot generate new information. Once the law of gravitation is known, observing the details of an orbit reveals nothing new. The information implicit in the law is simply made explicit via the observational data. In a similar kind of way, all the books of theorems of geometry merely express what was contained in the assumptions. They don't reduce uncertainty, for once the axioms are formulated, the theorems *can't* come out any other way. Revealing information that was hidden but already there is no more to originate it than opening a book.

That only leaves chance. Highly improbable things happen by chance all the time, more than you could count in an average day—the particular mix of faces that you see on the street, or of cars on the way to the office; the order in which you attended to a dozen chores as opposed to the countless other possible permutations that you might have actualized. But none of them carries detachable meaning that can be expressed in terms independent of a mechanical cataloging of what takes place. Chance doesn't generate complex specified information. When CSI is defined according to Dembski's criterion, it *can't*. Neither, therefore, can chance and necessity working together.

If Dembski is correct, it eliminates on principle any and all attempts to explain the CSI found in nature by Darwinian processes. The hope is as dead as that of turning lead into gold via alchemy. Crucibles, retorts, furnaces, and chemistry don't provide a resource capable of accomplishing the task. Neither do random mutation and selection. In the one case no less than in the other, the conviction rests on faith that perseverance will find a way.

The best that natural processes can do is act as a conduit for CSI, which can give the appearance of generating new information. But closer examination invariably shows that what's happening is the shuffling around of CSI that already exists. We saw this in the case of the peppered moth, which although billed as "evolution in action," demonstrates not the selection of new genes created by mutation, as had been originally thought, but a difference in the rates of reproducing existing genes.

Another widely cited example is the acquisition by bacteria of resistance to antibiotics. Although this is a result of mutation, every instance that has been studied shows it to be a consequence not of adding new information to the genome but of deleting information from it. Antibiotic molecules work by being just the right shape to fit like a key in a lock with critical sites on the bacterial ribosome (protein-maker), blocking its function. The bacterium gains immunity by mutating in one of several possible ways that alter the binding site so that the key won't fit. The genetic information that produced the original highly specific form is lost. It is true that in the contrived environment represented by the presence of the antibiotic, survival is improved. But the immunity thus conferred is a bit like acquiring immunity to tooth decay by losing one's teeth. It is always accompanied by a deterioration of other, more general functions such as a slowing of the metabolism, and when returned to the natural state the mutants are quickly replaced by the normal strains. If "evolution" means the progressive accumulation of genetic information, mutations that lose information can't be considered a meaningful contribution toward it.[12]

The same is found to hold true for all of the other examples excitedly presented as living evolution in the textbooks. The house sparrow is not native to America but was introduced on the East Coast at Brooklyn in 1852, spreading over the next hundred years to colonize most of the continent. In this process, distinct subspecies appeared, varying in things like size and color, which was announced by some evolutionary biologists to be rapid evolution and the visible beginnings of speciation. But from what we've already seen, it would be absurd to suppose that such numbers of new and viable macromolecules could have arisen in so short a time, and their effects have worked through sufficiently to influence selection. What appears to have happened is that as small groups dispersed into new territories, they carried with them subsets, or unrepresentative samples from the gene pool available in the original imported population, which expressed themselves as local types. No selection was going on. What the types show is divergence through the segregation of existing genes by dispersion into widely separated regions where remixing was unlikely. This applies also to Darwin's original Galapagos finches.

The same kind of thing, but this time with selection at work, can be seen in the case of the yarrow plant, whose morphology varies continuously from the coastal regions of California to the High

Sierra Nevada. In general, the lower-level variants are larger and more luxuriant, and there is a shift of growing season. These differences are not due to the effects of different environmental conditions on a genetically uniform species but reflect definite genetic differences—evidenced by the fact that plants taken from their normal habitat and raised elsewhere don't do so well, or even die. This indicates that although derived from a common stock, the genes have segregated into different mixes, and not in a chance fashion as was the case with the sparrows, but through selection to suit the varying local environments. This is precisely the kind of adaptive potential that has never been disputed—an organism with no inbuilt range for adapting to changing conditions would be precarious indeed, if not nonviable. But it comes up against limits. There is no evidence to suggest that anything other than segregation of existing genes has occurred. It sheds no light whatsoever on the question of where the genes came from. As with the various breeds of dogs, what's being demonstrated is the diversity that can come from a richly endowed—in some cases astonishingly so—ancestral genetic stock. (It follows that every such segregation results in a loss of diversity that was present in the ancestral species. Gene mixes separated out in this way can become so specialized that survivability is threatened. A notable example is the cheetah.)

Various models and algorithms are presented nevertheless that purport to show natural process generating complex specified information. One of the most ridiculous is a procedure that its proponents refer to as "cumulative complexity." The line from *Hamlet*,

"Methinks it is like a weasel" is used as a demonstration. Trying to obtain this sequence by pure chance, for example by randomly drawing twenty-seven Scrabble and space tiles in succession, would take on average around 10^{40} tries. Instead, the method offered is to enter the target sequence into a computer, say, and run an algorithm that randomly alters all the characters at every position. When one of them matches the corresponding character in the target it is held, and lo and behold the algorithm rapidly converges on the complete expression.

Is it not obvious that the required answer is being supplied by an intelligence, along with the directions for finding it? This is no more originating an English sentence than the search function of a word processor, which also compares a target string character by character until it finds a match. Yet it is seriously put forward and debated by senior members of prominent academic institutions. Professors of philosophy and biology rave about it.

Other evolutionary algorithms and genetic programs may be less transparent, but deeper looking always reveals that the CSI they seem at first sight to originate was already in there or smuggled in, often unwittingly, by the programmer. This isn't to say that they are not capable of arriving at remarkable solutions to the problems they are given, sometimes in ways that would never have occurred to a human. One of the better known is the "crooked wire" algorithm[13] developed for finding best solutions for radiating antennas in given circumstances. Contrary to expectations, the best answers come out not as neat, symmetric geometric forms but as weird tangles that no designer would have contemplated trying. This is certainly impressive and immensely useful. But it is not a manifestation of unguided natural processes mimicking the creative power of evolution in the way that enthusiasts claim.

Evolutionary algorithms work by sampling points in a "problem space" made up of points representing all variations that the solution to the problem could assume. Problem spaces are typically huge—otherwise we wouldn't need computerized algorithms to search them. You could think of one as a square mile of flat beach, with each grain of sand representing a possible solution. For the point that it has selected, the algorithm evaluates a "fitness function," which is a measure of how effective—or otherwise—that particular solution is. By comparing the fitness functions at different points, the algorithm is able to follow a path taking it from "so-so" to "good" to "even better." Visualize the fitness function as a hollow shell of valleys and peaks covering the beach like a bizarrely distorted circus tent. The fitness function evaluates the height of the tent at any spot. What the algorithm tries to do is move its sampling point around on the beach to locate a slope, and then follow it upward until it identifies a peak. The peak will represent an optimum value of the fitness function, which was the object of the exercise.

Where the programmer smuggles in the CSI is in defining the fitness function, which requires knowledge of the problem and awareness of the kinds of things that make one solution more desirable than another. We said that originating information equates to choosing from alternatives. Although such an algorithm appears to be making choices it really isn't, because it has no alternative but to follow the rules it has been given. The true choices were exercised in formulating the rules. What the programmer effectively does is choose an appropriate fitness function—circus tent—from among all the fitness functions that might have been applied. And fitness functions are almost always more complex than the formulation of the original problem, which means that they involve vaster search spaces. So what the algorithm has done is move programmer-originated CSI from the realm of fitness-function space into the problem space. Although not creating CSI, the valuable lesson that exercises like this demonstrate is that natural processes can combine with intelligence to produce results far exceeding anything that intelligence alone might ever accomplish.

We started out by noting that the spirit of true science is to follow where the evidence seems to be pointing, without preconceptions of where that should lead. It would appear that the evidence points to a powerful intelligence at work behind nature and the organization of the universe. Evidence of the kind we have been considering doesn't exclude the god of the Christian, or any other, religion, but neither does it endorse any such identification. It simply has nothing to say about the nature of such an intelligence, its competence or capability, its bearing on what we think of as moral behavior, or what its purpose might be. My own opinion if pressed is that it would do things for its own reasons, not what we would like them to be, and getting too hung up on thinking otherwise runs the danger of projecting ourselves into the center of our own Ptolemaic universe. Many think differently, of course, and they may be right; but these are questions to be addressed by theology, philosophy, and perhaps personal inner experience, not science.

But if we are departing from the hard evidence for a moment to touch on personal beliefs, one of my feelings is that modern science has blinkered itself so much with materialist-reductionist ideology that it gets a lot of things the wrong way around. The suggestion that life is an accident of macromolecules, and mind nothing but an emergent of neural electrochemistry to me is as preposterous as saying that *Gone With the Wind* is just a by-product of materials throwing themselves together to form film, speakers, and movie projectors. In the beginning was the concept. Concepts originate with intelligence and become manifest through design.

The objection is commonly raised that for an intelligence to influence events in the universe, it would need to intervene at some point to cause the particles to move in a way they would not otherwise have moved, which in turn implies injecting energy in a way that would violate the laws of physics, and that simply doesn't happen. But that's not the only way. An alternative way of influencing the way events happen is by imparting information. And that can be accomplished without involving any changes of energy at all by *altering the outcomes of probabilities*. After all, isn't that what living things do all the time? In fact, an indeterminate universe rising from a substrate of quantum fluctuations would seem ideally suited. Just a thought.

I would have thought that issues like these could be among the most exciting and significant that science might pursue. Instead, it has painted itself into an ideological corner of decreeing that there *must* be naturalistic answers to everything and forcing such an interpretation on any evidence that it considers. It seems ironic that in the cultural dominance that science now enjoys as a result of its contributions to creating wealth and securing material power in the modern world, it should in many ways have become a new voice for censorship and repression, shouting down those who disagree and proclaiming itself the sole purveyor of truth in a way that discomfortingly echoes the authorities that reigned in times gone by.

An increasing number of scientific and other professionals who have no religious ax to grind[14] are coming to the conclusion, purely from the evidence, that the possibility of intelligent design at work is a very real one that warrants serious consideration, and that this should be acknowledged by the educational system, along with the criticisms of the current theory. But any advocacy in this direction is greeted by outcries from scientific and legal quarters as wanting to "teach creationism" or "ban evolution." It is to be expected that such a movement will attract those of fundamentalist persuasions. But holding that the only alternative to one extreme is the opposite extreme, and that rejecting or even questioning Darwinism is automatically to insist on a 6,000-year-old Earth and literal Genesis, imposes a false dichotomy.

Truth doesn't demand a monopoly platform and call for dissent to be expunged from classrooms and bookshelves. It welcomes the open exploration of alternatives and grants to others the freedom to state their case. After all, if wanting to learn the truth is the object, what is there to lose? However, if the real objective, maybe rationalized to the point of being unconscious, is to defend a position of cultural authority and prestige, and the benefits that come with it, then there would be quite a lot to lose indeed.

Notes:

1 Ballantine Del Rey, 1977. To be reissued by Baen Books.

2 See, for example, "The Revealed Word of God," included in *Minds, Machines & Evolution*, June 1988 (Baen Books edition, December 1999, pp. 147–153).

3 Later research showed that the moths don't normally rest on tree barks in daytime, and bird predation isn't a big factor in controlling them. In some areas the moths changed color before the trees did. The photos in the textbooks were faked by gluing dead moths to trees.

4 Taken from the listing given in Michael Denton's *Evolution: A Theory in Crisis* (Bethesda: Adler & Adler, 1985), p. 279.

5 William Paley, *Natural Theology: Or Evidences of the Existence and Attributes of the Deity Collected from the Appearances of Natures*, 1802. (Boston: Gould & Lincoln, reprinted 1852)

6 Taken from David Swift's *Evolution Under the Microscope*, (Sterling, UK: Leighton Academic Press), a comprehensive introduction to the subject, written by a biochemist who started out unquestioningly accepting the conventional evolutionary paradigm.

[7] Swift, p. 138

[8] Fred Hoyle, *The Intelligent Universe* (New York: Holt, Rinehart and Winston, 1983)

[9] Swift, p. 155

[10] William of Occam, Surrey, c. 1300–1349, an English Franciscan monk and philosopher. Essentially, the principle named after him states that if a simpler answer will do—one requiring less to be assumed—then opting for a more complicated one is not justified. This doesn't guarantee that you'll always be right; but it's the way to bet.

[11] The following discussion is derived largely from William Dembski's *No Free Lunch* (Lanham, MD: Rowman & Littlefield, 2002).

[12] For a more detailed discussion, see Lee Spetner, *Not By Chance!* (New York: Judaica Press, 1997).

[13] Edward E. Altshuler and Derek S. Linden, "Design of Wire Antennas Using Genetic Algorithms," *Electromagnetic Optimization by Genetic Algorithms*, Y. Rahmat-Samii and E. Michielssen, eds. (New York: Wiley, 1999), pp. 211–248

[14] Denton, Swift, Hoyle, and Spetner cited above are examples. While Wells and Dembski do openly profess religious convictions, the works cited here deal purely with scientific and mathematical issues.

Old, Unimproved Model

Most people would probably think that a "hard" science-fiction writer whose universes are filled with intelligent robots, time machines, and galaxy-cruising aliens would be the ultimate technomaniac, surrounded by innovation and delighting in every improvement in comfort and efficiency that the further modernizing of life has to offer. They'd imagine his home to be a show house of cutting-edge gimmickry set in a proving ground of high-tech yard- and pool-care gadgets, with surround sound in every room and a kitchen like the control room of a nuclear submarine. His professional life would be managed by all the wonders of the electronic office against a backdrop of online banking, fingertip global information, and a sophisticated business and social networking community. Alas, for all those nodding in fond or even mildly envious agreement,

I have to shatter the image. I don't know if it's an effect of age, or of a falling threshold of tolerance that comes with it, but I find myself coming away from it all shaking my head with the conviction being steadily reinforced that everything invented since I turned fifty was unnecessary, and that the world would probably have been better off without it, anyway.

Computers played a bigger part in my life twenty years ago than they do today. In those days, I created graphical games for the children before most of the world had heard of them, sought out weird problems just for the satisfaction of writing programs to solve them, and meticulously verified all the orbital dynamics and energy calculations that my stories required. I was possibly the last user on Earth of the TRS-80. I could get into the command set, alter the printer codes, and make it do just about anything short of making toast. I remember buying an external eight-megabyte hard drive for it—the size of a shoe box. My mind boggled at the thought. What could one ever want with eight megabytes? It had redefinable partitions dividing the storage into four sectors, and I put some of my work in each, just to feel that I was getting full use out of what I had paid for.

Then came the catastrophe of unlimited brute force for pennies. Software grew in bulk and pointless complexity as cutesy graphics and overdone embellishments combined like the worst of Victorian furniture to pile up gaudier forms without function. Infuriating "enhancements" that presumed to know better than I did what I wanted persisted in opening browsers I hadn't asked for, dialing connections I didn't want, popping up messages I wasn't interested in, and leading me into disguised Web links that there was no way to get back out of. Finding out how to turn them off became a major part of every new learning process, along with automatically disabling anything described as "smart." As Web sites became more elaborate and annoying, I found myself more and more tuning out in frustration as the downloads of interminable frames and overlays grew longer without actually telling me anything useful. Nowadays I use a laptop that must be a million times more powerful than that old TRS-80 just for my writing and for e-mail. I don't read newspapers or own a TV, having long ago dismissed the mass media as a credible source of information on anything that matters. For research I prefer books and journals.

Beyond one's personal life is the havoc wrought by overcomputerization of the outside world in general. Besides the horrors of voice mail and automated information systems, the tentacles of electronic tyranny reach down from head offices floating in cloud cuckoo land to every real-world point of sale, service desk, and ticketing counter, where corporation robots stare in glazed immobility at screens flashing thickets of rules and restrictions, and the lines of waiting nonproductive humanity withdrawn from serving the economy grow longer. I've given up trying to fight my way through incomprehensible online order forms and address fields that recognize only U.S. formats. If I want the product badly enough, it's simpler—and often, in the long run, faster—to send an e-mail asking for a postal address that I can mail a check to.

I've never really figured out how to use cruise control. Oh, sure, I can twiddle the knobs and eventually find that it's kicked in, but I'm never sure exactly what I did sufficiently to be able to repeat it at will. Automobiles are another area where it seems that confusion and complexity are taken obsessively to points way beyond serving any worthwhile human need, purely for the sake of providing work for compulsive meddlers in design offices with nothing useful left to do. If it works, we understand it, the service department can fix it, and parts are available, it's a sure sign that it's about to become obsolete.

I have a suspicion that like airlines, banks, and any department run by government, car manufacturers have entire buildings filled with people whose sole function is to dream up more purposeless ways of harassing customers. I drive a twelve-year-old Pontiac because it's still mercifully that far behind the latest round of atrocities that regulators and the industry would inflict on us. A French car that I owned in Ireland would manage to set its alarm system while I was inside, with the result that it was impossible to get out without setting it off. The mechanic I took it to assured me that this couldn't happen. I agreed, but asked him to fix it anyway, since it did. How, he asked bemusedly, could he put right something that couldn't have gone wrong? How was I supposed to tell him? Well, was it possible to just disable the whole thing? Yes. Very well—and that solved the problem. Now, whenever I get a new car, the alarm system is one of the things that I have them disable automatically, like any software option calling itself "smart." So when I hear one going off inanely at three o'clock in the morning I can go back to sleep easily, knowing it's not mine.

Another of my cars had a steering-column lock that had a tendency to hang onto keys, necessitating the whole thing being replaced at exorbitant cost. When this happened for the third time, I asked why we couldn't just fit one of those old dash-panel ignition switches that didn't involve fooling with the steering at all.

"They're illegal in California," was the answer I received.

"I didn't ask if it was legal. I asked if you could do it."

"Well . . . I guess so, maybe."

"How much?"

"Say, fifteen dollars?"

End of problem.

With a car I had in England, I got so fed up with wrestling to get the key out of the column lock that I ended up leaving it in the car permanently. Since it was the same key as was used for the door, the door remained unlocked too. That was back in the days when I worked as a sales engineer in central London and would leave the car parked on the street or in convenient alleys all day. Nobody ever touched it.

I wanted a washer and dryer for a town house that I bought some years ago in Florida, but balked at the Starship *Enterprise* panel arrays and instruction manuals the size of the Manhattan phone book for the machines in Wards' showroom. Mastering them would surely require a pilot's license. (And anyway, no guy has things labeled "Delicate," et cetera in his wardrobe, or is going to mince around sorting his laundry into ten loads of four items each.) So I traced down the people who supplied the machines to the laundromat I'd been using to see if they would sell me ones that just had the couple of switches (Hot-Warm-Cold; High-Medium-Low) that I was used to. They did—and could supply them without the coin mechanisms. The machines were industrial grade and would come out best in an encounter with an Abrams battle tank. I was happy.

The combined washer-dryer in the flat I had over the pizza parlor in Ireland, however, was something else, with directions that might as well be in Swahili for all the sense I could make of them. So when the repairman came from the same supplier to fix the stove, I had him set up all the numbers and programs and options. From then on I could just hit "On/Off" and leave the rest alone.

Visitors despair when they see childproof bottles in my bathroom with the tops hacked off and the necks stuffed with tissue. The geniuses who design these things live in an unreal world inhabited only by incurious and inept young children and alert, fully functional adults. It doesn't include crotchety 60-year-olds half awake with a hangover at six o'clock in the morning, who can't remember where they put their glasses. My kitchen is a war zone of sliced and mangled boxes that refused to yield along the dotted lines, gouged containers with the easy-open tops still solidly in place, and resealable packages that wouldn't. I scour yard sales for "dumb" appliances that just work—and do nothing else—engineered in metal and fixed with screws, not pieces of pressed-together plastic with hidden catches to come apart like some Chinese puzzle that can never be reassembled. I have the hotel desk give me wake-up calls rather than attempt decoding the digital clock radio, while my own alarm at home has rotary hands, the way God intended, and is driven by clockwork, which by definition is what clocks were supposed to be.

Perhaps all this is Nature's way of leading us to the realization that the world needs teenagers. Those collections of gangly frames, splayed limbs, and toothy grins that we used to think of as assemblages of left-overs from the Creation with no practical use turn out to be indispensable to our survival. What is mindless irritation to us, becomes for the kids a boundless source of the delights of meeting challenge, demonstrating competence and virtuosity, and savoring the heady taste of achievement. Finicky and time-consuming? They have a lifetime of time; boredom is their enemy. Those intelligent "agents" we read about that will cruise the Web for us, applying personalized profiles of our interests and tastes, and communicate back in intelligible (well, almost) English are already here! The old joke about them being the only mortals (the geeks in manufacturers' back-room labs don't count as belonging to the real world) capable of programming a VCR is not only true; it's scary. I've watched them create intricate databases by just *playing* with the software, making it a game in which opening the manual would spoil the fun—like asking directions in the ways women can never understand, or copying the answers to a crossword from the solution at the back of the book. They revel in SUVs loaded with everything, and can click their way unerringly through a tree of Windows settings faster than I can follow with the eye, at the same time, as if just to rub it in, nonchalantly carrying on a conversation over a shoulder.

And maybe there's a good reason why it's all that way. It makes the bonds of dependency between generations two-way, creating cohesion in society. We—the older crew—are finally force-fed a little of that humility that we've always been told would be good for us, but nothing else so far in life has succeeded in persuading us to try. The kids get to develop the confidence and sense of adequacy that they're going to need a whole lot of before they really get into the thick of life.

There comes a time when the effort to keep abreast of the latest versions and on top of all the updates that will be history a year from now just isn't worth it anymore. It's time to pay attention to other things in life that never change and were there all along. Playing chess (that's the one where you push pieces of wood around on a board; the excitement is all in the mind; doesn't even need batteries) with the boys is more exciting than endlessly mowing down suicidally inclined monsters in mazes. I've even found time to take up the piano.

People talk about getting "over the hill," and they worry. I think they have what Americans call an attitude problem. What happens when you get over the hill on a bike? All the hard stuff is over, right? You can sit back, enjoy the view, and let gravity do the work. Life is no different. There's wisdom and justice in the ways of the world after all.

From the Web Site

Bulletin Board, "Miscellaneous" section, July 30, 2003 (http://www.jamesphogan.com/bb/content/073003. shtml)

CHILDREN NEED TO GET OUT AND PLAY

Something I discovered in the process of growing up in London was that bombed buildings make great playgrounds. All-round adventure parks without any admission fee. Makeshift rafts transform flooded base- ments into eerie pirates' caves. A surviving corner with some pieces of floor still attached becomes the neighborhood North Wall of the Eiger. After raising three sons and three daughters, I can testify that young people are not designed to sit for hours in silent, obedient rows, listening to droning adults. Their way of learning about the world is to explore it. When I came to the States in the '70s, I was astounded to learn of children commencing school at 7:00 a.m. and being passed like a production line from class to class with only a half-hour break in the middle of the day. It couldn't work.

And now, it seems, science has vindicated my suspicions. In an article entitled "Hyperactivity 'just high spirits'" (http://news.bbc.co.uk/1/hi/health/3102137.stm) the UK's BBC News reports that Profesor Priscilla Alderson, an expert in childhood studies at London's Institute of Education, believes that such conditions as attention deficit disorder and mild autism are being overdiagnosed, and millions of kids are perhaps being alarmed, bullied, and drugged into compliance and semisomnambulance unnecessarily. It could be that they're being cooped up in homes and classrooms too much, she says, and not allowed to run off their energies in parks and playgrounds. Really? My word! I mean, how *do* these people do it?

According to Professor Alderson, the mania for finding maladjusted kids everywhere is driven by money. (Surprise.) Psychologists want the work and lower the diagnosis threshold accordingly. Not surprisingly, the professionals on the other side disagree. A spokeswoman for the National Autism Society found it " . . . disappointing that reputable diagnosis is being questioned." Just imagine—*questioning* the need to drug millions of children. Whatever next?

*　　　*　　　*

Bulletin Board, "Science—General" section, March 15, 2003 (http://www.jamesphogan.com/bb/content/031503.shtml)

PIONEER 10 SIGNING OFF

A friend of mine in Florida who runs an auto-repair shop does a steady business fitting replacement engines into older cars for something like $2,000 a time. It seems that a lot of people don't trust today's overpriced, overelaborate computerized offerings and prefer to stay with the simpler, more solidly engineered designs of times gone by. Another friend tells me she won't buy toasters anymore because they don't last—unless she finds an old one in a yard sale.

Pioneer 10, the unmanned space probe launched in 1972 to observe the outer planets, sent its last message back to NASA on January 22, which took 11 hours and 20 minutes to arrive. Originally designed for 21 months endurance, the probe ended up performing what has been described as one of the most scientifically rich exploration missions ever undertaken. It's amazing what can be done when engineering is left to engineers, without government bureaucrats and lawyers muscling in on it. Full story at *News in Science* (http://abc.net.au/science/news/stories/s793584.htm). Thanks to Dave Schilling for sending me the link.

Providing it doesn't run into something else on the way, *Pioneer 10*'s next encounter will be with the red giant star Aldebaran in the constellation of Taurus, two million years from now.

The Falcon

Myriam lay at that halfway stage of knowing that she was waking up and not wanting to; that sleep was receding and would deliver her inexorably to another day of life that she would rather not have to face.

These were the moments when the afterimages of dreams that would quickly fade still lingered. The dream had been another of those she had been having lately that left her in a strangely mixed state of feeling a glow of well-being from the release she had briefly known, yet at the same time, troubled. There had been a town by water where boats were moored, and little shops and restaurants facing it across a quay. It was a colorful town, where people shared their thoughts with one another and smiled openly without fear. Then Myriam had found herself with a group of them inside a room somewhere. She had wanted to be one of them but she couldn't comprehend freedom from fear. There was a young man with black hair and pale-blue eyes, in his early twenties, maybe—just a few years older than herself. She had wanted to be with him because he made her feel secure. But he gave a porcelain figurine as a gift to another girl, with fair hair, dressed in green, and when Myriam was alone she had thrown it on the floor and then tried to hide the pieces. It troubled her that such a side to her could exist and be beyond her ability to control, even in a dream. She felt as if she had glimpsed a hidden part of herself that she didn't want to know.

Sounds from the world beyond filtered through her cocoon to peel the last shreds of sleep away. Air entering through the ceiling vent, accompanied by the judder of vibrations in the ducting; water flowing in pipes behind the wall, telling of others in the building already showering and bathing; early traffic on the street, punctuated by a public-address speaker babbling unintelligibly in the distance. She tensed. *It could come at any moment. Perhaps she had just a few more precious minutes yet . . . ?*

As if cued by her thought, strident wake-up music burst forth from the videcon commanding the room. Myriam forced her eyes to open. They felt as if they had been glued. On the screen high in the far corner, a troupe of showgirls in spangle panties and military-style tops were parading through a routine with toy rifles against a backdrop of clips showing tanks and slow-goose-stepping guards. She left it on to shake herself fully into wakefulness. At least the light and the colors were a distraction from the drabness and utilitarian furnishings of the room.

Myriam sat up and shivered. It was winter, and the heating was only just coming on with the morning power ration. The lamp across the street was still on, making an orange blur on the thin window blind. She tottered across to the closet, groped for a clean work tunic, and made her way through to the bathroom. A voice from the videocon behind was reminding her that this was another National Maximum Effort Day. Working together they would make it the best ever.

Leisha and Greg were already eating at the corner table when Myriam arrived downstairs in the apartment house's shared kitchen. She crossed over to the refrigerator and unlocked her personal compartment inside. There was dried-egg-and-batter mix that would have made a pancake, but the thought wasn't appetizing. She settled for the remains of some canned fruit with crackers and a pâté of cheese spread, and spooned coffee granules from the communal tin into a mug. As Myriam pulled a stool out from under the side bar, Dolores came in and went to the refrigerator in her turn. There were no words of greeting. The room with its stained and faded wallpaper, scratched appliances, and plain, greasy tiles behind the stove reflected the listlessness of its occupants.

Footsteps creaked on the stairs outside, padded their way along the bare floor of the hallway, and were cut short by the sound of the front door opening and closing. Leisha raised an inquiring eyebrow at Greg over a spoonful of soup heated from the night before. "Is Stefanie still seeing her visitor?"

"Sounds like it."

Nobody knew his name. He had been coming and going intermittently for the last few weeks. Stefanie said he worked around the city on telecom installations.

"It wouldn't be surprised if that's a shell job," Dolores said. "I think he's DoS."

"What makes you say that?" Leisha asked. Her tone conveyed that the thought was not new.

Dolores shrugged. "He's just got that creepy feel about him." A stranger in the place made everyone wary of saying anything that might seem out of line. Department of Surveillance agents had things that could hear through walls.

As Myriam watched Dolores putting items from the refrigerator out onto a plate, she remembered a part of another of her dreams. There had been a white-haired woman who prepared food for the others and served it to them at the table—not as a hired domestic in an upper-social-echelon house, but freely. It was one of those things that a person who is dreaming somehow "knows." None of the people present had shown discomfort at the display of servility and such needless acceptance of an inferior's role. Myriam had sensed a bond between them that she didn't understand but wanted desperately to share. . . .

Then the fleeting image was gone. Just a shell of the feeling she had known was left, dry and empty like a husk of wheat. She finished her breakfast and went back up to her room to collect her coat and purse.

*　　*　　*

The bus set Myriam down at a side entrance to the Peace Department building, inside the restricted-access perimeter on the east side of inner city Core Zone. Through the door, the line to the body scanner and sniffer at the security point was short, and she was not singled out on the far side for random screening. A corridor brought her to the marble-walled lobby concourse with its dominating central statue of the Leader. A series of frescos depicting the history of the Party and its struggle lined the walls on both sides. Above the high doors leading through into the main body of the building was a huge plaque bearing the State emblem of a swooping falcon, its wings spread and talons extended. Myriam took an elevator down to Sublevel Four, and arrived in the vestibule of Telesupport Operations less than fifty minutes after her wake-up call had sounded.

She arrived at the cubicle containing the station for Watch Seventeen and hung her coat on the rack by the entrance from the aisle. Nathan, who was on night shift that week, had already activated the handover screen. He was tall and lean, with dark hair cropped short above a wan, spot-marred face rendered all the more bloodless by his gray, high-collared work tunic. "There's been activity in the Abheradan sector," he told her as he stood up to let her take the seat at the console. "Alert condition is at Orange-Two. Analyzer returns Subversive Probability at eighty-two percent."

Myriam nodded as she scanned over the summary displays and checked the log, following procedure meticulously. Nathan watched with a neutral expression. Nobody would compromise their record and risk disciplinary action for failing to report an irregularity in procedure on the part of someone else. Personal affections undermined the first loyalty taught, which was to the State, and were discouraged from an early age. State enemies could appear in any shape or form. The complications that emotional conflicts led to were best avoided.

"Good." Myriam entered her ID and request to transfer the task supervisory status. A readout confirmed and requested her authorization code.

"What kind of a day is it?" Nathan inquired, pulling on a dark gabardine overcoat.

"Gray and cold. It rained last night."

"Okay, then. . . . I'll see you tomorrow."

"Tomorrow."

Nathan left. Myriam slipped on the headset providing phones and imaging spectacles, which at that moment were presenting a copy of the Sector Summary screen. She selected a surveillance drone making a routine circuit in the north-central plateau region, and switched the sensor channel to "Live." Moments later, she was looking down over a scene of sandy hills speckled by clumps of scrub and brush, with greener gullies carving their way down to a winding river. For several seconds, she allowed herself to savor the illusion that she really was ten thousand miles away above a valley in a distant land of strangeness and mystery, breathing the air of its warm winds. Just for a moment, she let herself forget that it was seditious even to think of such things, and imagined that there could be an escape from the gray world of gray tunics, gray clouds, and the city's gray, brooding facades, to one where the sun shone from clear skies over unfenced lands, and the water flowed free from the mountains to the ocean.

"*Item Check.*" The synthetic voice of the Activity Analyzer sounded in her phones. At the same time, a graticule appeared on the image, along with coordinate details in the margins. Myriam voiced a zoom command, and the graticule enlarged. The view showed some sheds approached by a track from the river's edge. Figures were standing in front of what looked like a pump house serving a pipe that ran up to an earth-banked reservoir feeding the surrounding system of irrigation channels.

"*Item Check.*" In a village two miles or so away, a crowd in gaily colored dress was gathering for what could have been a wedding celebration. Myriam directed the drone onto a course that would enable closer examination.

Peaceful and innocuous as such first impressions might seem, these were the sources who served the State's enemies by sustaining the rebel armies abroad, and traitors and saboteurs nearer home. They provided their recruiting and training grounds. The State's survival depended on being vigilant at all times, everywhere.

A red annunciator flag appeared in Myriam's visual field. The Analyzer intoned, "*Query condition. Intervention indicated.*" It meant that an AI assigned to monitoring a condition tagged as "Sensitive" had spotted something that warranted human assessment. Myriam decoupled from the drone and returned to Sector Summary. The highlighted item was the situation at Abheradan that Nathan had mentioned. She connected to the device on station there, which he had already brought down to lower altitude. Its transmission showed a warehouse or factory building standing amid narrow streets and alleys in a densely built part of a town. The area seemed to be primarily residential, made up for the most part of houses with balconies, arches, and high, flat roofs. In a small open yard at the front of the building, facing a crowded street, a truck loaded with lettuces was standing in front of a large, open door. A box inset above the image summarized the AI's reasons for determining an alert condition.

The estimated amount of lettuces shipped from the surrounding area in the past few weeks was out of line with the figures for rainfall, yields of other produce, and the statistics for earlier years. The truck type was unusually heavy for this kind of work. Two similar, overheavy trucks carrying lettuces had been observed on the road from this area in the past twenty-four hours. Other activity in this sector [*reference link provided*] has already yielded an alert condition at 82 percent.

Myriam consulted the referenced details. An independent intelligence report from some months earlier had identified the building as a suspected supply dump and meeting point for guerrilla forces operating in that area. Overnight electronic intercepts indicated a known recruiter and organizer of munitions shipments to be in the vicinity.

She returned her attention to the image. Figures had appeared and were moving around the truck in apparent agitation. Another alert flag appeared, accompanied by the announcement in her phones, "*Signal analyzer detects strong Q-band spectrum sweeping. Consistent with attempt to jam transmission. Executing countermeasures.*" This needed to be referred higher. Myriam consolidated the situation outline and sent a request for the Duty Operations Controller to patch in. A few seconds later, an acknowledgment flag appeared on her status screen. Then the Controller's voice came over in her phones.

"Let's see, what have we got here? . . . Oh, these guys again, eh? I've been expecting something like this. Uh . . . Uh-huh . . . And there's an ECM beam active, Watch Seventeen? That's definite?"

"JF evaluation positive," Myriam confirmed.

"Uh-huh." A short silence followed, giving way to the barely audible sound of the Controller humming to himself. Myriam waited. Ten thousand miles away, one of the figures by the truck was gesticulating wildly at the others. Somebody who had come out of the open door from the building was running toward the cab. In the street beyond the yard in front, people were milling around a bus with baggage and bicycles on its roof.

"Crosscheck affirms," another voice, female, said from somewhere.

There had been a bus in one of the dreams. . . .

"Okay. Are you there, Watch Seventeen?"

"Sir."

"It's a hostile. Code Red, authorization Seven-Peter-Bravo-Fifty-Six. Deliver for effect—the truck and the building."

Myriam brought up the equipment designator box, entered the clearance code, and selected two APX-3 explosive and fragmentation, followed by one IP-7 incendiary. Verification confirmed. Target locks confirmed. Warheads armed. Fire control showing *Ready.*

The bus in the dream had been white with painted designs along the side. Laughing children ran from it, down among trees to a lake where birds were swimming.

Myriam stared at the faraway people in the image being presented by her headset. They were . . . *people*. They had never been people before, people with homes, people with lives. They were always just incidentals—animations in a computer game.

The truck was starting to move out.

"You have authorization, Watch Seventeen."

Myriam saw the blood, the torn-off limbs and burning flesh, heard the screams.

"What is this? Seventeen, are you reading? We're gonna lose them. I said, *deliver for effect.*"

"No."

"What?"

"I can't. . . . I won't do it."

"This is an authorized Code Red operational order. You are a contracted facilitator. I repeat—"

"Not anymore. I've quit."

"That's not permitted."

"I've just permitted it."

"You do not have that option."

"Fuck you. I just told you, I've quit."

Strained silence. Labored breathing sounded through the phones. Then, "Security to Telesupport Ops on Sub-Four. We have a situation. Be prepared for physical removal and restraint."

Four of them sat facing her from the far side of the long, central table in a sparsely furnished meeting room at the rear of one of the upper levels.

The Resident Psychiatric Counselor, a thin woman with hair tied back and a pointy nose and chin, read from a screen pad open in front of her. "Her previous profile shows acceptable conformity on all indexes. No history of social pathology or deviancy. Graded B to B-plus on Loyalty and Dedication Indicators. Cerebral rhythms do show recent peakings consistent with unresolved stress, along with an anomalous decoherence. Further exploratory testing is recommended." The last statement was in reference to patterns recorded by the microsensor implanted in Myriam's scalp since birth, mandatory for health monitoring and maintenance.

"This isn't a case of physical breakdown, then?" the Human Resources Administrator checked.

"I see no indication of such."

The Security Officer turned his head toward the Assistant Departmental Director. "It wasn't some kind of temporary insanity," he interpreted.

The ADD looked across at Myriam. "You hear that? Scientifically validated. It won't do any good to try pleading anything along those lines." The thought of doing so hadn't entered Myriam's mind. She stared back blankly, resigned to the futility of trying to explain anything. Yet they seemed to be expecting her to say something.

"External subversive influences, maybe," the HRA commented, addressing the others. "Social contacts and organizations? Political affiliations?"

"Report being run and updated," the Security Officer said.

The ADD was still looking at Myriam. "Don't you have anything to say? We really are trying to help you,

you know. You clearly have some kind of problem. But you have to try to work with us."

The psychiatrist chimed in. "Don't be afraid to be frank," she urged Myriam. "We need to know the way you see things. If it turns out to be delusional, remember it isn't your fault. How do you feel inside, right at this moment? Confused? Afraid? Angry?" A pause. Nothing. "Are you too unsure to tell us?" She waved a hand invitingly. "Does the thought trouble you, secretly, that you might be insane?"

"I've never felt saner," Myriam told them.

She was taken to the medical facility in the adjoining building to undergo a battery of routine tests, and then put in one of the treatment rooms while reports were scrutinized and superiors consulted. The doctor in charge prescribed a sedative and tranquilizer. Myriam insisted that she was perfectly calm and composed. It made no difference.

The young man with black hair and pale-blue eyes was holding her chin to tilt her head, and looking at her intently. His hands were strong but gentle. He was smiling reassuringly. They were in a room with wooden bookshelves lining one of the walls, and paintings of sailing ships. Outside the window, the sun was shining on shrubbery and flowers. Myriam was fascinated by the shelves. She had never seen so many books.

Then he was seated, writing something at a desk. She knew that he was some kind of physician or counselor. But different from physicians that she had known. He really *did* care.

"—was asking after you," he said without looking up. Something inside Myriam prevented her from hearing the name. "I told her you're doing fine. You have a good friend there—" Again, the word failed to form. Myriam realized that she didn't know her own name. But she knew somehow that he was talking about the girl with the fair hair, dressed in green, the girl whose figurine Myriam had broken. It had been a figurine of a cat.

"It was an accident," Myriam blurted. It was what she had been telling people. She was having one of those strange experiences of knowing that she was dreaming. But more than that, she was aware of its connection to the earlier dream.

"Accidents do happen," the man agreed. He sat back in his chair and looked across at her. Myriam had the feeling that she could conceal nothing from his intense, pale-blue eyes. He knew. And why should anyone have believed her? If it had been an accident, why would she try to hide the pieces? Feelings of inadequacy among these people welled up inside her. She could feel tears of frustration in her eyes. Then the moment came that she had been dreading, when her dark side that dwelt within took control, and she could only listen to herself helplessly.

"You don't believe me! Nobody believes me! You all think you're so superior. I detest every one of you! . . ."

An officer from the Inland Security Service, accompanied by two troopers and a staff matron, collected Myriam from the Peace Department building later that day. They took her to her lodging, where uniformed police had already arrived and were waiting outside her room to conduct a search. Nobody else in the house or the vicinity showed any sign of noticing. Myriam had become a nonperson. The troopers went straight to the space in the bottom of the closet underneath the board on which she stood her shoes, where she kept her letters, private papers, and her books. The ISS officer picked out several of the volumes and held them up to inspect the spines. "Lane, *The Discovery of Freedom . . . Knowing Thyself.* Hm, interesting." He nodded to one of the troopers, who was carrying a canvas holdall. "Take all of them. The papers too."

Owning books was frowned upon. It was best to keep them out of sight. Everything the citizen needed to know was supposed to be supplied by the official brochures and videocon channels. Meanwhile, the matron was rummaging through Myriam's personal things and setting objects aside. Myriam registered sluggishly—maybe as a result of the drugs she had been given—that they knew just where to look. Her room had been entered before. It meant that one of the other tenants was an informer. Or maybe it was Stefanie's visitor.

Myriam stood numbly. Although she had known since her early school days that, for the better protection of all, property and private lives had to be accessible to officials of the State, inwardly she was unable to suppress feelings of insult and humiliation. The thought fluttered on the edge of her mind that maybe she really did have a maladjustment problem. But she had set her course now. She had little choice but to see it through regardless.

Refusing to act against enemies of the State was considered equivalent to abetting and allying with them, which constituted a Category 3 Political offense.

Myriam was taken to the district ISS headquarters
and charged accordingly, and a dossier opened,
detailing her case. From there, a gray, windowless
ISS van took her, handcuffed, to a detention facility
to await a hearing. It lay about a half hour's drive
from the center of the city—in which direction, she
couldn't tell. She stepped out to find herself in a
yard enclosed by high walls topped by wire, in front
of an entrance to a stark, rectangular concrete building broken only by rows of narrow windows. For a
moment she stood looking around her bemusedly. A
female guard jabbed her painfully in the lower back
with a baton. "*Move it!*"

They took away her clothes and subjected her to
degrading body searches, made her shower in cold
water, watched by two wooden-faced wardresses, and
administered the same series of medical tests that she
had already been through that day, along with more
that required her to work a treadmill. Finally, she was
given a bright-orange two-piece suit with beltless baggy
pants, a pair of canvas slip-on shoes, a coarse blanket,
towel, and wash kit, and then conducted through a
barred gate, up in an elevator, through another gate,
and along a white-walled corridor of doors.

The cell they put her in had a door of yellow-painted
metal with a peephole covered by a sliding shutter.
A small window sat high in the opposite wall. There
were four steel-framed bunks, two on either side, a
molded plastic table with two chairs, a plain shelf
with some hanging hooks below, a washbasin, and a
toilet bowl screened by a curtain. A graying woman
in a light-blue suit was seated at the table, braiding
some kind of design from colored string. A younger,

blond-haired woman, in her thirties, perhaps, wearing a brown suit, was lying on one of the bunks, her eyes closed. She lifted her head when the door slammed, regarded Myriam indifferently for several seconds, and turned away again. Two of the three remaining bunks had blankets folded at the foot, indicating that there was an absent occupant. The bunk that was left was presumably Myriam's. She deposited her things on the thin, foam-rubber covering and stood uncertainly, then turned and sat on the edge. She felt herself starting to tremble. For the first time, the fear that the pace of the day's events had suppressed was beginning to surface. The gray-haired woman at the table was studying her curiously.

"The blanket stays at the bottom of the bunk until lights out. Towel on the shelf, wash bag on a hook underneath. Don't give them any reason to find faults." She had a deep voice. Her tone was even—not hostile, but guarded. Myriam got up and complied, then sat down again on the bunk. She was still too disoriented to know what she was supposed to say. "Orange," the woman went on. "Political. That's all we want to know." She gestured briefly toward herself. "Blue's Dissident. It means I refuse to believe what they demand I believe. And that's all you want to know. Get the idea?"

Myriam stared at the floor, then across at the figure in brown. So what did brown mean? She looked back at the gray-haired woman and started to frame the question. The gray-haired woman shook her head. She seemed to read Myriam's mind. So, you didn't ask about other people? Or was it that you didn't ask about them in their presence? Either way, Myriam was starting to get the idea.

The shutter behind the peephole opened periodically. An hour or so after Myriam arrived, the door opened and another woman wearing orange, about the same age as the blonde, was pushed inside. Her mouth looked swollen and bruised. She and the gray-haired woman began talking in low voices. Myriam made a cautious approach at joining in, hoping to learn what she could. But the conversation revolved around trivia, with no mention of where the newcomer had been. The blonde lay on her bunk and remained silent.

Supper appeared in the form of four plates of thin soup with scraps of vegetable floating in it, dry brown bread, and mugs of an unidentifiable lukewarm beverage pushed through a slot in the door. "Eat it. You never know when you'll get the next chance," the gray-haired woman advised. It was the first food that Myriam had seen since morning, and despite its insipid taste, she needed no urging. The lights were turned out a half hour later. She lay awake in the dark for a long time, reflecting on the day that had gone and fearing whatever was to come. Eventually, exhaustion overcame her.

Books! Myriam would never have believed that so many books existed in the world. Shelves of them extended from the floor to the ceiling; large ones and small ones, thick ones, thin ones; some with cloth covers, some with paper, others with glossy wraparound dust jackets. She moved toward them wonderingly as if in a dream—no, she *was* in a dream—and ran a hand over them. The solid, rectilinear forms, standing in their resolute ranks, were firm and reassuring, like trustworthy friends. Stories, histories, poetry and pictures; conflicts, journeys, famous lives. Books about life; books about the stars; books about things that people know, things that people think, things that people love, places that people have been. Somehow she felt that she knew them. She took one off the shelf and opened it, savoring the smell of the newly printed paper, tracing its texture with a fingertip.

"Ah, there she is." She turned to find a man looking at her from the end of the row of shelves. He was small, with a rosy, puckish face, white beard, and wearing a blue blazer jacket with silver buttons, and a red bow tie. The man nodded encouragingly. He seemed pleased. "Go ahead. Browse around all you want. It's good to see you back here again."

Myriam looked around. The room opened into another, also lined with aisles of bookshelves. "They're all yours, aren't they?" she said. She knew, but at the same time she was at a loss to understand how such a thing would be permitted.

The man laughed. "Well, in a way you could say so, I suppose. It's our shop."

The notion of owning a place like this was too strange for her to frame a question. But she knew what it looked like from the outside. She had seen it. It was one of the little shops in the row along the quay facing the boats and the water. The water was a river. Farther along, around a bend, it opened into the sea.

And then the man wasn't there anymore, and she was peering from behind the shelves at a table near the door, where a woman was signing books. It was the fair-haired woman who had worn green. People had been standing around the table, but now they were gone. Then the man with the black hair and pale-blue eyes came in, the man who had given her the figurine. He was smiling. The fair-haired woman got up and kissed him on the cheek. She called him Rory. They exchanged more words that Myriam couldn't hear and left together without seeing her.

She came out from behind the shelves and moved over to the table with its stack of books. The rage that she knew and feared was starting to boil up inside, goading her. She stretched out a hand, drew the top copy off the stack, and curled her fingers around a wad of the pages. The demon inside her shrieked. *Crush them up! Tear them out!*

Her body shook. . . . A part of her was fighting against the compulsion. Somewhere in her writhing consciousness, a memory stirred of a world where thought was controlled and minds were not free. Suddenly, she felt horror at the meaning of the destruction she had been about to loose. The rage subsided. Slowly, almost reverently, she put the book back. And then happiness and jubilation surged up where the blackness inside had been. She had kept control. She *could* beat it!

Then the premonition came that a dreamer feels who is about to wake up. *No!* She wanted to stay in this place she had found, and remain this person that she had glimpsed she could be. But the image was receding relentlessly. She opened her mouth and started to wail . . . which became the sound of the morning siren dragging her to wakefulness in her cold, cheerless cell.

Two days went by. The girl in the brown suit, which Myriam had learned by then stood for common criminal, was led away one morning and didn't return. She was replaced by a younger girl who cried most of the time. Later that same afternoon, Myriam was taken to a bare room of painted brick walls, containing just a table, and some chairs, and interviewed by a man and a woman from the Department of Justice.

They asked her about her work and her disposition toward it, her personal beliefs, and if she had any criticism of the State and its policies. Myriam was resigned to letting fate take its course and answered sparingly. All the same, they managed to find enough to make copious notes and fill in all manner of forms. Their manner was mechanically routine and impersonal. Although they talked about "representing her," they seemed to interpret it as finding technicalities for obtaining a more lenient sentence. The question of whether or not, or to what degree, she was guilty of the political offenses she had been charged with didn't arise.

While the man was tidying his papers and returning them to his briefcase, the woman contemplated Myriam across the table. Her face was devoid of any emotion—a technician performing an assigned task. "You have had two days now to reflect on your actions," she said. "Have you had any regrets or second thoughts? The beginnings, perhaps, of a concession to being wrong? That you were in error?"

"No."

"Hm. That's unfortunate. . . . It will only make things harder for you, you know. Confessing one's faults, admitting weakness, and asking for the State's help toward improvement is looked upon very favorably. But this attitude that you display . . ." The woman indicated Myriam with a dismissive wave. "The arrogance of imagining that you have the right to question; this obstinacy that we see. . . . It makes the difference between working cooperatively for your own cure, or fighting illogically against it. Which would you prefer?"

Myriam looked at the talking mask that was the woman's face, the impenetrable surfaces of the eyes, and wondered if anything resembling a person comparable to herself dwelt within. Communicating anything meaningful would have been as impossible as with the wooden table between them. The man had closed his briefcase and was watching with a detached curiosity.

"I'm not ill," Myriam said. "How can we talk about curing anything?"

Two days later, a van similar to the one she had arrived in collected her and took her back into the city. It deposited her in a yard behind a complex of large stone buildings, from where she was taken down to a basement holding cell. There were somewhere between ten and twenty people there, some fearful, a few noisy and belligerent, most just blank-faced and resigned. After several hours, during which the numbers thinned as various individuals were taken away at intervals, the warden reappeared accompanied by two guards and called Myriam's name. She was taken along corridors and up flights of stairs to a large room set in somber courtroom fashion, and directed to a box. Two uniformed police guards stood behind her. Dark-suited people were arrayed along tiers of wooden seats and at paper-strewn tables facing a raised bench, where a presiding judge was flanked by two auxiliaries.

The wall behind them was draped with large tapestries showing the national and provincial flags, and the State emblem of the swooping falcon.

Myriam had little sense of being a participator in the proceedings. She felt more as if she were following them in an unreal kind of way, like a distant spectator. Facts were recited and reports read in monotonous voices, and a series of individuals in various capacities gave opinions as to her mental and emotional stability, educational record, work evaluations, and periodic health and attitude assessments. She only recognized her two Justice Department visitors when they rose to speak. Their contributions were matter-of-fact and perfunctory, for the most part addressing minor issues. As had been the case on the day they came to see her, the validity of the charge against her was unquestioned.

"The verdict of the court is, guilty on all counts. Does the prisoner have anything further to add before sentence is delivered?" Myriam realized that all the faces in the room were gazing at her expectantly. "Well?"

"I'm sorry. I . . ." Her mental processes seized up. She was unable to form words. One of the auxiliaries sitting at the judge's sides spoke.

"You have been found guilty. Do you have anything to say to the court?"

"Just that . . . I'm not sure what I did that is supposed to be . . . to be . . . No. I don't."

"You will serve ten years of adjustment therapy in a corrective facility to be determined. Case to be reviewed after three years with provision for remission as appropriate on evidence of satisfactory progress.

The hearing is closed." The *clack* of the judge's gavel echoed from the walls. . . .

And repeated several times to become the insistent tapping on a door.

"Vanessa? Are you awake yet? We have to go into town early, remember? Mr. Elms has something he wants to talk to you about."

Vanessa? Was that her name? She blinked her eyes open to find herself in a sunny room with yellow drapes. It had a white-painted closet and vanity with gold handles and trim. Brightly colored clothes hung inside the partly opened door of the closet. She was having difficulty recognizing any of it. The dream had been so vivid that it still seemed more real. She could still see the talons of the swooping hawk. In the corner beside the window was a fluffy beige armchair and a small table. And above it, several shelves lined with *books*.

"Vanessa, can you hear me?" The door opened and a woman looked in. Her face was familiar. It was the white-haired woman who had waited on others in a kitchen. "Oh, you *are* awake." She smiled good naturedly.

"Yes . . ." Vanessa—was she? She still felt like Myriam—realized that she didn't know what she should call the woman.

"How do you feel today?"

"I feel . . . fine." She wouldn't have known how to begin describing the peculiar disorientation that she felt, a feeling of not being really here but watching through this body's vantage point from some other, distant place. It was all too strange. She had no idea who Mr. Elms was.

"Well, that's good. Hurry up and get washed and dressed, then. Breakfast will be ready in fifteen minutes."

They ate in a warm, cheerful kitchen with a large farmhouse-style stove. There were pans hanging alongside, and a wooden dresser decked with dishes and chinaware. A black-and-white long-haired cat lay curled on the widowsill. It felt like the kitchen she had seen in the dream.

But that couldn't have been a dream.

Myriam—or was she Vanessa?—mulled over the paradox while the woman transferred eggs, bacon, mushrooms, and fried tomatoes from a skillet onto her plate. If that had been a dream, then didn't it mean that this was too? She wasn't sure which was which. The image of the courtroom and the tapestries of the flags and the falcon hadn't faded the way dreams usually do but were still clear in her mind. The recollection made her shudder.

She had never tasted food so delicious. After they had finished, she cleared and washed the dishes while the white-haired woman collected things from another room. She couldn't really remember being here before, yet she seemed to know where things went. When they were ready to leave, she knew which were her coats, hanging on a rack inside the back door to the house.

Outside was a yard by a kitchen garden, with an outbuilding used for garaging a car—a private car, like the ones issued to upper-echelon personnel, but lighter and less boxy, silver-blue in color. The house itself was built of red brick and yellow stone, two stories with a brown tiled roof. It had trees to the side and a small lawn enclosed by a hedge at the front, with flowers growing on bushes and in beds lining the driveway. The white-haired woman had to be some kind of senior State manager or Party official to live in such a place. But nothing about her manner suggested it, and she made no mention of such things.

The house stood on the outskirts of a jumble of similar dwellings clustered among greenery and trees around a few larger central buildings and a bridge crossing a river. They drove in the opposite direction from the bridge, along a road winding its way among forested hills, passing rocky outcrops, a lake. Scattered cottages stood among fields that seemed to make up small farms. Myriam . . .Vanessa? . . . said very little, taking it all in. She had never seen countryside like this. The only trip away from the city that she could remember had been with a school outing years ago, when they were shown a cement factory and the efficiency of a State agricultural scheme in operation.

The hills opened out into a wider valley with more houses that became the outskirts of a town. The road joined a larger one by a river, following its left bank, the amount of traffic becoming denser with all manner of vehicles. Surely there couldn't be that number of managers and officials. She knew before they got there that the road would lead to the quay where the bookshop was, opposite the boats and the water. She didn't know how. She just *knew*.

They came to the quay. The white-haired woman parked the car in a yard at the rear of the shop, and they walked back through an alley to the front entrance. Myriam-Vanessa walked through the door into her own half-forgotten dream, unable to resolve the confusion. It was all just as she had seen it: the aisles of shelves; the view outside the window, across the quay to the boats; the table near the door where Sylvia had sat, signing her books.

Sylvia? . . . She realized with a start that she knew the name of the fair-haired woman. And that Sylvia and Rory were engaged to be married. She remembered her own rage and the jealousy she had felt. A fear gripped her then, that it might seize her again now. . . . But she didn't feel any anger or jealousy. She felt ashamed.

The little man with the ruddy face and the white beard came out of a room at the rear. He was wearing a tan jacket and again a bow tie, green with orange polka dots this time. "Good morning, ladies," he greeted. "A grand one it is, as well."

"A nice morning for a drive into town," the white-haired woman agreed heartily.

"And are you well, Josie?"

"Ah, I can't complain, you know. Well, I could, I suppose, but it's not a lot of good it does you. You're looking fine yourself."

"Never better." The man turned his head. "And how is Vanessa today? Are you taking good care of your aunt? Did she tell you we have a proposition for you?"

"Only that you wanted to talk about something." So the white-haired woman was called Josie? And Josie was her aunt?

"I kept it as our little secret, Mr. Elms," Josie said. "Surprises make life pleasantly interesting, don't you think?"

"Well, so long as they're nice surprises." Mr. Elms

was leading them back toward the room at the rear that he had appeared from. It contained a couple of desks and chairs, a large side table, and was filled with books on shelves and stacks of cartons. He went on as they entered. "Rory thinks it's time you got back into the world a little more, Vanessa. Your aunt and I do too. So I wondered if there might be something I could do. I asked him what he thought about letting you help out here in the shop for a few hours a week to get you out and mixing with people. He said it would be ideal. We all know how much you like being around books. You could have that place there in the corner for yourself—and of course you'd be earning something of your own, to feel a bit more independent. What do you think?"

Her, working among books? Books that people were allowed to read freely? She still hadn't puzzled out how this could be. Only the State commissioned books. It all had an air of unreality about it. As if she were in a dream.

Officially she was no longer Myriam, but KP273416. She sat on a wooden bench seat in a boxcar of a train, among rows of others similarly clad in orange, brown, and blue tunics. Chains from rings secured to the side wall ran along the rows. One hand of each person was manacled to a chain. The car had small barred windows at intervals, beyond which a bleak landscape rolled slowly by, of marshy flats and distant rounded hills. Her memories of exactly how she came to be here since the hearing were muddled. She had been in a room filled with people watched by guards, listening to a gaunt-faced officer in a peaked cap delivering a lecture on how no infringements of discipline would be tolerated, and the importance of showing a cooperative attitude. She had been in a bare cell, being punched and beaten by three large female wardens wielding batons; she wasn't sure why. Her back and her breasts and her stomach still ached, and there were welts on her arms and her shins. The slow, monotonous rhythm of the wheels on the track had a quality of dread, carrying her relentlessly toward whatever was to unfold. There was nothing to hope for; no comforting thought to be drawn of what lay ahead.

The gray-haired woman from her cell was there also. She called herself Ada. Whether that was her real name or not, Myriam didn't know. "Your mouth is looking better," she said. "If there's fish with the food when it comes, don't eat it. The salt will make your lip swell up again."

"I'm not even sure what I did," Myriam said.

"You don't have to do anything. It's too bad that you couldn't summon up just the appearance of playing along with them some. This way, you'll have gotten yourself tagged as a recalcitrant. They have a special way of dealing with that. First they break you up into little pieces. Then they put the pieces back together the way they want."

"What else happens?"

"It depends. But knowing what's going on helps."

"You've been through this before, haven't you?"

"For some people it becomes a way of life."

All the resentments that had been building up inside Myriam came boiling up. They came out as malice that she didn't know she was capable of, directing itself at Ada. "You just know it all, don't you? . . . Sitting there, sounding so smart." She heard the venom in her own voice but was unable to control it. It was if another person from somewhere else were taking over. "How come *you* don't feel scared? Is it because you know *you'll* be okay? What are you, some kind of plant that they put in here?"

"Easy," a lean, hard-faced man cautioned. "That sort of talk won't help any of us."

Ada frowned at her in alarm and surprise. "*Never* call anyone that," she said. "It's the ones who stick together that pull through. Isolate yourself, and you won't last long."

The alien presence that had flared briefly in Myriam soon abated. She tried to be herself again, but she was too troubled and confused. Something about her seemed to be changing. A distance remained between herself and Ada that hadn't been there before.

Vanessa's aunt Josie had assumed she would drive her to Rory's office for her monthly visit as usual, but Vanessa said she wanted to go there on her own. Everyone told her how well she had been doing lately, and working at Mr. Elms's shop gave her a such a nice feeling of independence and confidence that she was sure she would be okay. She had expected some kind of ritual objection, but Josie had seemed pleased. "Make sure you remember the phone number here—just in case," she had said as Vanessa put on her coat and checked her shoulder bag. She had another reason for wanting to go alone too, a more personal one that she hadn't felt was for sharing with third parties. She hadn't told Josie about the package inside the bag.

She walked two blocks from the bus and turned into a tree-lined street of offices and town houses bordered by shrubs. The plate bearing the title Rory Macallum, M.D., I.Psy.P was fixed to the iron railing by the foot of stone steps leading up to a red door standing imposingly between pillars. Vanessa ascended and went in. Brenda, the receptionist, was putting folders into an open drawer of the file cabinet behind her desk at the end of a short hallway.

"Hello, Vanessa. You're early. But we've had a cancellation. Let me check." She picked up a phone and pressed a button. "And how are you today?"

"I'm fine."

"Vanessa is here, Doctor. . . . Yes . . . Okay." To Vanessa, "You can just go on through. Isn't your aunt with you today?"

"I decided to try coming alone. You have to start sometime, yes?"

"Well, good for you, Vanessa!"

Actually, there had been something about traveling on the bus that made her feel uneasy—as if it had unpleasant associations. She wasn't sure why.

Rory was waiting at the door to usher her into the familiar office with its bookshelves, paintings of sailing ships, and view of the garden at the rear outside. He looked along the hall behind her after she had entered. "What, no Josie?"

"No. I came on my own, on the bus."

Rory closed the door and moved back behind his desk. "Was it your idea?

"Yes. Working in the bookstore made me feel as if I could. I wanted to see."

"Well, that's splendid!" Rory sat down. "So tell me how you've been getting on."

Instead of taking her usual chair, Vanessa remained standing. "Actually, there was another reason too. . . ." She moved forward, taking the package containing the book from her bag, and handed it across the desk to him. He unwrapped it, looking puzzled. Vanessa watched anxiously. Mr. Elms had said that the shop would be happy to make it a small gift—a kind of bonus, since she was doing such a good job—but Vanessa had insisted on paying for it herself. It was important.

Rory held up a large, glossy volume with a picture of kittens on the front cover. "Cats?" he said, sounding mystified.

"It's for Sylvia—from me." Vanessa explained. "I know she likes them. Because I broke the one that you gave her. It wasn't an accident. . . . But you all knew that, didn't you? I don't know why I did things like that. Sometimes I feel as if I didn't . . . as if it was a different person."

Rory set the book down carefully. "Oh yes, a good choice. Sylvia will like this a lot." He looked back up. "You didn't have to, you know. She didn't hold it against you."

"But *I* did. It mattered to *me*," Vanessa answered.

"Well, thank you, Vanessa, very much. Have you any idea how significant this is? The way you've been remembering things, connecting things together again . . . You are like a new person. So do you like yourself more these days?"

Vanessa went back to the visitor's chair and sat down. "I think I'm starting to."

"Of course you are." Rory nodded toward the book lying on his desk. "That's what this means. And how about things in general? Eating and sleeping well? Any worries or depressions? Aches or pains?" Vanessa hesitated. Rory raised his eyebrows inquiringly. "Yes?"

"I still have bad dreams—you know, very vivid, frightening ones, that don't go away. I feel jittery all day when they happen. Kind of scared. Insecure."

"Still? That's . . . interesting."

"What does it mean?"

"I'm not sure yet, exactly. That's what we're finding out. You're a lot better, which is the main thing for now. Tell me about these dreams. . . ."

She was with lines of other people, wearing strange, colored tunics moving slowly along in a line. They were stepping down from the cars of a train that seemed endless, onto a loading platform of wooden planks. A chill wind was blowing. There were rows of ribbed steel huts stretching away behind a concrete building inside a doubled wire fence commanded by watchtowers. Beyond the fence lay a wilderness of marshes extending away to a line of jagged peaks silhouetted black against a watery setting sun. Birds circled over the marshes, emitting plaintive, raucous cries. The heads around were staring at her, but they were blank, devoid of features. She could sense suspicion and hostility. One of them had a woman's gray hair.

Guards shouted orders. The people without faces began marching woodenly, a section at a time, through a chain-link gate, watched by armed sentries in posts on either side. Above the gate was metal plaque in the form of a swooping falcon with spread wings.

"I got a letter from Orna today," Josie told Vanessa across the kitchen table. They were having a pot of tea and sandwiches. Vanessa had just got home from her job at the bookstore. Josie watched her face curiously. "Do you remember her?"

Vanessa thought hard. It had become something of a game between them. Visions came into her mind of hills and a lake . . . a farm with a big red barn and a windmill driving a water pump. People owned and worked their own farms. They could use their land as they pleased, without having to pay regard to any State plan. There were still so many strange notions to get used to. The part of her that felt new to all this seemed to coexist with deeper currents of reviving feelings and memories belonging to the person that those around her had known.

"Orna . . ." Vanessa saw a plump woman in an apron, energetic and cheerful, always busy. Baking bread and tending animals. Long walks with the dogs. "Your sister," she said to Josie. "She lives on a farm, somewhere far away. With an uncle . . . His name won't come."

"Tom," Josie supplied. She looked pleased. "Orna is my sister. They've invited us to go and stay with them for a week over the holidays." She lowered her voice, as if she were confiding something. "I think they've heard how well you're doing and want to see for themselves. But it's been such a long time since I've seen them. What do you say?"

"Well, yes, it sounds nice . . . as long as Mr. Elms doesn't mind."

"Oh, I'm sure there will be no problem. It's been even longer since you were there. You used to spend summers there when you were a girl. Do you remember those times?"

"I think so. Bits of it, anyway . . ." Warm, pleasant memories stirred. Vanessa smiled distantly. "Yes," she said, and nodded. "Let's."

She dreamed she was trapped in a maze of rooms and passages with gray concrete walls. The passages that led out were blocked by barred gates. People wearing uniforms sat at tables in the rooms, repeating questions over and over that she didn't understand.

"The books about thinking. Why were you reading those? Where did you get them? Why were you hiding them? We know you discussed them with others. What were their names?"

"Passing judgment on the decisions of your superiors? Explain why you think you have the right. What is the source of authority?" She was fearful of not answering, but her mouth was unable to form any words.

And then she was in a street, with terrified people running past her, screaming. Something in the sky was sending down falcons that flamed and exploded. People were falling, burning, coming apart into pieces. . . .

She woke up perspiring and shaking. It took several hours before she could feel herself again.

Vanessa and Josie left two weeks later. They drove all day to arrive in a region of mountainous foothills, where they spent the night in a small hotel on the edge of a township nestling in a forested valley. Vanessa remembered staying there before. Josie was surprised. She said that had been a long time ago.

The next morning they carried on through the mountains into more open and rolling farming country. Scenes and features of the landscape began looking familiar. By the time they reached Tom and Orna's toward late afternoon, Vanessa recognized it before Josie said anything. The place had acquired a few extra outbuildings and undergone some remodeling, but its essential character was still the same as the picture in Vanessa's mind. The red barn was green now, and although the wind-pump tower was still standing, it no longer carried any vanes. The old stable had been rebuilt as a tractor shed.

That evening saw a welcoming feast in the large, wood-floored dining room, attended by somewhere over a dozen neighbors and relatives from the surrounding area. A young man called Kenny seemed to pay special attention to Vanessa, making efforts at conversation and watching her, but she was too preoccupied with so much novelty to respond. There were more kinds of food than she was able to name, and keeping track of who was who was a struggle, especially since they all seemed to know her and were pleased to see her back. Much of the conversation was dominated by the chatter of Josie and her sister catching up on events and the accumulated gossip of too many years that had been allowed to go by. Yet she had a feeling of fondness toward him. Once she caught his eye and smiled. It was as if her mind were still holding back something she was not ready for.

After the dessert there came coffee and a cheese board with crackers, and then liqueurs and brandy,

chocolates and nuts. Tom took out his fiddle, someone else produced an accordion, and the table was
pushed back to the wall as the dancing began. Kenny
came over to where Vanessa was sitting on the arm
of a chair that had been rolled back into a corner,
watching the dancers. "Hello, Vanessa," he said. He
had a fresh, open face, faintly freckly close-up, that
smiled easily, with clear gray eyes and curly golden
hair. Vanessa could remember the freckles. His eyes
reminded her of Rory's. . . . Or had Rory's reminded
her of Kenny's?

"Hello," she said.

"You've grown up a lot and changed on the outside,"
Kenny said. "What about inside?" Vanessa studied his
face as if for a clue—as if it were some kind of game.
Fragments of memories were jostling around in her
mind just beyond the fringes of awareness, but they
wouldn't come out into the light to be recognized.
"You do know me?" Kenny said.

"Yes . . . That is, I think so. . . ." She shook her head
and tried to make light of it. "It's all so overwhelming, after so long."

"We heard you were having . . . troubles. And then
doing so well." Kenny waited for a few seconds.
"When we were kids, we both promised once that
if either of us had to go away the other one would
wait. It didn't matter how long." He looked at her
searchingly. "No? . . ."

"I'm not sure. Maybe . . . But I don't want you to
have to tell me."

He nodded understandingly in a way that said that
was okay. "Sure. When it wants, in its own time."
Vanessa wanted to hug him. He was watching her

foot tapping to the music. "Do you still remember the steps?" He took her hand. "Come on. Let the serious stuff wait. You're home again now."

And she found that she could dance. The whole room was laughing and applauding. Kenny was home from college at the moment. He was studying history and literature, hoping to work overseas eventually. Arty and Mark were better suited to take over at the mill.

It came back to her then. They were his brothers. "The sawmill!" Vanessa exclaimed. "By the waterfall, right? And the log bridge. Is it still there?"

"Sure it is." Kenny grinned. "I tell you what. Why don't I pick you up tomorrow? We'll go for a drive and some walks around all the old places. Just us, away from all these people and the commotion."

"I'd like that," Vanessa said.

They parked in a clearing by a stone wall, where a track led down to a lake glinting through the trees. Rocky bluffs rose from the opposite shore. "There was a bus here," Vanessa said. "It was white, with a painted pattern on the side. Am I right?"

Kenny laughed. It had been a happy day all the way through, with a hike up the highest hill in the area, followed by lunch in a riverside pub. "That was a picnic outing that we came here on from the school, long ago. The schoolhouse is a hardware store now."

Vanessa looked at the path winding away below. "I want to go down there again," she said.

"It won't be the same these days," Kenny told her. "They're building a bridge where the river enters into the lake, about a mile farther along. But sure. Let's take a look anyway."

They followed the track down and came out on a grassy bank fringed by rocks at the water's edge. A track led along the shore in the direction where the lake narrowed. The slopes above them grew steeper with fewer trees, breaking up into rocky outcrops. Around a curve in the shoreline, they came upon a scene of excavations being cut and some pilings already in position on both banks amid a litter of general construction debris, concrete blocks, stacks of reinforcing bars, and steel drums. Since it was the holiday, the machinery was standing idle and nobody was around.

"They'll clear all the mess up when they're done," Kenny said, reading her mind. "It will mean a much shorter road to town."

Vanessa didn't answer. There was something about the sight of concrete and steel construction workings that disturbed her. She wasn't sure what or why.

They walked on among the trenches and walls of steel forming strips where the foundation for one of the piers was being poured. To the side were mounds that had been bulldozed aside in the excavations. Mixed among the soil and rocks were pieces of broken, crumbling concrete and rusted steel that looked old. Kenny kicked the caked mud away from what seemed to have been a metal plate with letters formed on it, now illegible. "Looks like there was something here from long ago," he commented.

Vanessa wasn't listening. She had stooped to peer at a molding that looked as if it had broken off the top of the metal plate. It was discolored and corroded, but the general form could still be made out. It was a bird, possibly a falcon, swooping with spread wings, its talons extended.

"Kenny, what's this?" she whispered. She felt her blood run cold.

Kenny stepped closer. "Hey, interesting. You know what it is? There must have been something here that goes way back, to before the Long War. That was one of the emblems they had then." He watched her, puzzled. "You didn't know about that?"

She shook her head. The object evoked feelings of dread. She had a vision of cold winds blowing across marshes from jagged peaks outlined against a watery setting sun. Ghosts were coming up out of the marshes. Figures without faces. "Let's go back," she said tightly.

Kenny turned his head to look at her intermittently as they retraced their steps. She kept her eyes ahead, walking quickly. "All that was long ago." He spoke to alleviate the silence, puzzled by the sudden change in her. "Vanessa, I don't understand. What happened back there? You looked as if you were terrified. . . . It's over. This is a new world now. Those ways can't happen again."

Vanessa's pace slackened. Birds were wading among the rocks and gliding above the water. She stopped and sighed. "I'm sorry. It's just . . . Oh, it reminded me of bad dreams that I used to have. But I don't have them anymore."

She managed a smile. Kenny smiled back reassuringly. They resumed walking back up toward the clearing by the stone wall, where their car was parked.

Crossword Solution

(continued ☞)

ACROSS

6 SPIELER Anagram of "replies"
7 MACHINE Machine = contrivance. With "time," becomes "time machine"
9 ELEGY Anag. of "glee" with "y," start of "year"
10 CONSTRUCT siliCON STRUCTural
11 APROPOS Anag. of "a poor" and "P.S."—afterthought
13 SPUTUM "Put" inside "sum"
15 NUCLEAR FUSION Anag. of "run of lunacies"
19 PODIUM "P," capital of "Peru," plus "odium"
20 SPOUSAL Anag. of "uspo" inside "s" and "AL"
23 ENAMELLER Anag. of "real mean" and "le" = French "the"
24 WATCH A personal time machine
26 POLITIC Po, Li, Ti, C. Chemical symbols
27 NEGLECT Anag. of "Eng" and "Celt"

DOWN

1 TIME cenTIMEters
2 PLAY UP Double meaning
3 CRACKSMAN Double meaning
4 ECOTYPES "E"—musical note—"co" plus "types"
5 SITUATIONS "Sit" = pose, before "tau" rising, over "ions"
6 SEE SAW Double meaning
7 MANE Double pun on main and Maine
8 ENTOMB Anag. of "boatmen" after "a" removed
12 ROUND TABLE "Round" = ammunition. "Table" = columns of numbers.
14 OFFSPRING "Of," "F"—musical key—"spring"
16 LAUREATE Original meaning, one decorated with laurel leaves
17 UPKEEP "Keep" up = "peek"
18 OLD HAT Double meaning
21 ON WE GO Double meaning. Time to appear "on" stage.
22 BLOC "Block" less end letter
25 TREE In stREEt